CW01638906

Samuel's Girl

for Michael

By

H.K. Hillman

Welcome to the thing my mind produced b

HK Hillman

(Leg-iron)

Eternal Press
A division of Damnation Books, LLC.
P.O. Box 3931
Santa Rosa, CA 95402-9998
www.eternalpress.biz

Samuel's Girl
by H.K. Hillman

Digital ISBN: 978-1-61572-784-1
Print ISBN: 978-1-61572-785-8

Cover art by: Dawné Dominique
Edited by: Janet Slike

Printed in the United States of America
Worldwide Electronic & Digital Rights
1st North American, Australian and UK Print Rights

This book first took form on a critique group called Critique Circle. Without the help of many members of that group, it might have remained a 200,000-word monstrosity of irrelevant fine detail and scientific-report-style tedium.

I would like to thank all the members who derided my initial amateur attempts, and who set me on the right path, by their individual names, but that would be difficult and would probably violate the terms of the group.

Therefore I would like to thank Critique Circle in general terms, and another writer called Rob Shelsky in specific terms because he was the one who pointed me at that writing group when it was just starting up, and when I was just learning the writing ropes.

Next time I see Rob, it's my turn to buy the whiskey. Unless I can convince him otherwise.

Chapter One

Romulus slammed his palm on the table. "The tree, for God's sake. The tree!"

"I don't get it." Jim Patton, the interviewee, stared at the row of photographs. "Which tree? Where?"

Romulus pressed his hands on the top of his head and paced the interview room. "Right. One more time." He stopped, facing Patton, on the other side of the table.

"This is the situation. You've been approached by someone—a woman, let's say—who claims to have a photo of a ghost. Here." He pushed one of the photographs towards the confused Patton. It showed a car, with an old woman looking out of a rear window. A clear face shot.

"She claims this was taken after this older woman died. Her death was on New Year's Eve, and your claimant is sure the photo was taken later than that." Romulus folded his arms. "You now have the whole film. You have the photographs placed in order based on the negative numbers. You have enough information in front of those blank little eyes of yours to tell me whether that photograph shows the woman alive or dead. It's a simple question. Is she a ghost or not?"

"I—" Patton bit his lip and stared at the photos. "It could be. I don't see how I can prove it from what I have here."

"Idiot." Romulus bared his teeth. "You can't prove she's a ghost. She's not, and you have the evidence to prove that." His shoulders slumped. "Now I've even told you the answer, and you still can't see it, can you? Tell me what you're seeing when you look at these pictures. Little blurry squares of color, or can you discern actual images?" Romulus closed his eyes. Sometimes, his rages resulted in floaters crossing his vision. These blurry spots had grown worse in the last week since he moved here to Marchway University. Perhaps it was time to get his blood pressure checked.

"Professor Crowe, there are thirty-six photos here, and seventeen of them have trees." Patton's voice came out as a whine. "There are Christmas photos at the start of the film, then some summer-holiday sorts, a wedding, another set of Christmas photos with the ghost photo in among them and then some sunny outdoor shots. Which tree am I supposed to be looking at and why should a tree prove—or disprove—a ghost?"

"Start from basics, then." Romulus took a few breaths to calm himself, an action which rarely worked for him and which failed this time also. "Look at the whole film. What does it tell you about the photographer?"

Patton raised his eyebrows. "Well, most are in focus, but most are badly aligned. A couple have the subjects' heads missing. An inexperienced photographer?"

"Inexperienced, yes. Why would you say she was inexperienced?"

"I thought I just did." Patton's face showed despair.

"You described symptoms, not the cause." Romulus hissed through his teeth and thanked a God he had never believed in that this was the last interview. If he had to contend with another moron today he was sure to end up in a rubber room.

"Look. Really look. Oh, forget it, I'll just tell you. The photos start with Christmas. The camera was most likely a present because all those photos are after Christmas morning."

"How do you know that?"

"Shut up. You had your chance." Romulus tapped the line of photos. "Then the camera sat idle until holiday time. A few more shots. Someone's wedding. Three pictures only. Christmas decorations. Woman in car. Christmas decorations again." He stared into Patton's pale face. "That's a year, and still the same roll of film. Then some summer shots and the film finally gets developed."

"Ah." Understanding brightened Patton's face. "Inexperienced, because she hardly ever used the camera. I get it."

"No. You don't." Romulus scowled until Patton resumed his bewildered expression before continuing. "That film took a year and a half to complete. Your claimant can't possibly know exactly when each photo was taken, and she's forgotten about most of them anyway. She can't be certain whether she took the photo of the old woman before or after the funeral. I, and anyone else with any intelligence, can be certain. Because of the tree."

Patton's body sagged into his chair as though he was trying to fold in on himself. "What tree? Which one? I don't get it."

"That's not all you don't get." Romulus blinked away the floaters in his vision. It was time to end this nonsense. "That tree." He jabbed his finger onto a photograph and pushed it towards Patton.

"A Christmas tree." Patton shrugged. "What does that mean?"

"It's two photographs later than the alleged ghost photo. The old woman died on New Year's Eve. One last chance, Patton. Work it out. The answer is in front of you."

"It means nothing. People don't take their decorations down until January. That could have been taken after the woman's death."

"No. It was taken before. Tell me why." Romulus spoke through gritted teeth. "Oh, the hell with it. Look under the tree. What do you see?"

"Presents." Patton sighed. "People put presents under the tree. Everyone does it. So what?"

Romulus leaned in close but resisted the urge to grip Patton's throat. He spoke with slow, steady tones. "People do not put presents under the tree after Christmas. That's how I know the camera was a Christmas present, and how I know the so-called ghost photo was taken before Christmas day, the following year."

"Right." Patton's whole body sagged as the tension left it. "It's all so clear now."

"Well, that concludes the interview." Romulus picked up the photographs and placed them in their envelope. "You can go."

"Yes. Thank you, Professor Crowe." Patton headed for the door. "So I'll hear from you about the job in the next week or so?"

Romulus treated Patton to his fiercest glare. "No. You won't. Goodbye, Mister Patton."

* * * *

Elaine tapped twice on the interview room's door before entering. Romulus sat behind the long table, his seat tilted back, feet on the polished wood and his hands over his eyes. She closed the door.

"I saw that last guy leave." She walked to the table. "I'm guessing he didn't get the job."

"He's an idiot." Romulus lifted his hands. Fatigue showed on his face. "They all are. Eight interviews. A waste of a day."

"You tried the Christmas tree scenario on them, didn't you?" Elaine smirked. "You know hardly anyone ever gets that one. These are fresh from their first degrees, Rom. You can't expect them to act like experienced parapsychologists."

"Why not?" Romulus dropped his feet to the floor. The chair came forward with a thump. "All I'm asking of them is a little evidence of basic observational skills. You spotted it, when I interviewed you. That was four years ago. Nobody else has ever seen the obvious answer."

"Yes, but—"

"Oh, so you consider yourself special, is that it?" The gleam in Romulus's eye made his intention clear. He was looking for an argument.

Elaine had no intention of rising to his bait. "You're always like this after interviews. Forget it. I'm not in the mood for a fight." Grinning, she headed for the door. "Besides, you know I'm special. I'm the only one you've employed in seven years. I'm the only one to ever stay the course on a PhD supervised by you and I'm the only one who can put up with your temper. You need me, and it drives you nuts."

Elaine watched Romulus's face redden for a moment before she closed the door. Let him fume on his own for a while. There was no way he would ever fire her. He had never come close to finding a replacement. With his absolute perfectionism and short temper, it was unlikely he ever would.

Elaine's smile slipped a little. Her security in this position was not much different from the security enjoyed by a prisoner. She could leave whenever she wanted, but then Romulus was the one who had given her that first chance, Romulus who had seen her potential, Romulus who had ensured her continued employment when their last department had been closed. Walking out on him would be desertion. He would feel nothing if he ever fired her, but she would feel guilt if she left.

When Rom had informed—not asked—her of their new employment in Marchway, Elaine had been angry at first, then flattered. Whoever said "no man is an island" had never met Romulus Crowe. To have him insist she come along was the greatest compliment anyone could ever receive, and to receive any kind of compliment from Romulus was a rarity in itself.

They began their new department, with him heading it up, on Monday of this week. Today, Friday, Romulus had spent looking for potential employees, preferably PhD students, to justify the funding he had received to start this department. He had no need of the money. He had brought enough in grants and bursaries along with him. Yet he was not the sort of man who would turn down free cash, so the project money had to be used. Someone had to run a study on ghost phenomena. Elaine had the uneasy feeling it was likely to land in her lap since Romulus's opinion on the subject was clear. He had stated it many times. Ghosts are bunk.

She pushed open the door to her laboratory. Their entire department consisted of this one small laboratory and Romulus's office. Elaine had no complaints. The lab, though small, was far bigger than the tiny room Romulus had been assigned for his office, and the lab was hers. Romulus used intuition most of the time. He had little need of a laboratory. He understood almost nothing of the motion detectors, infrared cameras and other electronic equipment she employed, and nothing at all of the computer programs she used to log and analyze data. Romulus could spot a fake by looking at it, but he needed Elaine to provide the scientific proof.

The one thing he had never needed Elaine for was the denouncement of a fraud. His temper took care of that. It was never stated, but Elaine was sure the main reason their previous department closed was Romulus. He was investigating mediums, and when he found a fraud his denouncements were loud, vicious, and public. Too loud and too public for any university's tastes. Why the Marchway administration was so keen to have him run this new department was a mystery. Why Romulus so vehemently refused to believe in ghosts was another mystery. Some of the mediums he had denounced as frauds seemed to Elaine to be worth further study. His attitude seemed, at times, more attuned with the zealous witch-finder than the dispassionate scientist, especially where any suggestion of spirit communication was concerned. There was something at the back of her thoughts, trying to come through. An incident, forgotten, but her conscious mind tried to drag it from the past.

The phone broke through her thoughts. She picked it up. "Hello?"

"I thought you went to the library this afternoon," Romulus said.

"I did. They're setting up someone's retirement party. The woman on the desk told me I'd get no sense out of anyone there before Monday, so I thought I'd leave."

"Hmm. Libraries are supposed to be places of learning, not party houses. Isn't it open tomorrow?"

"They're open Saturday morning but it's always busy. I won't be able to take up any of the staff time, especially since they'll be one short. Don't worry, I can go straight there Monday morning. As for now, it's five o'clock and I'm going home for the weekend." Elaine paused. "Do you want me to study up on ghosts for this project, or are you interviewing more candidates next week?"

"I've interviewed as many half-witted oafs as I'm going to. You find someone or you do the project. And get to that library on Monday. I want to know about their old books." Romulus hung up.

Elaine replaced the handset and stuck her tongue out at it. So the ghost study was hers. For the moment. Romulus had a way of taking over projects. Perhaps if she could get him interested in Marchway Library's collection of ancient manuscripts, he would keep out of her way for once. He loved historical artifacts almost as much as he loved to expose fraudulent mediums.

Elaine picked up her coat and bag and left for home. *One day,* she thought, *one day the swine will find a medium he can't debunk.*

Chapter Two

Samuel Watson took a deep breath of the musty air. It smelled of old paper, worn leather bindings, dust, and money. A lot of money.

Beside him, Nathaniel Attlee sighed. "This will be my last visit to this room, Samuel. You're in charge now." He held out a long, steel key.

Samuel's fingers twitched. He wanted to snatch that key and usher Attlee out of there, but he hesitated. He let his gaze wander around the small room, taking in the spines of ancient books, the teak-faced drawers filled with unbound manuscripts, the small desk with its solitary reading lamp. Between two of the books, a thin brown line marked the edge of a folder. It looked modern, out of place here. Samuel squinted at it. He would investigate that as soon as he had control of the room.

Finally, Samuel reached for the key. His hands moved in slow motion, straining against his excitement, but once his hot, pudgy fingers closed on the key, his grip tightened.

Attlee still held the key, as though unwilling to relinquish it.

"I've looked after this room for thirty-two years, Samuel. I've supervised everyone who read these books. Turned pages for them. Shelved the books and locked the room after each visit. Nobody has entered this room without me since I became the head of this library. Nobody."

"It's a great responsibility, Mister Attlee. I understand." *Let go of the damn key.*

"These are old books. Irreplaceable. All handwritten, many of them unique. Some have been here since this building was part of the Marchway monastery, right back to the thirteenth century. A few of these books were considered rare, and very old, even then."

Samuel's fingers ached. "I'll take great care of them."

Attlee's gaze rested on the key. "This is the only copy. Apart from the one locked in the university's safe, in case this is ever lost." He raised his eyes to the wall. "And that one. The original."

The temptation to wrest the key from Attlee's grip was close to overwhelming. Attlee was retired, effective at the library's close earlier today, although Samuel's promotion was not technically effective until the library opened again in the morning. In this limbo, the two men held on to the small token that marked the power of the head of this institution. The key to the Old Books Room. It crossed Samuel's mind that they might be locked in this impasse overnight.

He followed Attlee's gaze to the small wooden frame on the wall, in which hung the original key to this room. An antique, too valuable to be used, and yet too much of a security risk to be displayed anywhere but inside this room.

Samuel turned his attention back to his cramped fingers. "You can rely on me, Mister Attlee. You know that."

A shadow passed over Attlee's face. He released his grip. Samuel put his hand in his pocket, his fingers still tight around the warm metal. Attlee shuffled. His hands rubbed his hips. He folded his arms, unfolded them, scratched at his chin.

His eyes strayed to Samuel's pocket. For a moment, it seemed to Samuel as though this tall, thin man might lunge at him, beat him to the ground, and take back his long-held property.

Attlee took a deep breath and released it slowly. "It's hard, retiring. Harder than I expected." He put his hand over his eyes, as if to block out the lonely, empty days ahead.. "I looked forward to it these past few years, but now that it's here..."

Samuel understood. His own retirement was a little more than ten years away, and he was all too aware of the pittance he could expect as a pension. Attlee would learn to cope with it, but Samuel had other ideas. Many of the books here had never been translated. Some had not been taken from the shelves since before Attlee took over. Some might not have been opened in decades, even centuries. These unknown books, transcribed, translated, and published, would ride the New Age fascination with the babblings of ancient eccentrics and earn Samuel a tidy sum for his own retirement in the process.

Attlee lowered his hand from his face, reached out, and gripped Samuel's shoulder. Samuel flinched. His fingers tightened on the key while an all-too-familiar tension clamped his chest. Attlee bared his teeth in a wide smile that served only to accentuate his already skeletal appearance. In this small, silent, and ancient room, the effect was like being grasped by Death himself. Samuel's free hand strayed to the center of his chest and pressed to relieve the pain there.

"You'll be fine." Attlee squeezed Samuel's shoulder. "I've shown you how things are done here. I've prepared you for this day for years. I know these books are safe with you." He sighed. "What I worry about is whether you're safe with them."

"Huh?" Samuel took a step backwards. Attlee's hand fell back to his side.

Attlee moved to a row of shelves and stared at the tattered spines. "I know you plan to read these books yourself. Oh, I don't blame you. If I'd had your gift and your training, your abilities with ancient languages, I'd have read them too. Some of them." He raised one eyebrow at Samuel. "Others are best left unread."

"Oh?" Samuel fought for a more coherent response, but none came. Heat flushed his cheeks. In his pocket, his fingers flexed to relieve the numbness in them, but did not release his key.

"You've heard the story of one of our earlier librarians, one Alfred Melchior, no doubt?"

"That was a long time ago. One of Marchway's few scandals. Must have been, oh, forty years ago, although the older members of my church still talk about it as if it happened yesterday." Samuel chuckled. "Surely you don't expect me to add to the Marchway knitting circle's compendium of gossip?"

Attlee's face remained serious. "The story went around that Melchior must have run off with a woman. He didn't. He disappeared in the most literal sense of the word. I was there. Here."

Samuel's chest constricted. He took a few breaths before replying. "Vanished? Like a magician, you mean?" Samuel massaged his chest.

Attlee snorted and turned away. "Something like that. He was a lot like you. He had a doctorate in languages too, and he was fascinated by the books in this room. He used to spend hours in here." Attlee leaned on the desk, his head lowered. "I was a junior at the time. I worked late often, because I was ambitious. Melchior was always here, in this room, while I shelved and sorted books in the public room. He had no wife, no family. I sometimes wondered if he ever left the premises."

Samuel's chest pains reduced in intensity. He took out a handkerchief and wiped a film of sweat from his forehead. "I see the similarity. I have no wife, and no relatives in Marchway, but still, I don't plan to run off. Heck, I have nobody to run away with. There's no need to be concerned about me."

"He didn't run anywhere." Attlee pushed himself away from the desk and glared at Samuel. "That's what I'm trying to tell you. He vanished. From this room." Attlee closed his eyes. His face creased in concentration. "I was in the public room. He would have had to pass through there on the way out. He didn't. Before I left, I always came down here to let him know, so he could lock up. That night, he wasn't in the room, and the door was unlocked."

"I don't understand. So he forgot to lock up? He could have slipped out while you were among the shelves. He'd hardly have said goodbye if he planned to run away with some rich widow." That was the story told by the gossips of Samuel's church, and he had heard it so many times he had come to accept it as the truth.

"No." Attlee pursed his lips. "I tried to tell myself the same thing, but he left this room unlocked. Melchior would never have done that. Nor would he have left any of these books open on the table."

Samuel took the key from his pocket. "We still have the key. He probably assumed you'd lock up."

"That's a duplicate. Melchior's key vanished when he did. It caused quite a furor, although that was never made public."

"Really?" Samuel gave a low whistle. The value of the books stored here was beyond anyone's ability to calculate, so the loss of a key would have been a security nightmare. "Why didn't they change the locks?"

"It was considered, but tampering with historical buildings isn't something that can be done lightly. Besides, none of the books were missing. If he planned to steal them, he would have done so that night." Attlee walked around the desk to the opposite wall and faced a row of books. "This is the one Melchior left open on the desk. It's this one, in particular, I'd advise you to avoid."

Samuel moved to Attlee's side. "Which one?"

"There." Attlee pointed to a red spine that showed no wear. It looked to be in much better condition that the books around it, as though someone had shelved a new book among these relics of the past.

Samuel tilted his head to read the lettering on the spine. It was Arabic, but what he read made no sense in any Arabic dialect he knew.

"I've never been able to read it myself. It's listed as an 'untranslated grimoire' in our records." Attlee pursed his lips. "It's been on this shelf since I put it back there that night. Nobody has requested it since, and I found no record of anyone ever wanting to read it, as far back as the library's records go."

Samuel wrinkled his nose. "If that's the title, I can't make sense of it. The script looks like Arabic but it doesn't translate into any Arabic I've ever read. The first word looks like 'Nooz' to me." Samuel straightened. "I think I'd have given up on this one without taking it off the shelf." He said what he knew Attlee wanted to hear, but his interest in this particular book was piqued by the old man's tale. Melchior had been a scholar of some note, with several translations published. If he was working on this book then it must be worth Samuel's time.

"I'm glad to hear it." Attlee's smile returned. "There are several books here whose contents worry me. Grimoires, magical texts, that sort of thing. I don't know why the monks kept them." He faced Samuel. "Still, I know you're an active member of the Church, so I needn't worry too much about you getting involved with those. This one, though, you should particularly avoid. I'm certain it had something to do with Melchior's disappearance."

"I'll leave it right there, on its shelf, Mister Attlee." *The hell I will.*

"Thank you." Attlee headed for the door. "And it's no more Mister Attlee. I'm retired, so you can call me Nathaniel. Or Nate." He held the door open for Samuel. "I prefer Nate, I think. Makes me sound younger."

Samuel walked past the door. Attlee closed it, then patted at his pockets. "Ah, of course." He grimaced. "Old habits die hard, I suppose. Samuel, you'd better lock up."

It took a moment for Samuel to remember the key in his hand. With a reverence more suited to a place of high worship, Samuel placed his key in the ancient lock and turned it. Together, they walked from the granite walls of this historical monastery into the smooth, painted plaster walls of the new part of the library.

The corridor led them into the main, public room. On one of the tables lay the remains of Attlee's retirement party, a small affair conducted by the staff immediately after the library closed. Samuel eyed the drying sandwiches and vol-au-vents, the empty wine bottles and used glasses with distaste.

"It seems nobody spilled anything." Attlee smirked. "You wouldn't want to start on Monday as head of a library that stank of booze."

"No, I wouldn't." Samuel vowed to allow no more parties on the premises, not even small ones like this. Donna and John, the two long-serving staff, had shown suitable restraint but Robert, the junior staff member, was so drunk Samuel had worried he might collapse. They had moved on to continue their revelries elsewhere, with a promise to return tomorrow to tidy up. Samuel followed Attlee to the main doors.

"You know, I think Donna might have something of a crush on you." Attlee winked. "You could do with a woman in your life, Samuel."

"She's just flirting." Samuel laughed off the suggestion. "Besides, she's ten years younger than me. It wouldn't be right."

"That's not such a big age difference these days." Attlee pushed open the street doors.

Samuel switched off the lights. "It is to me. And she drenches herself in perfume. The fumes are probably corrosive." He followed Attlee into the street and closed the doors.

"You'll need to lock up. I gave the rest of my keys to John." Attlee fidgeted on the darkened sidewalk.

Samuel took out his bunch of keys and locked the doors. He checked for the Old Books Room key when he returned the bunch to his pocket. It needed to be attached to his keyring, but doing that while Attlee watched felt like rubbing salt into a wound. It could wait.

"Well, I suppose it's time to go home." Attlee stared at the floor. "I feel as though I've been discharged from the Army, or let out of prison. Years of routine grind themselves into you, and when it stops it leaves you lost. You'll find that out for yourself in time. Find yourself a woman, so you'll have someone to go home to."

Samuel avoided looking at Attlee. He knew Attlee's wife had died years ago, so Attlee had only a cold and lonely house to go back to. The way things were going,

Samuel would have the same on retirement, but without even those memories of marriage that Attlee could bask in. He held out his hand.

"Well, goodnight. I hope we'll see you again soon."

Attlee shook Samuel's hand. "I'll be back, don't you worry. Only I won't be working. I'll be coming as a reader."

They paused for a moment until Samuel released his grip. Attlee nodded once then walked away along the street. Samuel stood at the base of the library steps and watched until Attlee turned the corner, then dashed back to the door, unlocked it, and ducked inside. He made his way directly to the Old Books Room and slid his key into the lock.

A vague unease drifted through his mind before he stepped inside. It took a moment for him to define the source. This was Attlee's domain. Nobody came in here without his supervision. Even Samuel was never here alone. The unease was similar to that first time in a car after passing the driving test. The first solo run. These books were now under Samuel's control, and his alone.

Samuel bared his teeth in a wide grin. "You're mine now," he said to the shelved rows, "and I'm going to read you, translate you, and then you're going to make me rich." He walked over to the red book Attlee had pointed out and ran his finger along its spine. "You first."

The spine glowed at his touch and sent a tingle through his finger. Samuel pulled his hand away. He moved closer, his eyes narrow. Did he damage the book?

The desk drawer contained several pairs of white cotton gloves. These books should not be handled with bare fingers. The oils in his skin might corrode them. Satisfied that he had caused no damage, Samuel stepped back.

The folder he had seen was new, so the gloves rule did not apply. Samuel reached for it and pulled it from between the books. It was slipped between a fifteenth-century tome recording regional taxes and another from the same period, listing property ownership in the area. Neither was of interest to any of Marchway's readers so it was likely they had never been off their shelf. He laid the folder on the desk, switched on the reading light, and examined the cover.

The name in the top right corner made him catch his breath. In a fine, steady hand, A. P. Melchior had labeled his property. Samuel licked his lips and opened the folder.

It was more than Samuel could have hoped for. Melchior was in the process of translating the "untranslated grimoire" that Attlee had pointed out. Samuel turned page after page of scribbled notes, diagrams, and attempted translations with lines drawn through them. None of it made any sense. Melchior had, it seemed, made no progress at all on this particular book. Maybe this work had driven Melchior mad, and he had run off into the night to get away from his failure. Samuel turned one more page. Across the top of the next page, in tall capitals, Melchior had written "Eureka!" Samuel leaned forward over the paper.

Laughter burst from Samuel at the simplicity of the code Melchior had finally cracked. The book was written in Greek, not Arabic. The Greek words were written in reverse, then phonetically transliterated into Arabic characters. The writers of these grimoires had done such things often, partly to hide the contents of the book from the religious authorities of the day and partly to boost its credibility among the gullible.

Even with this knowledge, translation was a challenge. Arabic letters were not a good phonetic match for Greek words. Nevertheless, Melchior made some initial progress with a few pages. Samuel yawned and checked his watch.

"Quarter to twelve!" Samuel rubbed at his eyes. He stood, the folder tucked under his arm. Facing the "untranslated grimoire," Samuel grinned. "I'll be back to finish you." He already knew the title from Melchior's notes but delighted in retranslating it directly from the spine of the book.

Geometria ton Zoon. The geometry of lives.

Chapter Three

Shadows moved across the barren yellow plain, flickering and twisting like a dark fire whipped by an unfelt wind. Samuel watched, fascinated and unafraid, although he saw nothing that would account for the shadows. There were no clouds, no trees, no hills. The land was flat and featureless in every direction.

The pale ochre sky spread from horizon to horizon. High above, the sun was... wrong. It was partially transparent, it had too many colors, and it seemed to be spinning. Or something was spinning around it. Samuel shrugged. It didn't really matter. He turned full circle, saw nothing and nobody, and was therefore surprised to hear a voice to his left.

"Are you going out? Can you take me? Can I come out with you?"

Samuel faced the speaker and smiled into the parchment face of the bedraggled old man who appeared beside him. The man cowered. His eyes swiveled left and right, although Samuel already knew there was nothing to see. Nothing to see, nothing to fear in this silent, restful place.

The man's clothing wrapped around him in shreds that barely disguised his wasted frame. The strips of cloth twitched with his movements, revealing long cuts in his flesh. New, open wounds crossed old and livid scars. Samuel observed this with a detached interest. He believed he should feel something, but his mind refused to leave its soothing calm.

"We can't go out," Samuel said, "because we're not inside anything."

The old man laughed, a dry sound like a cracking of twigs. "Oh, you're not all the way in." He clasped his bony hands. "You've touched it with skin, haven't you? One of them is calling you." He brought his wrinkled face close to Samuel's. "Don't answer. Don't—"

The air filled with a rapid and insistent drumbeat that drowned the old man's words. Samuel strained to hear. Screaming joined the drums, as did a high-pitched whine. The old man faded, the yellow world turned gray, and the sound resolved into something the modern world called "music".

* * * *

Forcing open one eye, Samuel reached for his clock radio and thumped the "snooze" button. How come the radio never played soothing, gentle music at seven in the morning? Whichever station he tried, it was always the same. They played soft ballads in the evening, when he set the alarm, and in the morning they put on something that sounded like a drum kit dropped down a elevator shaft onto a nest of cats.

"Well, I suppose it worked. I'm awake." Samuel stretched, made sure the alarm was definitely off so he would not have to hear more of the early-morning wailings of demented guitar-thrashers, and stumbled into his bathroom. The fingers of his left hand tingled. He rubbed them to restore circulation and considered visiting a doctor. It was cramp, he reassured himself. Just a cramp.

Showered, breakfasted, and dressed, Samuel sat at his kitchen table, where he had spread out Melchior's notes the night before. He yawned. Five hours' sleep was not enough for a man his age. Then there was the strange dream and the persistent tingle in his fingers, which now spread through his palm. Age, he thought, brings nothing good.

The notes were interesting, but they went only so far. They stopped at a passage that was neither Greek nor Arabic. It looked like runes, but Samuel had been forced to stop reading and go to bed. Today was his first day as the head of the library, and it would not look good if he showed up late. He checked the wall clock, yawned again, put the notes into their folder, and put the folder into the briefcase he had rarely used but which he now believed he should carry to work every day. Executives did that sort of thing. Head of Marchway library was hardly an executive position—it certainly did not command executive pay—but it was as close as Samuel was ever likely to get.

In the hall, Samuel donned his coat, straightened his tie, and ran his comb through his thinning hair. Outside, a fine drizzle filled the air. Samuel set his hat on his head, locked the door, and set off to walk the few streets to the library.

His pace was a little quicker than usual, a touch more sprightly than it had been for some years. Today he had the key to the Old Books Room on his key ring and Melchior's notes in his briefcase. All he needed was some time alone with the books and that first translation could be done, prepared, and sent off within a few months. A first step to financial freedom.

The library door swung open when Samuel pushed his key into the lock. A sudden terror formed a tight band around his chest. Had he forgotten to lock the door last night? Visions of ransacked shelves, ruined displays, and stolen books filled his head. Even in a small town like Marchway, the Friday night drunks could be rough. With mounting trepidation, he pushed the door open and stepped inside.

"Mister Watson. Good morning." The voice floated from the back of the room. Samuel stood rigid. His heart pounded, hard enough to send shooting pains through his chest and arms. Yet he recognised the voice. John Legg, once his subordinate assistant, now his second-in-command.

Donna Parfitt stood beside John, holding a large black plastic bag. Samuel recalled John's promise to tidy up today, before the library opened. He fought against the tightness in his chest and cleared his throat.

"John. Donna. Hello." Samuel took deep breaths. Pain subsided from his chest, but the sensation in his hand remained. He flexed his fingers.

John approached, concern on his features. "Are you all right? You've gone quite pale."

"Yes, yes, I'm fine. I forgot you said you'd be here early. Gave me a bit of a fright when I walked in. I'll just get a coffee and then I'll head up to the office." He almost said "Atlee's office.". It was now the office of Samuel Watson, Librarian, but somehow he could not quite bring himself to call it that. Not yet. It felt disrespectful.

"Why don't you just go on to your office? I'll bring up a coffee." Donna swayed her hips as she walked towards him. She looked good for forty, but she always exaggerated her seductive moves. Samuel's lips twitched into a smile at the sight of her. No way could she be serious. No woman could possibly try to seduce a man with those Betty Boop eyelashes, half a tanker load of perfume and hips that swung out so far Samuel half-expected her entire pelvis to rotate.

"No, Donna, you carry on with what you're doing." Samuel pushed himself away from the desk, swayed a little, and blinked spots from his vision. "I'll be fine," he said, as much to convince himself as the others.

"We're about done." John took the bag from Donna. "I'll finish up here. Donna can deal with coffee." He gave Samuel another concerned look and headed back to his clearing up.

Donna stood far closer than Samuel considered morally acceptable. He took a step back and coughed. "Well, I'll get on then. Have to find my way around this new job."

"You've been doing most of it for years." Donna followed Samuel as he crossed the room. "Mister Attlee backed off from most of his job when his retirement was close. The only thing he kept a tight hold of was his room full of old books." She moved ahead of Samuel when they reached the staff-room door and blocked his way for a moment. "That's the only thing you haven't already done."

Samuel wiped cold sweat from his forehead as he walked around her. "Yes, I know. Still, I have to get used to the responsibility." He turned and forced a smile. "I can't go to Mister Attlee with problems any more." His fingers gripped the handle of his briefcase too hard, and it took an effort to relax them. Mention of the old books brought back his reason for arriving early today. Now he had no chance of peace to read them. Samuel continued to Attlee's—no, *his*—office and was relieved to close the door behind him. He sat at the desk, checked the contents of the drawers, and finally opened his briefcase just as Donna entered with a coffee. Samuel dropped Melchior's folder back into his case, which he set on the floor until she left.

* * * *

It was a busy Saturday morning. Samuel barely found time for a coffee break. This was, he reminded himself, his first solo flight. Attlee had always been there as backup before. What Donna said was true. Samuel was doing most of the job already, but now he was doing it all. By the time the morning ended and the library closed, Samuel was exhausted. He did his best to hide his fatigue, but John must have noticed because he offered to lock up. He sent the staff home. Once they were out of the building, Samuel locked the doors, took Melchior's folder, a notepad, and pencil from his briefcase, and hurried to the Old Books Room.

That uneasy feeling came over him again the moment he entered the room, a sensation of eyes watching his every move. Samuel shook it off. Attlee was retired, and he was the room's keeper now. The eyes watching every future visitor here would be his.

Samuel switched on the reading lamp, put on the cotton gloves from the desk drawer, and lifted *Geometria ton Zoon* from the shelf. Pins and needles filled his fingers at once. He needed both hands to place the book on the desk.

"Dammit, what's wrong with my hands?" Samuel flexed his fingers until the tingling stopped. He knew that numbness in the extremities was linked to the pains in his chest. A heart condition of some kind. As long as he stayed away from doctors, as long as he had no idea what was wrong, it could be denied. One day he would seek treatment, but first he had to work on these books. He had not waited so long for access to this room just to give it all up and fade away on an invalid's pension. Oh, one day he would see a doctor. A good one. The best. When he could easily afford it, and not before.

Geometria's cover glowed beneath the reading lamp. Its surface shifted when Samuel moved his head, changing shade like mother-of-pearl but always a deep and clear red. Samuel opened Melchior's notes first. The first pages of *Geometria*, according to Melchior, contained invocations to several demonic forces. Azazael, Lilith, Asmodeus, Hu Gadarn. Samuel shook his head. Hu Gadarn did not belong in the group of demons Melchior named in his translation. Samuel turned to *Geometria* and lifted its cover.

Minutes later, Samuel sat blinking in confusion. Melchior was right. Pazuzu was named here also. Demons and gods from widely different cultures, from different historical periods, all gathered together in one tome. Samuel tapped his fingertips on the desk. Could he sell this? It was too fantastic even for the New Age crowd. They wanted deep mythology, but they needed it to be credible. Pazuzu, Hu Gadarn, and Asmodeus in one book? It was too much. Samuel breathed a heavy sigh and considered returning *Geometria ton Zoon* to its shelf. There were other grimoires here, most of them known but not all of them available as translated paperbacks. Something easier, something a little less controversial might prove to be a better starting point. He slid his fingers under the open book and started to close it.

A moan, soft and low, froze his action. Samuel sat still and held his breath. It had been a female sound, a little gasp of disappointment. He stood and walked to the door.

"Hello? Anyone there?" It was a stupid thing to say but it was out before Samuel could stop it. An intruder was hardly likely to give a little wave and say "Hey, only me. Just burgling the place. You carry on with what you're doing." Samuel's call had alerted the intruder—if there was one—to his presence and location.

He was sure the moan must have come from a woman. Women were seldom burglars, at least as far as Samuel was aware. He stepped into the corridor.

"Donna? Is that you?"

No, if it was Donna she would have responded by now. Samuel swallowed and edged along the wall until he could see the main room. Rows of shelves filled the hall, with tables and chairs at the back and the issues desk at the front, near the doors. The lights were off, but the gray afternoon provided enough illumination. There were too many hiding places in that room. Samuel could chase someone around there all afternoon and never catch them.

"Anyone in here? If you don't show yourself you'll be in a lot of trouble." A corner of Samuel's mind laughed at that. *Yeah? What are you gonna do about it, fat boy? You can't run from here to the door without turning blue and fainting.*

Denying the ache in his chest and arms was easy. Samuel had practiced that for years. Denying the more immediate danger of a potential burglar was an entirely different matter. Samuel was overweight, unfit, and neither physically strong nor fast. He had not been involved in fighting since his schooldays and even then, he had lost every time. The chest pains might or might not kill him. Tackling desperate criminals almost certainly would. Samuel backed away and returned to the Old Books Room, determined to simply pack up and go home. If he saw any sign of a break-in before he left, he would call the police. Otherwise he would just assume it was all in his imagination.

Perhaps it was. Samuel leaned on the desk and forced his shallow breathing to deepen. It was, surely, his imagination. The sound had been like a quiet moan. A woman's moan. It was the wind coming through a vent or a door shifting in a draft. He was alone in this large and empty building, and he was jumping at shadows. Buildings creaked all the time, and this part of it was over 700 years old.

All the same, he could not settle here. Not now. His translations could wait a day or two more. They could accumulate over coffee and lunch breaks. Perhaps, when he had become accustomed to the solitude of this room, he could continue on weekends and in the evenings. He would do no more today.

Samuel shuffled Melchior's notes back into the folder and reached for *Geometria*. It was open to a different page.

A breeze. A draft. Samuel had left the door open. The same breeze that made the noise must have turned the pages. Samuel rubbed his fingers against his thumb.

This page was not in Arabic. Samuel pulled Melchior's notes out again. Going through them, last night, he had noticed something but had been too tired to pay it much heed. Runes, he assumed, yet there was something odd about them. Melchior must have made a bad copy. Here they were again on the page before him and they matched Melchior's copy exactly.

Samuel slumped into the chair, still clutching Melchior's copy of this page. The characters looked Etruscan, but that could not be. The book would have to be a new fake, yet it was listed as being in this collection for at least 400 years, long before Etruscan writing was described by archaeology. The only other alternative was too preposterous to consider. The Etruscans had been crushed by Rome before the birth of Christ. This book, with its pristine cover and fine paper, could not have existed in Etruscan times. It even mentioned another book, *Clavicula Salomonis*, which also could not have existed then. Samuel reached for *Geometria*. The woman's voice whispered again.

Take me home.

Samuel swung his head from side to side, but he was alone. The voice sounded close, almost inside his head. He picked up *Geometria*, determined now to replace it on its shelf and get out of there. It was fatigue and his missed lunch, he was sure, combined with the stillness of the empty library and the creaking of the old structure, but the sounds spooked him, and all he wanted now was home. Something to eat and an early night.

Take me. I'm yours.

Samuel stared at the book in his hands. What if he took it home and studied it in peace? Some food and rest was all he needed. No, it was against the rules. These books never left this room. He could not break so stern a rule on his first day as the boss.

Yet it would be so easy. So logical. Nobody need ever know. All he had to do was get the book back early Monday morning. Tomorrow, after church, he would have the rest of the day to examine it and compare Melchior's notes with the original. Okay, it had some anomalies, but the translation could skip a few parts. The Etruscan characters fascinated him. At home he had a modern codex. Maybe he could translate some of it. Or all of it.

Samuel shook his head. "This is silly." He had the key now. Access to the books here whenever he liked. Breaking rules and risking unemployment was pointless. Yet even holding this book sent a thrill through his hands. The Etruscan...

Take me. Free me from this place.

Samuel reached a decision. Nobody ever requested this book. It was likely that there was no record of its existence other than that anonymous "untranslated grimoire" entry in the catalog. He would risk it.

Samuel put Melchior's notes in their folder, placed the folder on the book and, carried both to the door. He stopped in the doorway.

Geometria ton Zoon referenced *Clavicula Salomonis*. That was translated, so cross-referencing *Geometria* with *Clavicula* would be useful in his own translation. It might help when he tried publishing *Geometria*. Samuel considered the risk and decided it was acceptable. He took *Clavicula Salomonis* from its shelf, added it to his pile, then left the room in a hurry. With the Old Books Room locked once more, the books, gloves, and folder in a plastic bag and the library's doors secured, Samuel hurried home.

Chapter Four

Fed, rested, and comfortable in the familiar surroundings of home, Samuel donned the white cotton gloves and sat at his dining table with *Geometria ton Zoon*, *Clavicula Salomonis,* and Melchior's notes spaced out in front of him. Apart from his notepad and pencil, his copy of *Lost Languages* was the only addition to this collection.

Samuel stretched his face in an attempt to force his eyes to focus. Food and home was easy. Rest had helped, but rest was not sleep. Yet he could not—would not—even consider bed before examining *Geometria*'s Etruscan passage.

Samuel transcribed, letter by letter, until dusk fell and he was forced to add to his room lights with a reading lamp. Finally, he settled back to examine his transliteration.

Even allowing for the Etruscans' somewhat cavalier approach to vowel use, his notes made no sense. None. Not one identifiable word appeared from the phonetic garbage on Samuel's notepad. He dropped the pad onto the table and pressed the heels of his hands into his eyes.

"Waste of time." Samuel stretched his aching neck. "They look Etruscan, but that's probably a coincidence. Runes of some sort, maybe, or just random symbols copied from a slab of rock someone found. They look good but they say nothing."

Samuel pursed his lips. The rest of the book was in one language, written in reverse and in the script of another. Perhaps this passage was also reversed, and in another language? With trembling fingers he transferred his notes to another page, this time backwards.

It still made no sense. Samuel dropped his pen beside the pad and stared at his work. He could not recognize any language among the random-looking syllables on the page. If he read the phonemes aloud, maybe it would come to him. He pronounced the first line.

Dots of light appeared in his vision. Blues, reds, and yellows danced before his eyes. Whispered voices filled the room. Samuel's fingers tingled. His head swam with the intensity of the whispers. His temples throbbed with the urgency in their tone. The lights blocked his view of the page. Samuel's heart pounded. He folded his arms over his chest to stop it bursting and took in ragged breaths.

Among the whispers, a woman's voice came through clear.

Not yet. There are preparations.

Samuel leaned back in his chair, trying to find a position that would reduce the pain. Tears poured from his eyes, but his mouth felt as dry as dust. That paradox was the last thing in his mind when Samuel lost consciousness.

Chapter Five

Romulus dropped the thick wad of paper that made up the Sunday news onto his coffee table, placed his tea beside it, and relaxed into his deep leather armchair.

The sofa and the antique cabinets were among the items he brought with him when moving here. The house, though large, was well within his budget, but he had not yet found sufficient furniture to fill it. Romulus felt in no hurry. He had a seat to sit in, a place for his tea and newspapers, room for all his books. The kitchen and this sitting room were equipped, as were his bedroom and bathroom. There were two more downstairs rooms, one of which was filled with shelving, and two spare bedrooms, neither of which contained beds. Most of these other rooms were stacked with boxes Romulus had not yet unpacked.

Sunday morning was not a time for unpacking. It was a time for a cup of tea, a good cigar, and a read of the newspapers. Since Romulus saw no way to avoid sharing the planet with imbeciles, he felt obliged to keep up with what they were doing.

First, there was the ritual of filtering the pile of paper on the table. Out went the TV guide and the glossy celebrity magazine. Out went the fashion and sports supplements. That reduced the pile by half. The comics went to the bottom of the remaining pile. After reading the weekly woes, Romulus always liked to end with a laugh.

The stack of supplements would go, unread, into the recycling bin. It occurred to Romulus that the recyclers could save a lot of time and money by putting the same magazines back into next week's papers. Nobody with any sense read them anyway, and those who did read them were unlikely to notice.

Romulus took a sip of tea and picked up the first of the papers. He had just scanned the headline on the first page when the doorbell rang. Romulus ignored it. He was not at home to Sunday callers. Never had been and never would be. The doorbell rang again. Romulus opened the paper, held it up, and growled.

Another ring. Romulus crumpled the paper, folded it, and dumped it on the table. It was impossible to concentrate until whoever was at the door gave up and went away.

After a few minutes of silence, Romulus reached for the newspaper. He straightened it out and held it up.

Someone tapped on the window. This time the paper tore in Romulus's fingers. He would need more than a few cartoons to dispel the rage that filled him now. He glared at the window.

A small man with neat black hair and a black suit grinned and waved. Romulus strode to the window, fists clenched and jaw set. The man pointed towards the door. Romulus pointed at the street and closed the curtains. He had almost made it back to his chair when the doorbell rang again.

Romulus hung his head and tensed his shoulders. Even God managed a day off on the Sabbath. Could the buffoons who wandered the world not allow him the same? He yanked open the door to the hallway, stomped to the front door, and pulled it open just as the man in black reached for the doorbell again.

"Don't." Romulus put his hand over the doorbell. He was about to unleash every foul word in his extensive vocabulary, as well as a few he had invented on the way to the door when he noticed the man's straight white collar.

On Romulus's list of hated professions, priests were very near the top. His youth had been filled with his mother's devotion to the Church and to all its talk of sin, repentance, and punishment. Especially punishment. The sight of a priest was enough to bring back vague and unwelcome memories. Priests were interested only in hellfire and damnation. Well, this one came to the right place. Even so, a remnant of his childhood indoctrination forced Romulus to moderate his tone.

"What do you want? Make it quick, make it quiet, and then leave." Romulus folded his arms and leaned against the door frame.

The priest showed no sign that he had heard. "Hello. I'm Father Thomas Michael. I used to live here." He held out his hand.

"Irrelevant." Romulus stared into the priest's eyes. "This was once a manse, but now it's my home. There is no religion here now. Just tell me what you want and then go."

Father Michael stared at his open hand for a moment then let it drop to his side. "I heard you might be difficult."

"On the contrary, I am easy. All you have to do is stay out of the way."

"Let me start again." The priest puffed out his cheeks.

"I'd rather you skipped to the end. The part where you leave." Romulus started closing the door. "I think that's going to be my favorite part of this conversation."

"Perhaps I could come back another time?"

"Perhaps. A time when I'm not home would be best." Romulus stood with the door half closed and narrowed his eyes. "It's Sunday. Shouldn't you be at work? Don't you have people to indoctrinate?"

The priest shook his head. "Father Johnson is taking services today."

"I see. Well, tell him I didn't say hello." Romulus slammed the door, reached up to the doorbell, and pulled out its battery. He would replace it when he had finished his newspaper.

Romulus returned to his chair and finished his tea. The newspaper could wait until after he had smoked a cigar and calmed down. He hissed through his teeth.

"A priest. Here. On a Sunday of all days. What is the world coming to?"

He stared at the newspaper and considered skipping straight to the comics.

Chapter Six

Samuel knelt on the yellow soil, one hand outstretched on its surface. He pressed, but his fingers made no indentation in the ground. Puzzled, Samuel felt around with both hands. It was not rock. It felt like sand but it was impenetrable.

A pair of bare legs stepped into his line of sight. Samuel followed them up, his cheeks warming as he realized their owner was female, beautiful, and naked. He lingered a while before reaching her face, standing as he did so. She smiled.

"What's your name?" The woman reached out her hands towards him.

Over her shoulder, Samuel saw the ragged old man approaching, calling something. He ignored the man. This was his dream, and he preferred not to share it with the scarred and wrinkled wretch. He gazed into the woman's jet-black eyes.

"My name is Samuel. Samuel Watson."

The woman's face lit with pleasure. "Shemuel. Ah, it has been a long time since I heard that name. I have been waiting so long."

"Waiting? For what?"

She put her arms around him, pulling him close. "For you."

Her long black hair reached out as though alive, strands of it caressing his face and neck. Samuel inhaled her musky aroma, so much more natural than Donna's chemical-factory smell. His arms slid around her waist, and she pressed closer in response. Samuel glanced over her shoulder, hoping the tattered man had vanished.

He was still there, and he was getting nearer, the shreds of his clothing flying around him. Samuel picked up some of what he was saying.

"Don't tell her..."

A thunder filled the air, a hammering of steel and wood. The yellow world faded into darkness.

* * * *

Samuel woke to a pounding in his head. Everything ached, and his mouth felt desiccated. He shifted his head a little and groaned at the painful protests of his neck muscles. He became aware of cold, of pressure on his chest, and his seated position. The pounding came again, but it was outside his head. Outside the room.

He forced his eyes open. The light on the ceiling burned, so he closed them, shifted his head forward, and tried again.

A table strewn with papers and books came into focus. The books he took, the notes, his own attempt at transcription. Samuel groaned. He must have spent the whole night here, and a good part of the morning judging by the amount of light coming through the window. He winced at another bout of pounding but this time recognized it. Someone knocked at his door.

Samuel forced his numb legs to move. His feet had swollen and felt like footballs. Leaning on the table, he lurched upright and stumbled towards the hallway, wondering what the time was—what day it was. Should he be at work?

He tried to unlock the front door, realized it was already unlocked, and pulled it open.

The small, woolen-coated woman on his doorstep stuck out her gray-bristled chin. "Your doorbell doesn't work. Come along, Samuel. We'll be late."

"Late?"

"Late for church. My, you don't look well."

Samuel's sleep-dazed mind finally connected a name and a face. It was his neighbor, Mrs. Oldham. They always walked to church together. "Ah. Hello. Is it Sunday already?"

She frowned at him, deepening her collection of wrinkles in the process. "Samuel. I do hope you haven't been drinking. You look a mess. My husband used to look like that on Sunday mornings, until the drink finally killed him."

Samuel forced a smile. "No, I haven't been drinking. Just working very late. I fell asleep in my chair."

"Come on then. You'll have to hurry for church."

"Ah, I'm sorry. I think I'll have to miss church this morning. I'm really not feeling up to it."

"Well, I hope this won't become a habit. You have to look after yourself, you know. You're not getting any younger."

"I know, but I've just been promoted. It means more work, as well as more pay. I have to make a good impression."

"Not much good if you kill yourself. What kind of impression will that give?" Mrs. Oldham sniffed. "Well, I'll be off to church. You get to bed and get some sleep. You look like you need it."

"I'll do that. Goodbye for now." Samuel closed the door and stared at the doorbell. He had fitted a new battery just last week. Or had he? His memory was never good when it came to household chores. Samuel shook his head and resolved to add "battery" to his next shopping list. He walked to his kitchen, filled the kettle, and switched it on.

He spooned coffee into a cup and tried to recall how far he had progressed when he fell asleep. Something about the Etruscan-like passage. Perhaps he should leave that until later. Certainly he should avoid tiring himself out. If he had fallen forwards, and woken up with his face on *Geometria ton Zoon* or *Clavicula Salomonis*, drool soaking through their pages...

Samuel shuddered. It didn't bear thinking about. The sensible thing to do was to take the books back today and leave them alone until tomorrow. He could spend time in the Old Books Room on his breaks, and if the evenings proved too spooky, well the translations would just take a little longer. The Etruscan lettering could wait. It made no sense anyway.

His mouth twitched into a smile. It didn't need to make sense. It needed to be mysterious. The New Age folks loved this sort of thing. Translating this book, and some of the other ancient grimoires in the library, would make him rich. This one, though, was special. According to Melchior's notes, the only known copy of *Geometria ton Zoon* was here, in Marchway Library.

A twinge of guilt wiped his smile away. He never missed church. It was his one regular social event. Samuel stared at the floor. For many years, it had been his only social event. Once a week, every week, he attended church. What would they think of him as the author of such a book? Translations of ancient magical texts were the province of people like Crowley or Mathers, renowned devil-worshippers. Would they deny him communion if they discovered his plans? Would they ostracize him? There was also Nathaniel Attlee to consider. This was the one book Attlee had insisted Samuel leave alone.

The kettle clicked. Samuel made himself a coffee, and his smile returned. A false name would solve both problems. Writers did that all the time. Nobody need know it was him behind the translated texts.

Samuel sat at the table and sipped his coffee. Yes, he should take those books back today. A wry smile twitched his mouth. Later today. Perhaps this evening. Or tomorrow morning before the staff arrived. Yes, tomorrow would be fine.

A sneeze took him by surprise, then another. His coffee spilled onto the table. Samuel put the cup down and reached for a roll of paper towels. Sleeping in the cold left him with more than just a few aches and pains.

Chapter Seven

Romulus stomped along the tall, empty corridors of Marchway University. Perhaps he had been wrong to move here. Perhaps he should have left academia altogether. Self-employment had its attractions. The absence of interfering administrative staff would be top of the list.

He hefted the box of books and papers he carried and wondered if he had accepted the job out of spite. Spite directed against Grimshaw, his former boss, who had berated him often for his blunt exposure of fraudulent mediums and who had decided to close down his previous department. Perhaps it was directed against Imogen LeFevre, his only real competitor for this job. Perhaps both.

No, he took the job because it suited him to do so. If he had put both Grimshaw's and Imogen's noses out of joint in the process that was a bonus. All of that was in the past. Now he had a new target for his fury.

Romulus kicked open the door to his office, entered, and dropped his box on the desk. He stood with hands on hips, surveyed the compact room, and hissed through his teeth.

The room was almost filled by the plain desk, three chairs, two battered filing cabinets, and a few bookshelves. Romulus kicked the door closed.

His interview had provided some interesting insights into the arrangements here. As head of a new department, he would answer to Professor Chesterton, the head of Psychology, until his own department could stand alone. No problem. Romulus preferred to stand alone, and Chesterton clearly intended to stay out of Romulus's way. Above Chesterton was Chancellor Orson, a devious, politically motivated ball of blubber who Romulus intended to ignore as far as possible. Orson vehemently fought the formation of a parapsychology department in Marchway. Romulus was not to publish any paranormal "proof" of any kind unless Orson approved it. No investigation should produce anything other than a natural explanation.

That was fine with Romulus. Every medium he investigated had been a fake. A parasite, making a living on the grief of others. Romulus prided himself on his ability to root out the fraudulent, explain away hauntings, seek out and expose all the natural events that could be mistaken—or exploited—as evidence of the supernatural. He never failed.

There are no ghosts.

Neither Orson nor Chesterton were the focus of his rage this morning. He had called Chesterton's secretary's office in case there were any messages for him. Unlikely, since he had been here only a week, but there had been one.

With a tight and hateful smile, Chesterton's secretary had informed him that Jeremy Farquhar-Jones had arranged to visit him at ten o'clock. No one had consulted him.

Venting his anger on the secretary had been unsatisfactory. She refused to cancel the appointment since Farquhar-Jones would already be on his way. Romulus left her office after ensuring she would never again arrange any kind of meeting without first securing his approval. Now he had to prepare this little office to receive an unwelcome visitor.

The worn, though comfortable, swivel chair he reserved for his own use. He placed the solid wood, uncushioned chair opposite his desk and piled books and papers onto the third, cushioned chair to make it inaccessible. All of his books and papers could be shelved and filed later. Romulus opened the window and took a cigar from his pocket.

Smoking within the university buildings was forbidden, but Romulus reasoned that as long as the cigar was outside, he wasn't breaking any rules. He leaned out the window and lit his cigar.

Directly below him was the parking lot. Even from here, he could see piles of flattened cardboard boxes through the windows of his old Ford. Romulus blew smoke and wondered where Marchway kept its waste disposal facility. Deprived of his restful Sunday newspapers, Romulus had spent a large part of yesterday unpacking and now had to dispose of the residue.

Smoke curled from Romulus's cigar into the still morning air. Last night's rain had left the quiet town of Marchway fresh and clean. A few deep breaths of that cool air reduced Romulus's ire to mere anger, which he maintained for later rekindling.

A further puff of smoke swirled and twisted on eddies rising from below. For an instant it formed a face that stared at Romulus, its ethereal mouth agape. Romulus blew a smoke ring through the face and smiled as it fragmented. Smoke often formed face-like shapes in the air.

Romulus leaned on his elbows and took a long draw of his cigar. The human mind was programmed to find faces. So many times he had seen photographs purporting to show a shrieking, sad or kindly face among the interplay of leaves in a forest or in the grain of wood. Simple, natural structures, mistaken by the gullible as visits from the Other Side. He had nearly fallen for the delusion himself, when the smoke from his cigar formed into faces that resembled his long-dead mother or his Uncle Toby. Illusion, hallucination, self-deception. It was easy to "see" something recognizable in any structure that bore a superficial resemblance to a memory.

There are no ghosts.

The cigar reached its end. Romulus stubbed it out on the stone windowsill and dropped the butt into the bushes that lined the parking lot directly below his window. He left the window open. The lower the temperature in the room, the less time Farquhar-Jones was likely to stay. Romulus took his seat and picked up a book on cryptozoology. Bigfoot, black cats, yetis-these were tangible things with a faint possibility of truth in them. Romulus had considered pursuing such research. At the least it would involve a lot of free travel to exotic locations.

At a quarter to ten, someone knocked on his door.

Romulus clamped his lips together. *The weasel is early. He can wait.*

The door opened. Romulus filled his lungs, ready to explode at the impertinence, but instead exhaled slowly when Elaine entered, her long dark hair hanging loose around her slim shoulders.

"Romulus, you're here. I was wondering where you were."

"Well, this is my office, such as it is. This is where you'd expect to find me."

Elaine came into the room, closing the door behind her. "I see." Her eyebrows rose and a hint of a smile crossed her lips. "I was going to ask if you had a good weekend, but I guess not."

"Not much of a morning so far, either."

"So I gathered. What did you do to Chesterton's secretary? She practically ducked under her desk when I opened her door."

"I did nothing." Romulus looked at the ceiling.

"Come on, Rom. I know you better than that. What's ticking you off this time?"

"You know I bought that old manse? Well, I didn't know it came with a built-in cheery priest. Irritating little pest popped up yesterday to tell me how he used to live there. What are you smiling at?"

Elaine laughed. "Priests do that, you know, stop by to welcome new parishioners and invite them to the church. I had a visit myself when I moved in. He was pleasant enough. He said his name was Father Johnson."

"Well I had to put up with the other one. He's painfully happy, immune to sarcasm, and threatened to come back. He just won't take a hint."

"Other one? You mean one from a different church? I'd be surprised if he did come back. I've heard your 'hints.'"

"He said this Father Johnson was taking the services yesterday, so he must be from the same church." Romulus curled his lip into a sneer. "Hopefully he'll stick to welcoming people who care to be welcomed in the future."

Elaine took the seat opposite Romulus, squirming as she sat. "This chair is awful. Why don't you use that one?" She indicated the third chair, with its cushion covered in books and paper.

"Might encourage people to stay," Romulus muttered.

"Well, that's nice. I move to a new town for you, and you don't even want me in your office."

"I didn't mean you." Romulus waved his hand. "I meant Jeremy Farty-Jones or whatever he's called."

"Who?"

"Some rich kid. He wants to fund a project."

Elaine's brow furrowed. "That's good, isn't it?"

"No. He arranged the meeting, using his rich dad as a lever. First I heard of it was this morning."

"Ah. That's what's got you riled."

"I don't like having meetings arranged for me without being consulted. It's an idiotic project, too."

"What's it about?"

"Orbs." Romulus spat the word.

Elaine shrugged. "I don't get it. We're supposed to be studying ghosts now, and surely orbs are part of the whole phenomenon? Extra funding is always useful."

"Orbs are bunk. Ghosts are bunk, but orbs are extra-special bunk. They're dust, insects, something in your eye. Not even worth looking at."

"But—"

"But nothing. You know how to get orbs? You take a cheap digital camera, especially a small one, where the flash is close to the lens. When the flash goes off, it lights up dust particles in front of the lens. They're too close to be focused so they flare, looking like globes on the photo. Hey presto—orbs." Romulus finished with a flourishing gesture.

"Some people see orbs without cameras." Elaine wore a smirk. She was deliberately winding him up, he could tell.

"Floaters," he said.

"What?"

"Floaters. Bits of cells inside the eye. Gives the same effect."

Elaine shook her head. "That's not right. Floaters don't—"

A knock at the door interrupted her.

"That'll be Farty-Jones." Romulus leaned his elbows on the desk. "We'll have to finish this later."

"All right, but—"

"Later. Let the moron in, would you?"

Elaine rose, giving Romulus a look he knew well. It meant "control your temper." He nodded impatiently and waved her to the door.

As she opened it, Romulus heard a thin nasal voice. "Oh. I was given to understand this was Professor Crowe's office."

The voice gave Romulus the impression of a thin man with no chin. Elaine moved aside to let his visitor enter, and Romulus saw that his impression had been entirely correct.

"Come in. Take a seat." *Let's get this over with.*

"Good morning, Professor Crowe. Jeremy Farquhar-Jones, at your service." He settled himself into the wooden chair. Romulus watched the man wriggle, trying to get comfortable.

"Well, Mister Jones—"

"Farquhar-Jones."

"What can I do for you?" *Maybe I can ask the chancellor to loan you a chin or two.*

"It's more a case of what I can do for you. I'd like to provide you with funding for your work."

"Very generous. What's the catch?"

"Catch?"

"Normally, I have to write a proposal for a series of experiments and then find someone willing to fund the work. It's most unusual for someone to turn up and just offer me money. There must be a reason, surely?" Romulus smiled at the man's evident confusion.

"I see. Quite right, of course. Well, there is a particular aspect I'd like you to study—"

"Yes, there would be. I didn't think you'd hand over the money and just let me do what I liked with it."

"Well, no. The thing is, I have developed a preoccupation with the phenomena known as orbs. They're a kind of light, you see—"

"I know what orbs are." Romulus held up his hand, lowering it as he turned to face the window. "May I ask what's piqued your interest in these orbs?"

"Ah. Well, I was watching television late one night, and there was a program about ghosts. Amazing stuff. Anyway, I found these orb things particularly fascinating, so I thought, you know, let's get that new professor guy looking into them. I thought it might be a good project to get you started."

Romulus clamped his hands to the arms of the chair to stop them shaking with his building rage. His breath hissed through his teeth. *Get me started?* He spun his chair to face Jeremy, whose bland smile just made matters worse. Romulus spoke through clenched teeth. "I can assure you, I have already 'started.' I can also tell you about your little orbs, here and now."

"Oh, really? How fascinating. Do tell."

Romulus paused for a moment before continuing. "Those orbs have as much intelligence as you do."

Farquhar-Jones leaned forward. "Wonderful. You already know that?"

"There is no doubt." Romulus rubbed the end of his nose with his finger so that he could hide his smirk with his hand. "There's one more thing you should know."

"Yes?"

"Orbs don't exist. They're reflections from insects and dust." Romulus waited for Farquhar-Jones to make the connection. *This could take a while.* Instead of the expected outrage, the realization manifested on Farquhar-Jones's face as a spreading grin.

Romulus let his head drop into his hand. *The lunatic thinks I'm joking.*

Farquhar-Jones started laughing. "Hawr hawr hawr." Mingled with this appalling braying were assorted snorts and grunts. The whole farmyard was there, sounding through one revolting mouth.

Romulus found it difficult to decide which was more offensive, the man's laugh or his severely limited reasoning abilities. He raised his head to glare directly at Farquhar-Jones.

"If you make that sound again," Romulus said, his voice low, "I'll staple your mouth shut."

Farquhar-Jones stopped laughing and looked at Romulus with uncertainty. Romulus lifted the heavy stapler from his desk and raised an eyebrow.

"Well," Farquhar-Jones said. "I've never been so insulted in all my life."

"Oh, you must have been. You're just too dim to realize it."

Spluttering with indignation, Farquhar-Jones stood and strode towards the door. "I don't think I'll be financing your work after all. You, sir, are a mannerless clod."

"I couldn't possibly accept funding from someone with no more capability of understanding my work than an underdeveloped sponge," Romulus said, still smiling. "'Watched it on the television' indeed. You, sir, are the most offensive, repellent, hideous caricature of a human being it has ever been my misfortune to encounter. I'll spend the rest of my days fervently hoping that we never meet again."

Farquhar-Jones turned purple with rage.

"Goodbye," Romulus said. "Don't come back."

Speechless, Farquhar-Jones slammed the door as he left. Romulus grinned. He had lost what might have been a substantial grant today, but it had been worth it. Besides, how could he have sent reports to that idiot? What chance would the fool have had of understanding a word of them? Romulus would settle for much more modest funding if it meant dealing with people who could at least comprehend the reports on the work they were paying for. He settled into his seat with a contented sigh and looked at his watch, then turned his grin to the phone. *This shouldn't take long.*

* * * *

The man nearly upended Elaine's tray as she turned the corner.

"Watch it!" She looked up to see the same man she had left in Romulus's office. He looked furious, which could mean only one thing. He glowered at her, giving a "harrumph" before storming off towards the stairwell. Elaine, eyebrows raised, drew a slow breath and continued towards Romulus's office.

Bracing the tray on one arm, she tapped the door and opened it. Romulus was seated at his desk, grinning as though he hadn't a care in the world.

"I brought some coffee and doughnuts, but I see he's already left." She nudged the door closed with her foot as she entered.

"Yes, he's gone, and good riddance."

Elaine sighed and placed the tray on the table. "Well, you may as well pour the coffee. No sense in wasting it."

Romulus raised the lid of the pot and sniffed. "Ah, a decent coffee. Just the thing."

Elaine moved the papers and books off the cushioned chair and set them on the floor, then exchanged the chair with the uncomfortable one. "Rom, you can't keep on doing this."

Romulus poured two coffees and handed one to her. "Doing what?" he said, his face a parody of innocence.

"Antagonizing everyone you meet. That man might have been important."

"Oh, he is, or at least his father is. His dad's on the board, you know." Romulus sipped his coffee.

Elaine had the cup halfway to her lips. She set it down. "Romulus! We've been here one week and you've already thrown a governor's son out of your office. What if he goes to the chancellor?"

"I expect he's there now. The phone should ring at any moment."

"Sometimes I despair. Look at you. You're enjoying this, aren't you?"

Romulus set his cup down. "Do you know why he wanted to fund research into orbs?"

Elaine shook her head.

"He saw them on TV. So, he set up this meeting without consulting me, waltzed in here, and offered to give me a bit of a start in my new job."

Closing her eyes, Elaine sank back into her chair. The outcome had been inevitable.

"What about the chancellor?" she murmured.

"What about him?"

"He could fire you. He could fire us both."

"He won't. The grants and bursaries I have are more than enough to cover my salary. And yours. He has us here, effectively, at no cost to the university. Then there's my publication record, which will boost the psychology department's rating at the next research assessment. Plus, the students will be back in a couple of weeks, and they're expecting lectures on parapsychology. Orson won't just throw us away."

"Are you sure?" Elaine opened her eyes and stared at him. *Of course he's sure. He's never anything but sure.*

"You said it. It's our first week. If I'd gone along with Farty-Jones and his silly little scheme, you know what would have happened?"

"No. What would have happened?" A sudden fatigue gripped her. It was often like that around Romulus, as if his enthusiasm grew too large for one man and he had to absorb energy from those around him just to keep it going.

"Next time there was a late-night horror film, every chinless twit within a hundred miles would be knocking at our door. Can we investigate vampires? Werewolves? Mummies? Aliens? Can we assess the risk of being eaten by a brain on a stick?"

Elaine had to agree. There was rarely an option anyway, but this time he was right. "But what about the chancellor?"

"He'll see my point, I'm sure"

Yes, he probably will. She noticed Romulus blinking, shaking his head. "Rom? Are you okay?" She started to rise, but he waved her back into her seat.

"Floaters," he said.

"Floaters?"

"I get them occasionally. Nothing to worry about, I've checked up on them." He stretched his eyes wide. "That's how I know about floaters and orbs. I see them sometimes, but I, at least, know what they are."

"My father had floaters." Elaine half-closed her eyes, puzzled by his description. "A lot of them. He described them to me, often."

Romulus spread his arms. "Good. So you know what I'm talking about."

"Not quite."

"Oh?"

"Floaters are like little bits of dust or hair in your vision. They're not globes and they're not lights. They're dark, irregular shapes."

His eyebrows lowered, and his face formed a frown.

She sighed. "Whatever you're seeing, they're not floaters."

His face colored, his finger started wagging at her, and he opened his mouth to speak. The phone rang. Romulus's frown became a grin.

"Aren't you going to answer?" Elaine's fingers twitched. She had never understood how Romulus could ignore a ringing phone.

"In a moment." Romulus looked up. "I thought you were spending the morning at the library?"

Elaine took a gulp of her coffee then rose to leave. "Yes. I came here first to pick up some notes." She forgot about the library. "I'm going there now." As she reached the door, Romulus called after her.

"Take a look at their rare manuscripts. See if there's anything interesting."

"Right." Elaine pulled the door closed. Before it shut completely, she heard Romulus answer the phone, his voice light and pleasant.

"Ah, Chancellor Orson. How may I help you?"

The door closed with a thud. Elaine gritted her teeth and went to the laboratory to fetch her coat and handbag, wondering if she would still be employed when she returned.

Chapter Eight

The tree looked like glass. Its gnarled bark distorted the yellow plain behind. Samuel reached out to touch it. His hand stopped at where the bark would be, but his fingers registered no contact.

Samuel dropped his hand from the tree and looked around. He stood at the edge of a forest of crystal trees, all leafless, all twisted into grotesque shapes. Multicolored sunlight flared and glowed within the branches, which moved as if in a breeze. Samuel stood in the still air and enjoyed the display.

"You're getting further in. You must fight it." The tattered old man appeared among the trees, heading towards Samuel. His rags flapped around him, beard and long hair so matted with grime it was impossible to distinguish one from the other. He stopped a few feet away. "You can see some of it, can't you?"

"I see the trees. They're beautiful."

"They are hideous, just like those who form them." The old man's face wore a sneer, although he whispered the words as though he feared someone was listening.

"Where are they? Are they like the woman I met last time? I'd like to see them."

"No. You wouldn't." The old man lowered his head. "Don't look at her directly. See her in obsidian."

Samuel chuckled. "Obsidian? What are you talking about? I can't see through a stone."

"Please. Listen. Trust me." The old man reached out. His thin fingers touched the edge of Samuel's jacket.

Samuel moved out of reach. "Who are you?"

The man recoiled, his eyes wide. "No names here. Don't ask mine, and tell no-one yours. Names have power, especially here."

"So why should I trust you?"

"I can't tell you my name, but I have something." He dug among the filthy scraps of his clothing. "Here. You must recognize it. It links us. It proves you can—must—believe what I say." The man held out his hand, palm open.

The trees shattered. Shards flew in all directions, some passing through Samuel and the old man but causing no harm, no sensation at all. Samuel's vision narrowed into a tunnel. At the end was an old hand holding something. Samuel blinked his eyes but failed to identify the object.

* * * *

Samuel raised his head from his desk and took a deep and noisy sniff. He reached for his box of tissues, pulled out a handful, and blew his nose. The clock on his desk stood at ten past eleven, so he couldn't have slept more than ten or fifteen minutes. The cold he caught from sleeping in his chair had already made him late for work. He had no time for napping.

Sitting up, Samuel brought his office into focus. On his desk, a set of book request forms awaited his approval.

He picked up the forms and frowned, remembering part of his dream. He tried to picture what the old man had shown him. It was there, in his mind, if he could only remember, but concentration hurt his head.

It was only a dream. Forget it.

He blew his nose again, then tried to concentrate on the forms. Requests from patrons of other libraries for books in Marchway's stock. Donna or John would already have checked whether the books were currently available, out on loan, or no longer stocked. The forms were sorted and marked. All Samuel had to do was sign them, but he felt it his duty to know which books left his library.

The concentration Samuel applied to the forms made his head pound and his eyes water. He pulled the first form towards himself and looked at the requested title through tear-filmed eyes.

Geometria.

Samuel gasped. He grabbed a fresh tissue and wiped the tears from his eyes. After blowing his nose, he looked again.

Gematria.

He could have cried with relief. The request was for Aleister Crowley's treatise on numerical divination.

Must be my conscience acting up.

The phone rang. A light on the instrument indicated an internal call. Samuel wiped his nose with the tissue before dropping it into the rapidly filling bin beside the desk. He picked up the receiver.

"Yes?"

"Sorry to disturb you, Mister Watson, but there's a young lady here who'd like to see you." Donna's voice was tense.

"Oh? What about?"

"She wants to look at the old books."

Samuel's whole body sagged. *Geometria ton Zoon* and *Clavicula Salomonis* were still at his house. He had woken late, so he had failed to get to the library early enough to put them back. Samuel forced his fuzzed brain to concentrate. Donna was still speaking.

"...told her she had to have an appointment, but she insists on seeing you."

"All right, Donna. I'll be down in a moment."

"I'm very sorry about this, Mister Watson."

"It's not your fault, Donna. Have her wait in one of the side rooms."

"Very well, Mister Watson." Donna hung up.

Samuel stared at the phone in his hand for a moment. With slow precision, he put it back into its cradle. *She can't want to see Geometria. What if she wants Clavicula Salomonis though? How will I explain that?*

He stood, leaning on the desk for support, and stretched his aching muscles. After stuffing a few tissues into his pockets, he headed for the door.

I'll tell her I can't go sneezing and coughing in the Old Books Room. It's true anyway.

Closing the door behind him, he descended the stairs to the main room. Donna stood at the issues desk. She watched his approach, her hard expression fading to concern by the time he reached the front desk.

"Are you sure you shouldn't just go home, Mister Watson? You don't look at all well."

"I'm fine, Donna. Just a cold."

"You're sure? You look as though you might have the flu."

Samuel took a tissue from his pocket and wiped his nose. "Maybe. I hope not. So, who's our visitor?"

Donna's face hardened again. "Some new researcher from the university. She wants to get into the Old Books Room but she hasn't made an appointment. I told her."

"Yes, I know. She must be new. I'll explain the rules to her, don't worry." *And buy myself time to put the books back.* "Did she give a name?"

"Pettifer. Doctor Pettifer. She's in there." Donna pointed to one of the side rooms, where a dark-haired, slim woman was visible through the glass panel.

Samuel raised an eyebrow. "She looks very nice." He turned, smiling, to Donna, whose expression brought a whole new meaning to "stern."

"She was very rude. Just wouldn't be told." Donna folded her arms, wafting enough perfume into the air to cut through Samuel's blocked nose. Samuel took an involuntary step back.

"Well, she won't be seeing the books today. Not without an appointment," he said.

"Good." Donna's face relaxed a little.

Samuel walked towards the side room, his worries forgotten for the moment. Whoever this Doctor Pettifer was, she had made quite an impression on Donna. An impression the poor doctor would find difficult to modify, even if she stayed in the university for the next ten years.

* * * *

Elaine fidgeted in the little room, twisting her fingers in the strap of her small handbag. She looked up as the door opened. A short, rounded man with a pasty face and a red-rimmed nose came into the room, closing the door behind him. He held out his hand.

"Doctor Pettifer," he said, "I'm Samuel Watson, the librarian. How can I help you?"

Elaine rose, accepting the handshake.

"Elaine Pettifer. Doctor of Parapsychology. I'd like to see your collection of ancient books." She thought he winced, but couldn't be sure. He took a tissue from his pocket and blew his nose, motioning for her to sit. Samuel took the seat at the opposite side of the small table.

"I'm afraid you'll need to make an appointment," he said. "I'd have to supervise, you see, and I'm in no condition to do that today."

"Yes, the woman at the desk told me about the appointment system. I'm new here. I didn't know. Would it be too much to ask to see them this afternoon?"

Samuel squirmed in his seat, avoiding her gaze. "Ordinarily, I could make an exception, but I'd rather stay out of that room today. I don't want to risk coughing and sneezing all over those books." He took another crumpled tissue from his pocket and held it over his mouth.

Elaine waited while he coughed. "Perhaps you could supervise from outside the room?"

"Oh, no. I couldn't do that. I'm responsible for the books. Besides, how would you find the one you're looking for?" He frowned. "Which one are you looking for? You haven't said."

"No, I haven't. Actually, I'd like to browse."

"Browse?" The red color in Samuel's nose spread across his cheeks.

"Yes. I'm looking for local ghost stories, and I thought those old books would be a good place to start."

"Browse? Young lady, you don't browse in that room. You request a specific book, make an appointment, and I supervise you while you read."

"I'm sorry, I didn't mean to offend—"

Samuel covered his mouth with one hand, coughed, then continued. "Quite all right. You're new and unfamiliar with our rules. Besides, if you want information on local hauntings, the Old Books Room is hardly the best place to start."

"Oh?"

"We have a section on local history and folklore in the main library. I'll show you where it is. When you have something you want to trace, maybe the old books can help you, but I expect you'll find what you're looking for without them." He rose and held the door open.

"Thank you, Mister Watson. I'm sorry to have caused you so much trouble." She stood and walked to the door.

"Not at all. I'll show you the books I mentioned, and I can arrange to have an inventory of the Old Books sent to you."

"Oh, an inventory would be very useful. Could you send me two copies? One for my Head of Department, Professor Crowe?"

"No problem."

"Have you worked here for long?" she asked as they left the room.

"For quite some time, yes."

"Oh, so you'd know if there were any local ghosts?"

"I've lived in Marchway all my life. I think you'll find we're fairly ghost-free ."

"I see." Elaine noticed his voice getting quieter as they entered the main library and lowered hers to match. "Not even in the old monastery buildings of the library and university?"

Samuel laughed, a quiet sound that turned into a cough. "No, I'm afraid not. There were one or two sightings at the university, I believe, although they could have been student pranks."

"Really?" *Right under Romulus's nose. He won't like that.*

"Yes. No figures in monk's habits, I'm afraid. Just some lights."

Elaine stopped. "Orbs?"

Samuel took a few steps more and turned, eyebrows raised. "I believe that's the term, yes. Orbs."

Romulus described his floaters as looking just like orbs.

"Here we are." Samuel indicated a shelf. "This section is all local folklore. If there are any ghosts hereabouts—and I must admit I don't know of any—they'll surely be recorded here."

"So you haven't heard of any current hauntings?" Elaine stared at the books. They were unlikely to contain any recent reports, given the time it took for books like these to be compiled and published.

Samuel shrugged. "I keep pretty much to myself. Always have. You'd be better off asking my neighbor." He smiled, tapping the side of his nose with his index finger. "In Marchway, the old lady network knows everything."

"I think that's true in every town." Elaine took a pen and a piece of paper from her handbag. "I'd like to talk to your neighbor, if she's heard of any ghosts." She wrote her name and phone number on the paper, then handed it to Samuel. "Could you ask her to give me a call? I don't want to seem like I'm intruding, but I do need somewhere to start with this project."

"Certainly. I'm sure she'd be delighted to help. I warn you though, she does love to chat. You should expect a long visit with her." He grinned as he pocketed the paper.

"Thank you. Goodbye, Mister Watson."

One of Samuel's eyebrows rose. "Not goodbye, I hope, Doctor Pettifer. Just good day." He turned and walked towards the staircase that led to the upper level of the library.

Elaine's smile slipped a little. Samuel seemed pleasant enough, but he was twice her age and not in the least attractive. She hoped he hadn't just indicated a romantic interest, especially since she had just handed over her phone number. At least it was only her work number. Elaine sighed and turned her attention to the rows of books, scanning for anything potentially ghostly in the titles.

* * * *

Samuel closed the door of his office and leaned against it, wondering how he had managed to restrain himself from running up the stairs. He was sweating profusely, more from nerves than from his cold, and he soaked a tissue with the moisture from his forehead. Crossing to his desk, he sat and stared at the book request form on top of the small pile.

What's that for? Oh, yes, the request for Crowley's book.

He signed the forms without reading any more of them and put them in his out-basket. John would collect them later, and deal with them.

Paperwork completed for now, Samuel relaxed in his chair and considered the risk he took with the old books. If Doctor Pettifer had made an appointment with Attlee, Samuel might not have known in advance. Attlee was notorious for his ad-hoc systems. If she asked to see one of the two he took home, he might now be facing disciplinary action and unemployment. Perhaps even legal action. He shuddered at the thought.

Samuel took the Old Books Room key from his pocket, unclipped it from his keyring, and twirled it in his fingers. The light gleaming on its surface relaxed him. He smiled.

Ah, the power this represents. I, and only I, have a key to the room.

The copy at the university was for emergencies only, and the original, antique key was locked inside the Old Books Room. That made three. One more key had been lost, so Attlee said, when Melchior vanished. Samuel's hand stopped moving. His smile faded. The key lay across the palm of his hand.

He had seen this before. A hand, holding something, in this position. Where had he seen it?

The dream.

Fresh beads of perspiration formed on Samuel's forehead and beneath his thinning hair. He remembered what the old man had shown him. It was a key.

A key to the Old Books Room.

* * * *

"I'm going home, Donna. I feel terrible." Samuel placed his briefcase on the desk and leaned on it.

"Quite right, Mister Watson." Donna's tone was sympathetic. "You really shouldn't have come here today at all, you know."

"I know, but it's my first day in charge. I thought I should try, at least." Samuel coughed, covering his mouth with his hand. "I'd better let John and Robert know."

"Here's John now," Donna said, nodding past Samuel. He turned and saw John approaching the desk.

"John, do you feel like taking over for the rest of the afternoon?"

John smiled. "Certainly, Mister Watson. We've all noticed you're not well." He looked around the library. "It's a quiet day. I don't think there'll be any problems."

"Thank you, John. I expect I'll be back tomorrow, once I've had a good night's rest."

John shook his head. "You just get well. We'll manage."

Samuel looked from one to the other, uncertain how to proceed. He rarely took time off work. "Well, if anyone needs me, you have my phone number."

"Yes, we have, but I don't think we'll need it."

Donna leaned across the desk. "What about the woman who wanted the old books?" she asked. "Should I tell her there'll be no appointments until further notice?" Her self-satisfied grin suggested she would enjoy that.

Samuel suppressed a smirk. "Well, don't make any appointments before next week, just in case. I don't think Doctor Pettifer will be ready for the old books before then, anyway." He turned to John. "Right. I'm off home." He strolled to the main door.

It was when Samuel tried to use his right hand to open the door that he realized it was in his pocket, the key still gripped between its fingers. His left hand was occupied with his briefcase. Samuel put his shoulder to the door and pushed it open.

Chapter Nine

Elaine knocked once and opened the door without waiting for a reply. She smiled at Romulus, who rose from his seat in indignation.

"Hi," she said, taking the seat facing him at his desk. She dropped two books on the desk and looked up at him. "How did it go with the chancellor?"

"Where have you been?" He lowered himself into his chair, folding his arms. "I've been looking for you. We're supposed to be working, you know."

"I have been working. I went to the library, which is where, if you recall, you sent me."

Romulus looked down at the books. "Anything interesting?"

Elaine sighed. "No ghosts anywhere in the town, as far as I can tell. I couldn't get in to see the old manuscripts without an appointment. The librarian was very protective of them." She pushed the books towards Romulus. "There was a poltergeist over in Weston, a few years ago, but it's gone now. Not much in these books apart from old folklore, but the librarian did hint at one place that might prove interesting."

Romulus raised his eyebrows. "Local?"

"Very. But I'm not going to tell you."

"What? Why not?"

"Not until you tell me about your meeting with the chancellor. I want to know if we still have jobs, after your tantrum this morning." Elaine set her jaw and glared at Romulus, who glared back. This impasse lasted only a few moments before Romulus gave in. Elaine allowed herself a self-satisfied smirk. Few people could stare down Romulus Crowe.

Romulus sighed through his scowl, a difficult trick but one she had seen him perform countless times. "The fat controller didn't fire us. Now, where's this ghost of yours?"

"Not good enough. I want details."

"For heaven's sake, woman..." Romulus glowered, but Elaine held her ground. "Oh, all right. Orson and Chesterton were there, along with Farty-Jones. Orson gave me a ticking off, then Farty-Jones left. Afterwards, Chesterton burst out laughing."

"Laughing?"

"Laughing, yes. Are you going to shut up long enough for me to finish this? I told Orson what I told you—accepting money from that idiot would lead to a flood of chinless wonders wanting pointless investigations."

Elaine rolled her eyes. She knew Romulus would have used those exact words. "And?"

"He agreed. Turns out they despise the little pipsqueak almost as much as I do. They're actually pleased about what I did to him." He grinned and puffed out his chest.

"What about his father?"

"No problem. They don't like his father either. Apparently Farty-Jones the elder pressured them into opening this department in the first place, using his position and influence with the other board members. That's why I got the job. Orson didn't want anyone who would be looking for real paranormal effects." Romulus's grin widened. "Orson took enormous pleasure in phoning the old fellow while I was there, on the pretext of apologizing. Best of all, the old man was furious when he found out what his son had been up to. Turns out he knew nothing of this morning's meeting."

"So we're okay." Elaine could not decide whether to be relieved or apprehensive. Romulus had his bosses eating out of his hand. He was going to be insufferable now.

"Yes, yes, we're fine. Now tell me your news." He leaned forward, his elbows on the desk and his chin on his hands. "Where's this so-called ghost? We'll need to get rid of any local ones before we venture further afield."

Elaine pursed her lips. *He's not going to like this.*

"Well?"

Patience was never one of his strong points. Elaine took a deep breath. "There have been reports of orbs—"

Romulus snorted. "Orbs. Is that all? I can explain those away without leaving this office." He settled back in his chair and looked out of the window.

"You won't need to."

Romulus stared at her. "What? I won't need to explain them?"

"You won't need to leave the office."

His eyes narrowed. "Where are these orbs?"

Elaine sighed. "Here. At the university."

His eyes closed and his head shook slowly. He opened his eyes and stood, stepping to the window and staring through it. "Here," he muttered. "Right here. In a place filled with allegedly intelligent people. Who's seen them? Do we have names? Dates?"

"No names. Some of the students, apparently."

The cloud of fury over Romulus' features dissipated in an instant. "Students? Tell me it was on a Saturday night. Go on. Tell me that."

"I don't know. I only know what the librarian told me. Some students saw orbs, here at the university."

Waving his hand in a dismissive gesture, Romulus returned to his seat. "Some drunken students saw headlights reflected in a window," he said. "That's all. There are no orbs." He shook his head, blinking.

Elaine sat up. "Romulus? Are you seeing something?"

"Just these floaters again. They'll go away in a moment."

"Can you describe them?"

He stretched his face, mouth open and eyes wide. "That's better. Describe them? No need. They look like orbs. That's what I've been telling you."

No. Floaters don't look like orbs. He's not seeing floaters.

"Rom, I really think you should get those checked out by a doctor. They don't sound like floaters to me."

"I have a routine eye test booked in a couple of weeks. I'll mention it to the optician. Now will you stop going on about my eyes?"

"I'd feel better if you had it checked. It could be serious." *It could also mean something else, but I'm not going to mention that. Not unless I can do it from a safe distance.*

"Well, I will. In a couple of weeks." He looked at his watch. "It's time for lunch, and my car is full of cardboard."

Elaine struggled to make some kind of connection between his statements. "What?"

"Boxes. Left over from unpacking. I have to find a dump."

"I know where one is. It's only open in the mornings. If we hurry, we might get there before it closes." She stood and turned to the door. "Come on. We can get lunch at a cafeteria I know on High Street."

Romulus snorted as he rose. "As long as it's not some grease-laden fast food joint, you're on. Otherwise I'm leaving you there and going home for lunch."

* * * *

Romulus brought his battered Ford to a halt outside his house, bracing one front wheel against the curb to compensate for the uncertainty of his handbrake. He turned off the engine. The exhaust made a sound like a death rattle.

The cafeteria Elaine had mentioned had turned out to be little more than a burger bar. Well, she might be happy with a fat feast in a plastic tray, but Romulus preferred real food. There might be a decent cafe in the town but he had no time to search for it today. Home it was then, home for a ham salad sandwich and a cup of good coffee.

Romulus glared at the pile of cardboard filling the rear of the car before getting out and slamming the door. The dump had closed by the time he had arrived, so he would have to try again tomorrow. Without Elaine and her incessant complaints about the state of his car. It functioned reasonably well. It took him where he needed to go. It didn't need to be luxurious.

The iron gate leading into the long front garden screeched when he opened it, and screeched again as it closed on its rusted spring.

Must get around to oiling that thing.

As Romulus turned the key in his front door, he heard a voice directly behind him and froze.

"Hello, professor."

Romulus hissed through his teeth. *That priest again.* Still facing the door, he replied, "Good afternoon, Father Michael. I don't wish to be rude, but I think I'm about to be."

"I understand. The first few days at a new job can be tense. I may soon have some news that will interest you though."

"Oh?" Romulus quieted his sigh.

"Something is happening, here in town. I can feel it. I don't know for sure, but it's very bad news, I think. I'll know more later, after I've looked around."

The fool thinks he's a medium now. "Look, Father—" Romulus turned from the door to be confronted by his uncut lawn, his gate, and his car in the street beyond. The priest was nowhere to be seen. *He moves pretty fast.* Romulus shrugged. *He's gone. That's enough for me.* Romulus opened his door and went inside.

Chapter Ten

Samuel's whole body shook while he closed and locked his front door. It was a warm day, but he went to the kitchen and turned on the heat before switching on the kettle.

Samuel considered his situation while he waited for the kettle to boil. He took two books from the Old Books Room, something that would get him sacked on the spot if the university governors found out. After all, the old books, indeed the whole of the Marchway Public Library, actually belonged to the university. He just escaped one close shave. He was lucky Doctor Pettifer was so vague about what she wanted and that he had the handy excuse of this cold.

He had to put those books back tomorrow, no matter what. His translations must wait for another day. Samuel folded his arms, his eyes downcast. Why had he brought them home? He could have read them at the library on his lunch break. What could have possessed him to take such a stupid and unnecessary risk?

However awful he felt, he had to get up early and take them back. He could always come home again afterwards, if necessary. The kettle clicked and he made himself a coffee.

The scent of coffee brought a faint optimism to Samuel's thoughts. He still had the rest of the day. Not enough time for a full translation, but time for a little more work on *Geometria ton Zoon*.

What about the old man? The only other key to the room vanished when Melchior did. The old man had that key, so he must be...

Samuel shook his head. It was just a dream, something his mind had constructed from the notes he had read.

It seemed so real.

Samuel took a mouthful of his coffee. An unexpected coughing fit shook him. Coffee sprayed across the room, spattering the table and floor. Heat burned his nose as the coffee, under pressure, escaped through every available orifice.

Cursing, Samuel put the cup into the sink and grabbed a towel, wiping the hot liquid from his face and neck. He threw the towel onto the table.

"Damn it! I can't read those books in this state." His head swam. Cold-induced fatigue gripped him. "I wouldn't be able to make any sense of them anyway." He needed sleep. Without sleep he would be wasting his time with the books.

There was only one sensible solution. Samuel took a couple of aspirin and went to bed. He set his alarm for five o'clock. That gave him a little over four hours sleep, leaving the evening to study the books. With luck, his afternoon nap would help to clear his head.

Chapter Eleven

Romulus thumbed through the research project on his desk. It had been sent to him by a colleague in America and proposed an extensive study of several, probably mythical, creatures. Romulus pursed his lips. Cryptozoology was currently a minor interest of his, but if the bid were successful, the project would pay for him to spend several months in Mongolia, searching for the fabled Death Worm. The project also listed a number of visits to the States to look for Bigfoot, a lot of scientific conferences overseas, and other assorted freebies.

It was worth considering. The project was almost certain to draw a blank—they always did—but it included free worldwide travel for two years. Elaine could manage the ghost project during his absences. It was straightforward enough, and she was the expert with all that technical hardware anyway. The motion sensors, the automatic cameras, the computer programs that ran it all—they were Elaine's speciality. Romulus tapped his fingers on the desk. He decided to agree to his inclusion in the proposal. It would be at least a year before the project started, even if it were funded. By then, Elaine would be able to cover his lecturing commitments as well.

Romulus signed the form, wrote a cover letter, and slipped everything into an envelope. He had just finished writing the address when the door opened and Elaine came in.

"So, you don't even knock now?" Romulus put the envelope in his 'out' tray.

"Why? Were you doing something you shouldn't?"

"No. But I might have had a visitor. You should knock, just in case."

"I'll remember in the future." Elaine took the seat opposite Romulus and grinned. "I think I might have found a ghost to work on."

"Oh?" Romulus moved forward, resting his forearms on the desk. "More orbs, or is it something a little more interesting?"

"Better than orbs. I passed that church—you know, the one Father Johnson came from—on my way back from lunch. It's a very old building, so I thought it might be worth a look."

"And?"

"I spoke to Father Johnson. He told me that his predecessor died in a car accident and that several parishioners claim to have seen him since then."

"You have names, dates, places?"

"Well, he wouldn't give me details, but it seems the ghost has been showing up all over Marchway in the last few months."

"Really? It's not confined to one place? That's unusual." Romulus frowned. "So it's not likely to be hallucinations caused by vibrations or electric fields. Some form of mass hysteria, maybe? Does this ghost speak?"

"Not so far. It apparently tries to communicate but has failed every time. It disappears within moments." Elaine smiled. "I take it you're interested?"

Romulus straightened. "Fairly interested. We do need the names of the witnesses though, and times and dates of the sightings. Along with any other information that may be relevant—large-scale building works, particularly underground works, that sort of thing."

"Large-scale building works? In Marchway?"

"You know what I mean. Anything like that." Romulus swiveled his chair towards the window, his hands clasped beneath his chin. "Also, any information on the supposed ghost. Did you get a name?"

"I did. He was Father Thomas Michael."

Romulus swiveled his chair back to face Elaine. "What?"

"Father Thomas Michael. What's wrong? You look as though you've seen a ghost." Elaine paused, open-mouthed, then laughed. "Sorry, that wasn't the best analogy I could have used."

"That's the name of my visitor. He calls himself Father Michael." Romulus glowered at Elaine's look of astonishment.

"You don't think—"

"Of course I think. That's what I'm paid to do. Oh, I should have realized." Romulus leaned back in his chair, the worn leather creaking with his movement. "He's a local lunatic, dressed up as a priest and using the dead man's name."

"Or maybe—"

"Don't you dare." Romulus pointed his finger at Elaine, moving forward in his seat as he did so. "The man I saw was real. He didn't walk through any walls. He didn't float above the ground. He wasn't transparent. And he could speak, perfectly well." Romulus curled his lip. "Too well, and too much."

"So, it wasn't the ghost."

"No, it wasn't any kind of ghost." Something nagged at Romulus's thoughts. Something about his gate.

"Well, others have seen Father Michael. I don't know how we're going to get names though, if Father Johnson won't help."

"Easy. You go to church; get to know the congregation. Drop Father Michael's name into the conversation and see who bites."

"Church? Me? Why can't you do it?"

"It's your project. Besides, I have an impostor to unmask. Not too quickly. I want to find out what he's up to first." Romulus smiled. "You know, I've been thinking. It's time you picked up some experience at lecturing."

Elaine sat up straight, her eyes wide. "Really? I've been trying to persuade you to let me do that for ages. I'd love to get some lecturing experience."

"I think you're ready. You can sit in on a few of mine when term starts, then take one or two yourself. Start with something on the mechanics of all those devices you understand so well."

"Great! It's about time you let me expand a little. I'll get working on a couple of lectures right away."

"No hurry. You can think about them while you're in church."

Elaine deflated, her shoulders sagged, and her bright smile vanished. "Bribery. That's it, isn't it? I get to do the lectures as long as I work Father Johnson's congregation."

Romulus shrugged. "Does it matter? You still get to do the lectures."

"I suppose not." Elaine sighed. "I'd just prefer to think that I was getting this chance through my own merits."

"If I didn't think you were capable of lecturing my students, do you really believe

I'd let you?" Romulus lowered his head and looked at her through his eyebrows. "I may be using this as a lever but I wouldn't make the trade lightly."

"No, you wouldn't. You really think I'm ready for this?"

"Yes, I do." He rubbed his hands along the soft leather arms of his chair. "Now get out there and see what you can find out about the real Father Michael. I'll deal with the fake one."

"Right. Thanks, Rom. I won't let you down on the lectures." Elaine stood and hurried out through the door, closing it behind her.

Romulus grinned. *She'll make a good lecturer, and I'll get to take those trips abroad.* He stretched his arms and turned to stare through the window. *The day hasn't been a total loss, after all.*

Chapter Twelve

The crystal trees were darker this time, their structure permeated by an ebony stain. Samuel put his hand on the gnarled, twisted bark. It writhed at his touch.

"Why do you keep coming here? I told you to refuse their call." The old man's fresh wounds dripped red splotches on the yellow soil as he stood beside Samuel.

"I know your name." Samuel pointed at the old man.

"Don't say it." The old man's eyes grew wide, his hands held up beside his face, giving the impression of a monochrome clown from a silent film.

Samuel laughed. "Why not?"

"Just...don't." He gasped and clamped his arms across his chest. "They must never know my name. It will give them the power to use me."

"I'm bored with dreaming about you." Samuel returned his attention to the tree. "I'd rather dream about the woman."

"This is not a dream!" The old man grabbed Samuel's sleeve. Samuel pulled away and ran behind the tree, peering around it.

The old man danced, spinning in a rapid circle and cackling. "Notadream notadream notadream." He stopped, facing Samuel. His eyes glittered, and his lips drew back over yellow, decaying teeth. "I thought they were dreams, at first. The woman came to me too. She told me to read the book. I did. I got it backwards."

"You read a book backwards?" Samuel tilted his head, frowning.

"It brought me here. They torture me, trying to get my name. I won't tell them." He resumed his spinning dance. "Iwon'tIwon'tIwon'tIwon't." The dance ended, and the old man staggered, grabbing onto the tree for support. His face was inches from Samuel's.

Samuel recoiled from the old man's sewage breath. "Who are 'they?'"

"You met one. That woman. She's not what she seems." He jabbed his bony finger at Samuel's chest. "You don't know anything. The book will catch you too."

"I know one thing at least. I know you, Alfred Melchior."

Melchior shrieked, backing away and shaking his head. "You fool! You don't know what you've done." The sky darkened. "This place, the book, it's the same. The book is a trap." He looked around, frantic, as the trees turned black. A pink shape formed in the air beside him.

"Hello again, Samuel." The shape solidified into the woman Samuel had seen before.

Samuel grinned. Melchior screamed.

Dust devils whirled in the yellow soil, thickening and growing larger. Melchior's head darted from side to side, trying to follow their movements. His speech quickened. "She knows your name. How?" The dust surrounded Melchior now, dipping and weaving as they danced around him. He swung his arms at them, but his blows passed through, leaving no mark.

"I spoke to her, last time I was here." Samuel's eyes roved up and down the woman's body. She stepped towards him.

"Idiot. You've finished us both." Melchior sank to his knees.

Samuel glanced at him. The dust devils grew, whirling faster, until they towered over Melchior, their dance revealing the old man in intermittent flashes.

The woman's hand touched Samuel's shoulder, and he looked into her eyes.

"Don't listen to him. He's just a mad old man." Her smile was sympathetic as she inclined her head towards Melchior.

"I know." Samuel broke contact with her eyes and looked again at Melchior. The dust devils rushed in on the cowering old man, blending to form a single tornado which lifted into the air, taking Melchior with it. Screams echoed across the sky as the whirlwind faded into the distance.

Samuel was left alone with the woman. She took his hands in hers.

He drew a long breath. "You're beautiful. Like an angel."

She laughed and squeezed his hands. "Wonderful. You're exactly what I've been waiting for."

A warmth spread through Samuel. He stared into her eyes, those jet-black pools, a darkness he could welcome into his heart.

"Read for me, Samuel." With those words, she faded into the air.

Samuel stood alone on the yellow soil, watching the trees sway, listening to Melchior's fading screams. A hand touched his face. He looked around but saw nobody. The cool touch came again, and the world flew apart, brightening as it did so. The trees aligned themselves into regular patterns, lost their individuality, and became replicas, changing shape, changing colors but still translucent. Their pattern hung in the air before him.

* * * *

The pattern became Samuel's bedroom curtains, closed to block the daylight. Samuel scratched his chin, trying to hang on to the elusive remnants of his dream. The old man—his dream version of Melchior—had said something important, but the image of the woman filled his imagination, and Melchior's words faded.

Samuel stretched, then reached to his bedside cabinet for a tissue. The alarm clock showed four-thirty, but Samuel sat up in bed anyway. He canceled the five o'clock alarm before clearing his nose.

The throbbing in his head had subsided to a dull ache. Samuel drew a slow breath through his nose, finding it easier than he had that morning. The infection seemed to be easing off.

Clad in bathrobe and slippers, and filled with a corned beef sandwich and a hot coffee, Samuel donned his cotton gloves and examined the notes he had made on *Geometria ton Zoon*. Concentrating on these Etruscan characters was getting him nowhere, so Samuel turned to the next page.

There was a list of precautions to be taken when reading the passage on the previous page. Samuel smiled at the superstition of ages past and reached for his box of tissues. As he blew his nose, his eyes happened upon a particularly puzzling line. "Greek for inward, Arabic for outwards." He read it again. No mistake, that was what it said. Samuel frowned. He picked up his pad and pencil to record the line but stopped with his pencil poised over the paper. Translating little bits was interesting, but it was a slow way to proceed. The sensible approach was to start at the beginning of the book.

Melchior's notes helped him with the first few pages. The book offered riches, wisdom, and power to anyone who read the incantation aloud. Samuel snorted. This was standard fare for such a book. "Everything can be yours if you just say the words." Except the words of the spell were written in an alphabet few, if any, could have pronounced. He wondered how much the original author would have made on the sale of the book, and how many scholars down the ages had tried to read that incantation, only to find it a meaningless jumble of symbols.

Samuel passed over the Etruscan script and turned to the next pages. Melchior's notes suggested he had not read this far. Presumably he had fretted over the Etruscan and become stuck there.

These pages carried dire warnings to those who would read the script aloud. There were preparations to be made and precautions to be taken. The reader must choose the direction of transport and make careful preparations before reading a single word or the consequences could be terrible.

Transport? Transport what? Does it mean travel? Samuel adjusted his glasses and continued.

The next page was filled with diagrams. A sphere, made of apparently randomly joined lines, with a drawing of the book at its center. Intersecting lines, parallel lines, squares projected into cubes, cubes projected into confusing shapes. Most of it looked like a standard geometry textbook.

Samuel grinned. *So this is Geometria.* His grin faded as he read the accompanying words. Riveted now, he continued reading to the end of the book, then turned to the beginning and read again.

Stretching his aching shoulders, Samuel looked at his watch.

Ten-fifteen! No wonder I'm tired. Standing, he closed *Geometria*, took off the gloves, and laid them on the book. He went through to the kitchen, made himself another coffee and sandwich, and stood there, eating and drinking and considering what he read.

It was impossible, pure fancy, of course. Nobody in the Middle Ages could have understood the mathematics of multiple dimensions. Equally, there was no way the book could be a fake. It had been in the Old Books Room for at least four hundred years. It was there long before the first Etruscan codex was written. It had been there long before Einstein unleashed his new physics on the world. It could not be old, and it could not be new. Nobody could have written it.

Samuel finished his sandwich and swallowed the last of his coffee. A dizzy feeling swept over him. He braced his arms on the table, hanging his head.

I have to try it. If it's real, and Melchior tried it without reading the warnings, then it took him—somewhere. If I reverse the incantation, it might get him out. The dizziness faded and Samuel raised his head. *If it's not real, nothing will happen anyway.*

"Where did that come from?" Samuel said aloud. It was a ridiculous thought. Melchior had probably run off with a woman. The book was just a book.

Try it.

Samuel shook his head, hard. The room spun once more. His fingers tingled, and his vision hazed. The room took on a dream-like quality, unreal, vague. It made sense now. The book would work. He knew, somehow, that it would. A gentle, coaxing voice in his mind told him all would be well if he made the proper preparations.

Try it.

Samuel took a deep breath and returned to the book. The precautions included a chalk circle, filled with complex signs and with precisely placed candles, as detailed in *Clavicula Salomonis.* Samuel looked around. Carpeted floor was no place for a chalk circle, and anyway he had no chalk. His eyes widened. *Maybe I do.*

He hurried upstairs to the spare room and opened the chest that contained his mother's old possessions. She had been a seamstress, and he remembered she had used a triangular, flat chalk for marking cloth. Seeing it, he made a grab and recoiled, holding the chalk and staring at three pins that had been below it. These were now stuck in the end of his thumb. He pulled them out, grimacing as three red beads formed on his skin, and dropped them back into the chest.

There were candles in the kitchen, left over from the last batch of power outages. Clutching his chalk, Samuel rushed downstairs to the kitchen and retrieved a box of candles from the cupboard under the sink. His breathing was ragged, and his chest felt constricted, but the thrill of this adventure overrode any concern for his health. Samuel scanned the kitchen floor.

This would be a good place for a circle. It'll wash off the linoleum. He knelt and tried the chalk, brushing off the blood that had dripped onto it from the pinpricks in his thumb. The chalk slid on the smooth flooring, leaving no mark. Samuel stood, frowning at the chalk in his hand. *The basement has a concrete floor. That's bound to work.*

Collecting *Geometria, Clavicula Salomonis* and his transcriptions of the Etruscan passage from the dining table, Samuel went through the door below the stairs that led down to his basement.

A single bare bulb illuminated the basement, which stretched below almost all the house with thick stone pillars supporting the main walls. The concrete floor was mainly clear since Samuel had disposed of most of his father's accumulated clutter after the old man's death. What remained was loaded into cardboard boxes, stacked against one wall. Odds and ends of furniture occupied another wall. Chairs with unglued joints waiting for the day someone found the time to mend them. A drop-leaf table, functional but with nowhere to fit in the upper rooms. Old brooms, a stepladder, boxes of long-unused tools and books were stacked among the aging furniture.

Cheap wood paneling covered part of the back wall. A row of wooden moldings had been added at waist height, a decorative feature. It dated from the time his father had tried to make a habitable room down here, but his mother's protests had crushed the idea. Samuel had been only twelve at the time, and he remembered his father showing him the secret of the wall.

There was an alcove in the back wall, now completely covered, but a simple twist of one of the wood moldings released a section of paneling, swinging open on concealed hinges to reveal his father's hidey-hole. All those things he had bought that Mother shouldn't know about came here, until he could present it as "something that's been in the basement for ages."

Samuel grinned. He was sure his mother had been wise to the trick, but she'd let Dad have his fun. He looked down at the books in his hands.

I could hide them... No! I have to return them tomorrow. He placed the books on the table, picked up a broom that lay against one wall, and brushed what he considered sufficient floor space for his circle.

Laying the broom aside, Samuel wondered how he could draw an accurate circle. A nail and string could do it, but how would he drive a nail into a concrete floor? He looked around the room for inspiration and noticed the light.

Taking a sheet of paper from his notebook, Samuel formed it into a cone. Packing tape, found lying among the cardboard boxes, secured its shape. He placed the stepladder beneath the lamp, slipped the cone of paper over the bulb, and slid it along the cable until it produced a reasonably large circle of light on the floor. Satisfied, he secured it in place with another strip of packing tape, descended the ladder, and moved it aside.

Once the lamp stopped swinging, Samuel traced the outline of the circle with the chalk, taking care to leave no spaces, as *Clavicula Salomonis* instructed.

Another, inner circle was required, so Samuel retrieved the stepladder and moved the cone of paper lower to produce a smaller circle inside the first. He sniffed. The paper was turning brown in places. Samuel held the lamp as still as he could before descending the ladder and tracing the inner circle. Finally, he removed the smoldering cone and placed it on the floor well away from anything flammable.

Samuel paced around his circles, nodding his satisfaction. There was a lot more to do. There were complicated symbols and inscriptions to be drawn inside the circle, and a triangle outside to contain whatever the incantation called forth.

The triangle had to face east, and the symbols within the circle depended on the location of the triangle. Samuel oriented himself, using the door of the basement, to face the back of the house. In summer, the sun set there. So that would be west. East would be directly opposite. Samuel crossed the circle and made a chalk mark where he thought the apex of the triangle should be. Using a leg from one of the dilapidated chairs, one end held against the mark he'd made, he drew two arcs on the floor. The leg, placed so that its ends touched both arcs, provided the base of the triangle, and joining the base to the original mark filled in the sides. Samuel grinned at his work, pleased with his ingenuity.

He copied the symbols carefully, frequently erasing and repeating his work until he had an exact replica of the drawing on the floor of his basement. The chalk was now no more than a sliver, and he cast it aside. He placed the candles on their marks, outside the circle, and lit them. Samuel stood, hands on hips, and regarded his handiwork. He placed both books inside the circle and picked up his notebook.

"Right," he said. "Here goes nothing." He read his phonetic transcription of the reversed Etruscan passage, stumbling a little when he noticed *Geometria* flip itself open to the Etruscan page. The sounds he made resembled no words he could recognize, but they had a kind of musical cadence to them, a tonal resonance that flowed rhythmically as he spoke.

An intense white light appeared on *Geometria*'s open pages. It expanded, becoming more diffuse as it filled the circle.

Shit. I didn't really think it would work. Terror rose, clouding his sight, but his voice continued. *I can't stop. I can't control this.* The light took on colors, swirling and blending. It grew past him, past the circle, past the basement and the house. Somehow, the lights remained visible through the walls, ceiling, and floor, as though this world's substance was irrelevant to them.

Although he no longer looked at his notebook, Samuel's voice became louder, rising and falling in tone, uttering words he had never before spoken, words of age and power.

It's not me. Whatever's happening, it's doing itself. Through me.

The colors became a net of lines, centered on the triangle. His voice continued the chant. A smell of freshly turned soil drifted through the room, accompanied by the tinkling of far-off chimes. Samuel's head hurt under the pressure of the air. An epiphany shook him.

These are not words. They're the sounds that shapes make. The sounds of geometry. A tear rolled down his cheek. *I can't stop.*

The basement floor flickered grey—yellow—grey—yellow, the lines of Samuel's circle flashed between white and red. He was Samuel Watson, but he was also someone else, in another circle, on another world. Samuel raised his arm. The material of his sleeve faded, and long tears appeared in the fabric. It decayed before his eyes until it hung in shreds around wasted flesh, pale scars now livid with trails of bright red. It should have been agony, but Samuel felt nothing.

Something watched from the shadows outside the circle. Several somethings. They were tall, thin creatures, their angular bodies and multiple limbs dispeling any notion that they might be human. Samuel tried to put his hand over his mouth to stop the incantation, but as he turned his gaunt, wrinkled arm he noticed the blood pouring from a deep gash in his wrist.

His other arm had also been opened at the wrist. Blood ran to the floor and joined with the lines of the circle. His mind floundered in its attempts to reconcile what he saw with the absence of pain. If he had control of his voice, he would have screamed.

It's not me. It's an illusion. These are not my hands.

At the thought, the yellow world of *Geometria* faded, just as one of the shadowy creatures moved towards the triangle. Samuel's wrists healed, his arms filling out to resume their familiar, overweight appearance while the sleeves of his bathrobe reformed around them. The floor returned to concrete grey, the circle to white.

Samuel's voice rose to a crescendo as the incantation neared its end. A misty shape formed within the triangle. *Melchior?* The figure looked taller than the old man.

The sphere completed its disassembly, ending in points of light that flickered and went out. Samuel shouted the final words of the spell, dropped his notes, and fell to his knees. *Geometria* closed with a thud. Samuel shut his eyes, his breathing ragged, sweat pouring from his forehead.

What the hell just happened?

"Shemuel?" The voice was soft, sultry, and excruciatingly female. Samuel opened his eyes and looked up to the figure that stood within the triangle.

He put both hands to his head, pushing his glasses up by the side frames. "Uh..."

She was beautiful. Beyond beautiful. She was all the perfect parts of every perfect woman, blended into one figure. She was the woman from his dreams, and she was naked.

She stretched her arms over her head, bringing her breasts into sharp focus, and smiled at him. Samuel gaped, his eyes consuming every inch of exposed skin. Never, not in the hurried fumblings of his youth, nor in the slower, lights-off encounters of more recent years, had he ever imagined such a woman could exist in real life. He stumbled to his feet, wondering if he was dreaming now.

"Shemuel. Ruva tivr." She smiled as she spoke, holding her arms out to him.

Samuel tried to avert his eyes from the passion-made-flesh before him, but succeeded only in a flickering movement before being drawn back. It was enough to see the old woolen blanket draped across one of the chairs. Samuel hurried to fetch it, shook out its years of dust and approached the smiling woman, holding the blanket before him matador-style.

"I'm sorry. It's all I have." He tried to smile.

Her eyebrows lowered into a quizzical expression, but she turned and allowed Samuel to drape the blanket over her shoulders. He coughed. "I'm Samuel."

The woman turned so suddenly that Samuel jumped. She grabbed him, hands on either side of his head in a grip that belied her slight frame. He could see her glossy black eyes erupt into an ebony fire before she brought his head to hers, forehead to forehead, nose to nose.

Something rummaged in his brain, emptying filing cabinets and sifting through the contents. His head swam between ecstasy and agony as he was torn, sorted, read, and consumed in an instant.

She let go, dropping him to his knees.

I should have stayed in the circle.

"Samuel. Moon brother." She laughed, a delicate sound like a tinkling of crystal bells. "There was another Samuel, long ago..."

Samuel looked up. The blanket hung around her shoulders but she made no attempt to draw it closed at the front. "Where did you come from?"

She turned her smile down to his face. "From your dreams." She laughed again.

He didn't care what she said. His soul drowned in her eyes, sold for a liquid darkness he could neither resist nor understand.

"What's your name?"

She pursed her lips for a moment. "Call me Angela."

Chapter Thirteen

Professor Crowe.

Romulus groaned, trying to ignore the voice that cut through his dream.

Professor Crowe. The voice sounded again, loud and urgent.

Romulus snapped his eyes open. A single pale shaft of moonlight broke through the curtains, bisecting the darkness of his bedroom. He lay still, staring at the shadows.

Something moved. Romulus lay rigid, watching.

This is silly. There's nothing here. It was just a bad dream.

Nevertheless, he reached for the bedside lamp and switched it on. It illuminated a white face topped with jet-black hair, inches from his own. Romulus yelped and scrambled backwards across the bed.

"I didn't mean to startle you, sorry." Black eyes caught the light as the face moved back a little.

His heart pounding, Romulus curled his lip at the intruder. Father Thomas Michael. *That damned fake priest.*

"What in hell's name do you think you're doing?" Romulus fought to control the tremor in his voice. Thoughts flashed through his mind. He knew the real Father Michael was dead. He knew this man was an impostor. Was he some kind of psycho? A burglar? No. Why would a burglar wake him? A psycho then, possibly dangerous. Romulus regarded the man through narrowed eyes. He was at least a head shorter, and thin. Romulus could deal with him, if necessary.

"I'm very sorry to wake you, Professor, but it's important." Father Michael held his hands in front of him, palms outwards, and backed off a few steps.

Climbing off the end of the bed, out of reach of the intruder, Romulus grabbed his bathrobe and pulled it over his pajamas.

"If it's important, you can tell it to important people." Romulus placed himself between Father Michael and the door, knowing it was the wrong thing to do. If the lunatic ran off, he would have to go through Romulus. "The police should be important enough for you."

"Why would you call the police?"

"Why?" Romulus spluttered. He squinted at his bedside clock. "It's two o'clock in the morning. I wake up to find a madman in my bedroom, pretending to be a priest. Of course I'm going to call the police."

Father Michael shook his head. "I wouldn't do that if I were you."

"Is that a threat?" Romulus eyed the man while feeling for the doorknob behind him. He watched the priest's hands, but no weapon appeared.

"No, no, I'm here to help you, not threaten you. That is, I was supposed to help you, but now I need help."

Romulus found the doorknob and rested his hand on it. "What are you talking about?"

Father Michael ran his hand over his hair. "It's difficult. It wasn't meant to happen like this. I should have had more time."

"Time to do what?"

"To convince you. To prepare you."

Romulus sucked air, hissing, through his teeth. "You're making no sense. You need professional help, and I think we'd better get you some." He turned the door handle and opened the door, keeping his eyes on the priest while he backed through it.

Father Michael took a step forward. "Wait. I have to tell you."

"Tell the police." Romulus turned on the lights, illuminating the landing and stairwell. He stood beside the open door and jerked his thumb towards the stairs. "Move. I'm not letting you out of my sight."

"Okay, call the police if you have to. You're going to look pretty stupid though." Father Michael smiled as he walked through the door. "At least listen to me while we're waiting for them."

"Just get downstairs." Romulus followed Father Michael, a few steps behind, resisting the urge to push the lunatic down the stairs. He knew the vagaries of British law, where an intruder could sue a householder for assault. This intruder was clearly unbalanced, so Romulus had no intention of giving him any cause for complaint. Nor did he want to give the man an excuse to get violent. At the foot of the stairs, Romulus guided Father Michael into the lounge, where his only phone was installed.

The priest watched, smiling and shaking his head, while Romulus spoke to the police operator. When Romulus hung up the phone, Father Michael took a step forward.

"This is unnecessary. And pointless. The police can't do anything to me."

Romulus narrowed his eyes. "We'll see. They'll be here shortly." He furrowed his brow. Twice, the lunatic had claimed some kind of immunity from prosecution. Perhaps he had friends in high places. Romulus snorted. It must be a bluff. Even if this man were the son of the chief of police, there was no way he was going to avoid arrest tonight.

"Will you at least listen to me while we wait?"

"Might as well. The police will have to come from Weston anyway." *Damn, I shouldn't have told him that!* Romulus shifted to lean against the wall, a safe distance from Father Michael. "Okay, let's hear it."

The priest lowered his head, hands clasped in front of his chest. "One of the gamaliel is here. In Marchway. It arrived just a few hours ago."

"Really? Where did it land its spaceship?"

The look in Father Michael's eyes when he raised his head made Romulus press himself against the wall.

"It is not a joke! The gamaliel is here, and it will kill people." Father Michael took a slow breath and relaxed. "I need you to stop it. You're the only one I can talk to."

"Okay." Romulus decided it was safer to humor this small madman, at least until the police arrived. "What's a gamaliel?"

"It's a demon. Mentioned in *Key of Solomon*. The obscene ones, adversaries of the angels. Their queen is—"

"Lilith." Romulus finished the priest's sentence as an idea began to form in his mind. "In the Eliphas Levi translation. You know, I think I know what this is all about." He stepped away from the wall, towards the priest. "I have a copy of that book, including the fragment you just mentioned."

"You do? That's very useful."

"Very. My copy was a present from someone, a long time ago."

The priest shrugged. "Well, wherever it came from, you'll find it invaluable for this task."

"Oh, it's useful already. It's helped me solve one mystery." Romulus took another step forward, his index finger jabbing towards the priest's face. "The mystery of you."

"Don't be silly. The book has nothing to do with me."

"Not directly. It has to do with your boss. The one who sent you here."

Father Michael took a step backwards when Romulus made a particularly vicious jab towards his nose. "Well, in a roundabout way, I suppose. Solomon was a man of God, as am I."

"You are not. You're a fake, and this gamaliel story is all hokum. You've been sent here as some twisted joke, a petty revenge from a bad loser. This time she's gone too far."

"What are you talking about?"

"Give it up. You were sent by Imogen LeFevre. The demon story gave you away. That's her speciality. It was Imogen who gave me a copy of *Key of Solomon*, when we were..." Romulus closed his eyes briefly. "A long time ago. She was furious when I got the professorship here and she didn't. You're her revenge. A white-faced lunatic posing as a dead priest. Who are you, really? Some out-of-work actor?"

The priest drew himself up to his full height and looked up at Romulus. "I am Father Thomas Michael, as I told you. I am dead."

Romulus turned away, flinging his arms wide. "Oh, come on. Now you're pretending to be a ghost. She knows that's my current line of research, so naturally she'd try that one. Well, you can explain it to the police."

Father Michael exhaled. "This isn't how I expected it to be. I had hoped not to get too intrusive but—"

"What?" Romulus whirled to face the priest. "You break into my house at two o'clock in the morning, wake me with some insane story, and you don't consider that intrusive? Just how does that twisted mind of yours work? If it works at all." He filled his chest with air, so that the next blast of rage would not need to be interrupted with a breath, and opened his mouth to speak.

The doorbell rang. Romulus released his breath, his eyes fixed on Father Michael. "You stay there." He went through the hall to the front door, pulling it open with more force than was required. The night air blasted into the house, bringing a late-September chill mixed with the scent of wet grass. Two uniformed policemen stood outside, their faces registering surprise as the door flew open. There was a pause while they stared at Romulus and he at them.

"Well, come on inside. He's in the lounge." Romulus stood to one side to let the policemen enter and grimaced at their evident youth. Both policemen hurried into the hall, following Romulus's finger pointing to the lounge door. Romulus closed the front door, then followed.

"There doesn't appear to be anyone here, sir." The policemen checked behind the sofa, behind the chairs, then looked at Romulus.

"He can't have gone. I was only out of the room for a moment, and the lounge door is visible from the hall." Romulus stared at the empty room. "If he did, he must have gone out through the window." A quick check showed him that the window was securely locked from the inside. "The back door. Somehow he slipped out, while I was opening the front door for you."

The back door proved to be locked, as did all of the downstairs windows. The three of them checked the upstairs windows. Again, all were secure.

As they returned to the hallway, Romulus caught the glances and winks exchanged by the two policemen. There were smirks, wrinkled noses, and an avoidance of eye-contact with him. He clamped his teeth together and pretended to ignore them.

"There's nobody here now, sir." The taller policeman, almost Romulus's height, at least had the decency to keep a straight face. "We've met up with some slippery customers in our time on the force, but this is the first one who's locked up on the way out." His colleague turned away, caught by a sudden fit of coughing.

"I can assure you, officers, I did not call you out here on some fool's errand. There was an intruder, and I am particularly concerned that there are no signs of forced entry, and that everything is now locked."

"Oh? Why is that, sir?" The taller policeman raised his eyebrows.

"Because it means he must have a key." Romulus spoke through his growing rage. These policemen seemed unskilled in the basic techniques of logical deduction. He consoled himself in the knowledge that he had been solving mysteries for many more years than they had. The two officers exchanged a glance, their humor replaced by pensive concern.

"Is that possible, sir? How would he get hold of a key?"

"He's pretending to be a priest. He's convincing. This house was a priest's house until I bought it. Perhaps he borrowed one from the church, then copied it. Somehow he managed to get a key. I don't know how he did it. You figure it out."

"Perhaps we should get a description." The shorter policeman took out his notebook.

"Perhaps you should." Romulus described the priest as about five foot six, thin, black hair and eyes, white skin, black clothes. Monochrome man. The policeman wrote it all down.

"Did he give a name?"

"Father Thomas Michael."

"Really? My mother went to his church. He's —"

"Dead. Yes, I know. This one's a fake. I have an idea who put him up to this little stunt."

The shorter policeman stopped writing. The taller one lifted his cap and scratched his head before speaking. "You think someone put him up to this?"

"Absolutely. I think this was all a sick joke from the twisted mind of a woman called Imogen LeFevre."

The shorter policeman wrote the name in his book. The taller one pursed his lips. "Any idea why she would do that?"

Romulus nodded. "We were both applicants for an important job at the university. I got it. She didn't. This whole thing was just her way of getting back at me."

"You're sure? It seems a rather petty way for an academic to behave."

"I'm not a hundred percent certain, but I'm pretty sure. Some of the things the fake priest said pointed to her being behind it. And most academics can be petty, in my experience."

The taller policeman crossed his arms, one hand on his chin. "It's a potentially serious matter. If your intruder has a key then he could come back at any time. He might also have copied keys for other houses." He looked at his colleague. "I don't think there's much more we can do here. We'd better get going."

"What about me? What about this lunatic with a key to my house?" Romulus moved between the policemen and the door.

"You have bolts on both doors, sir. I recommend you use them tonight, and get your locks changed tomorrow." The taller policeman edged past Romulus, forcing him to move aside. As he opened the front door, he turned back. "We'll circulate the description, of course, and let you know if we find him. In the meantime, if you should see him again, let us know at once."

"And Imogen? Will you be talking to her?"

The shorter policeman shook his head. "Not at this stage. Unless you can produce some actual evidence to suggest her involvement, we have no grounds to visit her." He started to put his notebook away, then paused. "I wonder, sir, do you know where we might find Miss LeFevre? Just in case we do need to speak with her."

"I have her work address. Just wait a moment." Romulus hurried back to the lounge, where a recent copy of a professional journal lay on the coffee table. Imogen had an article in that issue. Romulus looked around for pen and paper. Finding none, he took the journal back to the policemen.

"Here, at the top of this article. That's where she works now."

The shorter man took the journal and copied the address into his notebook. He read the title aloud. "Reported sightings of Norwegian huldrefolk in recent times. Sounds interesting."

Romulus accepted the journal. "They're a kind of fairy. Nonsense, of course, but some people will believe anything." He tucked the journal under his arm, pulling his bathrobe tighter against the chill that drifted through the hall. "Put someone alone, on a dark night, and they can imagine all sorts of nonsense."

The policemen exchanged a glance. "Indeed, sir." The taller one opened the door. "Well, goodnight. We'll be in touch as soon as we have some news." He stepped outside, followed by his colleague.

"Goodnight, officers." Romulus closed the door. The front door had a sturdy bolt, fitted just above the lock. Romulus pushed it into place, then went through to the kitchen. There were two small bolts on the back door, one at the top and one at the bottom. The bottom one moved easily, but the top one required some force. Romulus resolved to get that fixed tomorrow, along with the locks. He had never bothered with such high-security measures in the past. If he had, he might have enjoyed a decent night's sleep tonight. After checking the windows once more, Romulus returned to his bed.

He lay awake, staring at the shadows cast by the moonlight while his body gradually warmed the cold bed. A glance at the clock told him it was now five minutes to four. Romulus groaned. Tomorrow was going to be a difficult day, unless he could find somewhere for a nap. Perhaps if he went to the library, he could find a quiet corner and a very large book to hide behind for an hour or so. Thoughts of napping made his eyelids droop, and he resumed his interrupted dream.

* * * *

"Ram her amidships!" Captain Crowe leaned over the rail of the poop deck and shouted the order to his crew. Five-chins Orson, the first mate, waddled up beside him.

"I don't think that's a good idea," he said in a disturbingly girlish voice. "You haven't had this ship serviced in a long time, and it might well fall apart—"

"Belay that whining and prepare to board. We ram them! We'll take what we can before she goes under." Waving his cutlass, Captain Crowe leapt to the deck below and charged to the bow, so that he could watch his ship, the Cortina, tear into the looming hulk of the Ghost. He could see shadowy figures moving on the decks of the other ship. One, dressed in black, looked familiar. Captain Crowe squinted, trying to make out the face, but the figure vanished as he watched.

"Professor."

Captain Crowe turned. "Who said that?" He gaped at the man before him. "A priest. On my ship."

"I'm sorry to interrupt your dream, but—"

"Oh, it's no problem." Romulus bared his teeth in a grin at the priest's evident surprise. "You can stay. After we sink the Ghost, I'll have you keelhauled. I'm going to enjoy this dream."

"You know you're dreaming?"

"Well of course I know I'm dreaming. Doesn't everyone? That's why I always win. I'm in control here."

"Not entirely. Not this time."

Before Romulus could question the little priest's impertinence, his ship and crew vanished. He stood, in his captain's finery, on a yellow desert. A short distance away, semitransparent trees stood, twisted and leafless. The branches moved, but there was no breeze. Romulus pointed his cutlass at the priest.

"Is this what you call a dream? It's rubbish. No detail, no imagination." Romulus concentrated his mind, and the planks of the Cortina's deck started to form beneath his feet.

"Stop that." Father Michael's voice was firm. "You can play at pirates another night. I have something to show you."

The deck faded, although Romulus still felt wood, not sand, beneath his feet. "Right. Well let's get it done and we can go back to my ship. I think, after I've keelhauled you, I'll give you forty lashes and then make you walk the plank."

Father Michael chuckled. "I'm not one of your dream characters. This place is all too real, as am I. A world formed from the geometries underlying the world of the living, constructed from the sounds of shapes. This is the prison of the gamaliel ."

"Oh, sure. Then that must be one of them, over there?" Romulus pointed at a bedraggled figure, staggering among the trees. The figure collapsed against one of the trunks and lay still. "It looks really scary." His voice dripped sarcasm.

"Just watch."

A second figure appeared, forming from the air, next to the ragged man. This figure was short, overweight, and wearing a dark suit. They appeared to talk for a time, then the ragged man walked into the trees, which closed around him. His visitor tried to follow, but dissipated into the atmosphere. Romulus snorted.

"What was all that about? I can make people appear and disappear in my dreams. I do it all the time. It must have been me that did it this time, too, since

you're nothing more than a nightmare. Cheese before bedtime, that's all you are. A bad cigar, or one too many whiskies."

The priest's face was serious. "The second man, the one who disappeared, is the man who released one of the gamaliel. Remember him. You have to find him."

"In my dreams? I have better things to do with my imagination than play detective."

"In life. He's real, and so is the monster he's released." Father Michael sighed. "I've done what I can tonight. We'll speak tomorrow." The priest, and the yellow world, faded into transparency.

Romulus smiled as the Cortina reformed around him, its ram mere inches from the hull of the Ghost. He braced himself for the impact.

Chapter Fourteen

The old man slumped at the base of one of the gnarled, bare trees, his hands open on his lap. Samuel approached him in silence. He recognized Melchior, but the man looked dead. Samuel stopped as Melchior raised his head.

"I'm surprised to see you here. She won't let you come again, I'm sure."

"What happened to you?" Samuel indicated the open wounds on Melchior's wrists. Black, dried blood covered the deep gashes.

"You know what happened. You were there." Melchior struggled to his feet. "They killed me."

Samuel laughed. "You're not dead. You're standing."

Melchior's eyes filled with despair, all trace of his former madness gone. "Death doesn't mean the same here. I have no blood, yet I live. They can still torment me."

"Not if I can get you out. I got Angela out, didn't I?" Samuel puffed his chest in pride.

"Idiot. I can't leave now, even if you had the power to do it. Which you don't." Melchior turned and walked into the trees. "Don't you see? I'm dead, or will be as soon as I leave here."

Samuel tried to follow but the branches blocked his path. "Wait. There must be something I can do."

"No. You can't stop her now." Melchior halted and stared at Samuel through the thickening branches. "Even if you get the book, she won't let you use it. She knows your thoughts."

"What book?" The network of branches meshed, closing Samuel's view of the old man. All he could see were the eyes.

"Liber Astaroth. Find someone who can use it, because you can't, not now. Find someone who can help you." The final gaps closed, leaving Samuel facing a wall of intertwined wood. The branches continued their growth. Fine twigs reached out towards his face, towards his mouth.

* * * *

Samuel woke with a start at a cool touch on his lips. Angela knelt beside him on the bed. She was naked, having shed the clothes he had loaned her the previous evening. Samuel stared, amazed that someone like her could even bear to be near him, never mind share his bed. Was it all just some hallucination, brought on by his illness?

"Angela." His voice was a croak. "You're real. I thought I'd dreamt the whole thing." Samuel tried to sit up, but she restrained him with a gentle hand on his shoulder.He realized he was still wearing his bathrobe and smiled at his own modesty.

"Poor Samuel. You've worked so hard. You're tired. You need to rest now."

Samuel shook his head, trying not to move it too far. "I still have the flu. I thought it had gone, but my head still hurts."

No daylight illuminated the curtains. Samuel squinted at the clock. "Four-thirty. No wonder I feel so tired. Angela, we need to work on your sense of time. It's likely to be different here than the world you've come from. Here, we like to sleep for more than a couple of hours before we wake."

Angela placed her hand on his forehead. Her touch was like ice, and relaxed him, easing the pains in his head and neck. Samuel closed his eyes and took a deep breath, inhaling the perfumed scent that floated from her as he allowed his head to sink back into the pillow.

"Angela, when you were trapped, did you meet anyone?"

She pursed her lips. "I met many, some pleasant, some not."

"Did you meet..." Samuel opened his eyes. "Did you meet Alfred Melchior?" He caught the smile that formed on her lips as she turned her head away. "Did you?"

"There's no need to concern yourself with him anymore. He won't trouble your dreams again."

"Why not?"

Angela shrugged. "He just won't." She leaned close to look into his eyes. "Don't worry, my little Samuel. Your sleep will be easier now."

"Sleep, yes. Tomorrow I have to return the books." Samuel's eyes lost focus. His eyelids closed.

"Return? Where?" Angela's hands pressed the sides of Samuel's head. He opened his eyes.

"To the library. They're not mine. I can't keep them."

"No." Her hands pressed harder. "There is only one *Geometria ton Zoon*. It must be safe."

"It will be. The book is kept in a locked room. Hardly anyone even knows it exists. Angela, don't get upset." Samuel tried to raise his hands to hers, to ease their pressure, but his own arms refused to obey him. He stared into her eyes.

Those deep black eyes held him. His breathing quickened. Somewhere in that soft darkness there was a hard edge. A black stone. Samuel trembled. He tried to move his eyes away from Angela's but could not.

"Who else knows about the book?" She wrapped her fingers in his hair and pressed her hands backwards, tightening the skin of his face.

"What are you doing?"

"*Geometria ton Zoon*. Who else knows?"

"Nobody. Only me. Angela, that hurts." Samuel's face burned.

"Don't lie to me, Samuel. I can read your lies in your face." Her voice sharpened. The darkness in her eyes engulfed him.

"Angela. What's happening?" Fear gripped his mind, twisted his insides.

"Just tell me, Samuel, and we can go back to being friends." She pulled harder.

"Attlee. Attlee knows. He was at the library when Alfred Melchior vanished." Samuel saw Attlee's face in his mind, saw Attlee's home, then gasped when the tension in his skin released. Angela sat up and broke eye contact.

He rubbed at his face, probing for the rips and tears he felt sure must be there. A pulse throbbed in his forehead, and pain clenched his chest. Samuel lay still while his pains subsided. "Why did you do that?"

"I have to be sure." Angela climbed off the bed and stood beside it, her arms folded. Her smile had returned, and a few strands of hair fell across her face. "I'm sorry, Samuel. I've been in that world so long. It's made me a little like itself, I suppose." She lowered her head and fluttered her eyelashes. "You can help me, can't you?"

"How could I resist?" The terror Samuel had seen in Angela's eyes was gone, and he wondered if he had imagined it. "But why are you so worried about the book? Melchior said..."

"I know what he said." She swept her hair back. "He fell for the trap, as I did. I won't fall for it again." She leaned across the bed, bringing her face close to his. "I just don't want anyone else interfering. It'll be just you and me. For now. Until I have time to find my way here."

Samuel shrugged. "Nathaniel Attlee doesn't know about you. He doesn't believe in magic. He suspects the book was involved in Melchior's disappearance, that's all."

"Nethaneel?" Angela laughed. "This new world is full of old names. Has nobody thought of any different ones, I wonder?"

"Nathaniel." Samuel corrected her. "It's the modern version. Nobody's used Nethaneel since the Old Testament." He paused, studying her face. "Angela, how long have you been trapped in that world?" *How old is that book?*

She leaned forward and kissed him fiercely, her arms encircling his neck. All his questions forgotten, he returned the kiss, running his hands along her back. When she released him, he gasped for breath, the airless agony indistinguishable from ecstasy. Angela stood up, her breasts bobbing in his vision.

"Time to get up, Samuel." Her wink betrayed her meaning. Samuel groaned.

"I'm ill, Angela. I couldn't—" His gaze followed the curves of her body, and his own body responded. He lifted the sheets and looked down, amazed. "Well, that hasn't reacted so quickly in years." The sheets flew from his grasp. Angela climbed over him. She lifted him, pulled his arms from his bathrobe and tugged it from beneath him, dropping it to the floor. "Angela. I'm all sweaty, and I stink. Let me have a shower first?"

"No. I've waited too long for this." She straddled him, pinning his shoulders back with her hands. "Feed me, Samuel."

"Feed you? What does that—oh." He lost his voice as she slipped over him, her internal muscles massaging and sucking at him until he released with a cry. Angela's hips pressed into him, her head back, a serene look on her face.

Samuel put his hand over his eyes. "Oh, God. I'm so sorry. It's just that—well, it's been a long time."

Angela laughed. "You don't know what those words mean." She lifted his hand. "Don't worry. It was enough. For now." She climbed off him and headed for the door, then stopped and looked back, frowning. "What's a shower?"

"Huh?" He stared, then nodded. "It's a water spray. For washing. There's a lot for you to see." Samuel yawned. "Later."

"Sleep now," she said. "We'll talk when you've rested."

"What will you do?" Samuel's eyelids dropped. He forced them open. "While I'm asleep, I mean." His eyes closed again.

"I'll amuse myself."

Samuel wanted to ask what that meant but fatigue silenced him.

Chapter Fifteen

The toaster discharged its load. Romulus reached for it, but stopped when he noticed the face at his kitchen window.

"Oh, for..." Romulus curled his lip at Father Michael's smile. "What the hell is he doing back here?" He considered calling the police again, but the small priest offered no immediate threat. Daylight made him seem even less imposing than he had last night.

The priest motioned towards the kitchen door, evidently wanting Romulus to open it. Romulus curled his lip and continued his breakfast. He hated to shout on an empty stomach. Father Michael disappeared from the window, towards the door. Romulus added milk to his tea, took another bite of toast, and stirred sugar into his cup. The priest reappeared at the window. Romulus sipped his tea. The priest's lips moved. Romulus couldn't hear him through the double glazing, even if he had cared enough to try.

Romulus watched the little man's agitation while he finished his breakfast. By this time, the priest was jumping up and down at the window, pointing at the door with such intensity that Romulus wondered if the man's trousers were on fire. He closed his eyes for a moment, savoring the image.

Romulus walked to the door. He recalled the impertinence of the man's invasion of his privacy and let it fuel his anger. With a hissing breath, he yanked the door open.

"What do you want?" Romulus sneered down at the shorter man.

"Ah, Professor Crowe. I'm glad I caught you before you left for work." Father Michael's easy manner confused Romulus for a moment. This was the same man who had trespassed in his house last night. Yet the priest acted as if nothing had happened. How deranged was he?

"The police have your description. I'll be calling them again, to let them know you've been back. If I were you, I'd get out of here, and quick." Romulus started to close the door. He paused, opened it wide, and held out his hand. "You have a key for this house. Hand it over before you leave."

"I don't need a key. The gamaliel has killed someone. I have to convince you."

Romulus opened his mouth, then closed it again. He narrowed his eyes to a squint. "You're babbling. I don't think Imogen sent you after all. I think you're just a nut." Romulus growled, deep in his throat. "Who are you?"

"Father Thomas Michael, as I told you. Look, can I come inside? I didn't want to burst in uninvited again. I thought I'd better be a little more polite this time."

"Father Thomas Michael is dead." Romulus leaned against the doorframe.

"Yes. It is a little limiting, but it's not so bad once you get used to it."

"Huh?" Romulus blinked, his head shaking in short bursts. "Are you still persisting with this ghost nonsense?"

"Well, I prefer the term 'spirit,' but yes. I'm dead."

"Ludicrous. It's broad daylight, full sunshine. Ghosts can't appear in these conditions." Romulus paused. "Ghosts can't appear at all. They don't exist." He leaned forward, jabbing his index finger to within an inch of Father Michael's nose. "I wish you were a ghost, because then you wouldn't exist either. You're a lunatic, and I am now going to give the police a far better description than the one I gave last night. Now get lost." Romulus stepped back and slammed the door. He stared at it for a while, a smile forming on his lips as he rubbed his hands. The aroma of tea drifted in the air, reminding him that the teapot held enough for at least one more cup.

Romulus poured himself another tea and took it through to the lounge. He glanced at the phone, but felt no immediate need to use it. He would phone the police later, after he contacted a locksmith.

Seated in his black leather armchair, Romulus sipped his tea and regarded the walls. The oak paneling had been the factor that had decided his purchase of this house. It gave the rooms an old, serious appearance. The solid floor-to-ceiling bookshelves lining one wall had been another selling point, certainly. Romulus took another sip of tea and reflected that he would have to get his books unpacked and shelved. Currently they were stacked in boxes in his spare bedroom. It would be a few days' work to sort and shelve them all.

"It depends on the type of spirit." The voice came from behind.

Romulus coughed, spraying a mouthful of tea across the room as he jumped to his feet. The teacup fell to the floor, spilling its contents across the carpet.

"Those of us who work for the light can appear in the light, but only to a few." Father Michael strolled around the coffee table to stand facing Romulus as he continued speaking. "Those who follow the darkness are restricted to darkness, mostly. They can appear to those less gifted than yourself, though."

Tears stung Romulus's eyes as he coughed the hot tea from his lungs. He raised his hand to point an accusing finger at Father Michael.

"Demons are different." Father Michael appeared unconcerned by Romulus's distress. "Once they gain entry to our world they can do pretty much as they please, day or night. The gamaliel can take any form it chooses, but it will most likely stick with whatever form it arrived in. No imagination, you see?"

Romulus blinked the tears from his eyes. "What the—" Another coughing fit interrupted him. "How dare you? You can't just walk into my house anytime you like. Get out. Now."

Father Michael continued as though Romulus were attentive to his words. "I can't find the gamaliel, and I can't find the man you saw in your dream. The demon has hidden itself and its caller from spirit eyes."

"This is insane." Romulus moved towards the phone, on its table against the wall.

"You have to listen, Professor Crowe. There's no more time to play the indignant householder. The gamaliel has killed, and it will keep killing unless you stop it."

Romulus lifted the handset.

Father Michael moved alongside him. "Don't use the phone." Desperation showed on his face. As Romulus dialed, Father Michael blurted a few words that stopped Romulus in the act of raising the handset to his ear.

"Your mother sent me."

Hello. Which service do you require?

The voice on the handset spoke, but Romulus stood motionless, staring at the wall. His mind flashed back to his childhood, to memories of his mother. The punishments, those hours spent in the small cupboard beneath the stairs. The beatings. His father, never around to stop them, pretending to believe his mother's protestations of accidental bruising. He knew, but did nothing. In retrospect, if his father had acted, it would only have made things worse for Romulus.

Romulus remembered his twin brother, their mother's favorite. He did what he was told. He behaved as she expected. He never saw the things Romulus saw, so he escaped punishment. In time, Romulus learned to keep quiet, to ignore the sights that appeared to him in his room, to pretend they didn't exist. Pretence became belief, then conviction. Romulus steeled himself against the visions, the sounds, and blocked them from his mind. They were lies. His mother had told him so. The workings of evil. It never occurred to him, as a child, that his mother could be wrong.

Hello, caller. Which service do you require?

The operator's tone became impatient. Romulus replaced the handset with a slow, deliberate movement, his hand resting on the cold plastic. He remembered the funerals. First his father, the sadness of loss and the fear of being alone with his mother. Her religious mania had worsened, until she finally followed her husband into the ground. Romulus could have danced on her grave. Her death released their inheritance, and Romulus and his brother were wealthy in their late teens. Romulus used some of the money to put himself through university and invested the rest. He had never contacted any of his family after his mother's funeral. That was over fifteen years ago. He had no intention of doing so now. Turning his back on Father Michael, Romulus rubbed his sleeve across his eyes.

"What do you know about my mother, you hideous little freak?" His voice cracked, and he faked a cough to disguise his emotion.

"I've met her."

"My mother is dead and has been for a long time." Romulus turned to face Father Michael. "She was almost certainly insane, but she taught me one thing. There are no ghosts." He took a step towards the priest, leaning forward so the smaller man had to crane his neck to look up.

The priest sighed and moved away, towards the window. "She was wrong."

"She was right! On that one thing, she was right. I have examined over a hundred so-called mediums, and every one was a charlatan. There's no spirit world, it was all fake. Cold reading and misdirection. I saw their assistants moving things around."

"But nobody else did." Father Michael's eyes glittered. "Nobody else could see these assistants."

Romulus shrugged and folded his arms. "They wanted to believe. Mass hysteria, self-hypnosis, whatever you want to call it. They fooled themselves into seeing objects move around on their own."

"You wanted to believe, Professor. You wanted to prove your mother wrong. Yet you didn't."

"What I saw convinced me. The mediums were fakes. There are no ghosts."

"There weren't always assistants."

"Oh? You were there? I think not. I saw the tricks, the lies, the deceit, with my own eyes. And I have perfect vision."

"Better than perfect, if you would only accept the fact." Father Michael held out his hand. "Go ahead, touch it."

"Touch your hand? Why?"

"Because you can't."

Romulus stared at the priest's outstretched hand. He could reach it easily. "What is this? Some sort of parlor trick?" Romulus made a sudden lunge for the priest's hand, hoping to take the man by surprise. His hand closed on empty air. An unexpected chill coated his fingers. The priest stood grinning, his hand still reaching out towards Romulus.

"Told you."

"You're fast, I'll admit. But I don't see what this has to do with anything."

"Try again, slowly this time. I won't move."

Romulus reached for Father Michael's hand and closed his own around it, intending to crush the priest's fingers. Once more, his hand closed on nothing, but the priest's hand was still there, apparently fused with his. Romulus blinked, and looked again. The cold in his hand spread throughout his body.

The phone rang. Romulus ignored it. One step brought him face to face with Father Michael. Romulus raised his fist and punched the priest in the chest. His fist connected with nothing. The momentum pulled him forward, merging him with Father Michael along most of the length of his body. The cold was biting this time. Romulus pulled back. The priest did the same.

"It's unpleasant, having you walk through me." Father Michael shook himself. "The heat can be unbearable." He nodded towards the still-ringing phone. "Are you going to answer that?"

"It's not possible." Romulus waved his hand through the priest's stomach. "Are you some kind of hologram?" He had read about a stage show, in London, where one of the actors appeared as a hologram on the stage. "Oh, that explains how you keep getting in here. Someone's projecting you from outside." Romulus strolled to the window as he spoke, then pulled the curtains closed. The phone stopped ringing.

Father Michael rolled his eyes. "I'm not a hologram. Nobody is projecting me."

Romulus slumped into one of the armchairs, staring at the drying tea stain on the floor. "Not a hologram. Not a real person. There's only one other possibility."

"Yes?"

"I'm hallucinating."

"No." Father Michael clasped his hands together on the top of his head.

"Overwork. Too much stress. I need a holiday. Just a few days' rest, then you'll go away."

"Listen to me. You're not mad."

"No, just overtired. Oh, I should have seen it coming. The gate made no sound last night, but you would have had to open it twice. Once to follow me to the door, then once more to get away. The policemen, their smirks and knowing looks. You appearing in my dream. It makes perfect sense. I can't touch you because you don't exist. You're only in my mind."

"I am not a figment of your imagination!"

"Yes, you are." Romulus straightened. "Well, at least I worked it out before I'd paid for new locks."

"How can I convince you? Look, I know about your grandmother, how she used to visit you when you were small. How your mother punished you for talking about those visits. Your grandmother died before you were born." Father Michael paced the room. “I could bring your grandmother here. Or your mother. Even your father. Would that be enough proof?”

“I’m imagining you, so you know everything I know. If I can dream you with such detail, it would be so much easier to conjure an image of my mother. It won’t prove a thing.”

Father Michael hung his head. “It’s hopeless. You’re the only one in Marchway with any chance of stopping the demon, and you don’t even believe I exist. How many have to die?” He raised his head. “There are two things I can tell you. One, a man named Nathaniel died this morning, just before I came to see you. Do you know him?”

“I don’t know any Nathaniels.” Romulus kept his gaze on the tea stain thinking of ways to remove it from his pale blue carpet. Perhaps he should rearrange the furniture.

“Good. So you’ll know I’m not just in your mind, when you read about it in the evening paper. There’s one more thing.”

“Go on.” *Maybe bicarbonate of soda would help.*

“Your assistant, Elaine. Talk to her about her brother. The one you met in Oxford.”

“Elaine and Oxford are part of my memories. That won’t prove anything.”

“Just do it.” On that final note of exasperation, Father Michael vanished.

Romulus lifted his head and looked around. The illusion was definitely gone. He relaxed and closed his eyes, muttering to himself. “I’m cracking up. I’ll burn out before I’m forty unless I relax a little.” A glance at his watch told him he still had a few minutes before he needed to leave for work. Romulus leaned into the comfort of the chair and closed his eyes.

Chapter Sixteen

Angela prodded the food on her plate. "What is this?"

Samuel sat opposite her and picked up his fork. "They're called hamburgers. It's not an exciting meal, I'm afraid, but I haven't been shopping in a while." He picked up his knife, cut into one of the burgers on his own plate, lifted the cut section with his fork, and stared at it. "They're the best of what was left in my freezer."

"What kind of animal?" Angela looked up. "It looks like slices of some large worm."

Samuel paused, mouth open, his fork inches from his lips. The meaty, fatty odor drifted into his nostrils, reminding him just how hungry he was. He glanced at the fork, lowering it before replying.

"It's beef. From cows. Minced and shaped." She was right, they did look like large worm sections. Samuel shrugged and put the meat into his mouth. He was hungry enough to eat it, no matter what it looked like. He wondered what she'd make of sausages.

Angela picked up one of the hamburgers between thumb and forefinger, sniffing at it. She wore one of his shirts and a pair of his jeans, both too short and too baggy, but they looked great on her.

"We'll go shopping," he said. "Get you some clothes, buy some decent food. Maybe we can call in at the library." Samuel wanted to show her off, and he wanted to check up on his library. This way, he could do both. He cut another slice and lifted it, then gaped as Angela tilted her head back and put the entire hamburger in her mouth. His fork lowered until it hit the plate with a clack. She hadn't even chewed, just swallowed the whole thing in one gulp. Samuel breathed out, a long, steady breath. It might be some time before he took her to a restaurant.

Angela lifted the second hamburger, tilting her head back again. Samuel closed his eyes for a moment, long enough to be sure she'd finished, then opened them. She was licking her fingers.

"Those were good. What's the other stuff?"

Samuel swallowed hard. "Potatoes and peas. The white ones are potatoes." He raised his hand when she picked up a potato. "Wait, Angela." She stopped, her black eyes fixed on his. Samuel cleared his throat. "I know you've been—away—for a long time. Let me show you how we do things these days." He lifted his knife and fork, held them vertically and nodded at hers. Angela dropped the potato onto her plate and picked up her cutlery, looking bemused.

"I suppose I should learn to fit in," she said. "It is best I am not noticed."

Samuel ducked his head, hiding the smirk that tensed his lips. "I doubt you'll be able to avoid being noticed, Angela." He looked up into her eyes. "I know what you mean though. You don't want people to think you're odd. I don't want that either." He didn't want people to think he was taking advantage of a simpleton, that was for sure. Samuel lifted the fork, turned it in a slow arc, and placed it gently into a potato. Angela followed his movement exactly with her own fork. Then a gentle press with the knife sliced the boiled potato in two. Again, Angela mirrored his movements. Samuel lifted the cut section to his mouth and placed the potato inside.

Angela laughed. "It must take ages to eat anything this way."

Samuel choked on his potato. He clasped the back of his hand against his mouth, chewing furiously to get the food down before he gagged. When he'd forced it down, he turned to her, his eyes filled with tears of laughter. "Normally we do it faster. I'm just slowing down to show you how it's done."

Angela grinned, then put the potato into her mouth. Her face contorted in an expression of disgust, as though she had tasted something vile. She spat the potato onto the plate, dropping her cutlery and rubbing her tongue with her fingers.

"Angela? What's wrong?"

"That was awful. Do you have any more of the round things?"

"Hamburgers? Here, have mine." Samuel exchanged their plates with a twinge of regret. He had only managed to eat half of one hamburger, but, being a gentleman, he would just have to bear it. He raised one eyebrow in disapproval when she reached for the burger, then smiled with her as she lifted her knife and fork and cut into it. Angela's dexterity with the cutlery improved with every piece she cut.

She learns fast.

Turning his attention to Angela's plate, now in front of him, Samuel picked up a potato on his fork and bit into it. It tasted fine, insofar as boiled potato could be said to taste of anything. He wondered what she found so offensive in this, the most inoffensive of vegetables.

"Angela," he said, "when you first arrived, you said there was another Samuel, a long time ago." Samuel kept his gaze on the plate in front of him.

"Yes." Angela swallowed the last of his burgers before continuing. "It was my father's name, and also the name of the man who trapped me in that book."

Samuel looked up. "Your father trapped you?"

"No." Angela's laughter brought a smile to his face, making him forget his hunger. "They were different, just with the same name. Except my father's name was pronounced Samael."

"Ah." Samuel rubbed his chin. She'd called him Shemuel at first, the old Hebrew version of his name. That seemed reasonable. The name "Samael" was unusual, though he'd seen it in a book somewhere. Which one? Thoughts of books reminded him of her arrival the night before.

"Angela." Samuel raised his index finger, bringing it to his forehead, between his eyes. "You did something to me, when you first arrived. Something in my head."

"Why, yes." Angela stood and walked around the table, one slow step after another. "I had to learn how to speak to you. Your language. Your name." She licked her lips. "Your desires." She reached his side, rubbed her thigh against his arm.

Samuel's breathing stopped. He took a moment to force his chest back into action. "You can use magic?"

"Some." Her shrug was noncommittal. She put her arm around his neck, pulling his head over to rest on her breasts. "I was in a magical place, remember?"

Her scent made his head swim. Everything she said made perfect sense. She couldn't help but pick up a little magic, trapped inside the world of that magical book for so long. There was nothing to fear, nothing at all. Samuel stood and gave himself to her embrace.

"Let's go to bed." Her voice was a cool breeze in his ear.

Samuel glanced up at the clock. "It's past ten. We really need to go shopping." He tried, but could think of no compelling reason to deny her—or himself.

Angela breathed a soft chuckle. "Shopping can wait."

Chapter Seventeen

Elaine unpacked the new equipment with great care. It took a lot of arguing to persuade Romulus to order these new motion sensors, and he was unlikely to authorize replacements if she broke any. She sat on a stool and tried to concentrate on the instruction manuals. Her old laptop computer might be able to handle these sensors, but only just.

Elaine glanced at her watch. Ten-fifteen, and still no sign of Romulus. In the years she had spent as his student, then as his assistant, she had never known him to be late for anything. She gave up on the manual and dropped it onto the bench.

She tried phoning Romulus at home, but there was no reply. He must have left already. Perhaps he took his load of cardboard to the dump. That would have taken no more than fifteen minutes, so he should still have arrived over an hour ago. Thoughts of Romulus's battered Ford drifted through her mind. The ramshackle vehicle was barely road legal and certainly unsafe—particularly with Romulus behind the wheel. Perhaps it had broken down. No, Romulus could have walked here by now.

What if he's finally crashed the thing?

Elaine still needed Romulus. She had to develop a name for herself, build up a background of research papers. Then she could apply for grants in her own right and be confident in her ability to win them. Besides, having a name like Romulus Crowe on her list of former employers would be a big help in applying for future jobs. She certainly did not want him dead, although if he were injured, there was a part of her that might laugh at his pain. It would be vindication of what she had told him for years; the derelict cars he insisted on driving were all potential deathtraps.

A knock at the door interrupted her thoughts. "Come in," she said.

The door opened, just enough to admit a worried face. It was Bethany, Professor Chesterton's secretary. Elaine smiled at the woman's nervous glance around the room.

"Is Professor Crowe here?"

"No. I haven't seen him today." Elaine covered her growing smirk with her hand when Bethany released her breath. It wasn't funny, really. Romulus had crushed the secretary's self-confident manner in less than a day, maybe in less than a minute after meeting her. He was a bastard sometimes, but he was usually correct in his assessment of people. Bethany might have carried on allowing people to set up meetings without consulting Romulus, but not after experiencing a blast of his uninhibited fury. Nobody pushed Romulus around twice.

Bethany pushed the door wider and stepped inside, her head raised and chest thrust forward. Clearly, Elaine posed no threat, so Bethany could let her self-importance shine. "Well, he has a visitor. Without an appointment."

No wonder you're worried. "I don't know where he is. Can I help?"

"His visitor is waiting in my office. If you could look after her until Professor

Crowe decides to show up, it would really help."

And you won't have to face him. "I suppose I could do that. Who is it?"

"Doctor LeFevre. As I said, he's not expecting her."

Elaine slipped from her stool and walked around the bench. "Imogen LeFevre? I've read some of her publications. I'd be glad to meet her." She followed Bethany back to her office, where a red-haired woman in a dark gray jacket and short skirt was seated. Imogen LeFevre stood as the two women entered. She lifted a square, black leather bag and put the strap over her shoulder.

"This is Doctor Pettifer, Professor Crowe's assistant. I'm afraid I can't find the professor." Bethany had recovered her composure. She crossed to her desk and sat, busying herself with paperwork and ignoring her visitors.

"Call me Elaine." Holding out her hand, Elaine approached Doctor LeFevre.

"Imogen." They shook hands.

"Would you like to look around?" Elaine led the way into the corridor. "Or maybe we could go for a coffee?"

"Well, I was hoping to see Romulus. I was passing through Marchway on my way back from a conference, and I thought I'd say hello. I could do with a coffee though."

"Conference? The one in Southampton? I wanted to go, but Romulus decided against it. Said we were too busy, what with starting up the department here."

Imogen laughed. "He must have read the conference program. I chaired two of the sessions and presented four papers."

Elaine led the way through the labyrinth of corridors towards the coffee room. "Why would that bother him? Although, now that I think of it, you and I have never met before. Even though we work in a relatively small field, our paths have never crossed."

"That's my Romulus. He can hold a grudge to the end of time." Imogen waved her hand. "It's a long story."

Clearly there was some history between Romulus and this woman. He never mentioned her, but Elaine would have been surprised if he had. Romulus never discussed his past. Elaine changed the subject. She would work around to Imogen's story, in the same way she normally wrung information from Romulus.

"I haven't seen Romulus today. It's the first time I've known him to be late."

"Really? I wonder where he could be?" Imogen raised perfectly plucked eyebrows.

"I phoned him at home but there was no reply. Maybe his car's broken down."

"Don't tell me. Battered, rusted, no maintenance, and blue. Always blue."

"That's right. He never seems to have any money to spend on his cars. And yes, they're always blue." Elaine stopped and opened a door. "Here's the coffee room. It'll fill up in about fifteen minutes, but we have it to ourselves for now. Have a seat, I'll get some cups." Elaine stood back to let Imogen enter.

Imogen laid her bag on a seat then sat beside it. She remained silent while Elaine made the coffee, apart from her response to Elaine's question regarding milk and sugar. She took neither. When Elaine sat opposite her, Imogen resumed the conversation.

"He's loaded, you know."

"What?"

"Romulus inherited a fortune from his parents. He's not too poor to run a decent car. He's too cheap." Imogen's eyes twinkled over her cup as she sipped at her coffee.

"Romulus is rich? He hates rich people. Only yesterday, he threw someone out of his office, someone who could have given him a substantial grant." Elaine set her cup on the table. "His reasons were valid, I suppose."

"They always are, aren't they? His arguments are so convincing."

"Well, yes."

"He's tiring to work with, don't you find? As though he's draining energy from you."

Elaine looked into her coffee. It was clear Imogen knew Romulus, and knew him well. Elaine decided to change topics until she could work out the relationship between Imogen and Romulus.

"Why blue? I mean, why are his cars always blue?"

Imogen laughed. "That's easy. He's colorblind. Red and green, and shades of those colors, confuse him. He can see them but can't always name them. That's what he told me when he tried to explain it." She leaned forward. "Blue is easier for him to see. If he bought a red or brown car, he would have trouble finding it in a crowded parking lot."

Elaine nodded. Romulus would never allow himself to appear confused or lost in public. He would never put himself in a position where he might have to ask someone for help. She looked into Imogen's green eyes. "Colorblind? I didn't know."

"No reason why you should. He never admits to any flaw." Imogen leaned back in her seat.

Elaine ran her fingers over the handle of her own cup. "There's something wrong with his eyes—floaters, he says—but what he describes doesn't sound like floaters."

"What he describes sounds like orbs." Imogen winked. "I know. He's seen them for a long time. I once made an appointment at an optician for him and went along, to be sure he didn't dodge out of it. There's nothing wrong with his vision apart from the colorblindness."

Elaine's gaze alternated between her coffee and Imogen's face. Romulus had never shown the slightest inclination for any romantic involvement with any woman. Was Imogen the exception, or perhaps the reason? Elaine set her cup back on the table.

"Rom says orbs are bunk. Dust, or insects. An artifact of digital cameras."

Imogen laughed, a high, yet soft and pleasant sound. "You sound just like him. I hope you're not spending too much time with him?"

It was a lighthearted remark, but it sounded like a serious question. Elaine covered her warming cheeks with her hands. "I work for Romulus. That's all there is to it."

Imogen sipped at her coffee. "There are rumors, you know. I mean, you and Romulus are rarely seen, but when you are you're always together."

"That's Rom's fault. He—well, he's just not the socializing type."

"He was, once." Imogen glanced at the bag on the seat beside her, as though checking to make sure it was still there.

Elaine saw an opportunity to change the subject. "Is that a laptop? The bag looks new."

"So is the computer inside. That's why I didn't want to leave it in my car."

Imogen placed one hand on the bag.

Elaine sighed. "I've been trying to get a new computer for ages. Romulus doesn't see the point, but some of the things he wants done need more processing power than my old laptop can provide."

"I told you. He's cheap. Not just with his own money, but with his research grants. Romulus won't spend without very good reason."

"He's never late without a good reason either. I wonder where he could be?" Elaine glanced at the door, even though she knew the chance of Romulus walking through it was slim. He rarely bothered with the communal coffee room. She turned back to Imogen. "You're still based in Edinburgh?"

Imogen nodded.

"So, you're driving from Southampton to Edinburgh in one day? That must be a tiring drive."

"I planned to stop over for a night." Imogen's eyes twinkled and a hint of a smile creased her lips.

"In Marchway? It's a little out of your way, isn't it? Did you book somewhere?"

"No, but I'll find a guest house or hotel later. I have to visit the library, to look at one of their ancient books. I have an appointment for this afternoon."

Elaine recalled what she knew of the little town. "There's only one hotel, although there are a few bed and breakfast houses. The students haven't come back yet, so there should be vacancies." She glanced at her watch. "Tell you what, I could show you the hotel."

"You're sure Romulus won't mind?"

"Why would he? He hasn't even shown up for work yet." Elaine stood and took both cups to the sink. She washed them while she considered what she had learned so far. There was something between Imogen and Romulus, of that she was sure, but the idea of Romulus having any romantic involvement seemed ridiculous. Why, then, did he go to such lengths to avoid this woman?

* * * *

Imogen's car was a two-year-old Rover in perfect condition. Elaine relaxed in the leather passenger seat and inhaled. No cigar fumes, no petrol or oil vapors. The floor was clear of junk. The car was spotless and started so quietly Elaine had to concentrate to hear the engine. She buckled her seat belt while Imogen pulled out of the parking space.

"I wouldn't mind driving to Scotland in this. When I said it was a long way, I was thinking of Romulus's car." Elaine ran her hand along the seat belt. There was no trace of grease.

Imogen laughed. "I doubt any car he bought could make it that far." She stopped at the exit of the parking lot. "Which way?"

"Oh—left. Then right at the traffic light."

While she directed Imogen to The White Monkey, Marchway's only hotel, Elaine tried to sort out what she knew of the woman. She was a well-respected parapsychologist, but Romulus never referred to any of her publications. Imogen had hinted that Romulus even avoided attending meetings if he knew she was going to be there. That suggested Romulus nursed a very deep grudge against Imogen. Knowing him, that was no surprise. He held many grudges. It was almost a religion with him.

Perhaps she had won a contract he was bidding for. Perhaps she had been promoted above him. No, he was a professor now. He would have gone to the Southampton meeting to gloat, if that were the case.

It all came back to a past romantic involvement, but the very idea was insane. Romulus never showed more than a passing interest in women, In fact, Elaine sometimes wondered if he were gay. He showed no interest in men either, though. She had assumed that Romulus was so self-absorbed there was simply no room for anyone else in his life. She shook herself out of her thoughts as the car drew to a halt in the parking lot of The White Monkey.

Imogen switched off the engine and turned to Elaine. "You're wondering why I've come to visit a man who obviously hates me."

"Well, I..." Elaine's thoughts had not reached that stage, but the question was an interesting one. "I don't want to pry." She shifted in her seat, avoiding Imogen's eyes.

"Don't be embarrassed. I could tell you were trying to work it out. The answer will surprise you." Imogen opened her door and climbed out of the car. Elaine did the same. They looked at each other over the car roof. "Romulus and I were together at college. We were... lovers."

Elaine suppressed a sudden urge to giggle. "Romulus? Romantic? It's hard to picture that."

"I'm sure it is. He changed, overnight. Wouldn't speak to me, wouldn't even look at me. I still don't know why." Imogen walked around the car. "I can remember the date exactly. It was the day before I heard my father had died." She took a breath. "I left for home the next day. By the time I was back at college, Romulus had transferred to another one. That's one reason I'm here. I still want to know what happened." She faced Elaine, and the two stood in silence for a moment. Imogen sniffed. "Well, let's see if I can get a room for the night."

Elaine followed Imogen into the hotel. "You mean you're here simply to find out why Romulus broke up with you at college?"

"Well, I really do have to visit the library, but there is another reason." The reception desk was empty. Imogen pressed the buzzer beside the "Ring for service" sign. "I want to write a paper about him."

Elaine frowned. "You mean with him? You want to co-author a paper with Romulus?"

"No. I want him to be the subject of the study."

"But you study demons. Monsters."

Imogen inclined her head and raised an eyebrow.

Elaine leaned against the reception desk. "You're not serious. I know he can get pretty demonic at times, but he's human, I'm sure."

"He's human all right." Imogen grinned. "If he were a demon it would be easier. We could just exorcise him. No, he's human. He's also the most powerful psychic I've ever met."

"You've lost me now. Romulus doesn't even believe in psychics. He's proved every one he's studied to be a fraud. I was involved in many of those investigations. I saw no evidence of any psychic abilities in Romulus."

"He sees ghosts. Full manifestations, so complete he thinks he's talking to live people. If you're within range, he can sap your energy. Everything he says to you is absolutely convincing. He's clairvoyant, clairaudient, and capable of exerting mind-pressure through some form of telepathy. The best part is, he doesn't even know he's doing it."

Elaine's shoulders sagged. The floaters. Romulus's description sounded like orbs, but they couldn't be. There were no orbs. She had seen the photos he'd produced, seen how he generated the fakes. Romulus had lectured on the fallacies of orbs many times. Yet his floaters were not floaters. Then there was that incident, over a year ago, where he claimed to have met her brother. She had forgotten it, dismissed it as a mistake on his part.

"He sees orbs. Spirit lights," she said, her voice low.

"He sees much more than that. Listen, Romulus has abilities beyond any medium or psychic I've ever met. I should know. I was closer to him than anyone has ever been. Romulus is definitely psychic."

"Have you ever told him this?" *Is that why he left you?*

Imogen gave a sharp laugh. "Can you imagine his reaction? No, I haven't told him." She turned her head towards the desk as a middle-aged man in a suit walked out of the room beyond. "Anyway, let's see if I can get a room. Then we can get some lunch and compare notes. I'm sure you have a few more anomalies to add to my Romulus file."

Chapter Eighteen

Samuel struggled from his bed, laughing as he dodged Angela's playful attempts to restrain him.

"Come on," he said, "we have to get going. I want to get to the shops before lunchtime, while they're quiet."

"Why?" Her pout made him reconsider for a moment, but he stood firm.

"Because you have no clothes, there's no food in the house, and I have to check up on my staff."

Angela folded her arms beneath her breasts. "I can use your spare clothes. You have plenty. I'm not hungry and I don't care where you've left your stick."

A snort of laughter escaped Samuel. "Staff, not stick. Staff means the people who work for me." He shook his head. "You have to wear clothes that fit you. I thought you didn't want to get noticed? And I'm hungry, even if you're not." He was, indeed, extremely hungry. He ate little in the past few days, and his joints ached with fatigue. The flu receded, although it left him feeling tired. Samuel smiled to himself. There was more than just the flu in his fatigue. He grabbed his bathrobe from the floor and moved towards the door. "I'm going for a shower."

"I want to see this shower." Angela threw the quilt aside and jumped from the bed. Still naked, she followed him to the bathroom.

Samuel looked into the mirror over the sink and scratched the stubble on his chin. His hand stopped when he noticed his reflection. The face staring back was old, wrinkled, and ashen. The grey in his hair had spread while the lines around his eyes deepened, making him look far older than his years. He groaned. The flu and lack of food took their toll.

"Something wrong?" Angela's cool hands rubbed his shoulders. Samuel jumped. He hadn't realized she stood right behind him. He turned to look at her, and her arms slipped around his neck.

"I look terrible. I feel terrible. Maybe I'm not completely over the flu."

Amusement flickered in Angela's deep black eyes. "You'll live for a while yet." She tightened her arms, drew his face to hers, and kissed him. Samuel responded, his hands moved around her waist and down over her buttocks.

Angela laughed and drew back. "Now, show me how this shower works." She pulled away from his embrace, moving to inspect the bath and the exposed pipework leading upward from the faucet. She tapped the bath. "Is this it?"

"No, that's a bath. You fill it with water and lie down in it." Her quizzical look amused him, making him forget his aches and pains for a moment. "It's for getting clean."

"So you won't smell as bad?"

Samuel tensed. He hadn't thought of it that way. One look at Angela's face told him it was an innocent question, not meant as an insult, but it cut him deeply all the same. It had been a few days since he last showered, so he must stink by now. His reply was muted. "Yes, that's the idea."

Samuel glanced at his reflection in the mirror. If anything, he looked worse than he had before Angela kissed him. He really needed that shower. Moving past Angela, Samuel reached for the hot water handle. He turned the shower valve on, sending thin streams of water into the bathtub. He looked up at her as he adjusted the temperature. "Want to join me?"

Her eyes grew wide. "It's a rain machine."

"I hadn't thought of it like that, but I suppose it is." Samuel tested the water with his hand, dropped his bathrobe to the floor, and stepped into the shower.

"I haven't seen rain for a long time." She put her hand into the stream of water and gasped. "It's hot! Hot rain."

"I like it hot." Samuel realized he was leering and straightened his face. "Want to join me?" He held her hand while she stepped into the bathtub, enjoying every curve, every jiggle of her body. His own response was immediate. All thought of hurrying left his mind as he took her in his arms, running his hands over every inch of her perfect skin. Not a blemish, not a single mole marred Angela's perfection. Samuel wished his mother were alive. She had never approved of any of his girlfriends, always telling him they weren't good enough for him. He raised his eyes to the ceiling as Angela sank to her knees, and defied his mother's ghost to find fault with this one. His brow lowered briefly. Hopefully his mother wasn't watching at this precise moment. Angela reached her target. Samuel closed his eyes and smiled into the shower spray.

* * * *

As he buttoned his shirt, Samuel remembered the books. Those priceless, rare books, down there in the cold and dusty basement. It was no way to treat such irreplaceable antiques. Samuel closed his eyes. He had left them on the concrete floor.

He couldn't get them back into the library today, but he needed to be sure they were safe. He finished dressing and raised his eyebrows at Angela, who sat naked on the bed.

"Come on. You'll have to get dressed." Samuel opened the wardrobe and took out a shirt and trousers. At the bottom of the wardrobe lay a pair of training shoes. He had worn them once, in one of his many failed attempts to improve his health and general fitness. Shoes and clothes laid on the bed, Samuel indicated the chest of drawers and the wardrobe. "Pick out anything you like, just until we get something to fit you."

Angela sighed. "Very well. I suppose I should learn the ways of your world, but it does seem like a lot of bother. It took you ages to fix all those clothes around yourself."

"It's cold outside." Samuel headed for the door. "I just have to check on a few things, then we can go." He hurried downstairs, his concern for the books growing with every step. *Geometria ton Zoon* was his ticket to an easy retirement, or his route to unemployment, even prison, depending on whether or not his theft was ever noticed. Either way, he could not risk damaging those books while they were in his possession.

Samuel drew a short breath and blew it out quickly as he opened the basement door. The light was still on. *Geometria*, *Clavicula Salomonis,* and his notebook lay as he had left them, within the chalk circle on the concrete floor.

"God, I hope I don't have mice down here." Samuel rushed down the stairs and reached for the books, stopping himself before his fingers made contact. The gloves lay a few feet away. He must have discarded them when Angela appeared, although he had no memory of doing so. Samuel put the gloves on and picked up the books. A quick examination of each book showed no obvious damage. Samuel exhaled in relief and reached for his notebook.

Standing within the chalk circle, holding the two books and his notes, Samuel found it difficult to believe he had done all this. Not only had he stolen from his own library, he had also constructed a magical circle, spoken an incantation, and conjured a beautiful woman from his dreams. He stared at the notebook in his hand. The words written there were real. When he spoke them aloud, Angela had appeared. It was all true. The dreams with Melchior were more than dreams. So *Geometria ton Zoon* was no fake. It was the real thing.

The events of the previous night seemed unreal, impossible now that it was day. Angela's existence was tangible proof that they had happened. What about Melchior? Samuel remembered his warnings, his insistence that Angela was somehow dangerous. Should he take them seriously? Samuel tried to recall the name of the book Melchior had mentioned. "Liber" something. That was no use. "Liber" just meant "book." It was the name of a demon, starting with "A." Samuel frowned. "Asmodeus"? No, it sounded like "Asmodeus" but that wasn't it.

Samuel moved towards the false wall his father had built. His brow furrowed in concentration. "Asmodeus" was the wrong name, but it meant something anyway. Somehow the word was connected to another thought, somewhere in his mind, somewhere among all the books he had read throughout the years. He turned the wooden molding that opened a section of the wall and stepped inside.

The air was dry inside the old hidey-hole. Samuel placed the books and his notes on a shelf, the gloves beside them, then stepped outside and closed the door. Even if his house were robbed, the books would be safe now. Melchior's notes still lay on his dining room table, but no burglar could profit from them.

The name "Asmodeus" still nagged at his thoughts. He tried to distract himself by thinking of the money he would make from a translation of *Geometria*. Angela could help him. She must know about the book. She was trapped there for centuries, at least. She might even be able to construct a full Etruscan codex with him—and that would mean fame as well as fortune.

As he climbed the steps, Samuel fantacized about an early retirement with Angela on his arm. A dream come true, in the most literal sense. Angela had been trapped by someone she called Shemuel and released by Samuel. It was almost poetic. He turned off the light and closed the door.

The sound of footsteps above signaled Angela's approach to the staircase. She must have found something to wear. Samuel's smile faded when his tired brain found the connection it had been seeking.

The demon Asmodeus was a fallen angel, so he originally had an angelic name. An old name, a Biblical name.

A name Angela had mentioned.

Samael. Her father.

Chapter Nineteen

"He'll never agree to it, but I'd love to be there when you tell him." Elaine lifted her sandwich. "At a safe distance."

Imogen, seated opposite, finished a mouthful of food. "I don't intend to tell him outright. He'd explode. I'm planning to convince him gradually. I'll get him involved in the experiments by telling him I believe in their effectiveness. He'll do it just to prove me wrong."

"It might work. He's not easily deceived, though, and he'll be furious when he finds out." Elaine looked around the rapidly filling cafeteria. Office workers mixed with shop assistants and laborers as lunchtime started. She wondered if Romulus had shown up for work yet.

"I don't think there's any way to avoid him losing his temper." Imogen turned her gaze to her computer, open on the table beside her. "That story about your brother is going to set his teeth rattling, for sure. Hard to believe he challenged a ghost to produce a visitor's pass, isn't it?"

"I'd rather you didn't involve me too deeply. You can leave when it's all done, but I'll be stuck here." Elaine picked at her tuna and mayonnaise sandwich. The memory of her brother's death was not something she wanted revived. Two years ago, Romulus mentioned he had spoken with her brother on his way to the lab. She had insisted he was mistaken. Archie was, at that time, mountaineering in France. Elaine heard of his death a few days later. He had fallen. A faulty piton had broken. Perhaps he had come to say goodbye, but she had not seen him. If Imogen was right, then maybe Romulus had met Archie after all. Her brow creased. Where was Romulus?

Elaine took out her cell phone. "I'll just find out if he's at work yet." She dialed and waited. "Hello? Bethany? It's Elaine Pettifer."

"I was just about to leave for lunch." Bethany's voice was terse.

"I'll only keep you a moment. I wondered if Professor Crowe had arrived there yet, or phoned to say where he is."

"No, I haven't seen him or heard from him. Is that all? I only have an hour for lunch."

"Yes, that's all I needed to know. Thanks, Bethany." The line went dead. Elaine put her phone away and looked at Imogen. "No sign of him."

"Well, let's finish our lunch and go look for him. Marchway's not that big. He can't have gone far." Imogen took a sip of her tea. "We'll try his house first. You know where it is, I hope?"

"I have the address, but I haven't actually been there. He's not the sort to encourage visitors." Elaine stared into her sandwich. Romulus couldn't have disappeared unless he found out, somehow, about Imogen's arrival. Elaine set the sandwich on her plate and stared at the people passing in the street. Her appetite had deserted her.

Imogen reached over and tapped Elaine's arm. "Don't worry about him. He wouldn't worry about you."

Chapter Twenty

Romulus rubbed sleep from his eyes and opened his front door. Two stocky men in dark suits stood, unsmiling, on his doorstep.

"Professor Crowe?"

"Yes. Who are you?"

The men produced identification cards. "Police. I'm Detective Inspector Crawley and this is Detective Sergeant Poole. We're following up on your report of an intruder last night."

"Oh." Romulus squinted at the cards. "That was nothing. I probably dreamt the whole thing."

"Perhaps, sir, but we'd like to ask you a few questions, if that's okay with you. Could we come inside?"

"Well, if you must. I really should be at work, so I'd appreciate it if you can make it quick." Romulus backed into the hallway, giving the policemen room to enter. "It's pointless really. There was no harm done. Nothing was stolen." He closed the door and waved his hand towards the lounge. As he followed the two policemen, Romulus considered his options. Somehow he had to explain last night's fiasco without admitting that his mental state might be less than perfect. "Well, have a seat, and ask away."

"Thank you, sir." The policemen sat on the sofa, leaving Romulus to sit on the armchair. Detective Sergeant Poole took out his notebook and a pen. Detective Inspector Crawley leaned forward, his hands clasped.

"It's about this man who calls himself Father Thomas Michael. Could you describe him for us? We have the officer's report, of course, but you might have remembered something more since then."

Romulus ran through the description of his hallucination, knowing this was all a waste of time but with no way to graciously escape the situation. The police might look around for a while, but with no serious crime involved they would soon lose interest. Better to let the matter fade out on its own rather than risk humiliation.

"Interesting. The description fits the real Father Michael rather well. He's been dead for about a year."

"I know. My assistant told me. That's how I knew this priest wasn't the real thing."

"You had your assistant check up on him? Why would you do that?" Detective Inspector Crawley shifted in his seat. His foot hit something on the floor. He leaned forward, picked up a china cup, and raised a questioning eyebrow at Romulus.

"I—it must have fallen out of my hand when I fell asleep." Romulus rose from his seat, retrieved the cup, and placed it on a coaster on the coffee table. "I had a rough night. I fell asleep in my chair this morning." He paused and took a breath. "As I said, my assistant found out the real Father Michael was dead. We investigate supposed hauntings. People have been reporting sightings of this priest after his death. It's not surprising. I've been seeing him myself." Romulus stopped talking. What he had seen was nothing more than a product of his own overactive imagination.

"So, he's been here before?"

"Yes, but he seemed harmless enough. Really, is there any need for this? There's no harm done, I don't expect he'll come back." *Unless I hallucinate again.*

Detective Sergeant Poole coughed. "There was an incident this morning. Some aspects of that case show a similarity to what happened here last night." He glanced at Crawley before continuing. "A man died in suspicious circumstances in his own home. No forced entry, and all the windows and doors were locked. It's a remarkable coincidence, don't you agree?"

Romulus shrugged. "I don't think this Father Michael could have done it." *He's not real.* "He was too small to be a threat to anyone." *A man named Nathaniel died today.* The priest's parting words came to mind. Romulus stretched his shoulders, feigning nonchalance. "Who died? Anyone I'd know?"

"We can't go into detail, not until the relatives have been informed," Crawley said. "We're very interested in tracking down Father Michael's double though. If he can get in and out of one house without leaving a trace, he can do it in another. Two such intrusions in one night are too much of a coincidence to ignore."

One of them was imaginary. Romulus ran his tongue over his teeth. The police would hunt for his dream-priest instead of the real killer. They'd realize their mistake soon enough, when they picked up evidence from the crime scene. It would only delay them a little. Romulus rose to his feet. "Well, I wish I could be of more help, but I've told you all I know."

"Yes, well, your cooperation is appreciated." The policemen stood and followed Romulus to the door. "We may want to call on you again to clarify a few details."

Romulus opened the front door. Poole stopped on the doorstep.

"One last thing, sir. You mentioned a name to our officers last night." He checked his notebook. "Imogen LeFevre. You seemed to think she was involved."

"No. I don't think so. I was a little confused last night. Lack of sleep. Besides, she might play a trick of this sort on me, but murder? No, she'd never get involved in anything like that."

"I see, sir. Well, good day to you."

"Good day, officers." Romulus watched the policemen leave, wincing at the shriek of his garden gate. As their car pulled away from the curb, another replaced it. Romulus raised his eyebrows at the sight of Elaine in the passenger seat. His eyebrows lowered and his lip curled when the driver of the car climbed out. An impulse to slam the door flashed through his mind, but he stood still while the two women approached his gate. Romulus hissed through his teeth, considering how close to let them approach before releasing his fury. A floater drifted across his sight.

The gate's hinges screamed again when Imogen pushed it open. Romulus noticed a flicker of movement across the street, and Father Michael formed where the floater had been, now standing on the pavement opposite. *Oh, not now. Not another hallucination.*

That settled it. The act of covering up his newly acquired disorder in his conversation with the police. This detestable woman appearing on his doorstep, apparently in collusion with the one person he trusted. That was surely stressful enough to bring on this vision of the priest. Thus was his theory confirmed. The priest was a stress-induced hallucination. The man he took to be a lunatic was in fact no more than a floater. A big, talking floater. Romulus took a deep breath to calm himself before addressing the two women.

"What now? Can't I get any peace, even in my own home?"

"If you'd turn up for work I wouldn't have to come looking for you. Why didn't you answer when I phoned?" Elaine stopped, concern creasing her face. "Romulus, are you all right? You look awful."

"Oh, thank you. If you must know, I'm feeling a little run down. A few days' rest and I'll be fine." He nodded towards Imogen "What's she doing here?"

"I was just passing." Imogen said.

"Nobody 'just passes' through Marchway. You came here on purpose. Why?"

"To see you."

"Well, you've seen me. Now you can leave." Romulus stared between the women at Father Michael, who crossed the street and walked through his gate, its rusted iron bars melding briefly with his body. Romulus blinked rapidly.

"What is it? Floaters again?" Elaine moved forward.

"Never mind." Romulus pressed his hand against his forehead. The more tense he became, the longer this hallucination was likely to persist. He needed to calm himself.

"He sees something." Imogen sounded smug, as though she knew what was happening. Suspicion resurfaced, but Romulus pushed it away. Imogen could not be doing this. It was all in his own mind. Romulus moved his hand down to rub at his neck.

"Tell them." Father Michael nodded towards the two women.

"Get lost." Romulus grabbed the door. His head swam.

"We're only here to help." Elaine sounded hurt.

"He's not talking to us." Imogen put her hand on Romulus's arm. He shrugged it off.

Father Michael walked between the women and brought his face close to Romulus's. "I'm sorry, Professor, but time is pressing. You'll find it hard to believe, but this is for your own good."

Before Romulus could speak, the priest stepped forward into him. His blood turned to ice water. Every muscle in his body tensed. Floaters clouded his vision, so many he could barely make out the shapes of Imogen and Elaine through them. Romulus gasped as his imaginary priest took a grip on his mind.

Voices roared through his head. Romulus closed his eyes tight and put one hand over his face, gripping the doorframe with the other. His fingers pressed into his forehead, his thumb into his cheek. The voices grew louder, clearer.

"Maybe we should call a doctor," That was Elaine. Romulus grasped at this one point of focus, his link with reality, but it slid away from him to be replaced by impossibility. Romulus railed inside against the loss of his mind, against his rapid descent into insanity.

Is this a nervous breakdown? Is this what it feels like?

His father's voice filled his head. "That's the trouble with life, son. Sometimes we just have to face things, like it or not."

"Doctors are no use to you." That was Father Michael. The hallucination, the sign of strain, the early warning Romulus had ignored. Religion had driven Romulus's mother insane. It was fitting that his own collapse was marked by a vision of a priest.

Father Michael spoke in soft tones. "You're not losing your mind. Just the opposite. You're coming to your senses at last."

"Go away. Leave me alone." Romulus cringed at the shrill fear in his own voice.

"I'm sorry, Romulus. I didn't know." His mother, the inquisitor of his childhood. The tortures she put him through, when he had only told her the truth.

The truth. Was it, really?

Gentle hands took Romulus's arms and he was moving, walking without caring where he went.

"It's all right, Romulus. You can tell them now. Nobody can hurt you any more." The quiet, calm voice of his grandmother stopped him. He was aware of the hands pulling, urging him onwards but he stood immobile. So many years had passed since he last heard that voice. His childhood, repressed, flooded back as though a dam had collapsed in his mind.

"Nana." Romulus was four years old, waiting in his darkened bedroom for his visitor. She came and told him tales of things past, things that had been in the world before he was born. He asked questions, spoke too loud. The bedroom door flew open. He was torn from his bed. Screaming, his mother dragged him downstairs to the small cupboard, beating him as he bounced on the steps. Shrieking "Devil. Hellspawn. Monster." More words, harsh words he couldn't remember. The cupboard door slammed and locked. Romulus shivered, curled into a ball, and cried.

There are no ghosts.

By the time he was five years old, he didn't cry any more. He never cried since.

By the time he was six, the visits stopped. Romulus refused to acknowledge them. They were deceptions, illusions, the work of evil. He could not admit them to his life.

There are no ghosts.

It made little difference. His mother regarded him as evil, latent perhaps, but ready to burst upon the world at any moment. The beatings continued, although their frequency reduced. It was her mission to remove the devil from his soul and this was apparently accomplished through pain. His lack of tears only enraged her further.

The young Romulus suppressed his emotions, one by one, until only vengeance drove him. He had to prove his mother wrong. His nocturnal visitor had been kind, his mother cruel. Surely there was no evil in his grandmother? Certainly there was evil in his mother.

There are no ghosts.

The spiritualist mediums had offered hope. They had failed him. Fakes, one and all. In his rage he destroyed their reputations. In his fury, he debunked and ridiculed. Others at the seances claimed to see objects appear or move around, but Romulus saw the hands that moved them. Fakes. Charlatans. His mother had been right all along.

There are no ghosts.

Time moved at random in his mind, to the awakening of feelings. Imogen should have been his salvation, but that one night had sealed him forever. Halloween, he had dressed up as a werewolf and crept to her ground-floor window. She was home, but not alone. A man stood over her while she wrote at her desk; a tall man, a handsome man. Standing too close, too familiar. Romulus crept away as silently as he had arrived.

His emotions he sealed once more, this time for good. Romulus became stone, hard and cold. It was in this state he met the mediums, the only residue of warmth in his soul fueled by hate. Romulus produced paper after paper demonstrating the techniques of the cold readers, the manipulators, the fast-talking twisters of words. Liars. Frauds. Failures.

There are no ghosts.

Yes, there are.

Romulus sank to his knees, ignoring the hands that tried to support him. A fly-buzz of sound told him of voices outside his head, but his mind was elsewhere, internal, rearranging itself. His grandmother was right. His mother was wrong. He had seen, and spoken with, the dead. More times than he knew. That damned priest was the real thing, after all.

Voices broke into his thoughts, voices that were not of his mind's construction. Panicked, frightened voices. Imogen. Elaine. Romulus opened his eyes.

Father Thomas Michael smiled into his face. "It wasn't meant to be so rough on you. I'm sorry." The priest dissipated into the air.

"What's wrong with him?" Elaine sounded scared.

"He'll be fine. Let's see if we can lift him." Imogen's voice quavered, despite her attempted confidence.

Hands pulled at his arms. Romulus groaned. "I can see ghosts." He blinked his eyes open. Had he said that aloud?

Romulus rose to his feet, brushing away the women's touch. His mindset was new, but he kept his feelings locked away. He wouldn't need them yet, if he ever did. They would be a hindrance, especially as he now knew many of his papers to be flawed, some entirely wrong. Guilt was a luxury for another day.

Imogen wore a wide grin. Elaine smirked, avoiding his gaze. So, he said it aloud. Well, it would have come out sooner or later. Best to get it over with.

He took a deep breath. "That's right. I can see ghosts." He waited for their gasps of amazement. None came. Their smiles widened as they exchanged a glance.

"We know," Imogen said.

Chapter Twenty-One

Samuel followed Angela from the house and tried to recall the question he wanted to ask her. He felt sure it was important, but the query thought had vanished when he looked into her eyes. By the time he reached the gate he felt a vague unease, but could no longer specify what worried him. He let the matter drop.

Mrs. Oldham appeared on her doorstep, her nose in the air. She folded her arms and leaned against the doorframe.

"Good morning, Mrs. Oldham." Samuel relished the unusually cheery tone in his own voice.

"Only just, Samuel. It's nearly lunchtime." Mrs. Oldham narrowed her eyes at Angela. "Day off work, is it?"

"Well, not exactly. I've had the flu. I'll be back at work tomorrow." He opened the gate for Angela.

"You do look tired. Exhausted, I might say." The implication was clear in the old woman's tone. Samuel winced. His bedroom backed onto Mrs. Oldham's house. The walls were thin between these houses, and like most old ladies, Mrs. Oldham was nowhere near as deaf as she pretended to be.

"Ah, you haven't met Angela. She's my—friend. From overseas. We're just off to get her some things in town." Samuel glanced at Angela. She returned Mrs. Oldham's frosty glare with a look of pure ice.

Mrs. Oldham was never going to approve of him sharing his house with a woman who looked thirty years younger than himself. Maybe, given time, she could accept the idea, but never approve. The looks between the two women threatened to develop into something nasty. Samuel searched for a way to break the deadlock, and remembered something that might provide a diversion. He put his hand in his pocket and withdrew a piece of paper.

"Oh, I forgot about this." Samuel leaned over the fence and handed the paper to Mrs. Oldham. "Someone from the university was asking about local ghosts. Doctor Pettifer, a very nice young lady. I said I'd give you her number, in case you'd heard of anything."

"Oh, I can tell a few tales that would make her hair stand on end. Not just about ghosts, either." In her lined face, Mrs. Oldham's eyes glittered.

"Yes, well." Samuel's face warmed. "We'd better get going. I'll see you later." Samuel took Angela's arm and started along the street, ignoring Mrs. Oldham's sniff. When they returned, he planned to move his things into the spare bedroom, away from the wall adjoining Mrs. Oldham's house.

"That woman is a relative of yours?" Angela said, her eyes still cold.

"No, she's a neighbor."

"She acts as though she has some control over you."

Samuel laughed. "No, she's just an old lady who disapproves of our relationship. She'll get used to it. You'll see. She's not so bad once you get to know her."

Angela stopped beside a bright red, polished Mercedes. "Why don't we ride in one of these? I saw them, while you were asleep. They move without horses."

"That's a car. I don't own one anymore. Too expensive, and everywhere I need to go is a short walk or a bus ride away, so a car isn't necessary."

"You are not wealthy?" Angela pouted.

"No, not very. That will change when I've translated *Geometria* though. I'll make a fortune when that hits the bookshelves."

"You plan to make a copy of *Geometria ton Zoon*?" Angela stared at him. "The holy men will not permit it. There is only one book, and they would destroy it if they could."

Samuel's brow creased. "Holy men? Oh, priests. Well, they don't own the book anymore. It's the property of the library now, and I'm in charge of that. Besides, these days—" He was about to say "nobody believes in magic," but for him at least, that was no longer true.

Angela drew in her breath. "So the holy men no longer rule. You can make a copy of *Geometria ton Zoon*?"

"Copies. Hundreds, perhaps thousands." Samuel resumed walking. "You don't know about the invention of printing. I'll translate the book, then a printer can make hundreds of copies in no time at all. Translations of old magical texts are popular at the moment. The New Age people will love it. It'll make me—us—very rich."

"They will all have access." Angela murmured as she walked beside him. "All of them."

Samuel glanced at her smiling face. She must realize how rich he was going to be, how rich they would both be. He had no looks to speak of, little in the way of charm, and failing health. If he wanted to hang on to a woman like Angela, money was the only reliable alternative. The book was his key to wealth. Samuel's eye twitched. He still needed to get the books back into the Old Books Room before their absence was noticed. Someone might request to see one of them at any time. This should have worried him more than it did, but all he had to do was inhale Angela's scent, and his troubles fled. Samuel walked in pensive silence until they reached the main street. He stopped outside the green grocer's.

"I need to get a few vegetables, maybe a little fruit. Everyone tells me I should eat more fruit." He led Angela inside.

She was clearly unimpressed, but then this must be similar to the market stalls she saw before she was trapped in *Geometria*. Samuel bought a few things, including some fruit he intended to eat this time, rather than watch it rot in a bowl as he usually did. For years he had ignored the advice of doctors and friends. Now that Angela was here, Samuel needed to take care of himself. Those chest pains might be more than heartburn, after all.

From the green grocer it was a short walk to the butcher. Here, Angela seemed much more interested in the goods on display. She pointed out cuts and joints she liked, including some that made Samuel grimace. Tripe. Chitterlings. Sweetbreads. He bought a small amount of each, along with some sausages and a few chops. It was going to take time to adjust to Angela's tastes.

His constitution was tested when Angela picked up one of the sweetbreads and popped it into her mouth. It burst as she bit down on it, and Samuel covered his mouth with his hand.

"Angela, that's raw," he said through his fingers.

The butcher moved around the counter. "You can't eat on the premises, especially not raw meat." He stood in front of Angela, hands on hips. "Please leave."

"Come on, Angela." Samuel led her outside, apologizing to the butcher as he left. "She's foreign. They do things differently where she comes from."

"That may be, sir, but here we have laws. The health inspector would shut me down if he saw what I've just seen."

"Sorry. It won't happen again."

Outside, Samuel placed his carrier bags against the shop front and took Angela's arms. "You can't do that here. Please, Angela, you'll draw attention to yourself. Just watch me. Do as I do for now. Okay?"

"Okay, Samuel. I prefer them fresh, but I'll follow your ways for now." Angela grinned at him, and ran her tongue over her teeth, using its pointed tip to pick out the residual flecks of meat. Samuel released her arms and picked up the bags of food.

"Okay. Just the clothes shop, then we can get home." The street was filling with people as lunchtime started. Samuel headed for the ladies' outfitters he had seen, but never entered, just off High Street. The admiring glances Angela drew from male passers-by made Samuel's blood boil with jealousy. He quickened his pace, ignoring the tightness developing in his chest. Once inside the shop, he could relax. Even if the lunchtime crowd made the ladies' outfitters busier than he liked, at least they would all be women. He rounded a corner and walked straight into a man stepping from a cafe.

"Hey, watch where you're going." The man stepped back and brushed at his sleeve where Samuel had bumped into him. "Oh, it's Mister Watson, isn't it? From the library?"

Samuel stared at the man. He recognized him, but couldn't place the face. Mumbling an apology, he walked past.

"Wait up. I didn't mean to be rude."

The voice triggered a memory in Samuel. This was Jeremy Farquhar-Jones. His father, Eustace Farquhar-Jones, was one of the wealthiest men in town and a member of the Board of Governors of the university, and therefore of the library. Jeremy was a shallow man with none of his father's character but with access to plenty of money. If anyone was going to make too much of a chance meeting with Samuel and Angela, it was Jeremy. Samuel turned to face him.

"Mister Farquhar-Jones. Sorry to barge into you, but we're in something of a hurry."

"A lot to do on your lunch break, eh?" Jeremy spoke to Samuel but his eyes were on Angela. "Funny thing is, I was at the library this morning. I heard you were ill." Giving Samuel a sideways look, Jeremy winked. "Looks like you're feeling better."

"I am ill. I mean, I was ill. I've recovered." Samuel stopped talking and gave himself time to breathe. "I had the flu. I'll be back at work tomorrow. Well, as I said, we have a lot to do. Goodbye, Mister Farquhar-Jones." Ignoring Jeremy's huffed "Well," Samuel led Angela to the ladies' outfitters and ducked inside.

The shop was almost empty. Two women browsed in a row of skirts and one more perused the lingerie. Samuel breathed a low sigh and glanced at Angela. She seemed only mildly interested in the displays before her, which was not what he had expected at all. Surely, after her long imprisonment, she should be overwhelmed at the variety of clothes here. He'd expected her to gasp, to cry out, to run wide-eyed into the shop, feeling this skirt, trying on that top, running her hands over a long evening dress. She showed no reaction at all.

One of the shop assistants caught Samuel's eye. She glared at him. Her head moved forward, raptorlike; her body moved beneath it as if it struggled to keep up with the speed of her face. She stopped a few feet from Samuel.

"Can I help you?" The woman's stern voice came from a thin-lipped mouth surrounded by wrinkles that led up to hard, steel-blue eyes. Narrow shoulders and hair in a tight bun completed the severity of her look.

Samuel swallowed. He and Angela were not an obvious match. She looked to be in her twenties, young, fit, and beautiful, while he was nearly fifty, although his recent illness made him look much older. This woman's disapproving look was understandable, under the circumstances. He cleared his throat.

"Ah, right. My cousin," he said, shifting his carrier bags to one hand then putting his free hand on Angela's elbow to bring her forward, "has just arrived from overseas. Unfortunately, all her luggage has been lost, so she'll need a whole new wardrobe." Samuel paused, astounded at the ease of his lies. He'd become something of an expert in deceit over the last few days. Angela smiled at him. He took a deep breath and continued. "Certainly enough to tide her over until her own luggage shows up."

Samuel exhaled a long, silent breath as the assistant turned her gaze on Angela. The thin lips tweaked themselves into a smilelike shape.

"Of course. I understand. If madam would like to come with me?" She stepped aside, allowing Angela to go ahead of her. Samuel moved to follow but the woman blocked his way. "If Sir would like to take a seat?" She indicated a row of three chairs placed near the cash register. Samuel opened his mouth to object, but the look she gave him made it clear she expected him to comply. With a mute nod, he moved to the chairs and sat, relieved at least to be able to set down his shopping for a while.

Angela and the assistant disappeared among the racks of clothes, leaving Samuel to look nervously around at this alien world. He had never been inside one of these shops in his life. He may as well have stepped onto the surface of another planet. The shops where he bought his own clothes were somber affairs, filled with shades of gray and brown and blue, silent and efficient. He'd go in, knowing exactly what he wanted, buy it, and leave.

This place was bizarre. A cacophony of color, an overdose of choice. Why did women need so many varieties of clothing? Worst of all, there was underwear, held aloft on rails like frilly flags. Samuel's cheeks warmed at the sight of the intimate garments, so he looked through the window instead. He found no relief there. The window display consisted of life-sized plastic women, more realistic than was strictly necessary, dressed in more of those erotic frills. Samuel sighed and stared at his shoes. Finally, somewhere he could look without blushing.

Contemplating his left toecap, Samuel considered his feelings for Angela. When she was with him, his world was wonderful. Everything she did or said was perfect. Was this love? He was sure it was far more than lust. When they were separated, as now, he was uneasy. An indefinable, unfocused sort of worry nagged at his brain. Samuel wiggled his foot, watching the shop lights reflected in the shoe-polish. What was bothering him? Was he worried she might leave him? That something might happen to her? To him? He nipped at his lower lip with his teeth. Those were all reasonable worries, but there was something else. Something he couldn't quite form a thought around.

Then there was Farquhar-Jones. An infrequent visitor to the library, too loud, too arrogant to follow the rules. He was an unpleasant character, filled with a malicious jealousy for all those more intelligent than himself, which was most people. If he gave a twisted account of his meeting with Samuel to his father, there might be repercussions. Samuel could not afford to draw the attention of his superiors at work, not while he was in possession of the books. The library was only a short detour on the way home from here. Samuel decided to call in there, after Angela had bought a few clothes, to head off any problems Farquhar-Jones might cause.

A pair of bare legs came into view beside his shoe. Samuel looked up into Angela's smiling face. His eyes met hers, and all his worries evaporated.

He pushed himself off the chair, his gaze fixed on the tight black dress she wore. It accentuated every curve perfectly.

Samuel took a deep breath. "That's perfect. We'll take it." He turned to the shop assistant, who held a pile of clothes draped over her arm. She raised a carefully plucked eyebrow.

"Would you like to see the rest, sir?"

"The rest?" Samuel recalled his earlier request for a whole new wardrobe for Angela, and his jaw tensed. In his mind, his credit card grew teeth. That convenient piece of plastic he used so sparingly over the years was about to take a hit that could paralyze it for months. It was for Angela. He could not make her wear his castoffs. Samuel half-closed his eyes as his hand moved to his wallet. "We'll take them too."

The assistant beamed. "Very good, sir. I'll have these wrapped." She turned to Angela. "Now, we can see about finding Madam some shoes."

Samuel sank back into his seat, glanced at his watch, and closed his eyes. His pulse throbbed in his temple, his chest cramped, and a film of sweat covered his face.

Chapter Twenty-Two

"What do you mean, you already know?" Romulus stood in his lounge, his arms folded, facing the two women on his settee. Part of him still wanted to throw them out, but first he needed information. Besides, they had witnessed his collapse. He needed time to produce a reasonable explanation before they went off telling imaginative stories.

"I've known since college." Imogen smirked, stretching her arms behind her head. "You were always talking to yourself, or rather you were talking to someone. Someone nobody else could see. I suspected for a long time, but I was certain when you told me about Julia's accident. Nobody else knew until she came in the next day. You knew why she hadn't turned up to class. You even knew she was cutting bread when she hurt her hand." Imogen lowered her arms. "Those people told you. The ones nobody could see. Ghosts. Most of the other students thought you were crazy, but I realized what was happening. We were close, remember?"

Romulus curled his lip at the memory of their relationship and Imogen's betrayal. He tilted his head to stare at Elaine.

"What about you? How could you possibly have known?"

"My brother." Elaine avoided his gaze.

"Your brother told you?"

"No. You did." Elaine turned her head to stare into Romulus's eyes. "You met him once."

"I meet people all the time." Romulus shrugged. "Few of them are worth remembering."

"In the corridor outside the lab, at Oxford. You told me you'd met someone and asked what he was doing there. He said he was Archie, my brother. I showed you a photo, and you said it was the same man."

The encounter raised only a vague memory for Romulus. He gestured for Elaine to continue.

"My brother died that day. A climbing accident. I didn't know at the time. I found out a few days later. I took a week off, to be with my parents for the funeral."

"I remember that." Romulus nodded. Elaine had disappeared for a week, on some family business, right in the middle of a series of experiments.

"I thought nothing of it at the time. I was too upset about Archie's death. Later, though, when I had time to think, I wondered if maybe you saw his ghost."

"You've never mentioned this before."

"How could I? What would you have said? You were busy destroying the reputation of every medium you could find." A sly smile developed on Elaine's face. "Now you'll have to admit they weren't fakes, won't you?"

"Certainly not. I'm better placed to detect fraudulent mediums than ever now." Romulus twisted his neck, stretching his muscles. "Just because I can communicate with the dead, it doesn't mean every jumped-up wannabe mystic can do it. If any of them produced a real spirit manifestation, I'd have known. I'd have seen it."

"You didn't know my brother was a ghost." Elaine raised her eyebrows.

"And you didn't know some of your college friends were dead." Imogen's grin flashed.

"There's no time for this." Father Michael appeared between Romulus and the two women. "Stop bickering. You have a gamaliel to find."

"Indeed I have, and with precious little help from you. What's the use of walking through walls if you can't find any useful information?"

Imogen and Elaine stared at each other for a moment. Realization dawned in their eyes.

"Yes, all right, it's the priest again. He wants me to find some demon, a gamaliel . Claims it's killed someone already, and it's attached to a man here in Marchway." Romulus hissed through his teeth. "Look, I'm not going to play parrot, repeating every word just because you two can't hear him. Go away, and I'll summarize later."

Imogen's grin vanished. "Gamaliel?"

"You know, the daughters of Lilith—" Romulus raised his eyebrows.

Imogen ignored his superior sneer. "And Asmodeus. Romulus, you do know what the gamaliel are?"

"Yes, yes, yes. The obscene, the debauched, adversaries of the angels," he replied.

"They have another name, a more familiar one," Imogen said, rising to her feet. She shivered as her shoulder brushed Father Michael's before he stepped out of her way.

"Do tell." Romulus affected a sneer.

"They are better known as 'succubi'."

The silence lasted only a few moments, but Romulus's mind raced through it as though it were eternity. A succubus kills men. Going against it alone was tantamount to suicide. The thing has no power over women, so realistically he needed these two involved. Imogen's knowledge of demonology would be particularly useful. The choice was clear. Face the danger alone, or admit he needed outside help.

"I'll cope," he said. "Make yourselves scarce while I get everything I can from this priest." Romulus turned his sneer on Father Michael. "I don't expect it'll take long."

"You can't do this alone, Rom." Elaine stood beside Imogen. "You don't know about demons, and neither do I." She inclined her head towards Imogen. "Swallow that damned pride of yours and let the demonologist help you."

Romulus raised one eyebrow, following it with the other a second later. "You might both be of some use eventually, but for now the most useful thing you can do is get out of the way. Neither of you can see or hear our visitor, can you?" He waited until both shook their heads. "So you can't help in this situation. Now, if you wouldn't mind..." Romulus indicated the door with a sweep of his arm.

"We'd better go." Imogen gave Romulus a contemptuous look as she took Elaine's arm. "I have to visit the library anyway."

Romulus adopted his own expression of contempt, confident that his was far more developed than Imogen's. "Good idea. I'll meet you there in an hour or so."

"If we're still there." Frustration showed in Elaine's voice as the two women left the room. Romulus waited until he heard the front door close with a bang, then lowered himself into the armchair opposite the settee.

"They'll be there. Neither of them will want to miss out on the action." Romulus nodded towards the settee. "Have a seat."

"I'd rather stand. They're right, you know. You'll need help with this."

"Maybe. First, I think it's about time you told me what you know."

Father Michael lowered his head and sighed. "Well, I've already given you most of it, although you weren't paying attention."

"Yes, I was. I didn't believe you. That's different." Romulus rested his hands on the leather arms of the chair. "Who was that man in my dream, and where was the world you showed me?"

"I don't know the man's name, but the world is in a book."

"Okay, so I can look it up. Which book?"

"No, not like that. It's one of the worlds within the pages of an ancient book. That world is accessible from ours. Through the book."

Romulus snorted. "A bit more challenging than walking through a wardrobe, I suppose. Is there a lion and a witch in this story too?"

"This is not a laughing matter!" Father Michael's figure blurred for a moment as his face contorted in fury. "Just shut up and listen." He paused, rubbing his face with his hands. "Right. There's no lion. There is a snow queen, and she's here. The gamaliel will have taken the form of a woman but I can't get close enough to see. As your friend said, it will drain the life of men. Not just during sex, but the effect is more pronounced when the victim's emotions are heightened."

"Really? So the sex thing isn't necessary? The creature can feed just by being close to its victim." Romulus wondered if Imogen's knowledge extended that far.

"It feeds through an emotional connection. The form it takes, the scent it produces, means it's irresistible to most men. During sex, the connection is strongest so feeding is faster." Father Michael moved closer. "First, it will probably want to kill the one who summoned it. He can call it back if it strays, so getting him out of the way must be a high priority."

"The man who died this morning? The one you called Nathaniel? If the summoner is already dead, what can I do?"

"Nathaniel wasn't the summoner. I don't know why it killed him. He was the librarian here, but he'd retired. I can't find any connection between him and the gamaliel."

Romulus shot to his feet, passed straight through Father Michael, and headed for the door.

"Where are you going?" Father Michael followed Romulus from the room.

"If you can't see a connection, you're an idiot." In the hallway, Romulus grabbed his jacket and put it on. His car keys were in the pocket. "You tell me the thing came out of an old book, then you tell me the librarian's dead. Where do you suppose this book is stored?" Romulus opened the front door. "You stay here. I want to talk to you when I get back."

Drops of rain fell from heavy, dark clouds as Romulus hurried to his car. If the library was the source of this demon, he just allowed Imogen and Elaine to walk straight into it. There was no time to waste. They might discover something important, while all he had so far was a dead priest.

Chapter Twenty-Three

Five yards from the library, Samuel stopped walking and lowered his bags to the ground. His chest felt as though it was encased in a tight steel strap. His vision was blurred, his breathing shallow.

"Samuel? Why have you stopped?"

Was that concern in Angela's voice, or merely interest? Samuel couldn't tell. Her voice sounded distant, echoing in his head. A fine rain drifted from the sky. Part of Samuel wanted to hurry indoors, but another part enjoyed the cooling drops on his head.

"Are you ill, Samuel?"

"I'll—" Samuel took a few deep breaths before he spoke. "I'll be fine. It's probably the flu. It's left me feeling a bit weak."

"Weak? Your strength is fading? Is the burden you carry becoming too great?" She made no move to take the bags.

Samuel thought he detected a flicker of amusement in her eyes, but spots flickered and flashed in his vision. He reached down and grasped the handles of the bags. The thought of appearing at his work with Angela carrying the shopping bags galled him, so he took a deep breath and braced himself against the weight.

"I told you, I'll be fine. The library is just here." Samuel set off, blinking away the spots, ignoring the pains in his chest. He set the bags down at the top of the library steps and took several deep breaths while he wiped rain and sweat from his forehead.

Samuel held open the library doors so Angela could enter. The bags cut into his fingers as he lifted them. A draft blew Angela's perfume into his face. The scent made Samuel forget the ache in his arms and the mounting pain in his chest, but the euphoric feeling was short-lived. Inside the library, Donna's perfume overwhelmed Angela's subtle scent.

His breathing came in short gasps, and sweat poured from his forehead by the time he reached the front desk. Donna looked up from her computer, concern flooding her face as she stood.

"Sam—Mister Watson. What are you doing here? You look terrible. Carrying all those bags, too." She shot a menacing glance at Angela to emphasize her last statement. "You should be at home, resting."

Samuel tried to protest when Donna took the bags from him, but the words wouldn't come. Instead, he put out his hand to grab the desk as crushing pains twisted his chest and shot along his arms. Samuel took a couple of deep, halting breaths before he managed to speak. "I'm all right, Donna. There's no need to fuss. I just need to sit down for a while."

"Mister Watson?" John appeared beside Angela. Samuel could hear their voices but the words were blurred, as though his ears were full of wax. John spoke again, something about the staff room, and Samuel was led away from the desk. He blinked, looking around for Angela. She followed, her head tilted to one side. Samuel shook his head to disperse the sweat that stung his eyes. He could have sworn Angela was smiling.

The staff room was too hot. Samuel lifted his hand to wipe his face, then dropped it to his side. It was too much effort. John held a glass of water to his lips, allowing him to take small sips. Angela sat beside him, silent and watching.

"Just take it easy, Mister Watson. You should really have stayed at home until you recovered." John placed the glass on the table.

Samuel's breathing allowed him only a few words at a time. "No food in the house. Angela. No clothes—no luggage. Had to get some."

"Why didn't you phone here? Donna or myself could have done your shopping."

"Felt fine this morning. Okay until a few minutes ago. Shopping. So heavy." Samuel gazed at the water. It was within reach, if he could only make his arms move. It hurt to speak. He needed rest, time to recover.

"You must be Angela. Hi, I'm John." Reaching across Samuel, John shook Angela's hand. Her smile broadened as her fingers curled around his.

Don't touch her. Jealousy surged within Samuel. John was younger and better looking. He wanted to push John's hand away but couldn't muster the strength. Donna appeared at the door.

"Mister Watson? There's a Doctor LeFevre to see you. She says she has an appointment to look at the old books." Donna's voice dropped to a whisper. "That Doctor Pettifer is with her."

"Do you want me to deal with this?" John sounded so reasonable, so calm. He would deal with things. He would deal with Angela, if Samuel allowed it.

"No. I'd better see to it." Samuel struggled to his feet, separating the linked hands of Angela and John as he did so. "I'll see if the appointment can be rescheduled."

"That might be difficult," Donna said. "Doctor LeFevre is from Edinburgh."

Samuel groaned. "We'll see what can be arranged. John, will you help me?" Leaving him alone with Angela was out of the question and besides, Samuel doubted he could walk unaided. With John's support, Samuel made his way to the main room, where Elaine Pettifer waited with a red-haired woman. They were chatting, but their smiles faded to looks of concern when they noticed him. The redhead stepped forward, her hand extended.

"Mister Watson? I'm Imogen LeFevre. I have an appointment to view one of your ancient manuscripts."

Samuel took her hand. His fingers felt swollen and flabby against her firm grip.

"Doctor LeFevre. Welcome to Marchway Library. As you can see, I'm not feeling too well. I wonder, would it be possible to reschedule your appointment?"

"Well, not really. I'm due to leave tomorrow. Could someone else help me?"

"I'm afraid the room is accessible only to the librarian." Samuel shook his head. The movement made him nauseated.

"That's unfortunate." Imogen frowned. "I suppose I could extend my stay for a few days. There are other matters of interest here for me."

"I'm sure I'll be better tomorrow. A good night's rest is all I need." Samuel coughed, then clutched his chest as pain burned his ribs. He paused while the agony subsided. "Tomorrow afternoon. Donna will arrange a time."

"I'm sure that will be fine." Imogen's smile looked patronising. Samuel wondered what she saw. Probably a short fat man, out of breath and on the verge of collapse. She wasn't far wrong, he thought.

"You must have made the appointment with my predecessor, Mister Attlee.

I wasn't expecting you. Could you tell me which book you wanted to see?" *Not Geometria ton Zoon. She can't want to see that book. Or—*

"My appointment is with *Clavicula Salomonis*, the Key of Solomon." Imogen's smile was brief.

Within Samuel's chest fire raged, though his skin turned so cold he was sure his sweat would freeze. He closed his eyes, fighting for breath. The world spun. Samuel leaned against John, grateful for that one point of focus. Without it, he was certain to fall into the maelstrom that raged around his head. Voices, worried voices, urgent voices came to his ears, but he could make no sense of their words. He opened his eyes in time to see Jeremy Farquhar-Jones, with three of his attendant cronies, enter the library. They laughed, too loud, at some comment of Jeremy's. Angela came into view, amusement clear in her eyes. Was she laughing at Jeremy's joke? The image faded. Samuel's legs crumpled, and he slipped to the floor.

The pain stopped.

* * * *

Samuel opened his eyes. He stood alone. Everyone else crowded around something on the floor. They huddled, blocking Samuel's view. Donna, beside the desk, shouted into the telephone. Only Angela looked his way. She detached herself from the group and strolled towards him.

"I feel fine now. Let's slip away while everyone's busy." Samuel reached for Angela, but she avoided his touch.

"It's over, Samuel."

"What?" Samuel recoiled. "What's over? You can't mean—" It must be John. His charm, his looks. She was leaving him for a younger man. "No, Angela. You can't leave."

"I'm not leaving, Samuel. You are." Angela moved to one side, allowing him a clear view of the group at the desk. There was a man, lying on the floor, his shirt open. A short man, overweight and unfit. John pressed his hands onto the centre of the man's chest while Doctor LeFevre covered the man's mouth with her own. As she raised her head, Samuel cringed. The man's lips were blue. He looked again at the face, and his jaw dropped.

"He looks like—"

"Don't you understand, Samuel? That's you, there on the floor." Angela leaned against a row of books and stretched, bringing every curve into sharp relief. "It's over for you, but it's also just beginning."

"I can't be dead. I'm standing here, talking to you." Samuel forced a laugh. He reached for a chair. His hand passed through the wooden back. Samuel stared at his fingers. "How?"

"You're a shade now, Samuel, but you'll get stronger. There is a way. You'll find it." Angela grinned at him. "You have work to do, Samuel."

John moved away from the body on the floor and went to comfort Donna, who was crying. Doctor LeFevre sat up. She said something, but the words were distorted, as was Doctor Pettifer's reply when she took John's place. Jeremy Farquhar-Jones and his friends left the building in silence. For a moment, before the two women continued their attempts to revive the prone man, Samuel had a clear view of the face.

"It is me. My heart." He put his hand on his chest, expecting to feel beating, but there was nothing. "I can't be dead. Not now. Angela, you know magic. Bring me back."

"No."

"No? You can, can't you?"

"I could, but why would I? You have nothing more to give me."

"I brought you here. I saved you. I helped you escape from *Geometria*. What about my translation? It would make us both rich."

"Someone will translate it for me." Angela inspected her nails. "The money is irrelevant."

"You can't leave me like this. Angela, help me. I don't know what to do. Should I find a light, or a pearly staircase, or something?"

Angela laughed. "Not for you. There's no rest for the wicked, Samuel, and you have been a very naughty boy."

"You mean hell? Why?"

"Not even hell. I told you. There's work to be done. You have yours, and I have mine." Angela walked towards the main doors, picking up the shopping bags as she passed the desk. Nobody tried to stop her. Samuel followed.

"Wait, Angela. I don't know what to do."

"Don't follow me." Angela snarled the words. "Go home. You'll work out what to do, how to keep your soul together. If you don't, you'll fade. It's happened many times. Work it out, Samuel, or you'll lose the last shreds of your sanity and end up as a wanderer." She smiled, but there was no innocent mischief in that look. This time it was an expression of pure cruelty. "You can hear them if you try. Mindless, they race without rest around the globe. Their howls are in the wind." She opened the door and stepped outside, into the rain. She looked into Samuel's eyes. "I've put a few there myself."

The door closed.

Samuel stared at it. *What now*?

Chapter Twenty-Four

Romulus considered the relative costs of buying another car or repairing this one as he struggled to see through the rain-lashed windshield. He pulled into the parking lot beside the library, sliding a little on the wet road. The car needed new tires, new wipers, new brakes, and doors that didn't leak. Another car might be the cheaper option.

A figure, blurred by the streaked windshield, strolled across the parking lot in front of him. Romulus hit the brakes and twisted the steering wheel. He missed the figure by a few inches and cranked open his window to get a good look at the idiot.

"Watch where you're going," he shouted into the roar of rain on tarmac. The figure turned. It was a woman in a short, tight black dress, no raincoat, laden with shopping bags. She smiled at him, then walked away.

"Stupid tart." Romulus's muttered words were lost in the screech of his window closing. He took a breath, jumped from the car, slammed the door, and ran for the library.

Speed was futile. In the few yards between his car and the library entrance, the rain soaked Romulus completely. He wiped water from his eyes and barged through the main door. A chill passed through him. He stopped.

There was a man lying on the floor with Imogen's face pressed to his. Elaine appeared to be leaning on his chest. Romulus hissed through his teeth. An old jealousy surfaced, but he pushed it back and looked away.

A woman wept at the issues desk. Beside her, a man tried to console her, his face drawn. To his right, a shadow flitted among the rows of shelves. Romulus raised an eyebrow. He had visited many libraries, many times, but never been faced with a scenario like this.

Elaine lifted her head and nudged Imogen. Romulus crossed the room to stand over them. From here it was clear the man was unconscious, maybe dead.

"What's going on?" Romulus indicated the body on the floor.

"It's Mister Watson, the librarian. He's had a heart attack." Elaine's voice cracked as she spoke.

"Dead?"

Elaine and Imogen nodded together.

"We think so. We're trying to keep his heart and lungs working until the ambulance gets here," Elaine said.

"Oh." *Another dead librarian*. Romulus pursed his lips. The book must be here. If only he had thought to ask Father Michael its title. He tapped Imogen's shoulder. "So, how do we get in to see these old books?"

Imogen's slap took Romulus by surprise. She twisted as she rose, her hand shot past his head, connecting with his cheek on the way back. In the same movement, Imogen returned to the man's face and forced another breath into him.

"What was that for?" He rubbed his cheek, checking for loose teeth with his tongue.

"You heartless swine. The man's probably dead, and all you care about are books?"

"A book. A particular book. It's the reason he's dead and the reason the previous librarian is dead. That's what the priest told me."

The woman at the desk looked up. "Who's dead? Do you mean Mister Attlee?"

Romulus faced the woman. "Depends. Was his first name Nathaniel?"

"Yes."

"That's him then. Died this morning."

The woman collapsed in a dead faint. The man caught her and shot a fierce glare at Romulus before he lowered her to the floor.

"Good God, Romulus. You just don't care, do you?" Elaine stared at him, wide-eyed. "How did you know?"

"Oh, the police were at my house. They confirmed the little priest's story, in general terms."

"Why would the police tell you about this man Attlee's death?" Imogen tilted her head to one side, a quizzical expression on her face.

"Long story." Romulus waved his hand. "No time for that now."

The door burst open. Two green-suited paramedics dashed into the room. They moved Imogen and Elaine aside, asking questions that held no interest for Romulus.

The dead face was familiar. Romulus furrowed his brow. The paramedics searched for pulse and breathing. Romulus blew a slow breath.

It was the man from his dream. The man Father Michael wanted him to find. Well, he had found him. Romulus rubbed his chin. If this was the man who summoned the gamaliel, it was loose now. Nobody controlled its movements.

A shadow flickered across his sight again. Romulus looked around. Imogen and Elaine watched the paramedics, as did the man at the desk. The body jerked as high voltage blasted through paddles on his chest. The shadow moved among the bookshelves. Romulus followed it.

"Where are you?" He squinted, trying to focus. There was something, an outline of a man, in the air. Only the blurring of the books behind it allowed Romulus to see the extent of the manifestation. Its arms waved, but it made no sound. Romulus concentrated, focusing on the vague shape. It was trying to communicate but failing.

"Stop." Romulus addressed the figure. "I can't hear you. Raise one arm for yes, both arms for no. Do you understand?"

The figure raised one arm.

"Good. Now, are you Attlee?"

Both arms were raised.

"Watson?"

One arm was raised.

"Ah, now we're getting somewhere. Do you know where the gamaliel is?"

The figure hesitated, finally raising both arms.

"Do you know what a gamaliel is?"

Both arms lifted.

"Okay, let's try it another way. Did you bring some kind of creature out of a book?"

The figure flapped one arm in the air. Romulus hissed through his teeth. How was he going to get the title of the book from yes-no answers? Perhaps this faint ghost could guide him to it.

"Is the book here?"

Both arms went up.

"Where is it?" Romulus spoke the thought aloud, not expecting a reaction. The figure gesticulated, arms flailing. It took Romulus a moment to realize it was pointing at itself.

"You have it?"

One arm was raised.

"At your house?"

One arm went up. Romulus rubbed at the back of his neck. He should be able to find the dead man's address from a telephone directory, as long as there weren't too many Watsons in Marchway. He jumped as a hand touched his shoulder.

"What is it? Can't you see I'm busy?" Romulus swung around, coming face to face with Elaine.

"Romulus, the police are here. They want to talk to everyone." Elaine spoke in a monotone, her face creased with worry. "They are treating Mister Watson's death as suspicious."

"Really? I thought you said it was a heart attack."

"That's what we all thought, but they want to question us anyway." She led the way back to the main desk. Romulus glanced behind him, but the figure had faded. No matter. He had enough information for the moment.

A white sheet covered Samuel Watson's body. The paramedics spoke with two uniformed officers at the desk. Beside them stood the two plain-clothes policemen who had visited Romulus earlier. They watched Romulus's approach with narrowed eyes.

"Professor Crowe. We meet again." Detective Inspector Crawley nodded a greeting. Detective Sergeant Poole folded his arms, a smug smile on his face.

"Good afternoon, officers. I don't think I can add anything to your investigation. Mister Watson was dead when I arrived."

"So I understand, sir. Perhaps we could take a statement from you anyway?" Crawley indicated one of the reading rooms, its door open. "Mister Legg is acting librarian for now. He's given us permission to use this room for interviews. We'll be as quick as we can."

With a heavy sigh, Romulus accompanied the two policemen into the room. Detective Sergeant Poole closed the door behind them. They sat, the two officers facing Romulus across the table.

"Marchway is a small town, Professor Crowe. Mysterious deaths are rare here. Even more unusual, though, are people with unexplained knowledge of those deaths."

Romulus lowered his eyebrows and pursed his lips.

Crawley consulted his notebook. "You told John Legg and Donna Parfitt about Nathaniel Attlee's death." He looked up. "Can you explain how you knew about that?"

"You told me." Romulus shrugged. "Just a few hours ago."

"We told you someone had died. We didn't give the name." Poole leaned on the desk.

"Oh, right. The priest mentioned—" Romulus caught his breath, seeing the hole he was digging.

"The priest? You mean Father Thomas Michael, or at least the man who looks like him?" Crawley leaned forward. "When did you speak to him?"

"This morning." Romulus turned his eyes to the desk. The truth might get him locked away as either an accessory or a lunatic. It would certainly cost him his job. "After you left. He babbled something about a librarian named Nathaniel. I put two and two together when I arrived here and found Mister Watson on the floor."

Crawley tapped his fingers on the table. "That's a pretty fast piece of detective work."

"Logical deduction is what I do for a living."

"True. However, I have a feeling you know more about this than you're telling us." Crawley interlocked his fingers and tapped his thumbs together. "Do you?"

Romulus looked into the faces of the two policemen. Their expressions showed suspicion, but he didn't think they believed he was involved in the deaths. Not yet, anyway. "I've told you all I can."

"I wonder." Crawley held his gaze. "Two bodies in one day, professor. Both of them librarians. Neither of them should have any connection to you and yet both seem to, somehow. How does your logical deduction explain that?"

"It doesn't, I'm afraid." Romulus sucked at his teeth.

"There is one link, professor. The man masquerading as a dead priest. You're the only one who's spoken to him."

"I don't think he's involved." Romulus shifted in his seat. "He's a lunatic but not actually dangerous."

"Really?" Crawley tilted his head. "What makes you say that?"

"I'm a psychologist. Also, he's been in my house and caused me no harm." No physical harm, although the extent of Father Michael's effect on Romulus's psyche had yet to be determined.

Crawley ticked off points on his fingers. "One. He broke into your house and left again, leaving no trace. Two. Whoever killed Nathaniel Attlee did the same, a few hours later. Three. He knew the dead man's name and occupation. You may have formed the opinion he's not involved in this, but I'm afraid we're of the opinion he is. Deeply involved." Crawley's eyes narrowed. "We're not sure about you."

"You're not serious. You can't think this has anything to do with me. I'm a professor, a respected academic."

"Academics go bad, just like everyone else. They're harder to catch, that's all." Poole smiled. "More of a challenge."

"Oh, come on." Romulus fought to control his temper. This was not the time to show how angry he could get. "I wasn't even here when Watson died. Besides, I thought it was a heart attack. Natural causes."

"We'll have to wait for the autopsy on that one." Crawley watched Romulus intently. "We have to regard his death as suspicious because it's happened so close to his colleague's murder. Poisoning hasn't been ruled out."

"Academics are especially good at poisonings." Poole's face parodied innocence.

"Chemists. Biochemists. Biologists. Not psychologists." Romulus maintained eye contact with Poole. These men knew the basics. A guilty man would look away. "We deal with behavior, with the actions of the mind. Not with chemicals. Believe me, I'd have no idea how to go about poisoning someone. Besides, I've never met either of these men. How would I poison them? More importantly, why would I? I have no motive."

"None that we can see." Poole's expression was flat.

Romulus hissed through his teeth. His fists clenched as blistering rage bubbled just below the surface of his mind. He pushed it down and forced his fingers to relax.

"We're not accusing you. professor. Just trying to work out what's happened." Crawley smiled below calculating eyes. He leaned back in his seat. "I think that's all for now. We'll speak to you again. Please keep us informed if you plan to leave Marchway for any reason."

Romulus stood, every muscle trembling, and walked to the door. As he opened it, he looked down at Crawley and Poole, who appeared to be ignoring him.

"What about Attlee? How did he die?"

Crawley grinned up at Romulus. "You tell us, professor. Surely you can logically deduce it?"

His fury approaching boiling point, Romulus stormed from the room.

Chapter Twenty-Five

Samuel hugged himself. There was one person, at least, he could communicate with. The psychic, Romulus, knew about *Geometria*, although he gave no indication he knew its title. It was a start.

As with Angela, Samuel understood Romulus's words. Everyone else's voice sounded like an echo in a long tunnel, indistinct and distorted by distance.

Romulus suggested Attlee was dead. Samuel shivered. Angela must have killed him, but Samuel was responsible. If he had listened to Attlee, Angela would still be in *Geometria*. The only recompense he could make was to send Angela back, and for that he needed help.

Samuel needed to get home. In his basement, he could show Romulus how the paneling opened. With luck, Romulus could use the book to free him from whatever evil fate Angela planned and work out how to trap her again.

Recalling the little he knew about ghostly manifestations, Samuel wondered whether he was constrained to the library, his place of death. There was only one way to find out. Samuel made his way to the door while Romulus walked into a reading room with two other men.

The glass door reflected the scene behind Samuel, but he didn't see himself. If he could have cried, he would have. With no reflection, he would never know if he looked the same in death as he had in life.

His books came to mind, his beloved books. He would never open them again. He was never going to translate *Geometria*, nor any other book. Never again would he enjoy a roast dinner or a glass of beer. Attlee had warned him, but he had dismissed the old man's words as fantasy. Melchior tried to tell him, but Samuel refused to listen.

Rain lashed against the doors. Samuel sniffed, but no rain-fresh scent entered his nostrils. Even Donna's perfume was gone. Samuel had sight. He had faulty hearing. Only certain voices were clear. The rain made no sound on the doors. Samuel had no sense of smell, taste, or touch. All lost forever, along with the job he had worked so hard to gain and the key to the Old Books Room he had waited so many years to own.

Samuel screamed his despair, raised his fists, and flung himself into the door. It was like falling through a net of needles.

A gasp replaced his scream as Samuel emerged into the rain. He had felt that, for sure. Passing through solid objects hurt him, something he'd need to remember. A niggling discomfort still raced through him, as though he were being whipped from within. The rain. Every drop left its trail in him. Samuel considered going back into the library until the rain eased off, but that meant passing through the glass door again. He had always found rain unpleasant, so this was no different. There was one benefit to being a ghost. He wasn't getting wet.

On the way home, Samuel pondered his new condition. When he put his hand through the chair, he had felt nothing. Or maybe he had. Maybe shock overrode the pain. Samuel reached for a bush overhanging a fence. The sensation as his hand passed into the leaves and branches was little more than a tickle. The iron railing below the bush stung his fingers. Samuel rubbed his chin, stopped, and stared at his hand. He rubbed his palms together. Apparently he could not pass through himself. He wondered whether he could see, hear, and touch other ghosts.

Head down, Samuel continued his walk, trying to ignore the possibilities his mind conjured. What if there were no other ghosts? What if everyone else who died was in either heaven or hell? What if he was alone, left to watch the world but never participate?

Samuel halted at his front gate. There had to be others. He reached for its handle but stopped himself before he made contact.

The gate was made of iron. This was going to hurt.

From the gate, the railings ran in both directions, surrounding his small front garden completely. Even if he went through the low hedge around Mrs. Oldham's lawn, he still had to cross the fence at some point.

The problem seemed to be one of density. To pass through glass or iron caused a lot of pain, water and wood merely discomfort. Brick, presumably, would produce more than discomfort but less than agony. Samuel sighed. Mrs. Oldham was unlikely to see him. He walked through the hedge and into the wall of Mrs. Oldham's house.

Brick proved less painful than he expected although the small pebbles on the outer facing of the wall felt like buckshot. Plaster and wallpaper posed no problem at all. Belatedly, he realized that he could have used the wooden front door.

Mrs. Oldham looked up from her newspaper as Samuel entered. He stood still. She stared directly at him, squinting. He stared back. It had not occurred to him to wonder if Mrs. Oldham were psychic. She shook her head and returned to her newspaper.

Samuel closed his eyes, opened them, and closed them again. It made no difference. His eyelids moved, but his sight was unaffected. One more thing he had to learn to cope with.

Moving with haste, in case Mrs. Oldham noticed something, Samuel passed through the dividing wall into his own house.

Books littered the floor. His shelves lay in a broken heap. Chairs were upended. The sofa lay on its back. Samuel looked around his living room, never the tidiest of rooms but now a total shambles. A burglary on the day of his death. Could things get any worse?

Shoulders slumped, he wandered through the house. The front door was closed although the doorjamb bulged, splintered at the lock. Even a breeze could blow it open. In the dining room, Melchior's notes lay in shreds, a litter of confetti on the table and floor. The kitchen, however, held the biggest shock.

On the kitchen table lay a mound of torn meat, gnawed bones and pools of blood. A ripped plastic carrier bag hung over one chair. In the corner, beside the washing machine, fruit and vegetables spilled onto the floor from a bag that looked like it had been thrown there. Samuel surveyed the mess, thankful this time for the absence of his sense of smell.

Angela had been here. This was the remains of his day's shopping. Alert now, Samuel scanned the room. He moved through the house again, this time with caution, checking every room until only the basement remained. He should have known she would come here. It was the only place she could call home. Why trash his house though? Some petty revenge, or was she looking for something?

She must want *Geometria ton Zoon*. Samuel put his head through the basement door. Below was chaos, just like every other room of the house. She had been thorough. Samuel passed into the basement, satisfied that Angela was no longer here. A quick inspection showed the false wall to be intact, undisturbed. Samuel risked a look inside. The books were still there. He withdrew, afraid Angela might appear and understand what he was doing. With *Geometria* she could release more of her kind. It was vital to keep that book hidden from her.

The day faded as Samuel returned to the dining room. Darkness coated the windows, but Samuel couldn't draw the curtains or switch on lights. He waited for the completion of sunset, bracing himself to spend the night here, alone, awake, without sight. The last glow faded from the sky. Samuel staggered.

Everything in the room came into sharp focus, a perfection of vision Samuel had never experienced, even in life. Until now, his ghostly sight had given the world an unreal, dreamlike quality. Now he could even see the fibers in the torn edges of Melchior's papers on the table and floor. Samuel moved to the table.

Perhaps it was for the best, this destruction of Melchior's work. The old man translated just enough to get himself trapped in the book. With Samuel's notes, someone else might have joined him. These papers must have enraged Angela, hinting at *Geometria*'s words yet incomplete, useless to her. Samuel reached for one of the pieces and picked it up. He turned it in his fingers, admiring the shredded edges with his new sight. Then he realized what he was doing and gasped aloud.

The paper dropped from his fingers and fluttered to the table.

Chapter Twenty-Six

Romulus slammed his car door, walked to his front gate, and kicked it open. He thrust his key into the door lock, twisted, and pushed the door hard enough to send it crashing against the hallway wall.

"Where are you?" Romulus roared the words into the house as he yanked his key from the door and slammed it closed. "Come out, you worthless gob of ecto-plasm. Show yourself."

Romulus removed his jacket and flung it at the coat rack as he passed. He found Father Michael in the lounge.

"There you are. Do you realize the trouble you've caused?" Romulus raised his fist, stared at it then dropped it to his side. He was denied even the satisfaction of thumping the priest. "Thanks to you, the police now think I'm involved in two deaths."

"Two?" Father Michael moved closer.

"Yes, two. Samuel Watson, librarian, and Nathaniel Attlee, ex-librarian. I knew the name because you told me. I knew he was a librarian, because you told me. The police haven't released that information."

"Watson." Father Michael frowned. "Yes, Watson. That's the man."

"Pity you didn't warn me earlier. He's the one who called the demon, the one you showed me in the dream. Why didn't you tell me his name then?"

"I didn't recognize him. Now that you mention it, I do remember him. Quiet man, kept to himself, always came to church with Janet Oldham."

Romulus covered his ears. "Don't tell me. If I let slip details of the man's life, I'll be arrested for sure."

"You have to know. If you're going to defeat the gamaliel you'll need all the information you can get. It's going to be even harder now, since its summoner is dead."

"Forget it. Find yourself another demon killer." Romulus slumped into a chair.

"What?"

"I said forget it. I don't want to hear about murders and monsters. I don't want to speak to ghosts. I'm going back to my old life, my real-world life. Out of this nightmare."

"You can't. You're the only one who can do this." Father Michael knelt in front of Romulus.

"You're a priest." Romulus accentuated his words with jabs of his finger into the priest's shoulder. "You talked to angels when you were alive. It must be easier to talk to them now. Angels are the natural enemies of the gamaliel. Call an angel."

"I can't." Father Michael shifted to avoid the finger penetrating his shoulder.

"Too bad."

"Angels can't get involved in this. A human needs to deal with the gamaliel. Specifically you."

"Oh, what? Don't give me the 'chosen one' crap. I'm not falling for it."

"Believe me, if I had a choice, I wouldn't choose you. You're just the only one here with the ability to deal with the creature." A smile twitched at the priest's mouth. He stood and turned his back on Romulus. "Of course, if you're not up to the job..."

"I didn't say I couldn't do it. I said I won't." Romulus glowered at the priest's back.

"Pity. I'll have to call on someone else then."

"Do that."

"Someone from a long way away. They'll have to travel. It'll take time."

"Book them a flight."

"The gamaliel will kill more people. There'll be quite a body count before it's stopped."

"You'd better get moving then. Don't let me hold you back."

"This new psychic will be quite a hero, I think. Solving all those murders, disposing of a demon. There'll be a lot of publicity." Father Michael looked over his shoulder at Romulus, who shrugged. The priest grinned. "Marchway will be famous for its demon, and for its parapsychology professor who couldn't deal with it."

Romulus surged to his feet. "Now hold on. There's no reason for me to be involved at all."

"You're the head of parapsychology, here in Marchway. You can't just ignore a demon on your doorstep."

"This is blackmail." Romulus seethed. If the priest brought in outside help, the whole story was certain to make headlines. Whether Romulus was involved or not, nationwide publicity would be bad for him. The case needed a level head, time to consider the evidence, detailed analysis of the data, and a proper write-up published in a respected journal. There was only one way to keep it quiet until that could be achieved. Yes, it was blackmail. Unless Romulus took care of the matter himself, his reputation was doomed. He narrowed his eyes and growled in his throat.

"Right. Let's talk. Why can't you just call in an angel?"

"For the same reason I can't get directly involved myself." Father Michael's smug grin nearly tipped Romulus back into refusal, but the thought of his career going down in flames held him back.

"Why is that?" Romulus walked to the window as he spoke.

"It's a question of allegiance. I've devoted my life—and afterwards—to the service of the Light. Angels are obviously creatures of the Light. The gamaliel is a creature of darkness."

"So? Aren't you therefore obliged to fight it?"

"In theory, yes. However, if an angel gets involved here, this gamaliel will call others. The angel will then have no choice but to call more of its own. The gamaliel will call more demons. The angel will call more of its kind. Do you see where this is leading?"

"War." Romulus blew a long breath.

"Worse than any human war. An escalation that will make nuclear war seem like a shouting match. The destruction will be enormous. It could mean the end of humanity." Father Michael sighed. "It all hinges on a book."

"Oh?"

"The one the gamaliel escaped from. If the creature has access to this book, it can release more. So, no angel can interfere unless the book is secure."

"You know its title?"

A long pause. "No."

"Great. You know where it is?"

Another pause. "No."

"I do." Romulus faced the priest, reveling in the ghost's shocked expression. "It's at Samuel Watson's house."

"What? How—?"

"I spoke to him at the library."

"But you said he was—"

"Dead. Inconvenient, but not so bad once you get used to it." Romulus could have howled his glee at the priest's discomfiture. "You seem surprised. Didn't you know I could speak to ghosts?"

"Okay, okay." Father Michael shook his head. "So, why aren't you at Samuel Watson's house now?"

Romulus laughed. "Oh, sure. I'm already a suspect in his death. Why don't I just go and burgle his house too? I may as well go all the way and conduct a magical ceremony in his basement while I'm there. Any other crimes you'd like me convicted of, or would that be enough for you?"

"Ah. I see."

"You ghosts can go around doing as you please, but those of us who still live in this world have a police force to contend with. I can't walk through walls. I can't make myself invisible. I can't wander into a dead man's house without a very good reason." Romulus returned to his place at the window. The sun had dipped below the house opposite. The late British autumn meant early darkness, cold, and gray skies for the coming months. Romulus hated this time of year, that twilight between summer and winter when the world was filled with dying things.

Father Michael narrowed his eyes. "You don't know the address, do you?"

"Not yet. A simple browse through the phone book will soon solve that."

"No need. He lives next door to Janet Oldham."

Romulus raised his eyebrows. "Well, that's a great help. Now I have two names, but still no address."

"I've visited Janet many times. I even called in there after I died. I think she saw me, but I couldn't communicate with her."

"Very neighborly of you. The address?"

"Eighty-eight Ballantrae Avenue."

"We're getting close. Watson's address?"

"Eighty-six. Are you going there now?"

"No. I need a reason to show up there. I also need more information. For example, if neither you nor the angels can take on this monster, what qualifies me for the job?"

"You're neutral."

"Explain." Romulus folded his arms.

"You rejected the Church from childhood, but you've never actually done anything evil. You belong to neither side. So the gamaliel can't legitimately start an escalation of forces against you."

Romulus nodded. "Surely though, I effectively choose a side by going against the thing?"

"No, you're fighting as a human. There are rules even the evil ones have to abide by. Unless higher powers are invoked, the gamaliel has to deal with you on its own."

"So, it's me against a magic-wielding, life-sucking monster who's already killed twice, and I can't rely on help from the good guys. Is that a fair assessment of the situation?"

"Yes. Unless the book is secured, no angels can come to your aid."

"Those are not good odds. How do I go about securing the book?"

"First you have to get it." Father Michael stood beside Romulus. Together they watched the gathering darkness. "It's more dangerous at night."

"So I'll leave it until tomorrow. I still have to think up an excuse to go to the house anyway." Romulus sniffed. "Besides, getting the book is second on my list. First I need to know what to do with it once I have it." He moved from the window, switched on the gas fire, and took a seat near it. His clothes were still damp from the rain and he was getting cold. Romulus considered a hot shower, but could he guarantee the priest would leave him in peace for long enough?

Father Michael remained at the window.

"What about Watson?" Romulus called from his seat. "He's been drained by the gamaliel. Is he under its power in some way? What can he do?"

"If he's still around, the demon's done something to him. I don't know what. I don't know if he has free will or if he's just a drone."

"That's not helpful. I guess he has some free will or he wouldn't have communicated with me at the library." Romulus pulled the damp material of his trousers away from his legs. "I need a shower. Why don't you make yourself useful and visit Samuel Watson's house? You can do it without being seen."

"I can't go there."

"Wonderful." Romulus sneered at the priest. "Where are you going?"

Father Michael had become transparent, fading still more as Romulus stared.

"Ghosts need to rest too. All this manifestation is tiring, you know. Usually I can last longer than this. It must be the excitement." The priest's voice became faint. "I'll return when I can. Concentrate on getting the book." Father Michael became a blur, a shimmer in the air, then he was gone.

Romulus stood. "Right. I can get a shower while he's out of the way." He stretched, enjoying the warmth of the fire, and wondered what the police had asked of Imogen and Elaine. Had those two inadvertently said something to condemn him? Romulus headed for the bathroom, determined not to worry about it. As long as news of this mess stayed away from the chancellor's ears, he could work it out.

Chapter Twenty-Seven

Shreds of paper filled the air, as though an indoor snowstorm raged in the dining room. Samuel laughed, arms spread, spinning in its midst. He could touch. There was no sensation. He could not feel the texture of the things he moved, but he could touch them. He could move things. He stopped spinning. Maybe he could open a book.

Excited, he ran through the dining room wall into the living room. Stooping, he picked up a book, relishing the experience before he opened it. A few pages later, he glanced at the wall behind him.

Did I just run straight through that?

Samuel dropped the book and faced the wall. He reached out his fist and tapped at it. The sound echoed in the silent room. Samuel extended his fingers and reached for the wall again. His hand passed through. Samuel withdrew his hand and scratched his head.

"So, if I want to go through, I can. If I want to tap it, I can." He held his hands out for inspection. "I can do anything. This is better than being alive. I can walk straight into the Old Books Room and read them all, at night, in peace." His thoughts turned to the wall dividing his house from Mrs. Oldham's. If he could make rapping sounds, he could communicate. Mrs Oldham might not understand, but she had Doctor Pettifer's phone number. The scientist would know what to do. Samuel headed for the wall.

Mrs. Oldham leaned forward in her chair, aimed her remote control at the TV, and flipped channels. She sighed, turned the TV off, placed the remote on the arm of her chair, and started to rise.

"Wait." Samuel rushed forward. "Don't go to bed yet. I need help."

Mrs. Oldham paused, halfway out of her chair, and squinted in Samuel's direction. She sniffed, shook her head, and stood up.

Samuel stood in front of her. "Mrs. Oldham." In panic, he reverted to his childhood name for her. "Auntie Janet. Wait."

She stood still, her eyes wide. Samuel tensed. *Did she hear me?*

"Getting old and daft." Mrs Oldham shook her head again and moved towards the door.

Samuel ran to the wall. He raised his fist and banged three times. The noise echoed in the small room. Samuel stood back, astounded at the force he had demonstrated.

Mrs. Oldham covered her mouth with her hands. Her face became deathly white. She swayed, her eyes half-closed. Samuel heard her heart pound, its beat erratic and halting. She staggered to her chair and slumped into it, one hand now on her chest, the other on her forehead.

Don't die. Samuel stood motionless until her breathing steadied.

Mrs. Oldham stared around the room. "Who's there?"

Samuel stepped forward. "It's me." She looked through him. Samuel stood in the center of the room, fists clenched, all-powerful and impotent. There was nothing he could not do, but he had no way to be identified for his actions.

On the mantelpiece, a china ornament held back a stack of papers. Samuel lifted them and dropped gas bills, electricity bills, and personal letters to the floor. With the slip of paper bearing Doctor Pettifer's phone number in his fingers, he advanced on Mrs. Oldham.

Her gaze was fixed on the papers littering the floor, her mouth and eyes wide. "A ghost." She breathed the word. "Father Michael, is it you?"

"No, dammit, it's me." Samuel waved the paper in Mrs. Oldham's face. "I want you to call this number. She'll know what to do. Doctor Pettifer—Elaine—studies ghosts and she works with the psychic man. I need them here. I can communicate with them."

Mrs. Oldham pressed herself into her chair. "Who are you? What do you want?"

"Isn't it obvious?" Samuel swore under his breath. Talking was futile. She heard nothing of what he said. Samuel dropped the paper onto Mrs. Oldham's lap. She squealed and writhed in her chair. He grabbed the phone and dropped it on her lap, then picked up the paper and held it to her eyes.

"Go away," she whimpered. "Leave me alone."

Samuel turned the paper and read the number. He took the handset off the phone and threw it to one side then dialed. Mrs. Oldham held her hands up beside her head. To Samuel's ears, the pounding of blood in her veins sounded loud enough to shake the foundations of the house. He picked up the handset and held it to her ear.

"No." She writhed away.

"Please. It's just a phone." Samuel placed the handset against her ear again and held her head with his other hand. "Please. Doctor Pettifer can help."

The touch of her skin warmed his hand. Through it, Samuel felt the movement of blood in old, hardened veins, the twitch of muscle, the chattering of nerves. He saw the confusion in her mind, the terror, the submission. Samuel was there, in her thoughts, while they faded. How he did it, he had no idea, but Samuel sucked the last vestiges of life from Mrs. Oldham's body.

Horrified, he stared at the corpse. What had he done? What had Angela made him do? Samuel flexed his fingers. New strength filled his body, strength he had never known in life. Stolen strength.

"Samuel Watson."

The voice came from a shadow over Mrs. Oldham's body. Her ghost floated into the air.

"Damn you, Samuel. Damn you to hell." She rose into a bright light, distant yet visible through the ceiling, and vanished. Her words drifted down. "You'll burn for this." The light winked out.

Samuel fled through the wall into his own house. In the basement, he screamed his silent horror into the empty room, into a darkness he could now only imagine. His eyes refused to close. His sight would not be denied. He had to face the disgusting reality of what he had become, what Angela turned him into. His existence depended on his absorbing the life of others. Samuel was no great and powerful specter, not even a lowly poltergeist. He was a parasite, no better than a tapeworm or a louse. Perhaps it would be better to sit here until he faded into oblivion. An eternity of madness, howling in the wind, must surely be less of an evil than the fate facing him now.

Chapter Twenty-Eight

Romulus whistled on his way to work. He had slept well, without interruption, and there was no sign of the tiresome little priest at breakfast. It was a fine morning, washed fresh by the night's rain, so Romulus's car languished outside his house.

Walking was good for his heart, or so the medical profession maintained, and the last few days had been particularly stressful. He even managed a "Good morning" to Chesterton's secretary, although he didn't go so far as to ask her name. There was, after all, a limit to familiarity.

Chesterton's secretary responded with a wide smile. A little too wide for Romulus's liking. It was that I-know-something-you-don't-know smile. He had seen it on women's faces in the past. It was a reliable indicator of imminent bad news.

"Professor Crowe." The tone in the secretary's voice confirmed his first impression. Romulus braced himself.

"Chancellor Orson would like to see you in his office. 'As soon as you arrived,' he said." Her grin spread across her face. Romulus hoped it might be a rictus grin, the onset of tetanus. He sighed. Wishful thinking.

"Really? I'd better hurry then." Romulus kept his expression impassive. "I'll just read my mail first, then maybe have a cup of tea. Then I'll rush right along to the chancellor's office." He watched the secretary deflate for a moment longer, before lifting the envelopes from his mail slot and ducking out of the door.

In his office, Romulus scanned the envelopes before dropping them on his desk. None looked urgent. He wondered what the chancellor wanted. Surely the news of his psychic conversion hadn't spread this fast. Unless...

Romulus half-ran to the laboratory. If Elaine and Imogen had returned here last night, and had been overheard discussing the events at his house, then Romulus might be in trouble. One of the main reasons for his winning the job here was his absolute scepticism, which just so happened to coincide with Orson's. If Orson heard about Romulus's ability to converse with the dead, his continuation as head of this little department was at risk.

Elaine was nowhere to be found. Romulus hissed. Just like her to be late when he had something important to ask. He rubbed his chin. There was now only one way to find out why Chancellor Orson wanted to see him. Romulus closed the laboratory door and made his way to the chancellor's office, near the top of the building.

Orson's secretary was an old, thin woman, somewhere between a praying mantis and a female Grim Reaper. Romulus presented himself at her desk. She ignored him, tapping away at her keyboard, her hands arched mantislike over the keys. Romulus wondered how many husbands she'd eaten on their wedding nights. He coughed.

"Wait." It was a statement, not a request, made in a thin yet imperious voice. She continued typing. Romulus coughed again, louder. The secretary ignored him.

"The chancellor asked to see me." Romulus placed his hand on the desk. The secretary stopped typing and stared at his hand. She didn't seem to be breathing. Romulus lifted his hand.

"I said 'wait.'" Her head turned on a neck that resembled a bundle of wire and thrust forward towards the computer screen. Her hands resumed typing.

Romulus narrowed his eyes. With this woman as secretary, how could Orson not believe in life after death? Her fingers jabbed at the keyboard, then one hand flew to the mouse. A few clicks later, she looked up and gave Romulus a smile that could curdle milk.

"How may I help you?"

"I am Professor Crowe. Chancellor Orson asked me to be here."

"Ah, yes, the new boy. Wait." She reached for the intercom beside her phone and pressed a button. "Chancellor, I have Professor Crowe here." The intercom crackled.

"About time too. Send him in."

The secretary inclined her head towards the door behind her, then returned her attention to the computer. Romulus blinked, breathed out slowly, and entered the office.

The chancellor's office made Romulus's look like a broom closet. Plush carpet, original paintings, and a desk big enough to sleep on. The room smelled of wax polish and old paper, with a hint of sweaty fat man. Despite the size of the desk, its only occupants were a telephone, an intercom, a nearly empty set of in and out trays, and a framed photo of a bulky woman, probably the chancellor's wife. Romulus scowled at the wasted space. A desk this size with nothing on it suggested a man with little to do.

Behind the desk, Chancellor Orson scowled back.

"Where have you been? I wanted you here first thing. I understand you didn't show up for work at all yesterday."

"Just because I'm not in the building, it doesn't mean I'm not working." Romulus approached the desk. "I was, in fact, investigating a haunting." He sat in the chair facing the chancellor.

"What? Where?"

"Here in Marchway. You might have heard of the alleged ghost. Father Thomas Michael?"

"Oh, yes. I read about that some time ago. An accident, as I remember. Who's seen this ghost?"

"I have a few witnesses. I'm working on it." Romulus leaned back and crossed his legs. "There's another thing I wanted to mention. I was thinking of branching into demonology. You've heard I have a visitor, Doctor Imogen LeFevre? She's an expert in the field."

"Research whatever you like. Just don't find anything. This is an old and conservative university. We don't want to fill the place with ghosthunting cranks."

"Understood." Romulus pursed his lips. It seemed news of Romulus's conversations with the dead had so far escaped Orson's notice. Somehow, he had to keep it that way. "So, will that be all?"

"Yes. No. Damn it, Crowe, don't play mind games with me. I called you here on a very serious matter."

"Oh?"

"The police called me at home yesterday. They asked about you. Who you were, how long you'd been here, what connections you had with the library. What's going on? Are you involved in some kind of scandal?"

"Not at all." Romulus shifted in his seat. "There have been some deaths, two librarians. I was at the library yesterday when the second librarian died of a heart attack. The police interviewed everyone, including me." He inspected his fingernails. "It'll be routine. I'm an unknown, a new face in town. It's only natural they'd want to check."

"Really?" The chancellor's jowls moved as his face rearranged itself into a sceptical expression. "So why are they coming to see you today?"

"Are they? I had no idea." Romulus's mind raced, sorting the information the priest had given him, separating it from what he could reasonably be expected to know.

"Another phone call, this morning. They'll be here at ten-thirty." Orson glanced at the clock on the wall. "Fifteen minutes from now."

"Well, I suppose I'd better go and wait for them." Romulus started to rise, but the chancellor waved him back into his seat.

"Something's going on, Crowe. I have a feeling I'm not going to like it, when it comes to light." He leaned his elbows on the desk. "If you embarrass this university you'll be out of here the same day. Understand?"

Romulus nodded. Orson mirrored the movement with his own head.

"Look, if you're in some kind of trouble, tell me now. I'm sure it can be swept under a carpet somewhere." Orson assumed a sly half-smile.

"There's no need—"

"Not for your sake, Crowe. For the sake of the university. That's what matters to me. I have influence. I can arrange to have evidence mislaid, charges dropped." He sat upright. "Of course, you'd still have to leave Marchway, but neither you nor the university would suffer any adverse publicity."

Romulus realized his jaw hung loose and closed his mouth. How many times had Orson hushed up indiscretions? How many of the staff who moved on to new positions did so with Orson's full knowledge of some crime they had committed? Did Orson later call in those "favors"?

"I can assure you, chancellor, none of that will be necessary. I have committed no crime. If the police wish to speak to me, it must be because they think I can help in some way."

Orson sniffed. "I see. Well, I'll let it go this time, but be warned. I don't like mysteries, Crowe. You will keep me informed with written reports of your conversations with the police. I will treat them as confidential, naturally, but you will provide them. I may call on you for clarification if anything in those reports causes me concern. Do I make myself clear?"

"Perfectly." Romulus glanced at the clock. "Now, if you will excuse me, it's just about time for my meeting with the police." Romulus rose from his chair. Orson remained seated, his gaze fixed on Romulus.

"I'll expect a report this afternoon. Include your interview yesterday."

Romulus felt Orson's eyes boring into his back as he left the office. He stalked past the secretary and into the corridor, where he paused and took a few long, deep breaths. That damned priest. If he hadn't given Romulus the name of the first dead librarian, the police would have left him alone. If he had made his spectral nature clear at the start, Romulus would never have called the police in the first place. Now he, Romulus Crowe, respected academic, was high on a list of murder suspects. Worse, he knew what was behind the murders but speaking up, with not a shred of proof, would certainly get him fired and subjected to public ridicule. Romulus headed for the stairs. He had no choice. Imogen knew more about demons than he did. He needed her help. How could he get it though, without admitting he needed it? His scowl developed into a grin. There was a way.

* * * *

In the corridor leading to his office, Romulus's grin vanished. The two detectives, Crawley and Poole, leaned on the wall opposite his door. Romulus forced down the curl in his lip and walked towards them.

"Good morning, officers. Can I help you?"

"Ah, Professor Crowe. We were beginning to think you ran out on us." Crawley's smile betrayed his disappointment. Romulus knew if he disappeared without explanation, they would have the case closed in no time.

"I have no reason to run anywhere." Romulus pushed open the door to his office and stepped inside. Crawley and Poole followed. Romulus sat in his swivel chair and waved his hand at the two chairs opposite his desk. "So, what is it this time? Another unexplained death?"

The policemen, now seated, looked at each other then turned serious faces towards Romulus.

"What makes you say that?" Crawley's eyes narrowed.

"Well, every time we meet, someone's dead."

"We have noticed that, sir." Poole's lips hardly moved. "Are you familiar with an elderly lady by the name of Janet Oldham?"

Romulus paused, a little longer than he should have. "No."

"She lived next door to Samuel Watson, the librarian who died yesterday." Crawley watched Romulus with unblinking eyes. "There was a disturbance at her house last night. Neighbors reported screams and sounds of a struggle."

"I've never met the woman." Romulus shrugged. That wretched priest's sole intention must be to get him into trouble. He decided to say as little as possible.

"Well, it's like this." Crawley scratched his head. "The uniformed boys were called out, then they called us. There was, once again, no sign of any forced entry. We found Mrs Oldham dead when we arrived."

"An unpleasant scene." Poole squirmed in the plain wooden chair. "Her face was contorted, as though she died in terror. As though she saw the devil himself."

Romulus swallowed. Next door to Samuel Watson, the one who called the gamaliel. Had it killed her just to prove women were not immune?

"She died holding the telephone." Crawley stared at Romulus.

"I don't see what this has to do with me." Romulus stared back. "I was home all night, alone. I've never heard of this Oldham woman. I don't even know where she lives."

"It seems she'd heard of you." Poole shifted again. "We're waiting for a list of her most recent calls from the phone company, but we think it'll just confirm what we found. There was a piece of paper on the body. There was a phone number written on it." He took out his notebook and flipped pages. Poole turned the book so that

Romulus could see the number written there. “Look familiar?”

Every muscle in Romulus's neck tensed. The number in the notebook was the direct line to a telephone in the university.

The phone in his laboratory.

Chapter Twenty-Nine

Elaine paused in the corridor outside Romulus's office. She checked her reflection in the window, tidied her hair, and straightened her clothes. She expected sarcastic comments from Romulus for being late, but it was best to give him no extra ammunition. Besides, what she had learned from Imogen should be useful, so hopefully Romulus would be mollified when she told him.

If only she hadn't drunk so much last night. Imogen could certainly put it away. She was still drinking when Elaine left the hotel to stumble the few streets to her home. The alarm clock failed to wake her from her alcohol-induced stupor, so she was late for work. A rare event, but one Romulus was likely to play on for months. Elaine took a deep breath, opened the door, and walked into the office.

"Romulus, I—" Elaine gaped at the two policemen who turned to stare at her. Romulus's chest inflated, and his eyes burned with fury.

"Out!" He pointed at her. Elaine moved back, pulling the door.

"Stop. Inside." Romulus beckoned her forward. Elaine moved into the room, her head sunk into her shoulders.

"Close the door." The command in his voice made her obey without thinking. Elaine stood, facing the seated men. Romulus rose to his feet.

"Do you know a Janet Oldham? Lives next door to Samuel Watson?"

"No." Elaine stammered the word. "Oh, wait. I don't know the name, but Mister Watson mentioned a neighbor who might know about some local hauntings. I gave him the phone number here to pass on to her. Is that the same woman?"

Romulus faced the two policemen, hands on hips, a triumphant look on his face. "You see? There's a simple explanation."

The policemen returned their attention to Romulus. "Please be seated, professor. We'll talk to Doctor Pettifer again in good time." The one Elaine recognized as Detective Inspector Crawley waved Romulus back into his seat.

The other, Detective Sergeant Poole, smiled at her. "Would you mind waiting outside? We have some matters to discuss here."

"Yes, get out." Romulus looked away as he spoke. "Wait in the laboratory, and next time, knock before you come in."

Elaine glared at him before leaving the room. She slammed the door behind her and hurried to the laboratory. Imogen mentioned the possibility of a job in Edinburgh last night. Perhaps it was time to look seriously at that offer.

Chapter Thirty

The sound of footsteps above brought Samuel from the depths of his self-pity and up to the top of the stairs. Before he passed through the basement door, he paused. There were two voices, neither of them easily audible, but one was definitely female. Doctor Pettifer, perhaps, with the psychic? Samuel risked poking his head through the door. The voices came from his lounge, and the female voice was not Angela's. Satisfied, he stepped through the door, then through the wall into the lounge.

Two uniformed police officers, one male and one female, stood among the debris of his room. The male spoke into a radio, describing the scene and requesting instructions. The female shook her head as she surveyed the devastation. Samuel moved closer as the male officer put his radio away.

"We're to wait outside until the plain-clothes get here with a forensic team," he said. "Don't touch anything. They think it's more than just a burglary."

"Too much of a coincidence, him dying and getting robbed on the same day." The female officer put her hand to her forehead.

"Mary, are you all right?" The male officer put his hand on her shoulder.

"I feel strange. Dizzy." Mary staggered. The male officer supported her as they approached the door.

"Fresh air, that's what you need. There's a heck of a stink coming from somewhere."

Samuel remembered the remains of Angela's feast in the kitchen. His heating system would have switched on this morning, warming the mess and increasing its pungency.

"Smells like something dead," Mary said.

Yes, something's dead. Me. Samuel swiped at an ornamental figurine, a relic of his mother's, that had escaped Angela's wrath. It toppled to the floor and smashed. The male officer looked back.

"What the hell was that?"

"Never mind." Mary's voice was thick. "This place gives me the creeps. Let's go outside."

Samuel stared at the shattered figurine. The two officers reached the door. Samuel decided not to follow, returning instead to his place in the basement.

Sulking in a corner, he considered this latest event. His power returned at the expense of Officer Mary. She became faint when he became strong. The male officer was unaffected. So, not everyone was susceptible to his influence. Therefore, he might be able to interact with some people without causing harm. Yet he needed to absorb energy from someone if he was to do anything.

Maybe he could learn to control this ability—to take just enough to communicate without causing damage to his victim. All he needed was practice.

He hoped he had enough time.

Chapter Thirty-One

"It's not that simple, Professor." Detective Inspector Crawley folded his arms. "While Doctor Pettifer's statement explains how your phone number was in Mrs. Oldham's possession, it does not explain why she called you, rather than the police, when she was being attacked."

Romulus ran his finger along his nose. Why would the old lady phone here? Even if she were being attacked by a supernatural creature, her first instinct must be to call the police. Something must have intervened. He swung his chair around to face the window.

"I don't know, detective. I'd be interested in finding out, but I have, at this time, no idea why this old woman phoned Elaine's number." Romulus curled his lip as the thin chirp of a cellphone filled the room.

"Excuse me." Poole stood and took his phone from his pocket. He walked towards the door and faced the wall, speaking quietly into the phone. Romulus and Crawley sat in silence, watching, until Poole put the phone away.

"News from Uniform. They've checked Samuel Watson's house." Poole glanced at Romulus. "It's been trashed."

"Right. Let's get over there." Crawley surged to his feet. He paused at the door. "We'll need more information from you later, professor. Fingerprints, too. To eliminate you from our enquiries, I mean." Crawley's grin lingered in Romulus's mind after the door closed behind the two men.

Romulus interlocked his fingers. This was getting out of hand. Orson suspected him of some undefined illegal activity. The police suspected him of murder. Not one, but three now. Furthermore, every corpse the gamaliel left behind was likely to be blamed on him. If he didn't stop the thing it would land him in prison.

He left the office and walked to the laboratory. Elaine tapped at her keyboard. She looked up, closed the file she was working on, and stood.

"I thought the police wanted to see me." Her voice was tense. She avoided eye contact.

"They've gone to look at Watson's house. Sit down. We have important things to discuss."

Elaine sat, still looking away. Romulus furrowed his brow. Something must be troubling her, but whatever it was, it could wait. His problems were worse. He sat down beside her.

"We need to catch the gamaliel, and soon. It's killed three people now. Before we can work on this though, we have to have some reason to do it. We need a funded project."

Elaine looked up. Her eyes blazed. "Why?"

"Because Orson will want to know what we're up to. If it's a legitimate project, he won't care. All he wants to do is balance his books."

"So, where do you intend to get money at such short notice? It takes months to secure a grant."

"Farty-Jones."

"Are you serious? I doubt he'll ever speak to you again."

"The feeling is mutual. He will, however, speak to you. I want you to convince him there's a demon on the loose and we need funding to find it."

"No."

"What?" Romulus almost slipped from his seat.

"No. You're taking advantage of me, and you're encroaching on Imogen's territory. If you want to hide this in academic research, you have to involve her."

Romulus trapped his upper lip between his teeth. Imogen must have filled Elaine's head with rebellious ideas. He released his lip.

"Of course she's involved. I'll speak to her later. First though, I need you to visit Farty-Jones. There's no time to go through proper channels or worry about protocol and professional courtesy. People are dying." *I'm getting blamed.* "In fact, you might have more luck if you mention her name rather than mine in your conversation with the chinless wonder."

Elaine folded her arms, tapping her fingers on her arm. Romulus played his trump card.

"It'll be your project. Your funding. Your name will be on the grant." This was a concession that came hard, but these were desperate times. If Elaine failed him, he was left with no choice but to give the glory to Imogen. Farty-Jones was the only funding source he could tap at such short notice, and he needed that to hide from Orson's scrutiny. With Orson mollified, Romulus could work on diverting the attention of the police.

"Really? You'll take a back seat?" Elaine was looking for signs of deceit. Romulus adjusted his body language to show openness.

"Really. You know Farty-Jones won't fund me anyway. Go there as yourself. Ask for funding as yourself. You can do it. Get the secretary. What's her name?"

"Bethany."

"Right. Get her to arrange a meeting today. I have to write a report, then I'll talk to Imogen." Romulus stood. "Where is she, by the way?"

"She stayed at the White Monkey last night. I don't know if she's planning to stay another night. All she had to do was visit the library today. Maybe she's already gone."

Damn. "I'll try the library first. You get Farty-Jones sorted out." Romulus strode from the room and headed back to his office to pick up his coat. If only he had driven here today. He had no time to waste, but he would have to walk to the library. Orson's report could wait.

Chapter Thirty-Two

Samuel prowled the basement, listening to the footsteps above. More police, most likely. They had no chance of finding the truth, no reason even to look for Angela. Mrs. Oldham knew about Angela living in his house, but she was gone. Attlee, Mrs. Oldham, Samuel, all dead. Only the library staff, and those few people who had been there when he arrived with Angela, now knew of her existence. They had no reason to suspect her involvement in any of these deaths. Angela's tracks were covered, and it was all Samuel's doing.

There was the butcher and Jeremy Farquhar-Jones. Samuel laughed. Why would the police bother to question the butcher? As for Farquhar-Jones, all he was likely to remember of their meeting was the size of Angela's breasts.

Samuel needed the psychic man. A psychic would surely understand about Angela and might know how to stop her. Footsteps thudded above. Maybe the psychic was up there now looking for him. Samuel had to check. If anyone became ill or dizzy, he could return to the basement. If not, he would stay up there. He wanted to see these people anyway, to know what they were doing in his house, to hear what they said about him. Samuel climbed the stairs.

Chapter Thirty-Three

There were a few people browsing among the library shelves, but Romulus paid them no attention. In front of the issues desk, a small table stood on the spot where Samuel Watson's body had lain. Flowers, in wreaths and bunches, filled the table and overflowed onto the floor. Watson must have been a popular man.

Behind the issues desk, a young man sorted books. Romulus strolled over to him and tapped the desk. The young man looked up.

"Can I help you, sir?"

"Yes." A chorus of hissing "shhh" sounds from behind made Romulus lower his voice. "Yes. I'm looking for Doctor Imogen LeFevre. She has an appointment to view one of your manuscripts. Is she here?"

"Yes, she is, sir. Mister Legg took her into the Old Books Room just a few moments ago. We had to wait for the police to return the key."

Romulus assumed a puzzled expression. "Oh?"

The young man indicated the flowers. "Mister Watson died yesterday. He had the key to the room."

"I see. So where is this room? I have to speak to Doctor LeFevre urgently."

"Oh, I can't let you go in there, sir. Not without Mister Legg's approval."

"So call him, and get his approval."

"I can't, sir. There's no phone in that room. Would you mind waiting?"

"Yes, I would." Romulus leaned forward so he could look down on the man. "This is an urgent matter. Tell this Mister Legg that Professor Romulus Crowe is here."

The young man cowered but held his ground. "As I said, sir, there's no phone in the room, and I can't leave the issues desk."

"Well, send someone else."

"There's only me and Mister Legg today. Donna isn't well, the rest of the staff are still on holiday, and Mister Watson is dead. Really, sir, it's best if you wait."

Romulus hissed through his teeth, drawing a chorus of "shhh" in response. He was about to demand directions to the Old Books Room when Imogen and the man he saw yesterday—who he presumed must be Mister Legg—appeared from a side door. Imogen was animated. Legg apologized profusely. Romulus headed them off before they reached the desk.

"Imogen. I have to speak to you now."

"I'm sorry, Mister Legg, I tried to stop him." The young man appeared beside Romulus, who turned on him.

"I thought you weren't allowed to leave your desk?"

Mister Legg held up his arms. "Quiet, please. Robert, it's all right. You go back to your desk." He glanced at Romulus and Imogen. "You'd better both come with me. We can discuss this in the staff room."

They followed him to a small room containing a few chairs and a coffee machine. Romulus turned on Legg as soon as the door closed.

"What's your involvement in this? Imogen, what have you said?"

"Shut up for a moment, Romulus." Imogen sank into a seat. "There's a valuable book missing."

"Really? What's its title?"

"It's the *Key of Solomon*."

"That's not the one." Romulus shook his head. "The gamaliel are mentioned in it, but it contains no instructions on how to call one out. There's nothing about a yellow world with transparent trees in there either." He realized the others were staring at him and closed his mouth.

"I'm John Legg, acting librarian." Legg held out his hand. Romulus ignored it.

"Professor Crowe." Romulus sat a few seats from Imogen. John followed, pulled up a seat facing them both, and sat leaning forward.

"Look, if you know where this book might be, it could save an awful lot of trouble." John's voice wavered, close to panic. "We could all lose our jobs over this."

"It's not the only book you're missing." Romulus said. "You'd better get an inventory and see what else is gone."

"What? How do you know? Which books are missing?"

"I've no idea. Your inventory should tell us though. Why don't you go and do librarian things while I speak to Imogen about more important matters. Once you know the titles of the missing books, I might be able to find them for you."

John Legg pushed his chair away and fled the room. Imogen turned on Romulus.

"What's wrong with you? Do you have to pick a fight with everyone you meet? And what's this about more missing books?"

Romulus rubbed his chin. "Samuel Watson conjured a gamaliel from a book, right? The book is at his house."

"How do you know?"

"Because he told me, just after he died. Now keep quiet and listen. He didn't tell me the title of the book so I can't find out if there's another copy somewhere. It's likely he has *Key of Solomon* too, but that's no problem. Translations of that one are easy to find."

"Incomplete translations. That's why I wanted to see an original."

"True, but the main parts of the book are easily obtained. There's nothing about calling a gamaliel in there, so that must be in a different book."

"Okay. What was all that about yellow worlds and transparent trees?"

"Never mind that now. The important thing is to get that book."

"Why?" Imogen moved a seat closer to Romulus.

"If the gamaliel gets it first, we'll be overrun with them. It might already have it. Watson's house has been ransacked, and I think the gamaliel was responsible."

Imogen's eyes widened. "You've been there?"

"No, I haven't." Romulus stood, flinging his arms wide in frustration. "Just trust me. We have to get into that house and find the book. If it's still there."

"We?" Imogen folded her arms. "You want me to help you?"

Romulus ran his fingers through his hair, scraping his fingernails against his scalp. Even if he found the book, Imogen was the only one likely to be able to read it. She spent most of her time with her face buried in those books, while his research had concentrated on contemporary phenomena. He needed her help.

"Elaine is currently securing funding for a research project on the demon. I'm inviting you to participate."

"You're working on demons now?" Imogen laughed. "Even you can't compete with me on that subject."

"I don't intend to. It's Elaine's project, not mine. I'm asking you to work with her, as I will."

"Are you serious?" Imogen rose from her seat and faced Romulus. "You're letting Elaine run a project?"

"She is perfectly capable."

"I'm sure she is." Imogen pursed her lips. "I think I know what this is about. Yes, I'll help Elaine with her project, on one condition. You don't take over."

"As if I would. I have enough to do without taking on someone else's responsibilities."

Imogen laughed. "Romulus, I can see right through you. I know what you're up to. Okay, I'll let you save face this time, but you owe me for this."

Romulus looked away. He had secured Imogen's cooperation, and that was enough. As long as Elaine convinced Farty-Jones to fund the work, he was left with only one problem. The police.

John Legg burst into the room, waving a sheet of paper.

"You were right. There are two books missing. One is *Key of Solomon*."

"And the other?" Romulus said.

John squinted at the page. "It's listed as an untranslated grimoire."

Romulus closed his eyes. A dead end.

Chapter Thirty-Four

The house was full of men. Samuel assumed they were all police, but few of them wore uniforms. Those that did stood at doorways, taking no part in the scrutiny of his home. Samples of the blood and meat on his kitchen table went into plastic bags. Men with rubber gloves investigated his books, his chairs, his tables, even the spilled bag of vegetables in the corner of the kitchen. Samuel moved from room to room, fascinated. His whole life was dissected as he watched.

The torn papers in the dining room captivated his visitors. All the shreds ended up bundled into bags. Samuel wondered how long it would take to put them all back together, if indeed they could be.

Upstairs, men searched his bedroom. They found hairs on the pillows, including a long black one. Samuel grimaced as one of the men bagged his find.

That's Angela's. It won't help them find her.

In the bathroom, they took his pills, his medicines, even his toothpaste. Samuel moved downstairs in time to see two of the men disappear into the basement. They looked familiar. Recognizing them as the men he saw with Romulus at the library, Samuel followed.

"I don't expect we'll find much in here," one of the men said as he turned on the light.

"Oh yeah? Look at that." The other man nodded at the floor. Both men descended the stairs and stood beside Samuel's chalk circle, now littered with the debris of broken furniture. "Seems our librarian was into some dark stuff on the quiet."

The first man shivered. "Creepy. What about the mess in the kitchen? Some kind of sacrifice?"

"Maybe. Or maybe he was just a messy eater." This man, obviously senior to his partner, bit into his lip. "Professor Crowe would know about this stuff. I wonder where he fits into all this." He walked around the circle. "Is he part of some devil worship group? Watson might have been part of the same group. What about Attlee?"

"There was nothing like this at Attlee's house."

"Nothing next door at Mrs. Oldham's either. If they always met here, there would be no evidence at the other houses. We'd find nothing at Crowe's house, I'll bet." The man folded his arms. "That Crowe is in this up to his eyes, I'm sure. He knew the name of the first librarian, showed up just as the second one died, then the old lady dies with his phone number on her lap. Then there's the LeFevre woman. He mentions her name and within hours, there she is. Too many coincidences, Poole. Too many."

Samuel raged at the men. *Idiots. There's no devil worship here. Nobody else was involved.* He balled his fists and concentrated, staring at the senior officer.

The man looked up. His eyes fixed on Samuel's. He shook his head and looked again, squinting.

"What is it?" The junior officer stared in Samuel's direction.

"I thought I saw something." The older man shivered. "Let's get out of here. Don't let the men touch anything in this room, and we'll go and find Crowe. I want to bring him here. I want to see how he reacts to this."

Yes, Samuel called as they climbed the stairs. *Yes, bring him here. He'll tell you. I can speak to him. He can tell you what I have to say*. The men closed the door. Samuel danced around his chalk circle. *Romulus will tell them about Angela. Then they can stop her.*

Chapter Thirty-Five

Romulus spoke to John. "Is there another copy anywhere?"

"No." John consulted his inventory. "We have copies and some translations, whole or partial, of many of the other books, but not that one. Oh, my God."

"What?" Romulus said. Imogen moved closer.

"It's marked as unique. That means we have the only known copy." John looked up. "It's invaluable." He folded the inventory. "Look, if you have any idea where these books are, tell me now. It'll go no further, as long as I get them back intact. I don't want to involve the police but—"

"There's no need for the police." Romulus picked the inventory from John's fingers. "Can I keep this? Good. I know who took the books. It was Samuel Watson."

"Mister Watson was no thief." John shook his head. "Although he was the only one with a key. Why would he take them though? He had full access here."

"I'll—we'll need time to find that out. You don't want to get into trouble over this. If I'm right, I can have those books back here by tomorrow evening. Nobody needs to know they were missing. Will you give me the time?"

John stared at the ground. "You know where they are?"

"I think so. I'm sure they were at Mister Watson's house, but they might have been taken from there. I have to talk to—some people, to get more detailed information. Can you hold off reporting these books missing until tomorrow?"

"Yes." John spoke through a heavy breath. "All right. I'll wait until tomorrow, but no longer than that." He looked from Romulus to Imogen and back. "This is my first day as acting librarian. If I've lost those books, I can forget any chance of making the job permanent. I won't have a job at all."

Imogen reached forward and squeezed John's arm. "It's not your fault. You didn't even have a key to the room until today. Don't worry. We'll get the books back."

Romulus moved away, making for the door. He looked back at Imogen.

"Come on, there's not much time. We have to get to the university and find out how Elaine's doing." He opened the door. "Then you need to contact the police and offer help with their investigation."

Standing outside was Robert, his hand raised as though about to knock. Behind him stood detectives Crawley and Poole.

Crawley smiled. "Very generous, sir. I hope you'll both be of great help in solving this matter."

Chapter Thirty-Six

Elaine paid for the taxi and accepted the receipt. This was going on Romulus's expense report, whether he liked it or not. She opened the gate to the Farquhar-Jones' residence and walked the hundred yards or so of the driveway to the imposing, ivy-garlanded house.

While she walked, Elaine wondered if the policemen who phoned had found Romulus yet. Perhaps she should not have told them he was at the library. He had nothing to hide but he was not going to like them bothering him. He would regard them as an inconvenience at best. Catching the gamaliel before it killed again was important, and the police were unlikely to be helpful in that.

It had been surprisingly easy to arrange a meeting with Jeremy Farquhar-Jones. Elaine had told him she was interested in discussing a project she was setting up in competition with Romulus. Farquhar-Jones told her to come straight to the house. Elaine sighed as she pressed the doorbell. Perhaps it was time to get away from Romulus. She used lies and deceit as easily as he did, and the last thing she wanted was to become as twisted and cynical as he was. The door opened.

"Good afternoon, madam. May I be of assistance?" The man's bearing, dress, and manner marked him as a butler. Elaine stared for a moment. She had never seen a real live butler before.

"I'm Doctor Elaine Pettifer. Mister Farquhar-Jones is expecting me."

The butler looked her over. "Indeed, madam. Would you care to wait inside?" He stood away from the door to let her enter, then closed it behind her.

Elaine gaped at the hallway dominated by a sweeping staircase flanked at its base by two square pillars. The pillars were clad in what looked like black glass. She reached out to touch it, but the butler's cough stopped her hand. Elaine gave a tight smile and allowed him to usher her through to a large, beautifully furnished drawing room. Left alone, Elaine admired the paintings, the antique furniture, the carpet with a pile so deep and thick it felt as though she were walking over a mattress. A stuffed fox snarled at her from a glass case. Ornate vases stood on tall, thin tables around the room. Elaine smiled, thinking of the paradox that was Romulus Crowe. He would love this room, while simultaneously despising the people who owned it.

"Doctor Pettifer. So glad you could make it." Jeremy Farquhar-Jones stood in the doorway. The woman on his arm stood a good six inches taller than he did, and she was built like a supermodel. Jeremy turned his head to speak to someone outside. "Chadwick, bring us some tea, would you?" He smiled at Elaine and walked into the room with his girlfriend, wife, whatever, staying alongside. Jeremy motioned for Elaine to sit and took a seat himself. The woman detached herself from his arm and sat beside him.

"May I introduce you two? Angela, this is Doctor Elaine Pettifer. Doctor Pettifer, this is Angela." He swelled with undisguised delight. "My fiancée."

"Congratulations." Elaine looked the woman over. Her short, tight black dress accentuated every curve, with neither a roll of spare flesh nor a panty line in sight.

In contrast, Elaine's jeans and pullover ensemble looked positively frumpy. Well, she was here to pitch for a grant, not compete in a fashion contest. There was something familiar about Angela, but Elaine could not place her. Angela formed a smile designed to show her superiority, but said nothing. Elaine turned her attention to Jeremy.

"I understand you're interested in funding research into the paranormal," she said.

"Well, yes, although your professor rather put me off the idea. I'm very interested in all this ghost and goblin stuff, you see. I'd like to get more involved in supernatural things. Properly, scientifically, not just as an amateur. You know, more of a 'hands-on' approach." Jeremy paused while Angela ran her hand along his leg. "I won't interfere, naturally. If I could come along on one or two trips, I'd be most grateful."

"I'm sure something could be arranged." Elaine avoided Angela's gaze. Something in those pure black eyes disturbed her. "Have you heard of Doctor Imogen LeFevre?"

"Can't say I have." Jeremy slipped his arm around Angela's waist. She purred and pressed against him. Elaine stared at her knees, wanting more than anything to end this interview now.

"Doctor LeFevre is visiting the university at the moment. She's mentioned the possibility of working with me on a study in demonology, but I'll need to secure funding." As long as she avoided eye contact, Elaine found these small lies easy to tell. They were not exactly lies. Imogen had suggested the possibility of Elaine moving to work with her in Edinburgh. Not real lies then, just a slightly dented version of the truth.

"Demons. How thrilling." Jeremy shifted forward in his seat. Angela sat bolt upright. Glancing up, Elaine saw Angela's eyes fixed on her. The smile was gone, replaced by a flat, unreadable expression. Jeremy started to speak again, but a knock at the door stopped him. The door opened to admit the butler, Chadwick, pushing a silver trolley.

"Tea, sir." Chadwick stopped the trolley beside Jeremy. Steam rose from the spout of an ornate china teapot placed next to three cups on saucers. Sugar, milk, and a tray of chocolate-coated cookies completed the offering. Chadwick lifted the teapot. "Shall I pour, sir?"

"No, thank you, Chadwick. We'll see to it ourselves." Jeremy waved the man away with a gesture that would have enraged Elaine had it been applied to her. Chadwick merely bowed and left the room.

"Now, do tell about these demons. Where are they? Do you know?" Jeremy leaned so far forward he was in danger of falling off the edge of the seat.

"We think there might be one quite close to here. That's what we want to study." Elaine glanced at the tea and cookies. Jeremy followed her look.

"Oh, but I'm forgetting my manners. Angela, would you be so good as to pour us some tea?"

Angela turned her dark eyes on Jeremy. "I think it may be best if you do it, Jeremiah." Her voice carried undertones of both melody and menace. Elaine pulled at her collar as an unexpected heat coursed through her body. She had seen Angela before, somewhere. How could she have forgotten such an impressive figure?

"As you wish, my dear." Jeremy laughed, then spoke to Elaine while he poured the tea. "She insists on calling me Jeremiah. I don't mind, really. It makes me sound important. Almost Biblical, don't you think? Now, tell me more about this demon. What does it do? Eat babies? Drag souls screaming into hell?"

"No, nothing like that. It sucks the life from men."

"Oh, a vampire. Wonderful." Jeremy filled the cups and passed one to Elaine. "Help yourself to milk and sugar. So it's cedar stakes at dawn, eh? Should I get cook to stock up on garlic?"

In that moment, Elaine understood precisely why Romulus had ejected this man from his office. It took an effort of will to stop herself from hissing through her teeth. Remember, she told herself, this is your first grant. Even if it is provided by an idiot, it still counts. Elaine added milk to her tea before continuing.

"Yes." *If that's what he wants.* "A vampire of sorts. We don't know for certain. It'll take some time to determine its nature." Elaine noticed Angela relaxed as she spoke.

"So you don't know what you're looking for?" Angela's honeyed tones barely concealed her contempt. "Do you at least know where it is or what it looks like?"

Elaine's cheeks warmed. "We have a good idea what we're looking for. True, we don't know its exact location or appearance, but if we did we wouldn't need funding for an investigation." She faced Angela, her jaw set in defiance.

"Ladies, please." Jeremy held his arms between them. "There's no need for this. I've decided to provide some funding for your project, Doctor Pettifer. I'd like to meet this Doctor LeFevre too, but we can do that later. Tomorrow, perhaps. Would three o'clock suit you?"

Elaine nodded, her eyes still locked with Angela's as she tried to recall where she had seen her before.

"Good." Jeremy seemed keen to separate them. "Look, Angela and I have things to discuss. Newly engaged and all that." He grinned and winked. "I'll have Chadwick call you a taxi. My treat." He stood, his arm entwined with Angela's, and half-pulled her from the room.

Elaine stared at the closed door. Her confrontation with Angela was more than a simple disagreement. It felt as though the woman was probing, trying to get into her mind. The effect was similar to Elaine's experiences with Romulus when his enthusiasm peaked. She felt drained, her limbs heavy. The door opened, and Chadwick's head appeared.

"Doctor Pettifer? I have arranged a car to take you home."

Numb, Elaine stood and followed Chadwick outside. Instead of the taxi she was expecting, a long limousine waited at the front door. Elaine furrowed her brow and inclined her head towards Chadwick.

"I have taken the liberty," Chadwick said with a sly smile, "of appropriating the young master's car for a short time. If you would like to make yourself comfortable," he said, opening the door, "I will drive you home."

Elaine started to climb in. "Won't they miss you? I don't want to get you into trouble."

"Believe me, madam, the young master is unlikely to notice my absence even if I stayed out for the rest of the day. The master, his father, is away for the day. As it is, I will only be gone for a few minutes." He ushered Elaine into the car.

Good for you, Chadwick, she thought as she settled into the plush upholstery. After asking Chadwick to drop her off at the university, she sat thinking in the back seat of the car, periodically wondering if she should open the window and wave at the poor pedestrians on the street. Mostly, though, she thought about Angela.

Every time she tried to pin down the memory of their previous meeting, her mind refused to focus on it. It was only after she had thanked Chadwick for the ride and started up the university steps that it came back to her.

The library, yesterday. Samuel Watson's heart attack. That was the one and only time she had seen Angela before.

Chapter Thirty-Seven

Romulus stared through the window of the police car as it turned into Ballantrae Avenue. The car stopped outside number eighty-six. Crawley turned in his seat to face Romulus who did his best to maintain an innocent expression.

"Where are we?" Romulus glanced at the house.

"Eighty-six Ballantrae Avenue. Does that mean anything to you?"

"Nothing. Should it? It seems an awful waste of taxpayers' money to drive us here. We could have walked."

"This is how the police work, Professor Crowe." Crawley opened his door and climbed out. He opened the door beside Romulus. "We do not march people through the streets."

Poole stood on the opposite side helping Imogen from the car. She gave Romulus a hard stare. He turned to face the house. By now, Imogen might have worked out the reason behind Romulus's haste, and his uncharacteristic generosity in allowing Elaine to take credit for securing project funding. It was unfortunate, but Imogen was hooked now. She was unlikely to walk away from the possibility of studying a real demon at work. Romulus sniffed and looked at Crawley.

"Why have you brought us here?"

"There's something I want you to see." Crawley led the way through the gate. "Something that might interest you."

Romulus ran his tongue over his teeth. Samuel Watson's house contained a great deal of interest for him, but could he investigate properly under police supervision?

"Whose house is this?" Imogen caught up with Romulus. He grimaced, knowing he should have asked that question himself. Crawley smirked.

"The late Samuel Watson lived here." Crawley nodded to the uniformed policeman at the door and pushed it open. Romulus and Imogen recoiled at the stench.

"Smells like he's still around." Romulus took a few breaths before crossing the threshold.

"That's coming from the kitchen." Poole said. Romulus noticed the small shake of Crawley's head. Poole shut up. Imogen staggered into Romulus, almost knocking him off-balance.

"I'm sorry," she said, grasping Poole's arm to steady herself. "I just felt a little dizzy."

Chapter Thirty-Eight

Samuel rested his arm on the wooden handrail beside the stairs. He tapped his finger on the rail several times before he realized he was, once more, touching the wood.

He heard voices upstairs. He brushed his hand along the wall, enjoying the rough surface of the brickwork. This must mean there was someone susceptible nearby, someone he could absorb strength from. He clenched his fists, hoping whoever it was would not get too close. Poor Mrs. Oldham had died because of him, because of his failure to control this parasitic ability. It must never happen again.

The voices moved closer to the basement door. Samuel retreated into the shadows at the far end of the basement behind the toppled stack of furniture.

Chapter Thirty-Nine

The shreds of an almost-dead emotion touched Romulus when Poole put his arm around Imogen, supporting her. Romulus fought his jealousy, conquered it, and flung it back into the abyss. He moved further into the house. All the doors were open. The living room was a shambles, the floor littered with books among the upturned furniture. From the doorway, Romulus scanned the floor, but the books he saw were modern hardbacks and paperbacks. No ancient manuscripts stood out among them. His fingers twitched. Perhaps he would find something under the upturned chairs, but he dare not try. The police already suspected him of some involvement with Watson's death, and the others. They would hardly balk at arresting him for tampering with a crime scene. Romulus backed into the corridor and walked towards the source of the vile smell at the far end.

"Hold on there, professor." Crawley's voice stopped Romulus in his tracks. "Where might you be going?"

Romulus looked back. Imogen stood, shaking her head, refusing Poole's offers of further help. Crawley walked towards him.

"You said you wanted to show me something. I'm guessing it has something to do with that awful stink." Romulus tilted his head as Crawley stopped in front of him.

"Maybe." Crawley extended his arm towards the kitchen. "After you."

Romulus entered the kitchen. The table in the middle of the room was covered in the remains of some hideous feast. Shreds of meat lay drying in pools of blood, some of which hung in drips over the edges of the table. A few pools of dried blood spotted the floor. A dozen or more flies, the remnants of the summer insects, crawled over the gory leavings.

"What is this?" Romulus moved aside to let Crawley and the others enter.

"We're not sure." Crawley said. "Forensics say there's not enough blood for something to have been killed here. They've taken samples, but as far as we can tell there's nothing human in that lot."

Imogen gasped, her hand over her mouth. Poole, beside her, had lost most of the color from his cheeks. Crawley motioned for them to leave.

"Wait at the basement door, Poole. We'll be out in a moment." Crawley turned to Romulus. "So what do you think, professor? You're an expert in the supernatural. Do you think this has some ritual significance?"

"How should I know? I study ghosts, not witchcraft." Romulus turned his gaze from the mess. "How long has this been here?"

"It's hard to tell. The central heating warmed it up, we think, but the extent of decay suggests it's been here some time."

"Or it's decaying faster than it should." The words were out before Romulus realized. Crawley moved closer, his face registering interest.

"How could that happen?" He stood directly in front of Romulus, his voice low. "Look, I'm going to be frank. I don't think you killed anyone. If I did, you'd be answering questions in an interview room at the station. It might still come to that."

"I can assure you—" Romulus began.

"I do, however, think you know a lot more about these deaths than you're telling me. Maybe you're involved somehow, maybe not, but you certainly have information that I want to hear."

"I doubt it." Romulus stared hard into Crawley's eyes. "I doubt you'd believe anything I have to say on the matter. I'm not involved in any deaths. I'm not responsible for them." He took a deep breath. "I suspect there might be some supernatural activity connected with them, that's all. That's my only interest in this."

Crawley rubbed his chin, the gesture failing to hide the smile that creased his lips.

Romulus folded his arms. "I said you wouldn't believe me. I'm used to this reaction, I don't expect the public to take my area of research seriously. I did, however, expect a more mature reaction from a supposedly educated, high-ranking member of the police force."

"I'm sorry." Crawley raised his hands. "I do, most certainly, take you seriously, Professor. It's just that in my own profession we find crimes are usually committed by the living, not the dead."

"Indeed." Romulus trembled with rage. "As are these. The culprit is living, though not human. I doubt your traditional arrest-and-charge scenario will work here."

"What are you talking about?" Crawley's smirk vanished. "Do you know who the killer is?"

"Not, who, detective. What." All thought of caution melted under Romulus's pride. His fingers interlocked behind his back as he assumed his lecturer's stance. "The creature responsible for the deaths of Watson and Attlee is an ancient demon, which escaped the pages of a book. Samuel Watson facilitated its escape. I suspect it is also responsible for the death of the old woman next door."

Crawley stared in silence, his mouth open. Eventually he lowered his head, shaking it slowly.

"I've already told you I don't suspect you of the killings. There's no need to try for an insanity plea."

"Insanity?" Romulus heard his voice rising, but in his anger he refused to control it. "How do you explain my knowledge of Nathaniel Attlee? I'll tell you how I knew. A dead priest told me. He also told me about a book. Samuel Watson himself told me the book is here, in this house. If I find it, will that convince you?"

Crawley pursed his lips. He folded his arms, tapping one finger against his chin as he walked around the room.

"You expect me to believe you get your information from the dead. You expect me to believe you've never met Samuel Watson, that you've never been to this house before, yet you know about a particular book he has here. If you've never met him, how did he tell you?"

"He told me at the library on the day he died."

"Was that before or after his death?" Crawley raised one eyebrow.

"After. Look, I know he has two very old books here—"

"Two? A moment ago it was one."

"Only one of them is important." Romulus clasped his head in exasperation. "Just let me look around. Let me find the book."

"Let you get your fingerprints over everything, you mean. Then you can say you've never been here, that any prints we find were the result of you handling everything today." Crawley faced Romulus from the far side of the table. He leaned forward, as though to place his hands on the table, glanced down then backed off. "How valuable are these books?"

"Very. I don't know their worth, but they're extremely rare."

"Worth a fortune, would you say?"

"Well, yes, I suppose so but—" Romulus's anger subsided. Caution reasserted itself too late.

"Worth killing someone for, worth ransacking their house to find?"

Romulus clamped his lips together. Crawley smiled and nodded, then moved slowly around the table until he stood a few feet from Romulus.

"What's in the basement here, professor?"

"The basement?" Romulus frowned, momentarily confused by the sudden change of direction. "I didn't know there was a basement."

"You surprise me. You seem to know everything else about the case. Why don't you ask your ghosts?"

"They're not here." Romulus tilted his head back and closed his eyes. "I've seen the priest Thomas Michael at my house. I saw Watson at the library. I hoped one, if not both of them, would be here."

"That's too bad. If you showed me his ghost, I might believe you. As it is, I want you to see the basement, then we can continue this conversation at the police station."

Romulus snapped his head down and opened his eyes wide.

"What? Are you arresting me?"

"Not yet. Although you have admitted to me that the priest you call Father Thomas Michael doesn't actually exist. The same priest you reported to us, the one we've wasted time searching for. I could charge you with that. You also know much more about the details surrounding these murders than you should. I have a lot of questions, Professor Crowe, and I think you can provide many of the answers." Crawley beckoned for Romulus to leave the room ahead of him.

Imogen glanced at Romulus as he entered the hallway, her face lined with what appeared to be some form of illness. She glared for a moment, then lowered her eyes. Romulus curled his lip. Evidently Poole's interrogation had been less expert than Crawley's. Most likely Imogen had learned more from Poole than he had from her. So there was no need to appraise her of his situation. She knew how much trouble he was in.

"Doctor LeFevre is unwell, sir. Should I take her outside?" Poole said as Crawley appeared at Romulus's side.

"Later. First, let's have a look in this basement." Crawley pushed past Romulus and opened a door, then reached along the wall inside. A light came on, illuminating a wooden staircase. Crawley pulled a few pairs of thin latex gloves from his pocket.

"Put these on," he said, handing some gloves to Romulus and Imogen. "Forensics hasn't been down there yet, and I don't want any extra prints turning up." Crawley pulled a pair of gloves over his own hands. "Poole, you wait here. I'll call if I need you." He led the way into the basement.

Romulus allowed Imogen to go ahead of him. Her forehead shone with a thin film of sweat. Romulus held his breath as she passed, in case she had something transmissible, then followed her through the doorway.

"Oh, wow." Imogen stopped on the stairway so abruptly that Romulus almost barged into her. "Look at that."

From above, the circle looked perfect despite the bits of wood scattered over the whole floor. Every sigil in its place, every line immaculate.

"I've seen that somewhere before," Romulus said.

"So have I." Imogen coughed and grasped the handrail. "Many times, in books and in places used in demonic ceremonies."

Another fit of coughing shook her. Crawley watched them both intently. Imogen's coughing subsided. She wiped tears from her eyes before continuing.

"I've studied enough translations to recognize it. That's the magical circle of King Solomon, although it's done with plain white lines. Its power is supposed to be at its height when each line is made with the appropriate color."

"Does it work?" Romulus followed the intricate lines of the symbols. It must have taken considerable time to prepare. Imogen's long silence made him repeat the question.

"If, as you say, there is a gamaliel here, then this is probably where it arrived. The lack of color would have reduced the caller's control over the demon. Perhaps that's why it escaped." Imogen started down the stairs, but Crawley blocked her way.

"I'm sorry, Doctor LeFevre, but as I said, our forensics experts haven't been down here yet."

"So why are we here?" Romulus growled over Imogen's shoulder.

"I wanted to see how much you knew about this. It's not something we cover in police training." Crawley's smile was tight. "It seems you both know exactly what this is, and what it's for. I'd be grateful if you would describe to me the details of whatever ritual was performed here."

"I can't be sure from up here." Imogen grasped the rail, swaying as she stood. "I'd like to examine the circle in detail. I'm especially interested in why the triangle there is colored in." She pointed to the large chalk triangle, some two feet from the circle.

Romulus squinted, but from his position on the stairs, the single bare light bulb hung in his line of sight. No matter how he shifted, there was no escape from its glare.

"What color is it?" he asked.

Imogen turned to face him. "Yellow."

Chapter Forty

In her laboratory, Elaine stared at the blank screen of her word processing program. Before her meeting with Farquhar-Jones tomorrow, she needed at least a formal outline of the project he was to fund, along with projections of the maximum cost and duration. Romulus, she knew, could write it in an hour, but he had given her this chance to do it herself. If she failed, he would never let her forget it. He might never let her try again.

Something nagged at her mind, disrupting her concentration. The woman with Farquhar-Jones, his fiancée, wore no ring. So they must have been engaged recently, perhaps even that day. Elaine closed her eyes. Everything about the woman seemed vague, difficult to recall. Her name was Angela. It was written in the notes Elaine prepared as soon as Chadwick dropped her off, but Elaine had no memory of being told the name. Angela arrived at the library with Samuel Watson just before he died. Farquhar-Jones showed up as Samuel collapsed, then left with his friends. Angela vanished after Samuel's collapse but before the police arrived. Then she turned up as Farquhar-Jones's fiancée. Why would Farquhar-Jones's fiancée arrive with Samuel? Why was she so difficult to remember? How had she vanished from the library without being seen? Elaine's eyes widened.

Romulus had used the word "gamaliel," which meant nothing to Elaine. Imogen called the creature a "succubus," a more familiar term, one that Elaine could visualize .

"Oh, my God." Elaine almost slipped from her stool. She grabbed for her handbag, pulled out her cell phone, and dialed Romulus's number. He carried a phone, though she knew he rarely remembered to charge its battery. She prayed he remembered today.

Chapter Forty-One

Peering through the wrecked furniture, Samuel watched the little drama being played out on his staircase. The psychic wanted to come downstairs, as did the woman, but the policeman blocked their path. Samuel considered his dilemma. The woman looked sick. She must be the one whose life he was tapping into. She should leave. Romulus, the psychic, must stay. If the woman left, conversation with the psychic would be difficult. If she stayed, he might harm her, maybe even kill her. It seemed likely that either all or none of them would stay. There was no choice but to reveal himself and hope the psychic could control the situation. Samuel stepped out from behind the chairs and walked towards the middle of the room.

On the stairs, the argument stopped at once. The psychic stared at him. The woman closed her eyes and gripped the handrail. Samuel stopped walking. It seemed his ability to drain her life varied with distance. If he stayed away, he might be able to muster the strength to communicate without seriously harming the woman.

"Watson?" The psychic stared at him.

"Yes. Can you hear me?"

"I can."

"Good. We have to talk quickly. Your friend is harmed by my presence."

"What do you mean?" The psychic turned his attention to the woman. She and the policeman were staring at him.

"Romulus, are you seeing something?" The woman forced herself upright, her breathing shallow.

"An invisible friend perhaps?" The policeman's tone dripped sarcasm.

"Can you make yourself visible to them?" The psychic leaned over the rail.

"I don't know. If I try, it might harm your friend."

"Never mind that. Just do it."

Samuel gasped, unable to believe a psychic could be so insensitive.

"Do it, man. It's the only way to convince him." The psychic indicated the policeman with a jerk of his head. Samuel moved closer. The policeman moved towards the psychic.

"Look, I don't know what game you're playing, professor, but—" The policeman stopped moving. His jaw fell open, and his eyes stared in Samuel's direction.

A thrill of mischievous satisfaction passed through Samuel as he realized what the policeman must have seen. In the middle of an empty basement, Samuel simply materialized from thin air. His enjoyment vanished when the woman collapsed, falling past the frozen officer to tumble down half the staircase. Samuel started forward, realized his proximity would make matters worse, and backed away.

Chapter Forty-Two

The color drained from Crawley's face with a speed Romulus had never before seen. His eyes opened so wide, Romulus was sure they would pop out onto his cheeks.

A flash of red hair signaled Imogen's collapse. She fell past the immobile Crawley and crashed down the stairs, landing in a heap at the bottom. Samuel moved back, his image wavering as he retreated.

Crawley leaned against the wall. Romulus prodded him, then nodded at the prostrate Imogen.

"Poole. Get in here." Crawley hurried down the stairs. Romulus followed, intrigued as to Samuel's involvement in this. He had said he might harm her. Did he use some otherworldly power to push her down the stairs? *Why Imogen? Why not Crawley?* Romulus leaned against the banister to let Poole pass. He stepped onto the concrete floor to get out of the way.

"What happened?" Poole leaned over Imogen to check her breathing.

She groaned. "I'm all right. Let me get up."

"You took a nasty fall. Let Poole check you over. He knows first aid." Crawley watched Poole examining Imogen. While the three of them were occupied, Romulus took the opportunity to wander across the basement towards Samuel. The ghost stood near the triangle. Romulus stopped on the opposite side and knelt to examine the yellow coloring.

The triangle was not colored with chalk. It seemed to be filled with a fine yellow sand. Romulus resisted the temptation to take a sample. Maybe later. He stood and faced Samuel.

"So, what did you do here?"

"I called someone from *Geometria. Geometria ton Zoon*, I mean. It's the title of the book, the one you asked me about."

"So it has a title. Legg knows it's missing. I promised to find it, along with the other book you stole." Romulus stopped talking as Samuel turned away. *So, ghosts can blush.*

"Both books are here. I'll show you."

"No. Not yet."

"Why not?" Samuel faced him again.

"I don't want the police to get them. I don't want them tied up as evidence while they mess about looking for a human killer."

"She looks human." Samuel's eyes lit with pleasure. "She's beautiful."

"Describe her."

"She's—" Samuel's face contorted. "I can't. My memory of her is faded. It's like looking through frosted glass."

"Ridiculous." Romulus snorted. "You've only been dead for a day." He took a step towards Samuel.

His foot made contact with the sand in the triangle and the basement vanished. Dark, twisted trees writhed against a windless sky, yellow ground climbed to the horizon. Something watched him from the trees, something inhuman. Romulus took a deep breath. Dozens, perhaps hundreds, of the creatures, all taller than him, with multiple limbs and long, snouted heads watched him. They rested, motionless, among the trees, all facing his way. Romulus glanced down. He stood on a gray concrete triangle, beside a circle drawn in red—or was it brown? It was difficult to be sure. One of the creatures shifted, drawing Romulus's attention. It separated itself from its tree and moved towards him.

The creature in front of him hesitated. Romulus yelped as something grabbed his shoulder and pulled him backwards.

Chapter Forty-Three

Space and time blended, indistinguishable in a blur of color and movement. Romulus closed his eyes, then opened them. The triangle was yellow, the floor gray. He was back in Samuel's basement. Across the triangle, Samuel stood, arms wrapped around himself, mouth and eyes wide. Fingers pressed into Romulus's shoulder from behind. Samuel spoke, his voice faint.

"It's still open." With those words, Samuel faded from sight.

"Wait." Romulus tried to move forward again, but the grip on his shoulder prevented him. He twisted himself free and turned.

Crawley stood with his arm outstretched as though he held the collar of some invisible criminal. His eyes, unfocused, stared past Romulus. Something buzzed. On the stairs, Poole half-carried Imogen towards the door. Something buzzed again. A thin trail of drool trickled from the corner of Crawley's mouth. Poole and Imogen made it to the door and left the basement. Romulus identified the buzz and took his cellphone from his jacket pocket.

"What?" he said, holding the phone to his ear. It buzzed again. Romulus swore under his breath, pressed the accept button, and tried again.

"Rom? Is that—" A burst of static interrupted the voice. Romulus shook the phone. It could only be Elaine. Nobody else had this number.

"What do you want?" He spoke into his phone's microphone before returning it to his ear. Romulus hated these small phones. He couldn't believe anyone would hear him.

"...hear you. Where...? ...about the succu...I know..."

Cellphones and basements don't mix. Romulus spoke slowly into the handset. "I can't hear you. I'll meet you at the university canteen in half an hour. You can tell me over lunch."

Elaine's voice sounded like a scream when he cut the connection. Romulus shrugged. The constant interference on these things made conversation impossible. He switched the phone off to pre-empt further interruption and returned it to his pocket.

Crawley's arms now hung at his sides, limp, his shoulders slumped. Romulus waved his hand in front of the policeman's face. No response. Romulus slapped the man's cheek. Crawley blinked. Romulus, beginning to enjoy himself, readied himself for another slap when Crawley moved.

"What in hell's name was that?" Crawley still stared past Romulus at the space above the triangle.

"You saw it?" Romulus twitched his fingers, still itching to slap this man.

"I saw something. Big, like a huge insect, a giant, thin beetle. Upright. It walked on two legs." Crawley stared into Romulus's eyes. "What was it? Did it have something to do with the man I saw earlier?"

"I believe so." Romulus sniffed. "I think it was a gamaliel." He moved towards the stairs, watching Crawley. The policeman regained his wits, but the experience might have unhinged him. It certainly changed him. Romulus narrowed his eyes as Crawley bent to examine the triangle.

"It was when I grabbed you." Crawley's voice was distant, as though he spoke to himself rather than Romulus. "You were interfering with evidence, standing on this diagram here." Crawley looked up. "I took hold of your shoulder, and everything changed. There were trees and some kind of monster." He shook his head. "It's fading, like a dream."

Romulus rubbed his chin. Was his power so great that a mere touch could transfer his gift to another? Or was it the circle? He started forward when Crawley reached out to touch the yellow sand.

"Don't!" Romulus shouted. Crawley snatched back his hand. "Watson said it's still open."

Crawley's face formed an unspoken question as he rose to his feet.

"That's what he said." Romulus nodded at the triangle. "I'm guessing that's some kind of doorway."

"So, that thing can get through?"

"I don't know. I'll have to speak to Imogen." Romulus winced at the admission, but this was outside his experience. In this instance, he needed Imogen's expertise. Romulus headed for the stairs. Crawley followed close behind.

From the hallway, Poole and Imogen were visible just outside the front door. Imogen took deep breaths, attended by the uniformed officer, while Poole spoke into his mobile phone. He finished the call just as Romulus and Crawley arrived.

"That was Control, sir. There's been another—incident." Poole stared at Crawley. "Are you all right, sir? You look as though you've seen a ghost."

Crawley choked back a laugh. "I think I may have seen just that, and worse." He inhaled, then exhaled slowly before continuing. "I believe I owe Professor Crowe here an apology. I've seen some weird things in my time, but this..." He blinked, his head moving in a slow shake. Crawley shuddered and put his hands into his pockets. "So, where's the new job, Poole?"

Romulus allowed himself a smile. The balance of power had shifted his way at last, and he felt comfortable with the situation. Even Poole's suspicious glance did nothing to dampen his spirits.

Poole inclined his head and spoke quietly to Crawley, so that Romulus could not quite make out what was said. Crawley's eyes widened and he gave a low whistle before turning back to Romulus.

"We have to go. I want to know what you two come up with on this, and I want to know today. Shall we say two-thirty, at the university?" Crawley raised an eyebrow. The color had returned to his cheeks, and with it, his confidence.

Romulus knew the experience was too much for Crawley to take in, so he must be treating it as some sort of hallucination. Soon Crawley would convince himself that's all it was and would look to Romulus for an explanation. He was unlikely to be happy with the answer.

"Two-thirty. My office." Romulus took Imogen's arm and led her out of Samuel's garden, hurrying along the street before Crawley changed his mind. As they rounded the corner, Imogen pulled free.

"What's going on?" she demanded. "What did Crawley see?"

"He saw what I saw. A gamaliel ."

"In the basement? You mean it's still there?"

"No, I think it was another one. Trapped in its own world and not alone. Watson said the circle was still open, and when I stepped on the triangle I saw into their world."

Imogen's shoulders slumped. She held on to a nearby railing for support.

"You're not going to pass out again, are you? You should see a doctor." Romulus pursed his lips.

"No, I don't need a doctor. Samuel Watson was there, in the basement. Didn't Elaine tell you?"

"Tell me what?" Romulus narrowed his eyes.

"The succubus drains men, but it doesn't just kill them. Their ghosts draw energy from women."

"Like an incubus?"

"Not quite." Imogen released the rail and resumed walking. "An incubus is a different demon. These ghosts are just parasites."

"Explain." Romulus caught up with her. "In particular, explain how Elaine knew this."

"We discussed it last night. The victim's fate depends on how the creature kills. If it kills someone it hasn't been draining, they just die. If it drains a victim's life, they become tied to it. Like Samuel Watson. The succubus made him into a servant of sorts. He'll drain women, even to the point of death." Imogen wiped at her eyes. "It was probably Samuel who killed the old woman next door."

"Why? What purpose do these parasites serve?"

"Who knows? Malice, perhaps, or some way of reducing competition for men? That poor woman."

"Does Watson know?"

"What he is?" Imogen shrugged. "Maybe. Or maybe he killed his neighbor by accident. Did he know what he was doing when he was taking energy from me?"

"He said he might hurt you if he came too close." Romulus braced himself against the breeze he walked into at the next corner. The university came into view. "Nearly there. Good thing too, I could do with some lunch."

"Only you could think of your stomach first! People are dying, Romulus. We have to do something."

"I'm thinking of eating in the university canteen. That hardly counts as putting my stomach first." Romulus sniffed. "Besides, according to the priest, it's me who has to do something. Unfortunately, he's rather vague on the details." They reached the worn stone steps leading up to the university's huge, Gothic front door. "I'd better work it out soon. If the circle is still open, more of the things could get through."

"Unlikely." Imogen shook her head. "There has to be an exchange. Someone must have gone through to let this succubus out. Someone else has to cross over to let out the next one. There are spells involved—oh!"

"What?"

"The books. The ones we're supposed to find. We've still no idea where they are."

"Relax. They're in Watson's house somewhere." Romulus pushed open the door and strolled into the musty atmosphere of the old building. "I'll find out more tonight, when I go back there."

"You're going back?"

"Of course."

"Why at night?"

"Something the priest said. His kind can appear any time, but the dark spirits are only strong at night. So I'll be able to get more out of Watson when the sun goes down."

Romulus led the way along corridors with vaulted granite ceilings, arched doors set into the sides. In a few days these halls would be thronged with students, but today they were silent.

Elaine stood at the door to the canteen. She started forward at their approach, but Romulus nodded towards the door. Elaine opened it, Imogen passed through, followed by Romulus. Elaine brought up the rear.

Romulus surveyed the canteen and curled his lip. The stainless steel and glass serving area was understandable, a product of modern health and safety regulations, but the Formica tables and plastic chairs were a revolting triumph of budget over aesthetics. The room, with its high ceiling and arched widows, deserved better. A few academics, in suitably depressed poses, sat at the tables, consuming whatever fare this place called lunch. Elaine tapped his arm.

"Let's get some food first," Romulus said. "Then talk." He examined the menu, settling on a chef salad as the least offensive option. He did nothing to hide his disgust when both Imogen and Elaine decided on hamburgers.

They sat at one of the plastic-topped tables, out of conversation range of any of the other staff. Romulus waited until Elaine had her hamburger to her lips before speaking.

"What was that phone call about? I couldn't hear a word you said."

Elaine hesitated, then lowered her hamburger. "The succubus is using the name Angela. It's currently engaged to Jeremy Farquhar-Jones." She delivered the statement in a calm voice.

Romulus choked, covering his mouth with his hand to stop bits of lettuce and cheese spraying out.

"It's what? Surely even a demon can't find that streak of slime attractive?" He wiped his eyes and mouth, swallowed, and stared at his plate. "If there's anything guaranteed to put me off my dinner, it's the mention of that moron's name."

"Who's Jeremy Farquhar-Jones?" Imogen glanced from Romulus to Elaine and back.

"He's a contaminant in the shallow end of the gene pool. A rich man's son, the product of centuries of careful inbreeding with the cognitive capacity of a lobotomized sardine." Romulus scowled at Elaine. "Have you met this Angela? Can you describe her?"

"I met her, yes. She's difficult to describe though." Elaine's face twisted in concentration. "We met her at the library, the day Mister Watson died, then she was with Farquhar-Jones when I went to his house."

"Wait. What do you mean 'we'? I was at the library that day. I didn't..." Romulus paused.

"I meant Imogen and myself. Angela left just before you arrived."

"Tall, dark hair and eyes, slim, tight dress." Romulus spoke half to himself. "Carrying a lot of shopping bags."

"That's right." Imogen slapped the table. A few of the other diners stared in their direction. "Mister Watson had a lot of shopping bags. I don't remember seeing them after he died."

"How did you know?" Elaine leaned forward. "Have you seen her too?"

"I nearly ran her over in the parking lot." Romulus chuckled. "Pity I swerved. It would have saved a lot of bother."

"I doubt she'd be that easy to kill," Imogen said. "Hey, the police said there'd been another death. You don't think—"

"Don't get my hopes up." Romulus toyed with his food. "On the other hand, if Farty-Jones is dead, we've lost our demon again. It galls me to say it, but I hope he's still alive."

Elaine finished her hamburger. "So, tell me what you two have been discussing."

"Oh, we've done more than discuss." Imogen leaned on the table. "We've been to Samuel Watson's house, and Romulus here nearly got himself arrested."

"Hardly." Romulus returned his attention to his salad. "The police know I have nothing to do with all this." He resumed eating, allowing Imogen to relate their recent adventure while he finished his lunch. Romulus pushed his plate away as Imogen reached the point in the story where she passed out on the stairs.

"You must have realized by then, surely?" Elaine said. "You must have known it was Samuel's ghost." She gave Romulus a hard stare. "You let her stay?"

"I didn't know what Watson could do." Romulus returned her stare with a haughty look. "Someone forgot to mention it to me."

"You didn't give me a chance!"

"Children, please." Imogen held her hands up. "There's no time for fighting."

"True. We should try to remain calm." Romulus raised one eyebrow at Elaine. She subsided, fuming. Romulus took up the story, since Imogen had been unconscious for much of the rest of it. Elaine sat back, arms folded, mouth tight, her eyes fixed on his throughout his narration.

"So, there's an open gateway to a world of demons in a basement haunted by a dead librarian." Elaine closed her eyes. "Tell me again how you managed to convince the police of this?"

"As I said, Detective Inspector Crawley saw the demon when I did. That was convincing enough." Romulus pushed his chair back. "We have to move fast. He had no real comprehension of what he saw, and he might persuade himself it was all an hallucination." He rose to his feet. "Some people have trouble believing what's right in front of their eyes."

Romulus strode from the table, pretending not to hear the astonished gasps from Imogen and Elaine. He also pretended to ignore Father Thomas Michael, who fell into step beside him as he walked.

Chapter Forty-Four

Seated on the basement floor, Samuel hugged his knees. He stared at the triangle, expecting a hundred Angelas to emerge at any moment. Nothing happened. Samuel laughed, chiding himself for his foolishness.

They can't be able to escape or they would have done so by now.

When Romulus stepped on the triangle, Samuel could see the yellow world of *Geometria* superimposed on his view of the basement. Only one demon came forward. None of the others moved. So, they only expected to send one. Samuel clapped his hands. One human in, one demon out. That must be how it worked. He furrowed his brow. Melchior had been in there for years. Why hadn't one of the demons escaped as soon as Melchior arrived?

Attlee's remarks held the answer to that. Melchior vanished from the Old Books Room. He had not drawn a circle. He just read the incantation. So his gateway only worked one way.

The circle must be the key. Identical diagrams on both worlds made a sort of bridge, a two-way door. Only one of the demons escaped because there was only one man on their world. Angela needed to send more humans through to release her comrades. Samuel shuddered at the memory of his intention to translate and publish the book. Humans would have changed places with Angela's kin all over the world as a result of experiments with the procedures he would have made available to them.

Samuel shifted around to face the wall. His dream of an easy, wealthy retirement by translating *Geometria ton Zoon* was no more, and it was for the best. The demons needed the blood from a human to make their circle. One human, one circle. The victims, like Melchior, remained undead in that world. No return was possible without blood. No death was possible in *Geometria*. Every released demon, like Angela, would kill more in this world, leaving them like Samuel, in a half-life, a sickening shadow of reality. It was better to be dead than to be responsible for the release of those demons. Samuel reached out to stroke the wall.

His fingers passed into the stone. He smiled. Nobody was within range of his parasitic powers. His smile faded. The only life he could know, the only way to feel, to touch the world, was by sucking the life from others. Mrs. Oldham. The policewoman. The red-haired woman with Romulus. Women.

Samuel tried to rest his head on the wall. It sank in so he pulled back. He tried to bite his lip, but there was no feeling. He needed to take life from women. It was his only way to maintain any form of solidity. A parody of reality, but there was nothing else for him now. Nothing but Angela's warning. Or was it a promise?

To fade until he became a mindless wanderer, a scream in the wind.

There was his dilemma. Suck the life from women, or lose what he had left of his own. His own thoughts betrayed him, told him his eventual choice.

Samuel was hungry.

Chapter Forty-Five

Romulus sat at his desk, skimming through papers and avoiding eye contact with the ghost that flitted across his vision.

"I know you can hear me." Father Michael's voice wavered. His fist swung down, passing through the desk instead of connecting.

"I can hear you. I'm just not listening." Romulus let the papers rest and looked up.

"At last." Father Michael's shoulders sagged. "I have something important to tell you. About a book."

"I know about the book. I know what it's called, and I know where it is." Romulus interlocked his fingers behind his head.

"Not that book. The other one. The one you need now."

Romulus groaned. He leaned forward, placing his arms on the desk.

"All I've heard from you so far are hints and riddles. Why didn't you tell me about Watson's little magic parlor in his basement? Why didn't you warn me about his circle? I could have been killed." Romulus scowled. "If you have something useful to say, tell me. Otherwise, clear off. I have work to do."

"I know. I'm sorry." The priest clasped his hands. "I have to be careful not to interfere too much, you know. I explained—"

"Yes, yes, yes. Well, tell me something I can use." Romulus rubbed the back of his neck where an ache had started. It seemed appropriate in the presence of this priest.

Father Michael nodded. "I'll get to the point. The book Samuel used to release the gamaliel is called *Geometria ton Zoon*, the Geometry of Lives. It's a forbidden book. It should have stayed forgotten in this little town. The Church never expected anyone to try to read it, never mind use it." Father Michael wandered the room while he spoke. "It was one of a pair of books, extremely ancient. The other was lost, hundreds of years ago ... "

Romulus coughed. "You mentioned getting to the point. I suggest you do so."

"Ah, yes. Well, I now know a lot more about that book and how it works. The gamaliel can only be released one at a time, since there is only one copy of the book. A human has to enter by his own free will. Then another has to try to get him out. The gamaliel then use the blood of their trapped victim in an obscene ritual, a reflection of the one performed by the victim's hopeful savior, and a gamaliel is released."

"I already know most of that. How do you get someone to enter of their own free will?"

"You nearly did." Father Michael smiled. "You walked straight into the triangle. If that policeman hadn't pulled you out, you could have been responsible for the next freed gamaliel. Walking into that world of your own free will is possible without knowing what you're doing."

"You were there?" Romulus narrowed his eyes. "I didn't see you."

"I have to be careful. I can observe events close to Samuel Watson but not interfere." Father Michael sighed. "Unfortunately he was only visible to me after he died. I can't see the gamaliel at all. I'm afraid I have no idea where it is now."

"I know where it is." Romulus smiled at the priest. "It's calling itself Angela and it's currently draining the life of a rich idiot."

"How do you know?" Father Michael's eyes widened. "Oh, never mind. You've found it. That's enough. Now you have to send it back. To do that, you'll need another book."

"Funny, I don't feel the same urgency as you." Romulus's smile grew at the thought of Farquhar-Jones suffering a demonic parasite. If it aged the little pipsqueak before Romulus dispatched it, so much the better.

Father Michael gaped, speechless for once. His obvious discomfort increased Romulus's enjoyment enormously. After a few minutes spent reveling in the priest's confusion, Romulus broke the silence.

"So what's this book, and where do I find it?"

Father Michael pursed his lips and frowned before replying. "It's in the library, in the Old Books Room. It's called the *Grimoire of Astaroth*, although it's listed simply as *Liber Astaroth*."

"The library?" Romulus laughed. "I doubt they'll let me take another valuable book. I've already promised to return their two missing books by tomorrow. No, I don't see them handing me another from their collection." He stood and crossed to the window. Opening it, he breathed the damp air. The wind was picking up, though it looked as if the rain was over. The pavements below dried slowly beneath the overcast sky.

"Nevertheless, you must get it. It tells you how to send this gamaliel into oblivion." Father Michael moved towards Romulus as he spoke, passing through the desk on the way.

Romulus took a cigar from the pack in his jacket pocket, unwrapped it, put it in his mouth, and lit it. He took several puffs, blowing smoke through the window, where the stiffening breeze whipped away the blue haze. He turned his head to the priest.

"How do you suggest I get this book? Steal it?"

"If necessary. You can return it later."

"Marvelous. You're determined to get me arrested for something, aren't you?"

"Nobody needs to know, if you're careful."

Romulus turned from the window, holding his cigar just outside the frame. "It has obviously escaped your notice, but I'm an academic, not a cat burglar. I'm also being shadowed by two detectives. Besides, even if I get this book, it's probably in Latin or Greek or something. I won't be able to read it."

"You'll find a way." Father Michael glanced at the door. "Someone's coming."

"Who is it?" Romulus took a puff of his cigar, then held it ready to drop out of the window.

"I'll see." Father Michael moved to the door and put his head through. A moment later he reappeared, grinning. "It's only that policeman friend of yours. You don't need to dump a good cigar. Considering what he has to contend with, I doubt he'd be interested in arresting you for that."

The priest faded into the air. Romulus could have sworn the ghost's grin was the last thing to vanish, Cheshire cat style. He curled his lip, then returned his attention to his cigar. A long, slow exhale sent a stream of fragrant smoke into the wind, which whipped and distorted it into a momentary image of a tortured face. Romulus stared at the place where the image had formed until a knock at the door broke his reverie.

"Come in, Mr Crawley." Romulus watched the door, prepared for the satisfaction of seeing Crawley's face as he entered. That should convince the plodding copper he was dealing with a real psychic.

Crawley opened the door, stepped inside, and closed it behind him. His pale face showed no expression, no indication that he had noticed anything unusual in Romulus's words. Suppressing his disappointment, Romulus motioned towards a chair. Crawley sat, silent, staring at Romulus.

"Surely you're not allowed to smoke in here?" Crawley inclined his head at Romulus's cigar.

"No." Romulus said, his indignation at the question overwhelmed by what he saw in Crawley's eyes. "I can, however, smoke out here." He took another puff of his cigar, watching for shapes in the smoke as he blew it outside. The increasing wind played mournful notes across the open window. Romulus shivered. He had felt something like this before, a long time ago. If only his memory were more certain.

Crawley stood beside Romulus, a lit cigarette in his shaking hand. A faint, acidic odor of vomit mingled with the smoke on Crawley's breath. This close, the fear in his eyes was clear. Crawley looked hunted, drawn, terrified. Whatever this man had seen, it cut beyond the veneer of police training and experience into the raw human beneath. Beyond the everyday world of murders and brutal assaults, into something primal, something buried in a race memory. A terror in the genes.

"What happened?" Romulus asked as he stubbed out his cigar on the stone sill and threw it into the parking lot below. It fell short of the chancellor's car.

"I've never seen anything like it." Crawley finished his cigarette. Romulus closed the window, blocking out the chill of the wind though not entirely muting its howls. They sat back down. Crawley took several deep breaths before continuing.

"When we left that house, I thought I'd imagined what I saw in that basement." Crawley shifted, his gaze roaming the room. "I thought maybe it was some psychology trick you'd pulled. Hypnosis or something."

"It was real."

"Well, anyway." Crawley interlocked his fingers and stared at them. "After you left, Poole and I went to visit the Farquhar-Jones residence."

"Poole said there'd been another death. Was it Fart—Farquhar-Jones?" Fast-moving thoughts filled Romulus's mind. The death of Jeremy Farquhar-Jones would be no great loss to humanity, but Romulus preferred not to feel responsible for that death. Would the succubus kill so quickly? Watson was old and ill, Farquhar-Jones young and healthy. He should last longer. Was it Jeremy's father?

"No. The victim's name was Chadwick. He was the butler."

"Really? I wonder why she killed him?" Romulus glanced at the window as the wind howled angrily. He shuddered.

"Why do you say 'she'?" Crawley's eyes narrowed, his policeman's manner returning. "Do you have some information for me?"

"I have a suspicion. Please, continue, then I'll tell you what I know." Something told Romulus that Crawley was ready to believe anything he said. He hoped that was the case.

"I doubt you're right. Nothing human could have done that to Chadwick. He was, well, shredded, for want of a better word. Something tore him to pieces." Crawley paused, swallowing several times. "According to our forensics, his limbs were pulled off and his chest ripped open by something with enormous strength. Something with claws. Something with a taste for raw meat."

"Claws?"

"There were marks. In the pillars, in the hallway where Chadwick died. Some kind of black glass. They were smashed, and their surfaces were scraped in parallel lines. Claws, they said, though you'd need chisels to make marks that deep."

"So, not human."

"No."

"Animal?"

"None that I can think of."

"What about..." Romulus pursed his lips. "What about that thing we saw in Watson's basement? Could that have done it?"

Crawley tapped his fingernails on the desk in a rapid beat. For a while, that and the howl of the wind were the only sounds. When he could stand the tapping no more, Romulus spoke.

"That's why you're here, isn't it?"

Crawley stopped tapping. "Yes."

"You want to know what that thing was."

"I want to know if it can get out of that basement. I mean, out of that magic circle or whatever it was."

"At the moment, it can't."

"Good." Crawley breathed a long sigh.

"However, another one has already escaped and is currently running loose in Marchway." Romulus permitted himself a brief smirk at the look on Crawley's face.

"Another one? How many are there?"

"I don't know. There's only one here though, and I intend to close down that circle so that no more of them get through."

"Oh, my God." Crawley ran his hands over his face. "There was nothing about this in police training. How do you close the circle?"

"Well, I don't yet know that either. I'll know more tonight, when I speak to Samuel Watson."

"Watson? He's dead."

"He is, but the dead can be chatty, I've found." Romulus curled his lip.

"Never mind." Crawley closed his eyes. "I'll take your word for it. What about the one that's here? How do we get rid of it?"

"I'm working on it." Romulus sniffed. Should he tell Crawley about the book he needed? Not yet, not unless he had to.

Crawley opened his eyes and spread his hands on the desk.

"I don't understand," he said. "How can something like that run around in a small town like Marchway without being noticed?"

"It can make itself look human. Currently it's a woman called Angela. The thing we're after is a gamaliel, more commonly known as a succubus."

"I thought a succubus was all about sex? Don't they visit men at night and sleep with them?"

"They take life from men, usually through sex. They can also eat meat. Remember the mess in Watson's kitchen? I'm guessing the thing was feeding there to keep itself alive until it found a new host. It's currently engaged to Jeremy Farquhar-Jones."

"I met her." Crawley's eyes widened. "She was..." His brow furrowed. "She was..."

"You can't recall anything about her, can you? That seems to be common." Romulus rubbed his chin. His own memory of the time he had nearly run her down in the library parking lot was clear. Why was he unaffected by the creature's induced amnesia?

"I'd better get on to Poole. He's still there." Crawley took his cellphone from his pocket.

"I wouldn't do that. Remember what it did to Chadwick. As long as Poole doesn't know what it is, he should be safe."

"You think Chadwick knew what it was?"

"Somehow, I think he found out. There's no other reason for it to kill him. It's getting sustenance from its host, so it won't need to eat at the moment. So Chadwick must have seen its real form. If we knew how he did that, it might help."

Crawley slipped his phone into his pocket. "Well, you know more about this than anyone. I hope you can spare the time to assist us in this investigation?"

"Certainly. All I need is for you to inform the chancellor of my involvement." Romulus turned the papers on his desk face down. There was no need for Crawley to know that almost all his information had so far been gleaned from Imogen's publications. Crawley's request for assistance would get him off the chancellor's hook. There remained the matter of Crawley's earlier suspicions. Romulus decided a sarcastic comment or two would be appropriate under the circumstances. Before he could formulate a suitably humiliating response, the door flew open, banging against the filing cabinets. Startled, Romulus looked up.

Elaine stood in the doorway, her face flushed. Romulus had never seen her so animated, apart from the times when she was angry about something.

"Sorry to barge in, Romulus, but you have to hear this." Elaine's eyes glowed with excitement. "In the laboratory. We've got it recorded."

"Got what recorded?" Romulus asked, but Elaine had already gone. Her running footsteps echoed along the corridor. Romulus raised his eyebrows at Crawley.

"Well, I suppose we'd better see what all the fuss is about." Romulus rose from his chair and led Crawley from the room.

As he closed the door, the wind rattled his window in its frame. Romulus stared at it for a moment, searching for a memory to match the feeling he had. It wasn't a good feeling.

Chapter Forty-Six

Samuel stared through his fingers at the basement beyond. The longer he sat here alone, the more he faded. Mrs. Oldham had provided hardly any life, and Samuel took very little from the other women. He needed more, and he was not going to get it sitting around here.

Upstairs, Samuel walked through his front door, past the single uniformed policeman who stood guard there. The hedgerow across the street rustled in the breeze. Moving air flicked at Samuel's shirt as though tiny, feeble fingers pulled at the material. The sun was lost behind gray clouds, and a few puddles were all that remained of the rain. His front gate lay open, which drew a sigh of relief from Samuel's lips. An agonizing trip through rusty iron held no attraction for him. With one foot on the pavement, Samuel paused.

He felt the wind.

Even at his strongest, he noticed no breeze, no draught. Yet now he felt the wind. It tugged at him, gaining in strength. Samuel recalled Angela's warning, and ran.

The wind pulled and pushed, sometimes hauling him forward, sometimes holding him back. It had no preference for the direction of his flight. Neither did Samuel. With no destination in mind, he ran through the streets, fighting the pull of invisible fingers. Stronger now, the hands clawed at him, pulling him in all directions as though they wanted to tear him apart. Each new contact held for longer than the last. Each new group of fingers dug deeper than before.

Samuel stumbled. The wind howled its glee, then its rage as he regained his feet. Dust devils whipped his ankles. Leaves soared through him like knives. Faces formed and dissolved in the air around him. Lunatic, unreasoning faces, eyes as dark as wells, tunnels to insanity. Their mouths opened to shriek and howl. Samuel waved his arms in an attempt to dispel them. They whispered in his ear, unintelligible sounds that spoke, without words, of madness and despair.

Raising his hands to ward off the shapes and sounds in the air, Samuel noticed his arms had faded to little more than an outline. He screamed, but the sound he made was a howl. The voices howled with him, triumphant in their capture.

Even the dead can die.

With his last shreds of reason, Samuel seized one final hope. Running was futile. His only chance was to escape the wind, to get indoors. Ahead loomed the university, its solid granite walls promising refuge. Inside, the wind would have no way to reach him.

Breaking free of the mindless ghosts, Samuel ran for the university's huge doors. The wind shrieked, racing after and around him. It followed him into the hallway, blowing papers from the porter's desk. With one headlong dive, Samuel passed through an oak door into the office beyond.

Outside, the wind screamed in fury, rattling doors and windows, shaking anything that could be moved, throwing litter against the building. Samuel danced at the window, mocking the faces that burst against the panes.

"Huff and puff all you want. You won't blow this house down."

With an effort, Samuel pulled himself together and forced down his cackling laughter.

That was close.

The wind nearly stripped his mind. All his thoughts, all the knowledge he had accumulated, through hard work over many years, all came so close to vanishing forever. Thoughts were all he had left, now his body was gone. He had to feed. There was no other choice.

What were a few years to a secretary or a technician? Samuel had no wish to kill, but if he took a little life here, a little there, it wouldn't be so bad. His victims need never know how their lives were shortened. Samuel considered his actions to be no worse than the results of a cigarette or a glass of whisky.

His intentions justified in his mind, Samuel moved upwards, through the ceiling, seeking someone to fill his ghostly form with life.

Chapter Forty-Seven

Elaine switched the phone's speaker on when Romulus and Crawley entered the room. Romulus seemed about to launch into one of his tirades, but Elaine waved him into silence.

"Just listen." With that, she replayed the message.

An electronic operator announced "You have one message." There was a hiss, then a shriek. A voice, far from the mouthpiece, spoke one word in a quavering tone.

"No."

Then they heard a second voice, closer, quieter, a sound like the breeze through bushes. Much of what it said was indistinct. Only a few words came through clearly.

"Please...Phone... Doctor Pettifer... Help."

Elaine stopped the recording. Crawley sank onto a stool. Romulus raised one eyebrow.

"There's more, in the same vein. It's not a perfect recording, but I'm sure that's Samuel Watson." Elaine watched Romulus for a reaction, but saw none. "Don't you see, Rom? We have his voice on tape after he died. It's proof."

"It's evidence. It's not absolute proof." Romulus picked up the phone and turned it over. "Strong evidence but not absolute. You and I know for sure it was Watson speaking, but would anyone else? Take the inspector here. He knows an old woman died in her house while she was phoning here. Listening to this, he now knows she wasn't alone. Someone else was there. Can we prove the other voice was that of a dead man?"

"It's evidence, certainly. I'd very much like a copy of that recording," Crawley said.

Elaine, her elation shattered, turned away to stare through the window. Romulus was right. The voice might not be as convincing to others, particularly to those who had never met Samuel.

"Where's the tape in this thing?"

Elaine looked over her shoulder, then laughed at the spectacle of Romulus turning the phone in his hands, examining it intently. Logical he may be, brilliant, undoubtedly, but modern technology somehow escaped him.

"There's no tape. The recording is in the phone system, not on the phone itself." She took the phone from his hands and laid it on the table.

"Oh. So, how do we get a copy of the message?"

"I'll see what I can do. It'll be digital, so it'll be on computer disk, not tape."

"Does that mean it's date-stamped? Like computer files?"

"Yes." Elaine noticed the gleam in Romulus's eyes. He was interested. The file would indeed be date and time stamped, which would place it after Samuel's death. If only they could prove it was Samuel speaking. Elaine made for the door.

"Wait." Romulus called after her. "Where's Imogen?"

"She went to get a few things. She said she'd be back soon. I'm going to get a copy of that file. Perhaps I can enhance it on my computer, pick up more of what was said." She dashed into the corridor, now confident that she had done something to impress Romulus. Perhaps, somewhere in the message, Samuel's name was mentioned. Her own name was in there. That much was certain. Elaine quickened her pace. She had given her phone number to Samuel to pass on to his neighbor. Why else would the old woman phone, if not to report a ghost? Who else could that ghost be, if not Samuel Watson?

Elaine chuckled. "Samuel, we're getting closer."

Chapter Forty-Eight

The young woman sat with her back to Samuel as he rose through the floor. She tapped away at a computer keyboard, oblivious to his presence. Samuel considered moving on and denying himself his horrible feast, but the urge was so strong and this woman was young. She could spare a little life. If he tried to take from an older woman he might take too much, as he had with Mrs. Oldham.

He completed his levitation and examined the room. He had passed through similar rooms in his progress upwards through the floors of the university, though this was the first he had found occupied.

The solid oak door opposite the woman's desk must surely lead into the corridor. Behind her, two high windows looked out over Marchway. To Samuel's left stood a row of tall filing cabinets, and to his right, more cabinets and another door. Samuel moved to this door and put his head through. The office inside was large, with a wide desk, but unoccupied. It must belong to some senior professor or administrator. Samuel withdrew, satisfied. The woman was alone.

He stood behind her, wondering what he should do next. His extraction of life from others had so far been accidental, requiring only their presence. A surge of panic took him. Was he now too weak to work his parasitism? Was the wind, having sapped his strength, waiting now for him to emerge from his sanctuary? He glanced at the window. Ethereal faces laughed at him. Scrawny hands beckoned. The wind pressed against the glass, mocking, calling to him. A thin draft cut through the window's seals, reaching for him, becoming vaporous fingers as it approached.

No!

This was no way to end. Samuel balled his fists and plunged them into the woman's back. She stiffened, arched against the seat. Her hands opened wide. She let out a small whimper.

An answering moan escaped Samuel as her life flowed into him. He grinned over his shoulder at the faces pressed against the window. They howled back at him, their forms dissipating, their voices merging into one. The window rattled in its frame. Samuel laughed.

"Can't catch me now, can you? I only need a little, a small dose of life from each woman I meet, and you can't get me." He returned his attention to the woman. His grin fell away.

Gray streaks shot through her hair. The skin on her hands wrinkled. Liver spots appeared on their backs. Samuel tried to pull away, but his hands stayed embedded in the woman's ribcage. She moaned again, a thin, reedy sound that finished with a rattle.

"I only wanted a little. Not all of it." Samuel tried to push life back into the woman, to no avail. His emaciated state allowed no control. All he could do was watch the woman's hair turn from gray to white, thinning in the process. Strands of it drifted to the floor, while her hands twisted into arthritic claws. Samuel looked away, silently thanking God that he had attacked her from behind. What this must be doing to her face, he could only imagine.

The flow of life slowed to a trickle, then stopped. Samuel's hands came free. He staggered back, stopping at the window, where the wind beat its fury against the glass. Fury at losing him or at what he had done? Samuel was no longer sure he cared. Go with the wind or stay as he was. He was damned either way.

The woman's clothes hung loose on her wasted frame. Under the chair her legs showed, withered and varicose, her shoes too large. Samuel fought the urge to move around the table to stare into her face. He should confront what he had done. It was his responsibility, but it proved too great for him to bear.

Samuel turned from the sight and faced the row of filing cabinets. It had never been like this before. With the policewoman and the red-haired visitor to his basement he had simply moved away. That was enough to reduce his effect on them. This time he had made contact and couldn't break it. He blamed the hunger, his drained state when he arrived at the university. He must never allow himself to get so hungry again.

Without looking back, Samuel walked through the filing cabinets. He ignored the pain of passing through the metal frames and continued into the next room, a laboratory where arrays of glassware suggested the practice of chemistry. One man, dressed in a scientist's white coat, worked at a bench. Bottles of powders and liquids surrounded him, and he seemed intent upon some reaction or other. Samuel settled behind the man, the observation of experimental diligence dulling his thoughts of the atrocity he had so recently committed. Brooding, he watched the mysterious actions of the scientist, not understanding the process but glad to have company, even though the man had no idea Samuel shared the room.

Samuel's reverie was broken by a scream from the room he had left. The scientist dropped a flask, spilling something along the bench that fizzed as it stripped the varnish from the wood. The scientist swore, jumped from his stool, and stood, his gaze alternating between the bench and the door. Another scream broke his indecision. His experiment forgotten, he ran from the room.

Samuel stared at the blistering varnish. He felt no impulse to follow the man. Samuel knew exactly what he would find.

Chapter Forty-Nine

"I didn't speak with Watson while he was alive, so I can't be sure. However, the voice on the recording did resemble that of the ghost in Watson's basement. I suspect this is evidence that Watson did in fact kill his elderly neighbor, shortly after he died." Romulus ran his finger along his nose and watched Crawley for a reaction.

Crawley shook his head. "This is a lot for me to take in. I know Mrs. Oldham phoned here, but like you I'd never heard either her voice or Samuel Watson's before that message, so I can't say for certain it's them."

"That's the problem. The time and date on the recording will show it was made after Watson's death, but unless we can get independent identification of the voice, it won't hold up as proof of anything paranormal."

"To hell with your paranormal!" Crawley stormed to the window. "Marchway hasn't had a murder in living memory. Now we have three. All different."

"Four."

"Four?" Crawley turned to face Romulus, his eyes narrow.

"You're forgetting Watson. He was killed."

"Watson died of a heart attack, in full view of witnesses. Nothing suspicious there." Crawley shifted his gaze back to the window.

"Watson was drained of life by the gamaliel . That's why he is now sucking the life from women."

"Right. So, we assume Watson was murdered by some means. That leaves Attlee, killed with one blow. The old woman, unmarked but apparently terrified to death, and Chadwick, torn to shreds. Two of these must have been carried out by someone—or something—with tremendous strength." Crawley faced Romulus again. "The thing I saw could have killed Chadwick, and it was certainly horrible enough to scare someone to death. But did it kill Attlee? How did it get into his house, which was locked? Why didn't it tear him apart?"

Romulus considered for a moment before replying. "What about Attlee? I haven't heard how he died."

"One blow, we think. He was lifted and pushed or thrown back, his head impaled on a coat hook. We assumed he'd disturbed a burglar, and since you reported someone in your house that same night, we were trying to connect the incidents. Both involved someone getting in and out of a locked house." Crawley folded his arms. "Nothing was disturbed at Attlee's house. It looked as though someone entered, encountered Attlee and killed him accidentally, then fled without ransacking the place. Watson's house was trashed, so we thought there might be a connection, what with them both working at the library. Then, of course, there was you. You knew details you shouldn't have known. That brought you into the picture."

Crawley took a deep breath. "If I hadn't seen that thing in Watson's basement, I'd have considered Chadwick's death unconnected. So, why is it killing in different ways, and why is it selecting these particular victims?"

Romulus tapped his finger against his lips. "Watson was unfit, overweight. He probably died too soon. The thing's been locked away for God knows how long. It must have been hungry and might have drained him faster than it intended. Attlee, Watson's boss, would surely have known about the books. He might even have known Samuel took them. So it silenced him. As for Chadwick, my best guess is that he surprised it, found out what it was. Then it killed him in a rage. Attlee's death was cold and calculated. Chadwick's wasn't."

"What about Mrs. Oldham?"

"The gamaliel didn't kill her. Samuel Watson did that. You saw the effect he had on Imog—Doctor LeFevre. He was sapping her strength as long as she was in the house."

Crawley closed his eyes. "So, you're telling me there are two killers loose. Neither of which I'm likely to be slapping handcuffs on. That sort of information doesn't sit well with me."

"At least two. I don't yet know about Attlee and Chadwick. They might be out there, sucking the life out of more people."

"Unlikely." Imogen's voice came from behind Romulus. He jumped.

"How long have you been standing there?"

"Long enough. Who's Chadwick?" Imogen walked to the bench and placed a plastic carrier bag on it.

"Chadwick was another victim." Crawley moved forward. "Why do you say it's unlikely they'd end up like Watson?"

Imogen leaned against the bench, smiling. "Samuel Watson was drained by the succubus. It had time to work on him, to control his mind. His soul, if you like. The others, from what I overheard, were simply killed outright. They're just dead. Now, who's Chadwick, and what has he got to do with this?"

"Chadwick was the Farquhar-Jones's butler." Romulus related what Crawley told him of the grisly remains of Chadwick. Imogen wrinkled her nose in disgust but brightened at the description of claw marks in the pillars.

"Black glass? You're sure it was glass?"

Crawley shrugged. "Well, I'm no expert, but it looked like it to me. Does it matter?"

"Oh, yes. Chadwick might have seen a reflection. Not in ordinary glass, but in obsidian. I don't suppose you took any pieces, for evidence perhaps?"

"Not me. Forensics probably has a sample."

"Would it be possible to get hold of a piece? Something fairly large, say six inches to a foot across? Without too many scratches?"

"For analysis? You think it's important to know what kind of glass it is?" Crawley reached for his cellphone.

"Very important."

"I'll see if Poole's still there." Crawley moved away as he pushed buttons on his phone.

Romulus caught Imogen's arm. "What's all this about reflections? And obsidian?"

"The succubus won't show itself in a normal mirror. It can control what you see of it, but only if you're looking at it. So it uses magic to negate any reflections." Imogen's eyes sparkled as she warmed to her subject. "It's very common with demons. Obsidian is their undoing. It ignores magic. Polished, it reflects their true appearance. If this man Chadwick saw the creature's reflection in obsidian, he saw its real appearance. The demon would be furious. It might even assume it's dealing with a witch or something similar, and it would dismember its victim to dispel any power he might have."

Romulus nodded. "I suspected he found out what it was. So that's how he did it."

"If I'm right. If the glass is really obsidian, then that's most likely what happened. We'll need a fairly large piece, but not too big to carry." Imogen pulled free of Romulus's grip and picked up the plastic bag.

"Why?" Romulus frowned at the assortment of paper and small boxes Imogen took from the bag.

"For a mirror. It'll improve your chances of defeating it. I've been out collecting some more things you'll need." She held up two boxes. "Candles and colored chalk." Setting the boxes down, she held up a diagram showing a circle like the one in Samuel's basement. Romulus took it from her.

"What are these?" He pointed to handwritten notes along the lines of the diagram.

"Colors." Imogen avoided his gaze. "I printed the diagram from my laptop, but I didn't have access to a color printer. So I wrote the colors on the lines."

"We have color printers here."

"Oh, this will be fine. As long as you know which color chalk to use for each line, there'll be no problem. My only worry is the incantation. I'm not sure the version I have is correct. It's one of the things I wanted to check against the original, in the library." She handed him a printed sheet. Romulus examined it. His lip curled.

"What language is this? I have no idea how to pronounce it."

"It's Latin. I'll take you through the pronunciation."

"Why can't you deal with this?" Romulus put the sheets of paper on the bench, beside the boxes. "You already know how to say this stuff."

Imogen laughed. "Oh, sure, as long as I can stay conscious long enough to say it. You know what happened last time I went into that basement. I'm not going back. You have to say these words. You have to close the circle."

"I see. I suppose if I want it done properly, I'd better do it myself." Romulus scowled at the floor. "So that'll stop any more of them getting out. How do we kill the one we have here?"

"Kill it? Romulus, you're talking about something older than recorded history. You can't kill it. It's immortal."

"Great. In that case, shouldn't we send it back through the circle before we close it down? Or do we just learn to live with it? Oh, my God. Something just occurred to me."

"What?"

"Farty-Jones. We have to deal with this thing before it kills him. Once he's a ghost, I'll be the only one who can see him. He'll follow me around like that priest. It's unthinkable."

Imogen's snigger became a fit of giggles. "Romulus, you crack me up sometimes. Don't worry. You can get that circle closed before nightfall, then we have to work on getting the gamaliel out of here. The circle Samuel drew won't work. The creature will simply refuse to enter it. You need something more...compelling."

"Like?"

"I'm not sure. I need time to look it up."

"You do that." Romulus put the papers, chalk, and candles back into the bag and lifted it from the bench. He had a gateway to seal, then he had to steal a book before the library closed. If Imogen wanted to spend time looking things up, that was fine. Romulus knew what he needed even if he did not yet know how to obtain it. He looked over at Crawley, who returned his cellphone to his pocket and walked towards them.

"Poole's on his way over. He has a piece of the glass, but there's more."

"Oh?" Romulus and Imogen spoke together.

"Something serious. There's been a death on the premises."

"What? Here?" Romulus drew a sharp breath. Had the gamaliel arrived here on his doorstep? He tapped his fingers on the bag in his hands. "Male or female?"

"A woman. Poole didn't know the name. On the fifth floor." Crawley moved towards the door. "I have to go. Are you coming? I could use your expertise." He coughed. "I could also use some directions."

"I'll come with you, but I can't stay long. I have to go back to Watson's house." Romulus turned to Imogen. "It's Watson. You'd better get out of here."

"I have to go to the library anyway. I'll take Elaine. Where is she?"

Romulus stopped breathing for a moment. "She went to look something up on the computers." He stared into Imogen's questioning eyes. "They're on the fifth floor."

Chapter Fifty

The varnish settled into a dark smear on the bench. Samuel sighed, then wandered out of the room to see the commotion in the corridor. The door to his last victim's room was closed. The scientist stood in front of it, holding a sobbing woman, murmuring placatory words to her. An older man arrived, breathless, bringing the news that the police had been called and were on their way.

Samuel moved past the office towards the stairs at the end of the corridor. He could take the easy route, through the floor, but if he conserved his energy he might not have to take so much life from others. Marchway was a small town with a limited supply of the female life he needed to continue his existence. When the students returned, that supply would be multiplied. With luck, and with care, Samuel might be able to pass unnoticed among the young lives of the students. Only during the holidays would he have to risk feeding from the local population.

Voices echoed up the curving staircase. Familiar voices. Samuel paused, uncertain. He recognized one particular voice and ducked into the stone wall, bracing himself against the pain.

From within the wall, his vision distorted by stone and paint, Samuel saw the psychic, Romulus, pass by with the red-haired woman and the policeman he had seen in his basement. Their images were blurred, but their conversation came through clearly enough.

"I told you to get out of here." Romulus spoke to the red-haired woman.

"Not until I've checked on Elaine. Besides, I can help. I know more about this than you." The woman's step faltered as she drew level with Samuel and she grabbed the handrail for support.

Romulus grimaced. "He's close. Look, you'll be no use at all if you're dead."

The policeman took the redhead's arm and helped her up the stairs. "I need you both at the scene. I appreciate the risk, but I'm going to need all the help I can get with this case."

"Make it quick," Romulus said. "I have to get back to Watson's house by nightfall."

The rest of their conversation faded. Samuel waited until he heard the stairwell door close before he pulled himself free of the wall. He stood for a moment to let the agony in his body subside, then ran down the rest of the stairs. If the psychic was going to visit his house, Samuel should be there to greet him.

The wind met him at the main doors. It gusted into the foyer to ruffle papers on the porter's desk. Samuel felt nothing. His stolen life left him immune to its fury. Tight-lipped, he hurried into the street, ignoring the litter that fluttered at his heels. The wind knew him now. It would follow him forever, waiting for the day when it added his soul to its collection. The voices in the air were indistinct, the faces barely discernible, but they were there. They would always be there whenever he ventured outdoors. Samuel started walking along the street, but stopped after only a few steps. *Why go around*?

Samuel estimated the direction of his house, then crossed the street after waiting for a gap in the traffic. He chuckled to himself. *Old habits die hard.*

Samuel walked through the front door of a house, along its empty hallway and out into the back garden. He was relieved to find a wooden fence at the end of that garden rather than a brick wall or iron railings. Across the gardens, into the next house, and into the next street. The wind flowed over the houses seeming to know exactly where he would emerge. Leaves fluttered around and through Samuel. Discarded papers and plastic wrappers collected in a whirl around his feet whenever he stopped moving. The whistles and groans of the wind constantly filled his ears. Only indoors could he escape it.

Through another house, an unpleasant trip through a concrete wall, and Samuel arrived at the back of a shop. He stood, blinking at the rows of shelves. It was the grocer's shop, and it was busy.

Women of all ages walked the aisles carrying wire baskets of shopping. Samuel moved between them trying to avoid contact. They staggered at his passing, placing hands to foreheads, dropping baskets, shaking heads to clear some sudden, inexplicable fatigue. Shreds of life drifted to Samuel from each of the women, though he saw no obvious effect on the appearance of any of them. As long as he did not allow himself to get too weak, he could control his curse. He could take a little here, a little there. Nobody would notice.

Pain lanced through his legs. Samuel yelped and stepped back. He had walked into the metal frame of a stroller. The baby within, wrapped in pink blankets, stared up at him while the mother reeled, holding on to the stroller handle and leaning against a shelf of canned food.

Samuel smiled down at the baby. He had heard that small children saw things denied to the sensible minds of adults, and there was no doubt this one saw him looming over its chair. Samuel tasted the pure, sinless life of the child for a moment before he realized what he was doing. The baby was a girl. Full of new life, fresh and succulent. Samuel skirted the stroller and ran into the street, heedless of the needle-pain of the glass door.

Taking life from women was bad enough, but to sap the essence of a baby? It disgusted him, all the more because of the relish he had felt while performing this foul act. It was worse than his murder of the girl at the university. Far more horrific than killing his friend and neighbor. Samuel felt unclean, a depraved child-destroyer.

Around him, through him, the wind laughed. It knew. It had seen, through the window. *Give it up,* it called. *Join us*, it whispered. *Know peace.*

Samuel shook his head and continued on his way home. Along the streets, not across them. The risk of encountering another baby terrified him, kept him alert to the people he passed, watching for carriages and strollers.

Baby killer. The wind blew the accusation into his ears. *You'll do it one day. Stop while you can. Come with us.*

Samuel grunted and quickened his pace, dodging shoppers as he half-ran along the street. A group of women made him veer into the road. Samuel did not notice the car until the steel shot though his body.

He screamed and turned, doubled over, in time to see and feel the windshield flash through his face. The woman in the passenger seat nagged at the man driving, but her words faded into silence when Samuel made contact.

He did not pass through her, as he expected. Stuck now to the woman's body,

Samuel raised his head. Her face contorted. Her eyes rolled back in their sockets. The driver glanced over.

"Are you feeling okay?" He switched his attention between the road ahead and the woman.

Samuel screamed again.

The woman aged while he straddled her limp form. Lines etched through the skin of her face. Her eyes, once bright, were now rheumy and filled with cataracts. She stared through Samuel, stared into the invisible face of death. Brown hair grayed, thinned, turned white. Her head fell back to reveal rapidly crinkling skin on her neck.

"Jesus Christ!" The driver lost all interest in driving the car, his knuckles white on the steering wheel as he stared at his passenger.

Try as he might, Samuel could not pull away. The woman's life flowed into him, filled him with power. Lust took him for a moment, and he revelled in the energy burning into his soul. Samuel glanced at the driver, at the man's gaping face, then twisted his head to stare through the windshield.

The car accelerated across a junction, careered off a passing truck, and smashed through the glass front of a shop. The impact inflated an airbag in front of the driver, but the woman, with her seatbelt unfastened, shot through the windshield. Samuel, now beneath her, suffered the torment of passing into the engine. Her life faded, and Samuel detached from her body to drop through, under the car.

He landed on another body, female, her life already faint. Samuel howled as he took the last of it.

A crowd gathered around the steaming car. Samuel fled, wanting to put as much distance as possible between himself and the carnage he had caused. He stopped when he reached his own street, empty of people, and sank to his knees.

"I wasn't hungry." Samuel sobbed the words. "God help me, what are the rules of this game?"

"It's no game." The voice surprised Samuel. He lurched to his feet and faced the dark-haired priest who stood before him. A familiar face. Samuel struggled for words.

"It's no game." The priest smiled, a twisted, pitying smile. "But the rules are simple. If you get close, you take a little. If you touch, you take it all. Finally, if you don't take life, the wind takes you."

"Father Michael? Father Thomas Michael? But you're dead." Samuel blinked. Could a ghost be haunted?

"Yes." Father Michael raised his eyebrows. "Did you think you were the only one?"

"You're like me?"

"Ah, not exactly. I'm not cursed with your particular abilities."

Samuel fell back to his knees, his hands clasped. "Help me. You can help me, can't you?"

Father Michael pursed his lips. "No."

Samuel slumped, head down.

"I do bring a small ray of hope. You must understand that I cannot help you directly. You have, shall we say, strayed from the path somewhat."

Samuel looked up, then climbed to his feet. "Anything. Any hope at all. I'm in hell, Father. I'll take whatever hope you have."

Father Michael nodded. "You've met Professor Crowe. He's your best chance. If he succeeds in getting rid of the gamaliel, its power over you will break. You'll be free."

"So I just have to wait?"

"Well, you could do that. When I say free, I mean free of this cursed existence. There's still the matter of your judgment. Eternal damnation still hangs over your head for the things you've done."

Samuel lowered his eyes. "It wasn't my fault. Angela did this to me."

The priest's tone grew stern. "Samuel, Angela is your fault. You performed an evil ritual. You brought her here. You are responsible for the deaths you've caused as well as the evil she has wrought. It's all your fault. If you won't accept that, you're damned indeed."

"You said there was hope."

Father Michael sighed. "I risk much by talking to you. It could be seen as interfering. Samuel, you have to help Professor Crowe in any way you can. It will count for you at your reckoning. That's all I can say." He stepped back, his body becoming translucent.

"One more thing. It will help if you stop killing people." With that, he disappeared, leaving Samuel with only the mocking wind-voices and the accumulation of litter at his feet.

Chapter Fifty-One

Romulus shifted in his seat. He kept his attention on the side window. Unused to being a passenger, he found it difficult to watch through the windshield without repeated applications of an imaginary brake.

Imogen parked in front of Samuel Watson's house, where two uniformed policemen sat in their patrol car. She applied the handbrake and turned to Romulus.

"Are you sure you'll be all right? I could go over the incantation one more time, if you like."

"I'm fully conversant with it now, thank you." Romulus opened his door. "As long as Crawley remembered to inform his people I'd be coming, there'll be no problems."

"You're sure?" There was a trace of concern in Imogen's tone, suggesting an old feeling, a relic of days long past. Romulus snorted.

"I've managed to stay alive for a long time without you around. I think I've got the hang of it now." He climbed from the car without looking back, afraid of what he might see in Imogen's eyes. This was no time for a lot of emotional nonsense. Romulus had put all that behind him many years ago.

Romulus closed the car door and waved Imogen away. She drove out into the empty road, reached the corner, and turned right, towards the library, where Romulus had arranged to meet Imogen and Elaine later.

The policemen had left their car and now stood facing Romulus. He took a deep breath and walked towards them.

"Good afternoon, officers. I am Professor Crowe. I hope you're expecting me."

"Indeed we are, sir. You caught us at the changing of the guard, as it were. I'm just going off duty, and Officer Mackenzie here will be taking over for the rest of the evening." The nearer policeman smiled and stepped aside, allowing Romulus access to Samuel's front gate. Romulus nodded as he passed, clutching the plastic bag with his chalks, notes, and candles. Officer Mackenzie followed him to the door, while the other policeman drove away.

"I was told you're not to be disturbed, sir. If you need anything, I'll be right outside the door."

"Thank you, officer. I won't need any help." *None that you can give, anyway.* Romulus pushed the front door closed, then made his way to the basement.

"Watson! Where are you? Come out, you transparent tapeworm. I saw what you did to that girl. I'm here to shut down your circle, then I'm going to deal with you and your girlfriend. Show yourself!"

"I'm here." The voice came from the shadows at the far end of the basement. Romulus squinted into the gloom, past a pile of old chairs. A shadow detached itself from the chairs and shifted into the shape of Samuel Watson. He moved forward, his steps hesitant, his eyes downcast.

"Watson." Romulus spoke through gritted teeth. "You're looking—well-fed."

The specter turned away. Its shoulders shook. Romulus curled his lip at the almost-solid appearance of the ghost. Samuel glowed with the life he took. It formed an aura, golden yet somehow tainted, around him.

There were many things in life that Romulus hated, but in that one moment they were all forgotten. Every ounce of his temper was directed at Samuel Watson, at the man who had perpetrated the horror he had just witnessed in the university. Watson was responsible for calling out a gamaliel. Because of him, Romulus had to deal with Father Michael. Because of Watson, he had been forced to adjust his beliefs, his convictions, his whole life into an entirely new mindset. Because of Watson, Romulus had been threatened with arrest.

The chancellor was angry. Watson's fault. His job was in danger, his reputation at risk. Watson's fault. Imogen was still in Marchway. Watson's fault. Now, Romulus faced the performance of a magical ritual, possibly dangerous, about which he knew almost nothing. Watson's fault again. Imogen was the expert for this job, but she could not come here—because of Watson. Romulus hissed again, a long, drawn-out hiss that ended only when his lungs were full. The ghost shifted, as though the thing that had once been Samuel Watson sensed his stare. Watson turned to face him, every movement in slow motion. The sorrow on his face was the equal of Romulus's fury.

"I'm sorry." Samuel avoided Romulus's eyes. "I didn't know how to control it. I know better now. It won't happen again."

"Oh? You expect me to believe that?" Romulus spat the words. Watson's apology served only to stoke the fires of Romulus's anger. "I should send you through this circle first, then close it after you."

Samuel's eyes widened. He stared straight at Romulus. "No. Not there. I'd rather ride the wind."

"What?" Romulus shook his head, momentarily confused. A memory surfaced, took form, and overwhelmed Romulus's thoughts.

* * * *

Romulus was sixteen, on a camping trip with his friends. The nylon tent rustled and fluttered in the darkness. Romulus woke to the sensation rather than the sound, of someone calling his name.

Cold air lifted the edges of his tent and whispered around his sleeping bag. The tent poles swayed with the wind. Romulus pulled his sleeping bag tighter.

Outside, the wind roared, as though impatient to be on its way, angry at the nylon obstruction on this otherwise open hillside. It whistled across the tent's zipper. It found every gap in every seam. It pushed and pulled at this flimsy shelter. Romulus imagined himself lying on the hillside, his tent in tatters on the rushing air. He pushed the thought from his mind. The tent would hold.

He considered checking outside to see if his friends were okay, but it was so cold now. Too cold for August. Romulus lay still. The tent bulged inwards at the wind's force. His breathing stopped when the bulge formed a face. A familiar face.

Uncle Tobias. His mother's brother, the one she rarely mentioned. The uncle who Romulus saw only at weddings and funerals. Tobias was a bad man, his mother said. He had done terrible things. The family never spoke of him, and rarely spoke *to* him.

In childhood rebellion, Romulus had defied his mother at one of the funerals—he could never remember which—and struck up a conversation with the dreaded

Uncle Tobias. It was his mother's own fault. She had instilled in him that curiosity about the Terrible Things, the things Tobias did. Her accusations were so vague, so lacking in detail that Romulus had to go to the source for answers.

He never managed to get the answers he wanted, but he decided Uncle Tobias wasn't so bad. His mother's punishment had been as severe as always, but Romulus expected it. He had, by this time, become almost immune to her reprisals.

Uncle Tobias died three weeks before this camping trip. It could not be him pressing his face to the tent. Romulus gasped and forced himself to breathe.

The face turned towards Romulus, who lay as still as a rock. He could not decide whether to stay silent or call for help. The nylon moved as the face mouthed words.

Romulus blinked. The face seemed to say "Goodbye." The rest of its message was lost to him. The nylon relaxed, hung loose from the poles, as the wind died down and the face faded. Romulus lay awake for the rest of the night, clutching his camping knife and watching the sides of the tent. He jumped at every rustle of grass, every distant cow or sheep calling into the darkness, until the dawn light glowed through the tent walls.

A chance remark the next morning brought quizzical looks from his friends. They heard no wind, felt no cold. Rather, they had shed their sleeping bags in the heat of the night. Romulus kept his other experiences to himself, suppressing them as he had taught himself over the years.

It was just a summer wind. His friends must have slept through it. The rest was a dream, brought on by an overactive imagination.

* * * *

"Are you all right?" Samuel's words broke Romulus's reverie. Romulus blinked, bringing the basement and its ghost back into his view. The memory faded but left a question in its wake.

Does Uncle Tobias ride the wind?

Romulus shivered.

"Never mind. I'm here to shut your gateway, and you're going to help." Romulus lowered his bag to the floor and emptied its contents. "You're a librarian, you've been messing about with old books, so I'm guessing you can read Latin." Romulus folded the empty plastic bag and slipped it into his pocket.

"Yes. Latin, Greek, Arabic, some languages you've probably never heard of. I wrote my doctoral thesis on a deconstruction of Zapotec glyphs. Did you know—"

"No, I didn't, and I don't care to. You're going to read the chant, or spell, or whatever it is. Just as soon as I've put the right colors to your piece of amateur necromancy here." Romulus picked up the box of chalks and opened it. He stared, his hand making uncertain movements over the chalks inside.

Samuel moved closer, still speaking. "All I had was white chalk. It's not necromancy either. I didn't call up the dead. Angela is very much alive."

"Will you stop babbling? I'm trying to concentrate." Romulus stared at the blobs of—color? Shade? What was the word he wanted here? He picked up one of the red chalks, paused a moment, then broke into a stream of curses. The chalk he held, though clearly a dark red, bore a paper label wrapped around one end and secured with clear tape. The label said 'Brown'.

"Brown chalk? Who ever heard of brown chalk?" Romulus held the stick in front of Samuel's eyes. "What color do you see here? Tell me. Brown or red?"

Samuel blinked and took a step backwards. "Brown."

"Brown." Romulus growled the word. He flung the labeled chalk across the basement. It broke against the paneled wooden wall.

"Don't do that. We might need it." Samuel knelt, picked up the diagram at Romulus's feet, and stood examining it. He breathed a sigh of relief. "It seems we don't. There's no brown here."

"Damn woman." Romulus picked the chalks from the box, read their labels, and dropped them back inside. "Never let a woman get too close, Watson. They have a way of interfering in your life, even when you think they've gone."

"Tell me about it." There was a hint of bitterness in Samuel's voice. Romulus regarded Samuel with a brief flash of empathy. They had both become what they were through the influence of women. Romulus because of his mother, and to a lesser extent because of Imogen. Samuel's present condition was caused by a demon, but one masquerading as a woman. Unlike Father Michael, Samuel clearly hated his situation and was probably filled with guilt and self-loathing.

Romulus shook himself. There was work to do, little time to do it, and here he was psychoanalyzing the dead. He reached to take the diagram from Samuel but stopped, his arm outstretched, his mouth open.

"You're holding it."

"Yes?" Samuel glanced at Romulus.

"You're a ghost. How can you hold anything?"

Samuel handed the paper over. "When I've taken life, I'm stronger for a while. I don't know how long it will last." His eyes slid away from Romulus. "I've never taken this much before."

"I see." Romulus pursed his lips. "Right. You can make yourself useful. Help me clear all this junk out of the way, then you can help with redrawing this diagram. You can do red and green. I'll do blue and yellow."

They worked in silence, referring to Imogen's diagram while they filled in the shapes within the circle. At last they finished and stood back to examine their handiwork.

"It's a little garish." Romulus wrinkled his nose at the multicolored floor. "Looks more like a child's play mat than a doorway to the supernatural." He turned to Samuel, but the ghost had moved from his side. "What are you doing? I need you to read the closing spell."

"There's something I have to do first." Samuel stood beside the triangle. "I won't be long." With that, he stepped into the triangle and faded from view.

Romulus gaped at the space where Samuel had been. He closed his eyes, then opened them. No, he had not imagined it. The wretched ghost went through the gateway, into the demon's world. Romulus grabbed the candles, set them in the places shown on Imogen's diagram, and lit them. He stood in the center of the circle with the Latin inscription in his hand.

"If he's not out in five minutes, I'll close it myself." Romulus glanced at his watch. Ten to five. The library closed at six, and he still had to work out how to steal a priceless book. He stared at the paper and wished he paid more attention to Imogen's coaching.

Chapter Fifty-Two

Samuel stepped off the concrete triangle onto the yellow ground of Geometria. Above him, the sun danced with orbiting colors, making the shadows of the leafless trees dance in muted shades. Something moved among the trees, something darker than shadow. Samuel shrugged.

"What can they do to me? I'm already dead."

The flat land stretched before him, identical in all directions, but Samuel knew where to go. He had no idea why, but something pulled him in a particular direction. There, in the distance, a hunched figure could just be discerned among the trees. Samuel ran.

Trees reached out with grasping branches at his passing. Dust devils sprang up and paced him for a while before they dissipated to fall in a fine spray to the ground. The shadows in the trees shifted. Unseen eyes pressed their attention into him from all directions. Samuel ignored them all. The exhilaration of speed overtook him. He ran faster than he had ever run, even when he was young and in reasonable condition. He ran at speeds unimaginable until the trees on either side blurred into fibrous streaks. The speck ahead took form, grew into the shape he knew it would be.

Melchior looked up, startled, when Samuel came to an abrupt halt in front of him.

"What do you want?" Melchior struggled to his feet. His face showed extreme age accentuated by a pallor tinged with blue. There were no tears in his eyes, though those withered, dry orbs were filled with lines. Not red, Samuel noted, but prominent, blue-gray lines that mapped the whites of his eyes with the paths to damnation.

"You look terrible." Samuel said. The spell of Geometria dispeled his worries. He felt no concern over Melchior's condition. Samuel fought against the deception with guilt, his strongest emotion. What happened to Melchior was his fault. What happened next was also going to be his responsibility, but he had to do it anyway. Samuel took Melchior's arm, avoiding the blackened blood dried into his tattered sleeve and started back the way he had come. Melchior pulled against him.

"I can't go there. The gateway. It's the link to your world—our world. The closer I get, the more I decay."

"I've come to take you home." Samuel stopped moving but held onto the old man's arm.

Melchior's eyes bulged. "Are you insane? I have no blood. I'll die if I go home."

"It's only death. It's not as bad as you'd expect." Samuel swept his arm taking in the bleak world. "Is eternity here really preferable?"

Melchior snorted. "What do you know about death?"

"I speak from personal experience."

"Oh, really." The sarcastic expression faded from Melchior's face to be replaced with realization and wonder. "You're not dreaming this time. You're really here?"

"Yes. I told you, I came to get you out before the circle closes."

"Really here." Melchior looked at Samuel's hand on his arm. "You can touch. You're not a ghost. Unless—oh, no. She killed you. It killed you." Panic filled Melchior's eyes. "You're her pet now. Her servant." He struggled to break free, but Samuel held him.

"No. I'm not her servant. Angela did this to me, but it wasn't my choice. I'm going to help destroy her. Come on. We haven't much time." Samuel pulled Melchior in the direction of the circle. The return journey was going to be a lot slower unless Melchior consented to being carried. Samuel considered throwing the feeble old man over his shoulder, but that would be unfair. All he had to offer Melchior was death, and he had caused enough involuntary deaths already. It was Melchior's decision.

Something snarled in the trees. Samuel moved his head trying to see what it was. Another growl came from behind, then another to the left. Melchior trembled in Samuel's grip.

"They heard you. They won't let you turn against her. We have to get out of here. Now." Melchior's voice quavered. He stumbled forward. Samuel caught him.

"Where are they? In the trees?"

"They are the trees. Don't you know anything?" Melchior let loose a short cackle. "They're her sisters. Waiting for her to call them, to let them loose in your world."

Behind Melchior, one of the trees writhed. Something split from the trunk, branches became arms, and twigs became fingers. Another tree writhed, then another. Black creatures, with multiple limbs, disentangled themselves in a slow ballet. Long heads, with rows of jet-black eyes, turned to face Samuel.

"They can't hurt me. I'm already dead." Samuel heard himself speak the words, though his belief in them wavered.

Melchior cackled again. "Death means nothing here. They killed me, but I still move. I still see. I still think." A sob cracked his voice. "I can still feel pain."

"They can't hurt me." Samuel stood, frozen, while the trees separated into their component creatures. Melchior tugged at him.

"You were in a hurry a moment ago. Be in a hurry now. I'll take your offer. Death must be better than what they'll do to me if you escape." Melchior slapped Samuel's face with his thin, bony hand. "You have to escape. If there's any chance of stopping her, it's got to be you."

Samuel flinched at Melchior's blow. The first of the creatures completed its release and crouched, ready to spring. Samuel crouched, drove his shoulder into Melchior's stomach, and stood, the old man draped over his shoulder. The snarling from the trees rose in pitch as Samuel ran back to the circle.

Trees broke and split at his passing. Melchior's weight slowed him only a little, the wasted frame of the old man bounced as Samuel ran. Thin fingers dug into Samuel's back.

"They're coming. Run faster." Melchior called. "Don't look back. If you stumble, they'll have us."

Whatever method the creatures used to communicate, it was faster than Samuel. Trees split beside him, then ahead of him. A wave of motion rippled through the trees. Growls and murmurs filled the air. Samuel pressed forward, concentrating on the dark circle on the ground ahead. Just a little further. Was that the hot breath of the demons on his back, or just Melchior gasping?

"Angela." Samuel grunted the words. "You'll pay for this."

"Is that the name she's using?" Melchior's laugh rattled in his throat. "She's taunting her adversaries. Her real name is Ailo. Remember that. Ailo."

Ahead, the circle took on a dull red glow. Several creatures now stood at the circle, each with four arms outstretched, long tails lashing. They seemed reluctant to cross it, instead moving around its perimeter to intercept Samuel at the triangle. Their movements seemed sluggish, as though they had awoken from a deep sleep, but they had less distance to travel than Samuel. The triangle of concrete, Samuel's basement floor, began to fade.

"No!" Samuel raced, summoning one last burst of energy. "It's closing. The bastard's closing it!"

Chapter Fifty-Three

Romulus turned the paper in his fingers. Latin. His father was fluent, a scholar of Roman history, but the subject never interested young Romulus. Oh, his brother took to it, reveled in the dead language, but Romulus had no idea where his brother was now. He had no real interest in finding out. He could call his father. If he could speak with Father Michael and Samuel Watson, complete strangers, surely he could speak to his own father.

Romulus closed his eyes and concentrated. He imagined his father's face, tried to think of happy times. All he could remember were the rows between his parents, his mother's religion conflicting with his father's fascination with those she regarded as her savior's killers. Romulus fought to keep an image of his father, but the face blurred, distorted, and developed a white collar. His father's face thinned and hair appeared on his head—black hair. Father Michael grinned in Romulus's thoughts.

"All right, if that's how it has to be." Romulus drew a hissing breath. "Priests study Latin, don't they?" He pressed his knuckles to his temples, willing the priest to appear.

"You shouldn't have called me here. It's very risky." The irritating whine could only belong to Father Michael. Romulus opened his eyes. The priest stood against the opposite wall, his fingers interlocked. Father Michael's gaze swept the room.

"We're alone." Romulus crossed the room. "If we weren't, I wouldn't need you."

"I told you. There's a limit to how much I can help."

"Oh, this is so simple even you can manage it. I want you to read this." Romulus held up the paper.

Father Michael shook his head. "I'm afraid not. Besides, you can do it. All you have to do is read it aloud."

"I don't know Latin."

"There's enough in your memory. Just start reading. The pronunciation will come to you. You don't need to know what the words mean. You just have to say them."

"What memory? I've never learned Latin. How can I remember what I never knew?" Romulus spread his arms wide in exasperation.

"I've seen inside your head, remember? It's in there. You heard enough Latin spoken as a child. Just do it." Father Michael backed into the wall and disappeared.

"A lot of help you were." Romulus glared at the brickwork, then stomped back to the circle. "Watson, where the hell are you?" He checked his watch again. Four minutes to five. Watson's time was up. Romulus checked through the Latin text, mentally pronouncing each word. He rechecked the incantation several times until his mind no longer faltered at the difficult words. Romulus bit into his lip. Whatever happened to Watson in there, it looked like he was never coming back, and there was no way Romulus was going in after him. He took a deep breath and started to read.

The words flowed from the page through his eyes and from his mouth without, apparently, passing through his brain. It was a strange sensation, and an oddly pleasant one. Romulus became detached, his thoughts able to wander while the incantation seemed to read itself through him. The circle pulsed with power. The walls of the basement appeared to bulge and flex. Within the triangle, the yellow sand started to fade into gray.

A shout, then a scream, came from somewhere far away. Romulus tried to move his head, but his eyes refused to break contact with the incantation. His voice, now out of his control, bellowed ancient Latin sentences into the chill, damp air of the basement. Romulus shivered, noticing the fall in temperature by the plumes of breath condensing in front of his face. Another shout. Something appeared in the triangle.

It had the height of a man but too many limbs. The top half of its body bulged grotesquely showing no clear head. The creature staggered, indistinct in the haze of the closing gateway. An arm reached from the air, grasping at the creature.

Romulus tried to blink away the beads of sweat running into his eyes, but his eyelids refused to answer. His vision blurred. In his chest, Romulus's heart pounded, blocking his ears with its pulse. Words poured from his lips, his voice rising and falling with the rhythm of the sound. The creature in the triangle solidified.

The spell completed, Romulus dropped the paper and rubbed at his eyes. The temperature of the room returned to normal, the walls steadied, and the pulsations in the circle ceased. Romulus stood still, facing Samuel and the burden he carried. Beside Samuel, on the floor, a chitinous arm with long, curved fingers leaked a yellow fluid onto the concrete. It must have been cut off when the gateway closed.

Forgetting Samuel for the moment, Romulus walked to the severed arm and knelt beside it. This was the stuff of dreams. A limb from a real demon. Evidence any paranormal investigator would give his eye teeth for.

"Shit." Romulus slumped as the arm crumbled into dry ash before his eyes. The yellow fluid dried and evaporated. The flakes of flesh turned to dust. Romulus sighed. He rose to his feet and turned to Samuel.

"What have you brought with you? Another monster?"

Samuel glared past the bundle of rags on his shoulder. "You closed it. I told you I was coming back. You wanted to lock me in there forever."

"It might have been better if I had. Now, I see, there are two of you."

"He's not like me. This is Alfred Melchior. He was the librarian a long time ago. They've tormented him for years." Samuel's face registered surprise as Melchior's body fell through him, to hit the concrete with a sickening clatter. Samuel stepped back. Romulus knelt again and examined the body.

"You've wasted your time. He's dead. From the looks of it I'd say he's been dead for some time."

The corpse's teeth were bared, lips drawn back by drying skin. His cheeks were sunken, his eyes like desiccated jellies. The tears in his clothing revealed deep wounds. There was little odor from the body, as though it had been mummified. Romulus stood and scowled at Samuel.

"It's what he wanted. He's free now." Samuel's lip trembled.

"I really should have left you in there." Romulus fought to keep his voice level. He wanted to bellow at Samuel, but too much noise might bring a visit from the policeman upstairs. "I've managed to convince the police I'm not their killer. They leave me here for a few hours and presto—another dead librarian."

"If I'd left him in there, those monsters would have tormented him forever. He'd never have died. They could torture him until the end of time." Samuel waved his finger in Romulus's face. "All you think about is yourself."

"It's probably escaped your notice, but I'm the only one alive here. I'm the one who has to explain all this. That's enough of a problem without you dropping another corpse at my feet. So I'd say I'm justified in worrying about myself at this point."

Man and ghost faced each other, their expressions grim. For a time, the only sound was Romulus's breathing. Samuel was the first to break the silence.

"Oh, this is pointless. I can't hit you, and you can't hit me."

"I thought you had the ability to interact with real matter?"

"I did. I used it all getting Melchior out. I'm about as powerful as fog right now." Samuel turned away. "The police can't blame you for Melchior's death anyway. Look at him—he's hardly a recent corpse."

"There's still the matter of how he came to be here. The police already checked this basement. I'd say they're likely to remember whether there was a body down here or not."

"We can hide him. They'll find him eventually, but they won't realize you already knew about him."

Romulus looked around taking in the basement and its contents. A few piles of broken furniture and some boxes. He shook his head. The police must have checked this place thoroughly. They would notice if something was moved, certainly if it was moved far enough to push a body behind.

"So where will we hide him, Watson?"

Samuel tapped the side of his nose with his finger. He motioned for Romulus to follow, then walked to the paneled section of the back wall.

"See that molding?" Samuel pointed to one of a line of diamond-shaped wooden moldings, set halfway up the wall. "Turn it to your left."

Romulus reached for the molding while watching Samuel through narrowed eyes.

"A secret door in a terraced house? I'm impressed." He turned the smooth wood. There was a soft click, and a section of the paneling swung open. Romulus pulled the door wide and looked inside. It was little more than a cupboard, some two feet deep and three wide, with shelving set into one wall. Romulus blinked against the gloom, finally focusing on two large books on one of the shelves. On top of them lay a notebook and a pair of white gloves.

"Are these the books you stole?" Romulus raised his hands to take them.

"Don't touch them!" The tone of Samuel's voice stopped Romulus in mid-reach. He looked over his shoulder at the ghost.

"What? Did you wire them up to the mains?"

Samuel laughed. "No. You have to wear those gloves before you touch them. They're priceless books. The oils in your skin will damage them."

"Still the librarian, eh?" Romulus put on the gloves and lifted the books. "I have to get these back to the library. They've been missed."

"Not *Geometria*, not yet. That's safer here until Angela's been dealt with."

"Oh?" Romulus examined the books. *Clavicula Salomonis*, its title embossed in its heavy leather cover, looked and smelled ancient. *Geometria ton Zoon* was a different matter. The cover looked new. The title—Romulus assumed it must be *Geometria*—was written in what looked like Arabic script. It could have been embossed into the cover days, rather than centuries, ago. Romulus weighed the books in his hands, considering his options. The only one that made sense was to return these books. That would give him the chance to get into the Old Books Room where he might be able to find a way of getting *Liber Astaroth* out. Although, if it was as big as these books that was going to be difficult. He frowned at Samuel.

"Why? What can she do with this book?" Romulus placed the books back on the shelf. They were too heavy to hold for long.

"That book is the reason she trashed my house. With it, she can call out more of her kind. She'll send in humans, one at a time, and call her own creatures out the same way." Samuel paused before continuing. "I was planning to translate it. A nice little earner for my retirement. It's a good thing I didn't. As long as there's only one copy, she can only call one at a time."

"I see. In that case, I'll take the *Key of Solomon*. I'll need one of them to get into the room." Romulus checked his watch. "Hell. It's nearly half past five. I'll have to get moving."

"What about Melchior?"

"I'll deal with him." Romulus knew he could not leave Melchior's corpse in plain view. It should take no more than a minute or two to drag the corpse into the cupboard. Romulus started towards it, but Samuel stood in his way.

Samuel coughed. "Gloves."

"What?"

"You can't touch him with those gloves on. They're for handling the books."

Romulus stared at his hands. "You expect me to handle a corpse with my bare hands?"

"Yes."

"To hell with you." Romulus pushed through the specter, ignoring the chill where his body blended for a moment with Samuel's, and grabbed Melchior by the ankles. The body weighed surprisingly little, and Romulus had it safely stowed within the cupboard in under a minute.

"I'm surprised at you, Watson. I thought you'd insist on a decent Christian burial," Romulus said as he took *Clavicula Salomonis* from the shelf, then closed and locked the door.

"I doubt Christianity would approve of the way Melchior died." Samuel turned his eyes to the floor. "I know it doesn't approve of the way I died."

Romulus headed for the staircase holding *Clavicula Salomonis* in his gloved hands. Samuel flitted around him, agitated, trying to take the book with his insubstantial fingers.

"You shouldn't touch the book with those gloves. They need to be cleaned. You can't walk out of here with the book. What if it rains? It's irreplaceable. Why do you need to get into the Old Books Room? The book's safer here, with *Geometria*. Nobody will find them."

Romulus paused. There was something in what Samuel said. Romulus took the plastic bag from his pocket and placed the book inside.

Samuel nodded his approval. "The gloves, too. They're not for everyday use." Samuel watched as Romulus removed the gloves and stuffed them into his pocket.

"I'll need these again. I have to take another of your old books."

Samuel's jaw dropped. "You mean you're going to steal from my library?"

Romulus chuckled. He held the wrapped book in front of Samuel's face. "A little hypocritical, aren't you? Besides, you're the reason I have to steal it. Borrow it. I, at least, intend to take it back afterwards."

"Which book?" Samuel's brow furrowed. "Liber something? Starts with 'A'?"

"*Liber Astaroth*. How I'm going to get it, I don't know yet. I have about twenty-five minutes to work it out."

"That's the one. I've been trying to remember it. You can't get it. The room is locked, and you won't be allowed to stay in there unsupervised. You might not get in at all."

Romulus started up the stairs. "Suggestions? Make them quick."

"Well, I..." Samuel followed Romulus into the hallway, muttering to himself.

Romulus ignored him. His concern now was getting the book past the policeman at the door. He had entered carrying this bag, so as long as the policeman didn't notice the increased bulk, he should get through without incident. Responding to Samuel's muttered speculations would draw unwelcome attention. Romulus hoped to get out with no more than a "good evening" between himself and the officer on duty. He took a deep breath, opened the front door, and stepped outside.

"All done, sir?" The young policeman grinned at Romulus.

"Yes, for now." Romulus held his bag on the opposite side from the policeman, hoping to obscure it from his view. "I'll be back later. Is that all right?"

The policeman shrugged. "I suppose so, sir. I should check with Detective Inspector Crawley, but I doubt there'll be any problem." He shivered and moved back against the wall, avoiding an unexpected gust of cold wind.

"Well, good afternoon, officer. I'll see you later." Romulus backed to the gate, his bag rustling in the breeze.

"Good afternoon, sir." The policeman glanced up from buttoning his coat, too busy to notice Romulus's bag. Romulus headed for the end of the street. Samuel appeared beside him, his eyes wild with fear.

"What are you worried about?" Romulus muttered the words, not wishing to be seen talking to himself in public. "I'm the one taking all the risks."

"The wind." Samuel hunched, as though hiding. "It knows me. I'm not weak enough for it to take me, but it's waiting. It'll always be waiting."

"Interesting. Why do you think the wind's after you?" Romulus glanced at his watch and quickened his pace. Not long ago, Romulus would have written off Samuel's comment to paranoia, but recent events made him more open to alternative explanations. The memory of Uncle Tobias resurfaced. Romulus pushed it away. There was time enough to consider Tobias's fate later. He turned the corner and increased his pace to a jog.

"That's what happens to those like me. Other kinds of evil ghosts too, I suppose. The wind takes us. It strips our minds, and we scream and wail for eternity. That's what the wind is, I think. That's why it damages things. It's the place for those too bad for heaven but who somehow never make it to hell. Or maybe it's an aspect of hell. I don't know."

"Do you consider yourself evil?"

"No. Definitely not. But I've done things. Evil things. I'm not like other ghosts, I'm something Angela made. Not like Father Michael."

Romulus stopped dead. "Who?"

"Father Michael. Father Thomas Michael. He used to be the minister at the church I went to. I met him, this afternoon. He told me to help you."

"Did he really? He told me he wasn't allowed to interfere. Something about starting a war."

"He said he couldn't help me, but if I help you it will count in my favor."

"I see. So you have to help me. Well, tell me how I can get that book out of your library. If you can't do that, you're no use at all." Romulus resumed walking.

"There is a way."

"Tell me."

"You won't like it."

"Tell me anyway." Romulus rounded another corner, where a gust of cold air took his breath for a few seconds. The library stood halfway along the street.

"I know where there's another key to the room. It's hanging on the wall. The original key. It's an antique, so it's too valuable for everyday use. It should still work though."

"Sounds good. Where is it?"

"Inside the Old Books Room."

"You're an idiot." Romulus reached the base of the library steps and started to climb.

"I can get it. I just need a woman nearby, and I can get it. I can open the door from the inside."

At the top of the steps, Romulus paused, one hand on the door. He had fifteen minutes before the library closed. Samuel's plan revolted him but there was no time to think of another. If he agreed, it meant giving Samuel the opportunity to feed, to suck life from some innocent woman. The alternative was to let Angela run loose for another night. Romulus pushed the door open.

Inside, Imogen looked up from her place in front of the issues desk and smiled at him.

Chapter Fifty-Four

"It's done." Romulus walked to the desk, beside Imogen, and placed his bag in front of her. "I've also found the book you wanted. So, now you can read it and go."

"You closed the circle. Good." Imogen opened the bag and peered inside. "And this is *Clavicula Salomonis*. What about the other one?"

"I know where it is. I'll have it by tomorrow." Romulus glanced around, but Samuel had vanished. So had the young man behind the desk, but he reappeared with John Legg a moment later.

"You have the books?" Legg's face radiated enthusiasm, as though Romulus had presented him with a map to untold riches. Or at least a means of avoiding unemployment.

"I have one of them. I'll have the other tomorrow." Romulus grimaced. He hated having to repeat himself.

"Which one?" Legg opened the bag. His face fell. "Oh, well, we have one of them. You're sure you can get the untranslated grimoire tomorrow? Early?"

"Yes. Why?"

"It's just that one of our patrons, one with particular privileges, has requested to see that book. As soon as possible."

"Let me guess." Romulus rubbed his chin, pretending to consider the matter. "Would it be Jeremy Farquhar-Jones?"

"How did you—" Legg took a moment to compose himself. "The identity of our client is confidential, of course." He peered into the bag, presumably inspecting the book for damage.

"Romulus." Imogen's eyes were wide. She leaned close to speak quietly to Romulus. "How deep do your powers go?"

"Logical deduction, nothing paranormal. The gamaliel wants that book translated so people everywhere can be sucked in, just as Watson was. It's not magic. It's just thought. You should try it sometime." Romulus turned his attention to Legg. "You'll need to put this one away safely."

"Yes, indeed." Legg lifted the book and headed for a door in the far wall. Imogen walked alongside him. Romulus followed, deep in his own thoughts. Samuel died too soon. The gamaliel can't have wanted to kill him yet. It might have been Samuel's idea in the first place, but the translation of *Geometria* was obviously to the demon's advantage. There was no way a moron like Farquhar-Jones could do it, but maybe the demon itself would perform the translation. Or maybe Farquhar-Jones planned to hire a professional. He could afford it. Either way, there was little time left. If even a partial translation appeared, it would draw others to complete the task. Samuel was right. The book was safer in his secret basement closet. Perhaps it should stay there. Romulus almost bumped into Legg when they reached the door.

"I was hoping to examine that book," Imogen said.

"I know, Doctor LeFevre, but the library is closing. I can arrange an appointment for tomorrow. We don't usually allow appointments on such short notice, but under the circumstances I think I can make an exception." He smiled at Imogen as he opened the door. She didn't return the smile. Instead, she ducked her head and pouted.

"Well, I should really be getting back to Edinburgh. Still, if you can arrange it for tomorrow morning..." Imogen's little-girl voice made Romulus wince. She had used this technique on him in the past. He was amazed to recall it had worked every time.

"I'm sure I can." Legg's smile broadened.

Sucker, thought Romulus, though he kept his mouth shut. Imogen was doing a good job of distracting Legg with her short skirt and fluttering eyelashes. She wanted to see that book, and she knew how to get her way. As long as Romulus kept quiet, Legg might not think to ask why he was tagging along. Samuel was nowhere to be seen, and Imogen showed no signs of feeling his presence. Romulus drew his lips tight, hoping Samuel was telling the truth about his control over his parasitism.

Imogen carried a parcel, brown paper wrapped with string, under her arm. Romulus had to bite his lip to keep himself from asking what it was. He endured Imogen and Legg's small talk along the short corridor, past white-painted doors to the point where the smooth, magnolia-covered walls ended. Here, it seemed as though time had slipped, flat plaster blending into bare stone blocks. The linoleum flooring ended, changing into worn flagstones. They turned at the end of the corridor, and Romulus let out a breath. This was what a library should look like, in his view.

Two doors were set in the wall to Romulus's left, both of them solid oak studded with black ironwork. Against the wall, to his right, was a long wooden bench. Romulus ran his hand over the aged wood, enjoying the delicate carvings in its surface. Fifteenth century, he guessed, or maybe sixteenth. Ahead, there was a tall, arched window at the end of this corridor. A hiss escaped Romulus when he noticed that, at some point, it had been double-glazed. It had a PVC frame wedged into the original stonework, and the top half of the window was filled with a badly-fitted pane, the edges bulging with sealant.

Legg jumped at Romulus's hiss. He turned, *Clavicula Salomonis* in its bag under one arm, a long silver key in his other hand.

"Oh, Professor Crowe, I didn't realize you were there." He followed Romulus's gaze. "Ah yes, the window. It's been like that since before I came here. It should be restored, but you know what budgets are like."

"I do." Romulus sighed. "Well, it can't be helped, I suppose. While I'm here, I'd like a quick look inside that room."

"Well, I don't really have time for a tour." Legg smiled, but shook his head.

"It's just that antiquities are a particular interest of mine. I won't keep you."

"I'm sorry. Some other time. Perhaps you could accompany Doctor LeFevre tomorrow?" Legg pushed the key into the lock of the right-hand door and turned it. The ancient door swung open on well-oiled hinges without so much as a creak. Legg disappeared into the room, leaving Romulus and Imogen in the corridor. Romulus glanced at Imogen.

"So, where's Elaine? I thought she'd be here."

"She called here on her way to the Farquhar-Jones house." Imogen moved closer. "Something to do with project funding. She was in too much of a hurry to explain."

Romulus stepped back. "Here's another bit of logical deduction for you. I'm guessing Farty-Jones has a different project in mind. I bet he's not funding any demon hunt."

"Oh?" Imogen raised an eyebrow. "You mean he might be getting into translation, of ancient texts?"

"Good thinking. I knew you could do it if you tried."

"Oh, come on, Romulus. You don't need to be such a hard-nosed swine all the time. You know you'd be floundering now if it wasn't for me. Here. You'll need this." Imogen thrust her parcel at him.

"What is it?"

"It's a slab of obsidian from Farquhar-Jones's pillars."

"For what?"

"Try thinking, professor." Imogen tapped her forehead with her finger. "Anyone who looks directly at Angela sees Angela. Chadwick saw something else. Best guess—he saw it reflected in this." She indicated the parcel.

"So?"

Imogen rolled her eyes. "So, if you use this as a mirror, you can see what you're up against. You'll also avoid being taken in by her hypnosis. She's a seriously compelling woman."

"I see." Romulus weighed the parcel in his hand. "How did you get this?"

"Elaine left it with me. Detective Poole took it to the university after we left."

"Hm." Romulus pulled at the string securing the package.

"Don't open it yet. It's a broken piece. The edges are sharp. You'll need gloves." Imogen placed her hand on Romulus's arm. "Whatever you do, don't cut yourself. Blood is a powerful thing in magic." She closed her eyes. Her grip tightened.

Legg returned to the corridor, carrying the empty plastic bag. He closed and locked the door behind him, then slipped the key into his pocket.

"Well, that's one valuable book replaced. Now, if you could—" He stared at Imogen. "Doctor LeFevre. Are you all right? You look ill." Legg dropped the bag and reached for Imogen.

At the sight of Imogen's pallor, Romulus realized what was happening. After a glance at the Old Books Room door, he grabbed for Imogen with his free arm, while Legg supported her weight. Between them, they manoeuvred her into a sitting position on the bench. She was unconscious, breathing heavily. Romulus placed the parcel beside her and looked at Legg.

"Some kind of fainting fit. Perhaps a glass of water?"

"Yes. I'll just be a moment." Legg dashed along the corridor.

Romulus muttered under his breath. "Hurry it up, Watson. We don't have all day."

Behind him, there was a click. Romulus looked around to see the Old Books Room door swing open. Samuel stood there, holding a huge book, fully twice the thickness of *Clavicula Salomonis*.

"Get the bag. Don't touch this without gloves."

Romulus grabbed the plastic bag from the floor and held it open, supporting it as Samuel slid the book inside.

"How do you propose I get this out of here?" Romulus held the book in both hands. Its weight pressed into his forearms.

"That's up to you. I'll see you back at the house." Samuel winced at the sight of Imogen. "I hope she's not too badly affected."

"Get going, Watson."

The door closed. There was a click as the lock turned. Imogen groaned. Romulus looked around for somewhere to hide the book, somewhere he could retrieve it later. His gaze fell on the window.

"Thank God for low budgets." Romulus opened the window, reflecting for a moment on how difficult it would have been had the window been original, and dropped the book outside. He winced at the thud, and hoped the grass was not too wet. Legg's footsteps echoed along the corridor. Romulus closed the window and returned to Imogen's side just as Legg turned the corner, carrying a glass of water.

"How is she?" Legg handed the water to Romulus.

"She'll be fine." Romulus held the water to Imogen's lips as she revived. "I'm sure it's not serious."

Imogen spluttered and pushed the glass away. Her green eyes flared at Romulus.

"He's here, isn't he?"

"Who?" Romulus passed the glass to Legg, who looked from one to the other in confusion.

"You know who. Samuel Watson. He's here." Imogen struggled to her feet.

"Mister Watson is dead." Legg gave Romulus a questioning look.

Romulus raised his hands. "I can assure you, Watson isn't here."

"Don't lie to me. I felt just as I did in his basement. He was here."

"But—" John Legg held the glass with both hands. His brow furrowed.

"It's just a relapse." Romulus took Imogen's arm. He picked up the parcel and led her along the corridor, speaking to Legg. "She was here when your boss died. A delayed shock reaction, I expect. She's confused. She just needs fresh air."

Legg stopped walking and looked back, his eyes searching the ground.

Romulus patted his pocket, where the gloves bulged. "I picked up the bag you dropped. I'll dispose of it later."

Legg nodded and followed Romulus and Imogen to the main room.

Imogen pulled free of Romulus's grip. "Delayed shock indeed. You know what's going on here, Romulus. I wouldn't be surprised to find you had something to do with it."

The last few patrons stood at the issues desk. They turned at the commotion.

"I'm telling you, he's not here. Now can you keep it down? This is a library, after all." Romulus tried to motion Imogen to silence. He preferred not to arouse Legg's curiosity.

"You mentioned you were in Mister Watson's basement?" Legg frowned. "Is that where you found *Clavicula Salomonis*? Perhaps the other—"

"I'll have it for you tomorrow. Don't worry." Romulus propelled Imogen out of the library, keeping up a rapid pace until they reached the parking lot.

"Where's your car?" Romulus had seen it once before, at his house, but took little notice of it.

"There." Imogen pushed Romulus away. "I can drive. I'm picking up Elaine from the Farquhar-Jones's house anyway. I expect you'll want to get back to your dead friend."

"Look, you passing out in there had nothing to do with me." Romulus held the parcel in both hands, staring down at it. He sucked at his bottom lip. "Thanks for this, anyway."

"You're welcome." Imogen's tone softened. "I hope it's of some use. I'm afraid I found nothing else to help you in the library. Their paranormal section is severely limited."

"I have all I need, I think. Some information from a dead priest." Romulus felt as awkward as a teenager. "Well you'd better go. You can't leave Elaine alone with Farty-Jones too long. Stupidity might be catching." He watched Imogen climb into her car and drive away, wondering at the meaning of the emotions in his mind. Then he remembered the book.

"Oh, hell. I hope it's not in a puddle." Romulus rushed around the building to where the window should be. He found it easily but had to climb a fence to reach it. The book lay on the wet grass below the window, its protective bag flapping in the breeze. Romulus grabbed it and pulled it half-out of the bag. It seemed dry. He wrapped it again, returned to the fence, and clambered over, his two packages making the task difficult. A gust of air brushed his face. Romulus paused, but sensed no menace in this breeze. Watson must have gone home. The malicious wind would have followed him there.

Romulus headed for his own home. It was going to be a long night, and he'd need some decent food before he started.

Chapter Fifty-Five

Samuel paced his basement floor. He had no idea how much time had passed since he left the library, probably hours. Where was the psychic? Had something happened to him? What about the book? Samuel took halting steps towards the stairs, then paced back to the circle, a performance he had repeated many times since arriving home. He'd spent all the power he had gained at the library. If he went outside, the wind would take him. The fate of Romulus, and of the priceless *Liber Astaroth*, were beyond his reach. There was nothing he could do but wait. If only there were a woman in the house.

Samuel gave a harsh laugh at the thought. His rare female visitors left quickly. No woman with any sense would come here now.

Samuel inspected his fingers. He could no longer bring their transparency under control. He could not make them appear solid. His time was running out, fast. Samuel clenched his fists. He had three options.

He could wait until he faded altogether. Then, either he'd be trapped forever in this basement, or whatever was left of him would join the lost souls in the wind. He could move through the houses on this side of the street until he found a woman, preferably more than one. They would give him enough power to walk the streets again. Both of these options damned his soul, but the second was less awful to him.

His third option depended on Romulus. If Father Michael was right, then helping the psychic dispose of Angela might just save him. Samuel considered this option as his best hope but only if Romulus arrived soon. They still had to work out how to use *Liber Astaroth*, then make the preparations, then perform the spell. Did he have enough time left?

"Where are you?" Samuel shouted at the ceiling. As if in answer, the front door creaked against its hinges. Footsteps sounded above. Low voices murmured through the ceiling. Samuel floated up the stairs.

There was a soft thud. The voices stopped. Samuel paused but heard no further sound. Curious, he reached the basement door and passed through.

The hallway was empty. Samuel looked towards the front door, then towards the kitchen.

"Hello, Samuel." The voice was honey-sweet. Samuel shifted to face the speaker, his terror making every movement slow.

Angela leaned against the frame of the lounge door wearing the tight, short dress he had bought for her. Her jet-black eyes bored into him. She swayed, every movement reminding him of the lust he had felt when alive. He was not immune to her, not in death, not even in the knowledge of what she really was.

Angela backed away from him. She placed her hand on the front door.

"Oh, but I'm forgetting my manners, Samuel. Someone wants to see you. I believe you've already met." She swung the door aside and stood in the opening, her smile filled with undisguised evil. The wind blew her long, raven hair forward as it rushed around her. Faces filled the hallway, elongated, wasted faces with dead, mindless eyes. Bony fingers formed in the air, reaching for him. He heard laughter among the howling. High, tinkling laughter. Angela held her arms out to him.

"It's this or me, Samuel. My way or the wind's way."

"No!" Samuel shrieked and pulled away from the fingers that penetrated his form. He dived headlong at the floor, passing through it to emerge in the basement below.

Samuel floated to the basement floor, his fingers now little more than thin wisps on his transparent hands. *This must be it. This must be the end.* The basement door flew open, and the air moved. Samuel looked up. Angela stood in the doorway. The wind tried to reach around her, but she held it back with a murmured word. Angela stepped onto the stairs and closed the door behind her.

"So, are you going to help me, or do I let your friends in to play with you?" Angela traced her finger along the banister as she descended the stairs. "They're so very eager to play, Samuel. Won't you join them?"

"Leave me alone." Samuel hung his head, wishing he had tears to cry. "I'm dead. Isn't that enough for you? Why do you keep tormenting me?"

"It's what I do." Angela's tone was gentle. Her voice sounded closer. "Besides, we have unfinished business, you and I. Something about a book? A translation?"

"You're not serious. I won't help you now. I can't. I'm almost gone." Samuel jerked his head up. Angela stood directly in front of him.

"That's true. You look faint, Samuel. Here." Angela opened her hand and thrust it into his chest. A pain like hot needles coursed through him. Spots of light flared in his vision, everything turned yellow, and a whistling noise grew in his ears. He sank to his knees when Angela pulled her hand back.

"That's enough. It'll keep you active long enough to help me." Angela purred above him.

"I won't do it. I won't translate the book for you." Samuel's pain subsided. He looked up at Angela's smile, through her cleavage. Part of him still wanted to reach up and cup those breasts, but he knew they were illusion. He had seen what she really looked like, in the trees of Geometria.

"Oh, but it was your idea, remember? I might never have thought of it if not for you." Angela clamped one hand onto Samuel's head and pulled him to his feet. "Besides, I don't need you to translate it. I have another sponsor for that work. All I need from you is the book."

Samuel glanced left and right. "It's not here. The police—"

"Liar." She spoke the word quietly, even as she hurled Samuel across the basement floor. He slid into the circle, smearing the chalk. Angela strolled towards him.

"Don't lie to me, Samuel. The book is here. You hid it before we went out. Don't you remember?"

"The police must have found it. They must have. They searched." Samuel ran to the nearest wall and tried to pass through it. He pressed against the brickwork. It was cold, it was hard, and it smelled of dampness. His body refused to melt into it.

"I searched. I didn't find it. You expect me to believe your pretty uniformed men did what I could not?" Angela's voice remained calm. She pulled his head back then smashed it against the wall.

Samuel slid to the floor, his hands to his head. He took them away, expecting to see blood. There was none, but there was so much pain his skull must have split open. Angela spun in a circle, sniffing the air. Samuel flinched, expecting another blow.

"What's that smell?" Angela moved around the basement, her hips swaying. "It's a new smell. Something that wasn't here before. Something dead." She stared at Samuel. "Surely you haven't been entertaining one of your lady friends here?"

"No." Samuel cowered against the wall. Angela sniffed at the wooden paneling on the wall opposite the stairs.

"It's in here, Samuel. How does this open?"

"It doesn't. It's just a wall."

"Just a wall." Angela smiled as she walked towards him, hips and breasts swinging in unison. Samuel stared, mesmerised by her beauty. She stopped and reached down, grasped his head, then dragged him back to the wooden wall.

"Just a wall? Let's see." Angela pulled Samuel upright and used his head as a battering ram to break the wood. He screamed at every blow, praying he would lose consciousness, but such mercy was denied him now. The wood cracked, then splintered, under the relentless hammering. Finally it gave, leaving a gaping hole in the paneling. Angela released her hold, letting Samuel fall to the floor. She looked down at him.

"Not just a wall, it seems."

Samuel curled into a ball, clutching his head. Behind him, the sound of tearing wood marked Angela's entry into his secret cupboard. When the noise stopped, Samuel turned to see a harsh expression on Angela's face. She held the corpse of Alfred Melchior at arm's length, towards him.

"I see you've been meddling. You took my sisters' favorite toy, Samuel. What will you give them in return?" She threw Melchior at Samuel. The rigid body bounced on Samuel's prostrate form and fell beside him. Melchior's dried eyes landed level with his own. Samuel scrambled backwards.

"You tortured him. You're evil. All of you."

"Evil and good are trivial human definitions. They mean nothing to me." Angela tilted her head to one side. "You'll have to make amends, Samuel. You'll have to replace Alfred in my sisters' affections."

Samuel choked back a laugh. "Too late. I'm already dead."

"Dead, but not gone. When they get here, they can still play with you. Even if you run with the wind, they can still reach you. Now, let's see what else you have in your little hideaway here." She reached inside and took out *Geometria ton Zoon*. "Ah, my book. You see, I knew it was here somewhere."

"It's not yours. It never was. It was made to trap you and it worked. It'll work again." Samuel struggled to speak through the agony in his head.

"No, it won't. Traps such as this work only once. I won't fall for it again." Angela moved to stand over him She reached down into his chest. "Now, I loaned you a little something. I'll just take it back."

The hot needles burst in Samuel again. He screamed. Angela withdrew her hand. All Samuel's pain left him. He lurched to his feet.

"What did you do to me?"

"I loaned you power, Samuel. It's a pity you didn't work out how to use it." Angela laughed and headed for the stairs. Samuel followed. Halfway up, Angela stopped and spoke over her shoulder.

"Are you following me? Before you do, I suggest you remember who waits outside that door." She continued her ascent.

Samuel watched her, his eyes fixed on her buttocks. Even now, Angela's allure overrode his knowledge of her reality. "What are you going to do?"

Angela opened the door. "That's no concern of yours. You should concentrate on finding sustenance, Samuel. You look unwell." She stepped into the hallway, where the wind shrieked, and closed the door behind her.

Samuel sank through the stairs, to the floor, where he knelt and howled his anguish. The wind battered at the door and howled louder.

Chapter Fifty-Six

From the moment Imogen picked her up outside the Farquhar-Jones house, Elaine had said very little. She watched the countryside turn into town through the car's side windows. Marchway had been a beautiful place when she first arrived here. Now the houses pressed around her, every arrangement of windows and doors a terrible face that threatened to bite.

Losing the grant was a small issue. Chadwick had lost his life. A mere research project could not compete with that. Jeremy's gleeful description of the scene had horrified her to such an extent she would not have accepted his money if he had offered double.

In any event, he offered nothing. He would spend his funds elsewhere. Elaine suspected the demon, Angela, had diverted Jeremy from interest in Elaine's project. It could not allow her to discover its true identity.

Imogen's attempt at conversation had forced Elaine deeper into her shell, rather than draw her out. Imogen mentioned something about obsidian, and about Chadwick's death, but her tone had been clinical. Detached. Very like Romulus. Imogen had never met Chadwick, but that was no excuse to crow about how Chadwick's death had enabled her to deduce that the Farquhar-Jones's hallway pillars were clad with obsidian.

The ten-minute drive passed in a sullen silence. Imogen concentrated on her driving, for which Elaine was grateful. It was not until they turned into Ballantrae Avenue that Elaine sat upright in her seat, her brooding thoughts forgotten.

"What's going on?" Elaine stared at the flashing blue lights outside Samuel's house as they passed. Several neighbors stood around, held back by uniformed policemen. Imogen cruised past the house, looking for somewhere to park. Both sides of the street were lined with parked cars. The first space she found was at least a hundred yards from the house.

Elaine had the door open even before the car stopped. She slammed it closed and ran along the street. Had she seen—yes. There was Romulus's car, its rust and blue color scheme unmistakable even under the yellow streetlight glow. She pushed back her hair, holding it against the wind that whipped it around her face. Flattened cardboard boxes still filled the car's rear windows. She glanced behind her, saw Imogen following, and made for Samuel's house.

Imogen caught up with Elaine while she tried to push through the small crowd of people. Together they reached the front of the crowd, where a policeman stopped them.

"I'm afraid you can't come any closer, ladies. This is a police investigation." He held out one hand to stop them, the other holding his helmet against the blustering air.

"Our friend is in there. He's—oh, God." Elaine covered her mouth. Three stretchers were carried out of the house, one of them covered completely. Of the other two, one was a man, one a woman, neither of whom she recognized. The white sheets fluttered but had been securely tucked under all three bodies. The two stretchers with uncovered faces were lifted into an ambulance, while the covered body was placed in a plain white van with the single word "Police" stenciled on the side. Imogen squeezed Elaine's arm.

Crawley emerged from the house. Elaine called to him, but her cries were drowned out by the ambulance's siren as it pulled away. The white van flashed blue lights but did not use its siren. It had no need to hurry. Crawley spoke to another uniformed officer. Elaine and Imogen called and waved. The other officer nodded and entered the house. Crawley lit a cigarette. Only then did he look towards the crowd and notice the two frantically waving women. He walked towards them.

"You can let these two through, officer," he said. Elaine and Imogen followed Crawley through Samuel's front gate. He stopped them before they entered the house.

"I don't want you going in there. One of our female officers passed out as soon as she crossed the threshold." He puffed at his cigarette, making it flare in the night air. "The two officers who dragged her out said she aged ten years in a matter of seconds. They came to check on the constable who should have been on duty, when he didn't check in by radio." Another long draw at the cigarette took almost an inch of its length. "We found him babbling in the lounge. All he says is 'beautiful,' with a mad smile plastered over his face."

"Where's Romulus? Is he—" Elaine moved her head, trying to see inside the house.

"Is he alive?" Imogen choked on the words.

"I'm afraid so." Romulus appeared in the doorway, carrying a brown parcel tied with string and a roughly square package wrapped in a plastic bag. "You can't get rid of me so easily."

"Romulus." Imogen ran to him and flung her arms around his neck. Romulus disentangled her and stepped back.

"What's wrong with you, woman? Show a little professional decorum." Romulus's face was hard, but Elaine thought she saw something in his eyes. Embarrassment? Maybe a hint of satisfaction? He was extraordinarily hard to read.

"We saw the body carried out. We thought, well..." Elaine looked at her shoes.

"You thought a mere demon killed me? It's not that easy. So, what are you two doing here? It's not a safe place for women," Romulus said.

"I'm hoping one of the three of you can tell me what happened." Crawley finished his cigarette and dropped the butt, stamping it out on the concrete path.

Elaine looked at Romulus. "Was it Angela? She'd left Farquhar-Jones's house before I arrived there."

"Where's the grimoire?" Imogen stood beside Elaine, wiping at her eyes with a handkerchief.

"Yes, she was here. No, the book isn't." Romulus looked from one to the other. "She's taken it. Her name's not Angela. It's Ailo."

"What?" Imogen stepped forward. "Ailo? How can you know?"

"Watson's inside, half out of his mind. I asked him if Angela had the book, and all he said was 'not Angela.' I kept at him. Eventually I found that Angela does indeed have the book, but her real name is Ailo. Watson says she's the daughter of Samael the Black, also known as Asmodeus."

Imogen's lower lip jutted. "One of the daughters of Asmodeus and Lilith. I've heard the name. I think Ailo was one of the first."

"Does that matter?" Elaine furrowed her brow.

"If I'm right, she's more than just a succubus. She's one of the originals. She might be almost as powerful as Lilith," Imogen said. "She can probably call on Asmodeus for help if she's cornered."

"Oh, for Christ's sake." Crawley lit another cigarette. "Look. I have a basement smashed to bits. I have two officers carted away in an ambulance, one in a coma, the other apparently insane. I have another corpse, looks like it's been dead for a hundred years. I've seen a man reduced to mince and a woman who should have been twenty-six die of extreme old age." He took a long draw and blew smoke into the wind. "All that's just this afternoon. I'm not a happy man. I don't care who's the daughter of whom or the original of what. Just tell me who to arrest."

"There's one arrest you can make." The light of mischief danced in Romulus's eyes. "By now, Jeremy Farquhar-Jones is in possession of a rare and valuable book stolen from the library."

"Jeremy Farquhar-Jones." Crawley's voice was flat. He threw his half-smoked cigarette to the ground and stamped on it. "Shit," he said.

Chapter Fifty-Seven

"I don't see the problem." Romulus shifted the weight of his parcels. "He's the only one in all this who's eligible for your handcuffs. Plus, we have to get that book away from him before he does something extremely dangerous with it."

"Oh, it's so simple, isn't it?" Sarcasm dripped from Crawley's words.

"Well, yes. You just get a search warrant, grab the book, and it's done." Romulus looked around the group, wondering at Crawley's attitude. Elaine and Imogen shrugged.

"Getting a warrant outside working hours isn't so easy. We have to visit a magistrate at home." Crawley took out another cigarette and lit it, cupping his hands around the flame. "This isn't Hollywood. British magistrates aren't happy about police visits after hours."

"Okay, so a magistrate gets a little upset. This is an emergency." Romulus shook his head. It seemed logical enough to him.

"You do know who the local magistrate is?" Crawley raised his eyebrows.

"I don't think I've ever met one." Romulus looked to Elaine and Imogen who shrugged again. "Besides, I've just moved here."

"Eustace Farquhar-Jones." Crawley accentuated his words by jabbing his cigarette at Romulus. "He's the damn magistrate. You want me to ask him for a warrant to search his own house?"

"Oh." Romulus looked away. "Well, try another approach. Tell him his son's in possession of stolen property. He'll likely force the chinless idiot to hand over the book to avoid a scandal. Getting the book out of there has to be our top priority."

"I see." Crawley looked up and down the street, took a long draw on his cigarette and nodded. "So, when my superiors ask what I'm doing about the deaths and other insane things happening in Marchway, you want me to tell them I was chasing an overdue library book. Oh, I can imagine their reaction now. Tell me, would you have any jobs for an ex-detective in your university?"

"It's too dangerous, anyway." Imogen moved between Romulus and Crawley. "If Angela—Ailo is confronted by someone trying to take her book, she'll kill to keep it."

"We have to get it. Do you know how long it'll take her to call another one through? No? I thought not. We're out of time." Romulus ran his free hand through his hair, shifting the weight of the packages under his arm.

Elaine nodded at them. "What's that?"

"That's the piece of obsidian I gave him." Imogen narrowed her eyes. "What's in the bag? It looks like a book. A big one."

"Something the priest told me I'd need. I have to get Watson back into some semblance of sanity so he can tell me what it's about." Romulus moved so the packages were partly hidden by his body.

"Where did you get it?" Imogen stared at him, her eyes narrow.

"I'll tell you about it later. Look, you two have to go. Watson's getting hungry again. He didn't take much from the policewoman he attacked. The wind's keeping him inside for now, but there's no telling what he'll do if he gets desperate." Romulus backed towards the house. Crawley walked to the front gate, which Poole was opening.

"You took it from the library while I was unconscious." Imogen's small hands formed into fists. "Didn't you?"

"Don't be ridiculous. The room was locked. And how would I smuggle out something this size? Besides, I was far too busy looking after you to worry about a book." Romulus held Imogen's gaze. Breaking eye contact would give away his lies, and he had no time for a confrontation now.

Elaine stepped forward. "What do you mean, the wind keeps him inside?"

Romulus rolled his eyes. Did he have to explain every detail?

"It's a long story. Get going, both of you. See what you can find out about this Ailo. I need to know the risk of this demon calling for reinforcements." Romulus already knew the answer. As long as Father Michael and his like kept out of the way, Ailo had no right to call for backup. It was Romulus against the demon, one demon. He paused, staring at nothing. How had it come to this?

Only a few days ago, Romulus had been secure in the knowledge there were no ghosts, demons, goblins, or anything of the kind. Now he was expected to battle a demon helped by a dead priest and a man who was, himself, a dangerous ghost. He was aware of Elaine leading Imogen away, of Imogen's suspicious looks, and of Crawley and Poole approaching him. Most of all, he was aware of the wind. There were voices in the wind, and one of them whispered his name.

Chapter Fifty-Eight

"You can't be sure." Elaine hurried to keep up with Imogen on the way back to the car.

"Oh, I can be pretty sure." Imogen jammed her key into the car door, then yanked it open. "To think, all these years, I imagined we'd be back together someday. He's changed so much. Oh, he was always arrogant, but there was a time he had feelings. He's completely heartless now."

Elaine ran around the car and climbed into the passenger side just as Imogen started the engine.

"Maybe he found the book somewhere else."

"Where?" Imogen grated the car into first gear. "Where else, in Marchway, could he possibly have found a book like that?"

"We didn't see it. We don't know it was one of the old books." Elaine clung to the door as Imogen roared the car into the street.

"No, we didn't see it. But what else could it be? He must have used me, Elaine. He must have let Samuel Watson take life from me so he could get the book." Imogen blinked away tears. She slowed the car, concentrating on the road ahead. They sat in silence until they stopped outside Elaine's flat. Elaine paused with her hand on the car door, ready to open it.

"What will you do?" She avoided looking into Imogen's face.

"Tomorrow, I'll visit the library, do the work I need to do with *Key of Solomon*, then I'm leaving. I won't be back."

"Romulus still has to deal with the succubus. Surely you can't leave until you know how it turned out?" Elaine narrowed her eyes. Imogen turned her head away.

"Why not? I can't do a damn thing here. I don't want the demon to win, obviously. I'm sure Romulus can beat it, but can you imagine how smug he's going to be?"

Elaine could, indeed, envision Romulus with smugness oozing from him. She had seen it before. "Can't we do something to help?"

"Nothing." Imogen banged her hand on the steering wheel. "I'm the demonologist, not him. I should be in there, I should be studying this. I can't even enter the house, or I'll be sucked dry by Samuel. That's the worst part. We just have to wait."

There was a long pause, in which the low hum of the car's engine sounded unnaturally loud in the quiet street. Elaine sucked at her teeth. She shared Imogen's frustration at being excluded from what was possibly the greatest find in any parapsychologist's career. Her frustration was tinged with concern for Romulus's safety, although Romulus gave the outward impression of indestructibility. Elaine sniffed to disguise a sudden chortle. He probably was indestructible. She should feel sorry for the demon. Elaine took a deep breath before speaking.

"The job you mentioned. Is it still open?" Elaine examined her fingernails. It wasn't a good time to ask, but she had to know.

"Yes." Imogen's tone softened. "Yes, of course. I'll send you an application form, but it'll be a formality. The job's yours."

Elaine stared through the window at the building that housed her flat. Did she really want to move to Edinburgh? She was a long way from her family now, but Edinburgh was so much further.

Doubts flashed through her mind. Was Imogen really that much better than Romulus? Was she offering the job because of Elaine's abilities or because it would be a stick in the eye for Romulus? Elaine didn't want to be a pawn in their fight. She licked her lips. Maybe she thought this way because she was trained to have an analytical mind. Maybe she thought this way because she'd spent too long with Romulus. Was she ready to move on? She turned to Imogen.

"He's not as bad as he seems, really. I think he cares about you. He's just in denial."

Imogen snorted. "His whole life has been one long denial. Forget him. What about this job?"

Elaine opened the door and climbed out of the car before replying. "I'll have to think about it." She started to swing the car door closed, but caught it before it met the frame. She put her head back inside. "Why don't you come in for a coffee, or something stronger? I have internet access. We can look up this Ailo together."

"I thought you'd never ask." Imogen switched off the engine.

Chapter Fifty-Nine

In Samuel's hallway, Romulus took the white cotton gloves from his pocket and put them on. Crawley pushed the front door closed, then turned to face him.

"I've sent Poole home. No sense in both of us staying here all night." Crawley shivered as the door blew open, letting the cold wind into the hallway. He pushed it closed again, then slipped the bolt at the top of the door to hold it.

"I don't get it. You say this monster of yours killed Nathaniel Attlee, yet there was no sign of forced entry at his house. Here, it broke the lock to get in. Why?"

"Why ask me? The expert's in the basement." Romulus took the book from its bag, and stuffed the bag into his pocket.

"What's this?" Crawley moved closer, inspecting the book. "Looks like an old and valuable book to me. Like the ones you wanted us to find. I hope you haven't been running us in circles, professor."

"No, of course not." Romulus cradled the book in his hands, the package containing the obsidian slab still under his arm. He couldn't very well tell the police how he came into possession of this book, but Crawley's raised eyebrow indicated he wasn't prepared to let the matter rest.

"So, how did you get it?"

"Samuel Watson took it from the library as well as the other two. One of those two is back at the library. I took it there this afternoon. The other is at the Farquhar-Jones's house, as I told you." Romulus decided to leave his part in the theft unspoken. Samuel was immune from prosecution, but he was not.

"I see. So how many books are actually missing?" Crawley clasped his hands behind his back. "An approximate figure will do."

"As far as I know, two. I returned the other one." Romulus fought down his rising anger. "Now, if you've finished hunting for reasons to arrest me, I suggest we get into the basement and talk to Watson."

"Let's go. Bear in mind, though, that as far as I can tell, you're talking to yourself. I can't see this ghost."

"You've seen what he can do." Romulus opened the basement door.

"Well, I've seen some killings, but nobody saw Watson commit them. Not even you. Plus, there was the incident in the grocer's shop and the car crash."

"What?" Romulus stopped in the doorway.

"Oh, you don't know about those? That's encouraging. It seems your ghosts don't tell you everything." Crawley's face developed a grim smile. "A mass fainting fit in the shop, and two women reduced to decrepit husks in the car crash. Rather like the husk we found in the basement here."

"Surely you're not thinking of blaming me for that?"

"Ordinarily, no. In other circumstances, I'd have said the body's been dead far too long for you to have anything to do with it. After those women this afternoon, though, I can't really say how long he was dead." Crawley ran his tongue over his teeth. "You told me Watson only kills women. The body we found here was male."

"Watson didn't kill him. I don't think he did, anyway." Romulus started down the stairs. "The dead man is Alfred Melchior. Apparently he used to be the librarian."

"Really? Must be before my time. I'll have to look it up." Crawley followed Romulus down the stairs. "So we're safe?"

"From Watson, yes. From the gamaliel, no. You don't have to be here, you know."

"Last time I left you alone here, the place got trashed again and our body count went up by one. I'm staying."

"Well, unless you can read this old book, you're not going to be much use." Romulus reached the bottom of the stairs and placed the book, and his package, on the floor. He unwrapped the jagged stone fragment and laid it beside the book, wondering if his thin gloves offered enough protection from the sharp edges. Crawley stood beside him, pulling on a pair of latex gloves. Romulus shot him a quizzical glance.

"It's still a crime scene. Remember that." Crawley looked around the basement. "So where's your ghost?"

"He was under the stairs earlier." Romulus walked around the staircase. Samuel sat huddled into a ball, muttering to himself. Romulus stared down at him, hands on hips.

"Watson. Pull yourself together. It's time."

"No time. No time left. No book. No life." Samuel stared at his fingers. "Fading. She's won."

"She has not won." Romulus wished he could slap this phantom, but Samuel was insubstantial, partially transparent. "Not unless you let her. I have *Liber Astaroth*, and I need you to read it."

"Can't. You have to read it. I can't." Samuel looked up. "The words have to be spoken aloud. I have no voice. Only you can hear me. Only you can save me."

"Oh, no." Romulus held up his hands. "Don't make me out to be some kind of savior. I'm a scientist. This is an investigation, an experiment. The only difference is we get just the one chance at it. There'll be no second attempt."

"You can save me."

"No. You have to save yourself." Romulus considered the hapless specter. Watson needed some hope, something to cling to. "I can give you the chance to do that. Help me, and you'll be helping yourself."

"What's going on?" Crawley stood beside Romulus, his eyes searching the space beneath the stairs. Romulus motioned him to silence.

"Will it work?" Samuel's voice wavered.

"Of course it will. Once the gamaliel is gone, you'll be free."

"Really?"

"Definitely." *Maybe*. Romulus watched Samuel. Somewhere behind the madness in those ghostly eyes, a spark of sanity ignited. "There's not much time. If we're going to stop this demon, we have to do it now."

"Shouldn't we wait until midnight?" Crawley said.

"That's three hours away. Watson might be too weak to be of any use by then." Romulus pursed his lips, then spoke to Samuel.

"Does it matter, Watson? Do we have to do this at a particular time?"

"Don't know. I don't remember what time it was when I called Angela—Ailo here. That's the only time I've done this. I don't know."

"Well, we have to try. Come on, Watson. Tell me how to use this book." Romulus walked back to where he had left *Liber Astaroth* and lifted it. Samuel appeared at his left, then moved to his right to avoid Crawley. Romulus opened the book and held it so that Samuel could see.

Samuel shook his head. "These books don't come with an index, or a table of contents. We'll have to work through it."

Romulus groaned. "That could take all night." He lowered the book to the floor and knelt in front of it. It was far too heavy to hold for long. Samuel waved his hand whenever he wanted Romulus to turn the page.

"Is this going to take long?" Crawley shuffled his feet.

"I hope not. Watson, have you seen anything useful yet?" Romulus glanced at the ghost, whose face showed something close to rapture as he studied the ancient pages.

"Turn the page," Samuel said.

Samuel's eyes lit up at a particularly detailed set of drawings, inlaid with spectacular colors. "Wow," he said. Now this is interesting."

"What? Have you found something?" Romulus examined the page. The drawings showed plants that looked like nothing he had ever seen, curled around images of women. The writing flowed around the drawings. Romulus squinted. It didn't look like Latin to him.

"This is a coded script. I can't read much of it, but it looks like it describes the origin of *Geometria ton Zoon*, and another book, *Arithmetike ton Kosmon*. It's fascinating stuff." Samuel leaned closer to the page.

"Is it what we need?" Romulus drew back, avoiding contact with the ghost.

"No. It's amazing, though."

Romulus hissed through his teeth. "We don't have time to indulge in academic details now. There'll be time for that later."

Samuel looked up. "For you, maybe. For me, I'm not so sure."

This might, indeed, be Samuel Watson's last chance to read this, or any, book. Nevertheless, time was against them. Romulus checked his watch.

"It's nearly ten. We have to move on." Romulus tried to make the comment as gentle as possible, but his impatience made it sound harsh. He reached past Samuel and turned the page. Behind him, the snick of a lighter preceded the smell of tobacco smoke. Romulus turned his head. Crawley sat on the stairs, a cigarette dangling from his lips.

"Getting anywhere?" Crawley looked hopeful.

"Not yet." Romulus returned his attention to the book. Samuel waved his hand, indicating he wanted the page turned.

By the time they passed the mid-point of *Liber Astaroth*, Romulus had trouble keeping his eyes open. The pages blurred in his vision, colors blending with the multitude of different scripts in a dozen different hands. It looked to him like nothing more than some Dark Ages scrapbook, a collection of the deranged ramblings of semi-literate magicians. When Samuel gasped and jabbed his finger into the parchment, Romulus automatically turned to the next page.

"Wait. Go back." The urgency in Samuel's voice startled Romulus out of his torpor. He turned the page back, then stood, stretching the cramp from his legs while Samuel scanned the page.

Crawley sat slumped on the stairs, a scattering of cigarette ends and ash at his feet. Romulus nudged him with his foot.

"Huh?" Crawley rubbed sleep from his eyes. "I must have dozed off for a moment. What time is it?"

"Nearly eleven. Looks like we'll be playing our game at midnight after all."

"Shit." Crawley checked his watch. "I'd better phone my wife. She'll be worried sick." He ran up the stairs. At the top, he called down to Romulus. "How long do you think this will take?"

"I have no idea. Maybe all night."

Crawley groaned and stepped into the hallway. Romulus stood over Samuel. He could see the book through the ghost's head.

"Well? Have you found it?"

Samuel sat back, his face grim. "There are two parts. The second part is where you banish the demon." He looked up. "The first part is where you call it here. I didn't realize it would have to be this way. I hoped the banishing spell would work at a distance."

"Can't be helped. How do we contain it once it's here?"

"There's a circle." Samuel indicated a diagram in the open book. "We stay outside the circle. The demon's trapped within it. If it works." Samuel hugged himself.

"What are you worried about? You're already dead. It can't hurt you."

"Yes, she can. You have no idea what she can do. Being dead doesn't make me safe."

Romulus sniffed. "You're in less danger than I am, that's for sure. What about the circle we already have. Can we use that?"

"No, we'll need to redraw it according to this plan." Samuel looked around the basement floor. "The chalks you left are still here, and the candles. We'll use the outline of my circle, but the inner sigils will all have to be redone."

Crawley reappeared at the top of the stairs. Romulus called up to him.

"Bring down a wet cloth from the kitchen or a washcloth from the bathroom. Hurry up. We have a lot to do."

Crawley leaned on the banister. "What do you want that for? I hope you're not going to mess around with evidence."

"Just do it." Romulus glared at Crawley. His brow tightened as he pressed a silent insistence into his words. Crawley flinched, then left the room. Romulus turned back to Samuel, who was regarding him with a strange look.

"You have a very persuasive manner." Samuel said.

"So I'm told." Romulus picked up *Liber Astaroth* and carried it to the circle, keeping it open at the page Samuel had indicated. He placed it just outside the circle, then retrieved the fragment of obsidian. Its shattered edges pressed into his fingers. After placing it beside the book, he inspected his gloves. Frayed in places, but not cut. Romulus rubbed his fingers together.

"You'll need to direct this, Watson. I realize you're no practical use, but you'll have to show me where to draw what. I take it we erase the whole thing, apart from the circle?"

Samuel examined the book. "Everything except the outer and inner circles. It'll take too long to redraw them. It's important to keep both circles intact. No gaps."

Romulus shook his head. "It's hard to believe something can travel from the depths of hell, yet can't cross a line of chalk."

"The chalk's just a symbol. The demon is held by the spell. The boundary of the spell is defined by the visual symbol of the chalk. I thought you were an expert."

"No. The expert in this sort of thing is Imogen. Doctor LeFevre." Romulus curled his lip. "Your red-haired feeding station. We're denied her expertise because you can't help knocking her unconscious every time she shows up."

Samuel said nothing but knelt in front of the book and stared at it. He was losing visibility at an alarming rate now. Romulus hoped he wouldn't vanish altogether before their work was completed.

A clatter of footsteps on the wooden stairs announced Crawley's return, accompanied by the odor of fresh cigarette smoke. He arrived beside Romulus carrying a dripping towel.

"Best I could find," he said.

"Watch what you're doing with that." Romulus pushed Crawley back, away from *Liber Astaroth* and the circle. "Wring it out a little. I need you to wipe out everything except the circles here, but do it carefully. Don't break the lines of the circles."

Crawley looked from Romulus to the circle and back. "You want me to destroy evidence?" He dropped his cigarette and stamped it out.

"We're going to redraw it. A little different, but nobody will know."

"I don't know." Doubt showed on Crawley's face.

"I promise you, nobody will know the difference. It'll be a circle filled with bizarre symbols, just like before. The symbols will be different, but who will know?"

Crawley wrung the towel until it stopped dripping. Water pooled on the concrete floor. He held the damp towel in both hands.

"We're running out of time." Romulus was running out of patience. "Once we've done this, the killings will stop. It's the only way. Face it, you can't arrest this killer. The only way to be rid of it is to help me." Romulus paused. "Besides, what harm can it do? Really? The circle, as it is, tells you nothing. There's also the risk it could be used to bring more of the gamaliel through. It's best to get rid of it."

"I suppose..."

"Good enough. Wipe out the chalk marks, but try not to break the circles. And don't get the floor too wet."

Crawley knelt and rubbed at the chalk. The markings disappeared, but the towel left a wet streak behind it. Romulus puffed out his cheeks. His chalk was unlikely to stick on the wet floor, and the basement was too cold for the water to evaporate.

"Watson," Romulus said. "Do you have a hair dryer in the house?"

Samuel looked up from the book. "I used to, but it's broken. Never felt the need to buy a new one. What do you want it for?"

"The floor. It's going to take ages to dry on its own." Romulus racked his brain for an alternative. "Well, what about a space heater? Anything that blows hot air."

"There's a space heater in the spare bedroom." Samuel rose to his feet.

"Show me." Romulus ran up the stairs, Samuel floated up through the ceiling. A few moments later, Romulus carried an aging plastic heater into the basement. Its cord was frayed in places, and the plug was blackened from overheating. Brown streaks showed along the once-white casing.

Crawley looked up. "Is that thing safe?"

"It's safer than calling up a demon," Romulus said.

Samuel pointed out a socket on the wall. Romulus plugged in the heater, and it whirred to life, belching dust into the air. Seconds later, the stench of incinerated dust filled the room. Romulus followed Crawley's path around the circle. The room grew uncomfortably warm, but he ignored it. Before he reached the far side of the circle, the heater cut out.

"What's up? Is it broken?" Crawley stood and flung the towel aside. All of the complex sigils were gone, and the circles were intact.

Romulus looked behind himself. "Damn. The plug's pulled out. The cable won't reach any further." He pushed the plug back into place, and the heater resumed its whirring. "Crawley. Aim this at the damp areas. I'll start filling in the details on the dry parts."

With Samuel's guidance, Romulus copied the diagram from the book onto the floor, pausing once to search the far corner of the basement for the brown chalk he'd flung there earlier. The small piece he found was enough, although it had lost its label, so Romulus had to keep it apart from the other chalks. Finally, the circle was completed, the heater switched off, and the candles lit. The smell of burning dust lingered in the air.

Crawley flexed his fingers. "That thing was hot, and I'm sure I could hear arcing inside. You get into some dangerous practices, professor."

Romulus held the book in both hands. "To coin a phrase, detective, 'you ain't seen nothing yet'. This is where the dangerous part begins." He nodded to Samuel, now little more than a faint wraith. Samuel pointed to a passage in the book.

"This one first. It calls her here."

Romulus took a deep breath. "*Oculi Tetragrammaton.*" With each word, the pronunciation became easier, as before. "*Asperges me, Domine, hyssopo et mundabor. Lavabis me, et super nivem dealbabor.*"

The bare light bulb buzzed, brightened, then dimmed. Within the circle, a dark mist twisted the air. Crawley moved towards the stairs. Samuel backed up against the wall.

Romulus's voice deepened, took on a hollow, echoing timber. "*Geburah, qui rex secundus est, unde Bittul atque Corruptio Achuraïm Patris hoc nomine indignatur.*"

The mist spun faster, reaching but never breaking the boundary of the circle. Romulus blinked sweat from his eyes. He continued reading. Deep in the swirling vapors, something moved.

Chapter Sixty

Imogen placed her glass on the table with careful precision. Elaine poured vodka into it, keeping one eye closed as she did so.

"What time is it?" Imogen asked. She stared at Elaine's computer and whistled.

Elaine squinted at the clock. "Nearly midnight." She slumped into the chair beside Imogen's. "Did you find something?"

"Most of the internet is crap. It's full of modern derivations and made-up stuff, and searching on demonic names brings up a heck of a lot of game sites." Imogen scrolled the screen. "This site, though, is a good one. Lilith's brood is called the lilin, and there are subsets, including the gamaliel." She shook her head. "I already knew that, of course, but I forgot this part." Imogen pushed back from the computer and picked up her glass.

Elaine narrowed, then widened her eyes until they focused on the screen. "Hey, she has a heck of a lot of names. Laylah, Agrath—Agrath bath—what is that?—Mahlath?"

Imogen swirled her drink. "The Sumerians knew about her. Later, the Assyrians called her Lilitu. She's been long known as a succubus and a demonic wind-spirit."

"Wind." Elaine pursed her lips. "Romulus said something about wind. It kept Samuel inside."

"She can control the wind. I suppose Rom will be safe from that aspect as long as he's in the house." Imogen frowned. "Though why should Watson be scared of the wind? He's a ghost."

"No idea." Elaine leaned back in her chair. "If we were at Samuel's house, we could get Romulus to ask."

"He probably already has, though I doubt he'll share that information with us. Oh, this is futile." Imogen switched off the computer. "The greatest find in demonology is happening right now, and I can't be part of it. Worst of all, that selfish shit is going to get all the glory." Imogen sipped at the vodka. "It wouldn't be so bad if I weren't right here in town."

"We could go there." Elaine raised her own glass. "My own research suggests that alcohol blocks psychic ability."

"Only in the drinker. It's not necessarily protective." Imogen smiled. "I read that paper. I suppose you did most of the work, and Romulus's name just slipped in there?"

Elaine flushed. "Well, sort of. It was while I was writing my PhD, so naturally—"

"Yes, of course, your supervisor's name would be on the work." Imogen took another sip. "Sorry. I'm blaming him for things he hasn't done now."

"It's only fair. He's avoided blame for a lot of things he *has* done. Anyway, what do you say? Let's go and see how he's getting on." It was the courage of drink, Elaine knew, but she was supposed to be Romulus's assistant. She had as much right as Imogen to be present at the summoning of this demon, if not more. She swayed a little as she stood. "You know what? I bet Romulus doesn't have a camera or a voice recorder with him." She pulled open a drawer beneath the computer desk. “He leaves all that stuff to me, and he’s going to blame me when he doesn’t have it.”

“Oh?” Imogen took another sip. “What about those EMF meters and infrared thermometers you ghost types use?”

“Cameras and voice recorder. Sound and vision. Romulus says those are the only things that will ever provide any kind of evidence of anything. The rest is just baggage.”

“Right.” Imogen set her glass down. “So how does this help us get involved?”

“It means we have an excuse—no, an obligation—to turn up at Samuel’s house with the proper equipment.” Elaine lifted two cameras and a tiny digital recorder. “He’d never forgive us if we didn’t.” She assumed an innocent expression.

Imogen grinned. “Great, but I can’t drive. I’m a little tipsy.”

Elaine giggled. “This isn’t Edinburgh, it’s Marchway. It’s only eleven streets wide and two miles long. The only place I’ve needed transport to is the Farquhar-Jones mansion.”

“So, how far is it to Samuel’s house?”

“Let’s see. It’s about fifteen minutes to the library from here. We can be there in twenty minutes, thirty if we stagger too much.”

Both women laughed. They grabbed coats. Elaine found two pairs of gloves, two woolen hats, and a bag for her equipment. Outside, the biting cold wind plucked at their clothes and played with their hair. Ignoring the unease she felt at the wind’s apparently personal attention, Elaine led Imogen through the sodium-lit streets of Marchway.

Chapter Sixty-One

The incantation ended, and Romulus drew a breath. The mist within the circle dissipated to reveal a beautiful woman with a confused expression. Romulus stared. Once he had considered Imogen beautiful, but this was beyond anything his imagination could have conceived. She wore a long, blue dress, split up the side, which did nothing to disguise the contours beneath. Romulus had often heard the term "sprayed-on" used to describe tight-fitting clothes, but never before had it seemed so apt. There was not even the suggestion of a wrinkle in the material, not a trace of a line revealing any undergarments. He tore his gaze away from her with an effort.

Crawley clung to the banister, his mouth hanging open. Samuel was on his knees, his eyes downcast. It took Romulus a moment to bring the faint ghost into focus.

"Back where I started." The woman regained her composure. "Well, magician, what is your bidding? I believe those are the correct words, although it's been quite some time since I stood in a circle of constraint."

Romulus ignored her. "Watson. Come here. I need you to tell me what to do next."

Samuel rose to his feet. He avoided looking at Angela as he approached.

"Oh, the magician has no power." Angela's sultry voice filled the room. "He needs the help of poor dead Samuel." She took a step forward. "Come to me, Samuel. Let me help you. I can give you solid form again."

"Only so you can hurt me." Samuel stopped walking. "Like last time."

"You refuse me? Your Angela?"

"Yes, I refuse you—Ailo."

"So, you've learned my name. It would help you, if you found a magician of any ability. This worthless creature doesn't know how to make use of your knowledge. You deny me. Then accept the consequence." Angela's lip curled.

"Come on, Watson. The sooner we do this, the better." Romulus spoke through gritted teeth. The demon's insult made this personal.

"There's another here. I've seen him before." Angela turned her jet-black eyes to Crawley. Upstairs, someone knocked at the door. Crawley jumped.

"Ignore it." Romulus wished the policeman hadn't decided to stay. He looked as though he might lose his mind.

"Might be important." Crawley's voice answered, but his eyes never left Angela. "I bolted the door. I should let them in."

"Whoever it is, they're best kept out of this." Romulus wondered if moving, relinquishing his place, would release the demon. Imogen would know. For the first time in many years, he found himself wishing she were here. He decided it was best not to take the chance, so he was powerless to stop Crawley from running up the stairs and out of the basement door. He faced Angela.

"Demon. Ailo. I'm going to send you somewhere. I don't know where, but I hope it's far, far worse than where you came from."

Angela raised her eyebrows. "Why?"

"Because you kill people. Because your presence forced me to accept things I preferred to ignore. Because you messed up my life. Because you described me as a worthless creature. Most of all, because I don't like you."

Angela laughed and ran her hands over her body. The dress vanished, leaving her naked. Romulus gaped. The book slipped in his gloved hands. He clutched it with numb fingers. Desire surged within him, flushing logic and reason from his mind.

"Am I that dangerous?" Her voice thrummed in Romulus's ears. "I have no weapons. I stand naked before you. Come to me. Be with me." She held out her arms.

Romulus took a step forward. Somewhere in the distance, a voice said "no." It sounded like Watson, but it couldn't be. Watson was dead. Romulus took another step. His foot hit something hard and heavy. He looked down.

The slab of obsidian lay at his feet. Reflected in its black depths was a creature like the one he had seen when he stepped into the triangle. Its slender appendages reached out to him. Its multiple eyes stared. A mouth, ringed with needle-points of teeth, slavered. Romulus jumped back.

"You're a monster. I won't fall for your illusion."

Angela screamed at the stone and at Romulus. "Foul, pathetic little magician. You can't win. You don't know how. Without Samuel, you are nothing."

Romulus tensed his arms, battling the fatigue the heavy book pushed into them. "Watson. Come on. What do I read next?"

Samuel moved forward. Upstairs, a howling filled the passageway. The basement door flew back against its frame. Crawley appeared in the opening, moving backwards, his feet not touching the floor. Crawley's head made contact with the doorframe and he crumpled, his body slumped half inside the door.

The wind shrieked into the basement, whistling its glee and triumph. Samuel screamed and fled into the stone wall. Angela laughed, part sweet tinkle, part malicious cackle. Romulus half-closed his eyes as the wind ripped across them. The candles blew out. The light bulb swung in circles. In his hands, the wind turned the book's pages, first one way, then the other.

"What will you do now?" Angela wasn't shouting, but her voice carried easily over the whine of the wind. "Samuel can't help you, magician. You will fail. I will be free."

"I won't free you."

"You'll die, or you'll leave. Either will break the spell. Either will do." Angela said. "I can wait years if necessary."

"Watson. Come back." Romulus called into the brickwork. The wind pressed into him, breathing contempt for his flesh.

"If he comes out, the wind takes him." Angela lowered her head. "Won't you reconsider? Won't you come to me?"

Don't.

Romulus shivered. The word didn't come from his mind. It came from the wind.

Listen.

Angela's face contorted in rage. "Mindless. You cannot speak."

She's wrong.

Romulus took a breath. The voice was familiar.

Broken, not mindless. Mad, but not insane.

Pages flipped in the book Romulus held. Forwards and back, as though searching. They stopped. Romulus recognized the page with the incantation he had just read. One more rustle of ancient paper, and the wind showed him a new page.

Tobias.

The wind whispered the name. Romulus stared at the open book. "Uncle Tobias?"

Yes. Read. Left hand page.

"No!" Angela raged within the circle. "You can't help him. He fights for the angels."

"I most certainly do not." Romulus grinned at the creature's fury. "I fight for Romulus Crowe. And for these." The wind dropped around him, though it still whipped through the room. "You and your kind put these souls into the wind. Why would you think they'd want to help you?" He started reading.

"They are mine." Angela's illusion faded. She almost doubled in height. New arms appeared, long and chitinous. A tail curled around her legs.

Romulus read more.

"Stop. I can give you power. Wealth. Women."

Romulus stopped reading.

Angela reformed into her beautiful, naked self. "So, you consider my offer."

The word Romulus stalled at was "nom". The Latin word for "name." Did he say that, or speak the demon's name? He looked up at the smiling, naked woman. "Ailo".

She bared her teeth, first perfect, white and human, then pointed, thin and vicious. Romulus continued his reading, replacing every "nom" with "Ailo".

The demon's rant became unintelligible as it reverted to its own language. The sounds it made stirred ancient terrors in Romulus, but he suppressed them with the ease of long practice. Visions assaulted his mind, sights of sexual depravity and lust. He brushed them aside. The guiles of female flesh had no effect on him. Imogen's betrayal had seen to that, a long time ago.

Motes of light swirled around the circle. Romulus stumbled over a complex word. The motes dissolved, then reappeared when he continued. The chalk lines forming the outer and inner circles glowed, though the new sigils were unaffected. The demon, now fully in its real form, fell silent. It bared its teeth. The chalk circles turned a dull red, then ignited. Thin sheets of flame surrounded the creature. The wind, still circling the room, tore at them.

Ailo laughed, using Angela's delicate tone. "Fool. You made the circle with blood."

Blood in the circle.

Uncle Tobias's voice quavered. The wind accelerated, moaned its fear, and rushed upwards, to the door. It fluttered Crawley's coat as it left, taking, for a moment, most of the air in the basement. Romulus stopped his chant. He gulped at the air. The flames reduced in height, licking around the demon's feet.

"Blood? There's no blood." Romulus checked his gloved hands. The obsidian had rubbed the gloves thin in places, but there were no tears in the cloth, no cuts in his skin.

"When the fire dies, I am free." The demon crouched, ready to spring.

"There's no blood. Only chalk."

The burning circle flickered, its energy almost spent. Blue flames, mere inches high, danced around the chalk lines. Ailo snarled and flexed her claws.

There was little point in running.

Chapter Sixty-Two

Elaine pushed open the gate of Samuel's house and held it for Imogen. Their walk in the cold night air had sobered them a little, though they were both still prone to occasional fits of giggles.

"No police. That's odd." Imogen surveyed the front of the house. "And the door's wide open."

"Open house. Let's go." Elaine moved forward.

The wind rushed from the door, knocking both women off their feet. Elaine landed on a flower bed, among damp soil and weeds. She fought for breath as the wind forced itself past her face. It whined and moaned with almost-human voices. Elaine closed her eyes and pressed her hands over her ears until the air stilled.

"What was that?" Elaine opened one eye.

Imogen sat up on the overgrown lawn. "I don't know. Whatever it was, it sounded scared."

"It came out of the house. How can a hurricane form inside a house?"

"Hell. I thought the demon wouldn't be able to do that indoors." Imogen stood, brushing at the damp grass stains on her clothes. She held her hand out to Elaine. "Up you go."

With more caution than before, they entered the darkened house. Elaine flipped the switches on the wall, then looked up. The hall light bulb was shattered, its wire and jagged glass visible in the faint light filtering through the doorway. The basement door stood open, some light flickered up from below, and a large bundle lay on the floor.

Imogen sniffed the air. "Smells like something's burning."

They crept forward, watching for obstacles. The bundle on the floor moved. Elaine grabbed Imogen's arm and stood as still as she could. The sound of their breathing filled the air.

A snarl issued from the basement. The bundle lurched upright and faced them. It was Crawley. Elaine let out a long, relieved breath and stepped forward.

"Inspector Crawley. Thank God."

"Stay there, please." Crawley smiled, a soft, placating smile that seemed out of place among his normally morose features. His eyes seemed unfocused, but Elaine put that down to the poor lighting. Nevertheless, she nodded at Crawley's request. He disappeared into the basement. Imogen moved to follow him, but Elaine stopped her.

"He said we should wait."

"Yes, he did. Well, we've waited. Let's go." Imogen led the way to the door. She halted and put her hand over her mouth at what she saw there. Elaine joined her and looked down on the scene below. She screamed, even as her hands moved of their own volition to her camera bag.

Chapter Sixty-Three

The scream came from behind. Romulus moved his head and came face to face with Crawley.

"What are you smiling at?" Romulus backed away. There was something inside Crawley, something not quite human.

"Keep reading. You have to finish before it gets out of the circle."

"Who are you? What are you?"

"Never mind. Just read."

The flames died on the inner circle. Ailo took a step forward. The long head dipped, as though willing the outer circle's fire to die. Instead, the flames intensified. They brightened, their blue giving way to yellow, then white. Ailo roared in fury.

Crawley closed his eyes. "I can't hold her for long. Read the spell."

Romulus glanced from Crawley to the demon. He found his place on the page and read.

"I know you." Ailo extended one thin finger towards Crawley. "You should not be interfering in this."

Crawley said nothing. Romulus continued reading.

"I know you. Why can't I see what you are?" The demon paced back and forth in the circle. It extended its arms. All its deep black eyes glowered at Crawley.

Only four lines left to read. Romulus stopped.

"I see through your disguise, Michael." The demon bellowed its triumph. "Your intervention means I am free to call my own here." She moved her arms in a shifting pattern. Their movements left lines in the air: shapes, images, symbols.

Crawley faced Romulus with panic on his face. "Finish the spell!"

"I can't." Romulus licked his lips. The last four lines were written in an unfamiliar alphabet. He had no idea how to pronounce them.

Brief light filled the room. Elaine took the stairs one step at a time, a camera to her eye. Imogen followed. The flash fired again.

"Get out of here." Romulus glanced from Elaine to Crawley to Ailo. "She's going to escape."

Imogen pushed past Elaine and ran to Romulus's side. Elaine took a voice recorder from her bag, slung it around her neck and switched it on. She continued taking photos. Romulus groaned. Sweat beaded on Crawley's now-flushed face.

Ailo's long, pointed tongue licked the outside of her mouth, where lips should have been.

Chapter Sixty-Four

Through the mist of brick and mortar, the scene in the basement unfolded before Samuel's dead eyes. Romulus was failing. The woman, Imogen, stood beside him. She might be able to help. Romulus said she knew about demons. Ailo, in her circle, looked Samuel's way, and he shook with terror. Even through the wall she saw him, and Samuel had no doubt she could reach him.

Doctor Pettifer took photographs like some bizarre suicidal tourist. Samuel shook his head at the sight. Was she as fearless as she seemed? Ailo would pull her apart.

The policeman blurred in Samuel's vision, part long-coated officer, part something else. Something bright. Brighter than the flames of the circle, which had fallen to ankle height and parted in places. Samuel moved to within an inch of the wall's surface and listened.

"I can't read this." Romulus slapped the book. "I don't even know what alphabet it's in."

Imogen leaned over the book and shook her head. "Arabic, I think." She gripped Romulus's arm. "I can't read it though. Given time, I could do it, but not like this."

Ailo laughed. "Your time is short. Michael's power fades, while mine grows." In the circle, dark shapes writhed. Serpentine, spider-like, low and tall, no two alike and none pleasant. Ailo called her armies, her demonic associates. Not her sisters, but things more depraved and disfigured. The dregs of hell.

"When the flame dies, she's free. They all are." The policeman and the brightness within him called out in a voice filled with defeat. "I should not have interfered. I've let hell loose in the world, and it's going to escalate. I have to call on help."

"No," Romulus shouted. "Wait. Give Imogen a chance to work it out."

"There's no time." The policeman sank to his knees.

"No time." Samuel echoed the words. He stepped from the wall. "I can do this, I can finish it." He took a halting step towards Romulus and Imogen. "There is a price. My salvation and her life." Samuel took another step. "I have to pay it."

Chapter Sixty-Five

"It's not just us." Romulus held the book as steady as he could. "If you don't read these lines, the whole planet's done."

Imogen looked up from the text to stare into his eyes. "Us? There used to be an 'us'. Why did that end?"

"Don't get sentimental on me now. Just read the damn thing." Romulus looked away from the hurt in Imogen's eyes to the circle of flame, now mere inches high. A shadow flickered on the wall, a shadow of a short, pudgy man. Watson? It moved closer, one arm outstretched towards Imogen.

"No!" Romulus moved between the shadow and Imogen. Cold shot like a shaft through his chest, flowed into his arms. Imogen's grip on his arm felt like a steel claw.

Just a little. Just enough.

The thought, like a flutter of torn paper, fell through Romulus's consciousness. Imogen's life burned through him into the cold shaft in his chest. Samuel took form, his arm through Romulus, his eyes wide.

"I can read it." Samuel's desperation filled his words. "I'll be damned for this, but I can read it."

"Enough. You've taken too much already." Romulus gaped at the gray threads in Imogen's hair, at the dark circles beneath her closed eyes. His own joints ached. He focused his mind, brought pressure to bear on the cold within him, and expelled it. Imogen slumped against him. With both hands grasping *Liber Astaroth*, Romulus could not stop her sliding along his body to the floor. "Don't die," he whispered.

"Ah, such a pretty scene." Ailo laughed aloud. "It will be so much prettier when the flames fall. My friends will play with you for a long time. Their games are slow and delightful, you will find."

"Do something. Finish the spell. I have to call help, and soon." Crawley's skin bulged and stretched with the power it contained. "I can't hold her."

"Hold the book." Samuel took form beside Romulus.

"If you've killed her—"

"I don't know." Samuel avoided Romulus's gaze. "I don't think so. I can't touch anything so I might not have. You stopped me. Just hold the book where I can see it."

Romulus held the book as steady as he could. Another flash from Elaine's camera made him snarl in her direction.

Samuel sniffed and began to read. *"Ailo, utukku limnuti..."*

Ailo snarled and crouched. The flames flickered, their ethereal fuel almost gone. Crawley closed his eyes. Romulus glanced at Imogen's still form. Elaine took more photographs.

Samuel finished the spell with a shout. "*Ishtah*!"

"Too late," Crawley said.

Horrified, Romulus stared at him, but Crawley had spoken to the demon.

The flames went out, leaving the dim overhead bulb as the only illumination in the room. A darkness grew within the circle, where the demon and its shapeless companions bellowed in anger.

Romulus closed *Liber Astaroth*. The darkness in the circle solidified, became a pillar too black to focus on. The demons within were lost to sight and sound. Romulus moved closer, fascinated by a darkness more absolute than any he had ever seen. Crawley stood and held out his arm across Romulus's chest.

The pillar rose until it engulfed the light bulb. Sight was extinguished. Afraid to move too far, Romulus stood still. A flash of light illuminated the scene for a second, but the black pillar reflected nothing. Crawley's arm tensed.

"Don't move." It was Crawley's voice, but there was an echo of someone else. Romulus tried to place it.

Light returned to the basement as the column descended. With a smooth movement it sank into the floor, giving Romulus the impression of an express elevator to hell. The chalk lines were carbonized. An occasional puff of smoke drifted upwards from them.

Crawley's arm dropped to his side. "It's over. For now."

This time, the voice was unmistakable. "It's you. You've possessed Crawley." Romulus pointed a shaking finger at the policeman. "You're that priest."

"Father Thomas Michael, at your service." Crawley performed an exaggerated bow.

"You said you couldn't interfere. Why didn't you help me before? What's a priest doing possessing a body? I thought that was evil." Curiosity battled anger in Romulus's mind. He wanted to flatten the priest, but he wanted answers, so many answers.

"I had no choice. You left blood in the circle. It was a risk, but it worked out okay."

"There was no blood. I'm not cut." Romulus placed the book on the floor and grabbed Crawley's hands. He turned them over. "You're not cut. Where did the blood come from?"

"I can answer that." Samuel moved forward, his eyes downcast. "When I first drew these circles, I pricked my thumb getting the chalk. There must have been a few drops of my blood on the original lines. I'm sorry."

"As for the possession, it's not evil when the host gives his permission. Elijah Crawley is one of ours. He understands the necessity," Crawley said.

"Elijah?" Romulus smirked at the name. "I doubt he'd want you telling everyone."

"Oh my God!" Elaine ran across the room to where Imogen lay.

In the intensity of the last few moments, Romulus had forgotten her entirely. He knelt beside her, while Elaine lifted her head. Imogen groaned. Something tugged at Romulus's feelings, some emotion he could not now remember. He shoved at it, but it refused to leave.

"What happened?" Elaine pressed her fingers to Imogen's neck. "There's a pulse. She's alive. Was it Samuel?"

"He tried to take all her life. I stopped him." Romulus glared at the ghost, who kept his distance. "You'd better get out of here before he starts on you."

"No need. Samuel is harmless now." Crawley/Michael folded his arms. "With the creature gone, Samuel's powers are gone too." Crawley knelt, then lay on the floor. "I don't want him to fall when I release him." Father Michael rose to his feet, leaving Crawley asleep.

Romulus touched Imogen's hair, now shot through with gray. He examined the wrinkles around her eyes and mouth, then stared at the back of his own hand. It was the hand of a much older man. Romulus surged to his feet.

"Damn you, Watson. What did you do?"

Father Michael raised his hands. "Calm down, professor. You stood between Samuel and the woman. Your intervention saved her life, but it cost you a little of your own. You'll live, just not as long as you would have."

"What? You mean this parasite sucked life from both of us?" Romulus clenched his fists.

"Rom? What's happening?" Elaine asked. "Are you talking to Samuel?"

"Him and that wretched priest. Watson took some of my life as well as some of hers." He glowered at Father Michael. "Will we recover? Will the effect wear off?"

Father Michael pursed his lips. "Somewhat, but you won't get back to where you were. There's always a price to pay when defeating something as powerful as a gamaliel. I'm sorry." He stood over Elaine. "You're still alive. It could have been much worse." The priest reached down to stroke Elaine's cameras and voice recorder, then stood and walked to where Samuel stood, eyes closed, beside the wall. "It's time to go, Samuel."

Samuel glanced at Romulus. "I'm sorry. It was the only way." Watson faded from sight. Father Michael offered a sympathetic smile as he, too, faded.

"Wait." Romulus blinked away the floater that formed in his vision. "I have questions."

The priest's voice echoed from the spot where he had stood a moment ago. "I can't answer them. There are very good reasons why not, which I think you'll understand one day. Goodbye, Professor Crowe."

Crawley groaned. Romulus resisted the urge to kick him. Instead he returned to Imogen's side.

Imogen opened her eyes. "Is it over?"

"Yes." Romulus took her hand. "It's over. For the moment at least, there are no ghosts."

Chapter Sixty-Six

Romulus puffed cigar smoke through the open window of his office. Tomorrow he would give his first lecture to a new batch of bright-eyed, hopeful students, full of anticipation for the easy life of academia. His first task was to disabuse them of any such notion.

His lecture notes sprawled across his desk along with his notes of the last few days. Romulus stubbed out his cigar and flicked the butt towards the chancellor's car. It fell short, but it was closer this time. He needed more weight, a longer butt. Romulus blew the last of the smoke through the window then closed it. Hating the chancellor must be good for his health if it made him smoke less. He stared through the window for a moment. Smoking was the least of his worries. His encounter with Watson took more years off his life than any cigar ever could. If this was the price of fighting evil, then someone else could take care of the next monster.

Elaine opened the door, knocking as she did so. Romulus slumped in his seat and watched her as she sat opposite.

"Well? Did you get the book?" Romulus swung his chair as he spoke.

"No problem. Farquhar-Jones was only too eager to get rid of it, as soon as he found out it was stolen. Since he thinks his fiancée's run out on him he's dropped the idea of translating *Geometria ton Zoon*. I've handed it back to the library."

"Good. I hope he was suitably distraught at the loss of his demonic true love?"

"He's getting over her. He asked me out."

Romulus opened his eyes wide. "You didn't accept?"

"Of course not. I'm not that desperate," Elaine said. "What about you and Imogen? Are you friends again?"

"She's gone back to Edinburgh. We'll speak when we have to."

"You know she offered me a job?"

"I suspected as much. You, naturally, declined."

"Not yet." Elaine shifted in her seat. "The job's open for a while. I'm going to wait and see if you keep your promises."

"Ah." Romulus swivelled his chair to face the window. "Blackmail."

"I learned from the master," Elaine said. "Besides, we have a lot to write up. A demon, ghosts, your own psychic abilities. There must be a few papers in all that."

"None of which we will publish. Not for a while anyway." Romulus swiveled back to his desk.

"What? We have the photos, don't we?"

"No photos. The film you shot came out blank." Romulus opened a drawer and dropped an envelope onto the desk. He waited while Elaine perused the blank negatives.

"How?" She dropped the negatives. "My camera was working, I'm certain."

"It was. The priest did that. He also wiped the voice-recording you made."

"Why?"

Romulus steepled his fingers. "Ghosts are elusive buggers. The priest didn't want us proving what we've seen. I don't know why yet, but I'm working on it. We have to catch them unaware, like that recording you have of Watson's voice." Romulus sighed. "The living present us with more immediate problems, unfortunately."

Elaine wrinkled her nose. "What are you talking about?"

"You know our great leader, Chancellor Orson? He of the heart-shaped face. By which I mean lumpy, purple, and covered in veins. Well, he's put a clamp on the whole thing. So has Eustace Farquhar-Jones, because of the murder at his house. None of the governors are happy about the library's involvement. If it's any consolation," Romulus picked up a pen and twirled it in his fingers, "Crawley isn't faring any better. His superiors told him to rewrite his report without all the witchcraft. The murders remain officially unsolved. His words, not mine. If any of us go public, we're all out of a job."

"They can't do that. We're only doing what we were hired to do."

"That's a good argument. Unfortunately it won't work. In the chancellor's mind, we've just done exactly the opposite of what he hired us to do. He wants debunkers, not psychic demon fighters."

Elaine slumped, her arms folded. "Maybe I should take that job with Imogen. They can't shut me up then."

"I think you'll find Imogen will get the same treatment. Moving won't help. We've annoyed some important people this week. I, for one, thoroughly enjoyed finding that out."

"So, we just forget it? Tear up all our notes and go back to busting fake mediums?"

"Not quite. We'll have to be careful what we report for now, but eventually we'll have enough data amassed to thumb our noses at them all. Then we publish. We'll cause enough of a sensation that even Orson won't dare fire us. Even if he does, we'll have no trouble finding other jobs." Romulus leaned forward. "But it has to be absolute proof. That recording of Watson's phone call isn't absolute, but it's a piece in the whole picture. Store it away. All of it. All the data. Save it until we have a landslide of evidence."

"That's going to take years. What do we do in the meantime?" A sly smile formed on Elaine's face. "You know, Farquhar-Jones might be persuaded to revive his orb project."

"No."

"No? You know for sure the supernatural is real now. You've spoken with ghosts and demons. So what's different about orbs?"

Romulus curled his lip. "Orbs are still bunk."

About the Author:

H. K. Hillman is a self-employed researcher, also known as a rogue scientist, who works with dangerous and stinky things and would rather write for a living. He has produced a number of short stories but has now let his natural verbosity blossom with the writing of novels.

On the internet he exists in many forms, none of them really him. One such is Phineas Dume, who can be found at http://docdume.blogspot.com/ and contacted via email at docdume@gmail.com

Also by H.K. Hillman:

Jessica's Trap
by H.K. Hillman

eBook ISBN: 9781615723690
Print ISBN: 9781615723706

Horror Thriller
Novel of 60,019 words

In a corner of the Civil War, a demonic battle is stirring.

An inexperienced young witch calls on demonic help to capture an ancient creature, an evil as old as Time and which inhabits the one known as 'Witchfinder-General'.

Inexperience is no match for the wiles of demons and Jessica soon loses control. The demons will build the trap she wants but...

She is to be the bait.

Also from Eternal Press:

Halo of the Damned
by Dina Rae

eBook ISBN: 9781615726042
Print ISBN: 9781615726059

Paranormal Horror
Novel of 87,133 words

A chain of advertising agencies, a new breed of humans, and a fallen angel to worship...

Andel Talistokov is known for his slick advertising agencies across the globe. He is a fallen angel that uses advertising as a weapon for Satan's work. His growing power emboldens him to break several of Hell's Commandments. Furious with his arrogance, Satan commands him to return to Hell after finding his own replacement. Yezidism, an ancient angel worshiping religion, quietly expands throughout the West. Armaros appears as a guest of honor during their ceremonies. He mates with young women to produce nephilim, a mixed race of humans and angels. They are alone and unprepared for their supernatural power. Joanna Easterhouse, a recovering drug addict, steps out of prison shortly after her mother's fatal accident. She and her sister, Kim, unravel their mother's secretive past. Intrigued, they learn their bloodline is part of a celestial legacy. Both worlds collide. Halo of the Damned is a horrifying tale that weaves research together with suspenseful twists and turns.

Eternal Press

Official Website:
www.eternalpress.biz

Blog:
http://eternalpressauthors.blogspot.com/

Reader Chat Group:
http://groups.yahoo.com/group/EternalPressReaders

MySpace:
http://www.myspace.com/eternalpress

Twitter:
http://twitter.com/EternalPress

Facebook:
http://www.facebook.com/profile.php?id=1364272754

Google +:
https://plus.google.com/u/0/115524941844122973800

Good Reads:
http://www.goodreads.com/profile/EternalPress

Shelfari:
http://www.shelfari.com/eternalpress

Library Thing:
http://www.librarything.com/catalog/EternalPress

We invite you to drop in, visit with our authors and stay in touch for the latest news, releases and more!

Lightning Source UK Ltd.
Milton Keynes UK
UKOW041552131212
203618UK00001B/12/P

9 781615 727858